TIME HEIST

Anthony Vicino

TIME HEIST
Anthony Vicino

Visit:
OneLazyRobot.com

To those who came before.
To those who are coming with.
To those yet to follow.

Thank you.

CHAPTER ONE
Georgie Gets Himself Killed

The numbers on my arm said I'd be dead soon. Staring at them won't change that fact, so I don't. When you're a kid they tell you the numbers are never wrong. But part of you hopes that's a lie grown-ups tell children, 'cause seventy years doesn't seem very long.

When you're a kid, dying's pretty much the worst thing in the world.

It's not.

Explaining that to the guy jabbering on the barstool beside me, however, would be a tough sell. One I didn't care to make. He called himself George, but it wasn't difficult imagining his friends and loved ones in the Uppers calling him Georgie.

Now, say what you will about Georgie and his perspective on life and death—the kid had balls. The fact that he was down deep, drinking in this particular corner of the Lowers, however, didn't suggest he had much for brains. Oh well, can't win 'em all.

There are good reasons why lost souls from the Uppers don't wander past the Middles for their life-affirming brushes with death. Mainly because you don't just brush death in the Lowers. Around here, death is an all or nothing sort of gig.

Georgie cradled a glass of beer as if holding the damn thing was the same as drinking it. "How much time you got?" he asked.

It's not polite to ask a man about his time. It's a social faux pas, if you will. But when you spend as much time on a barstool as I do, you allow for a certain amount of faux pas-ery.

Georgie didn't understand the delicate interplay between this social custom and not getting stabbed in the Lowers. Didn't understand that there's a time and place for everything. Walking out of Lucky Lou's with blood in your veins is all sorts of wrong if you go flashing the world your remaining time—especially if you have as little as me.

People get weird around a dead man. They get to thinking they can do things that maybe they shouldn't. 'Cause murder is murder, but you'd likely find the Lord Almighty in a more forgiving mood if the asshole whose clock you'd cleaned only had a couple hours to live anyways.

If there's a God I'm sure he'd understand the economics of the situation and give his blessing. If not, well, I don't suppose that's any kind of god a man in the Lowers would worship anyhow.

But I had nowhere else to be and anyone wanting my time could have it for all the good it had done me—so I humored the kid. I pulled back the faded leather sleeve of my jacket and showed him what remained of my Life Tracker: three half-moon circles glowing red. The outermost circle shrank with every passing second.

Georgie's eyes tried to jump out of his skull. The vein running the link between heart and brain via his throat did some sort of throbbing dance.

"You have less than a day," Georgie said, shouting his mathematical prowess for the room to hear.

On the tail end of such a bold proclamation it was in my best interest to give at least a half-assed look over my shoulder. In my experience, that's where people prefer to sneak up on you.

Neon tubes buzzed and flickered on the ceiling, casting beams of light through the smoke-hazed room. Bass, loud enough to be heard in the Middles, shivered across the floor before ascending the legs of my stool and rooting itself to my ass like a leech.

Lucky Lou's clientele come in a variety of shapes and sizes. A little bit of everything. Unity's grand mixing pot.

In one corner guys with shifty eyes hawk their mind-altering nanites: Angel Dust, Quick Sliver, Pandora's Shame—you name it, they've got it. And they know you want it. Life in the Lowers isn't worth facing without something blunting the ragged edges.

I had my fix of the Quick sitting at home waiting for me. It occurred to me, then, that being there, wrapped in the drug's loving embrace, might be preferable to Georgie's company. I would have made that exodus if not for the half glass of someone's bastardized interpretation of alcohol staring me down from the bar top. Soon.

A squat metal cage sat in a shallow pit behind the dance floor. It was big enough for two fools with more aggression than brains to jump into the Stream and dream up ever more creative ways of killing one another for the amusement of Lucky Lou's patrons. Normally that's where I'd be. Fighting in the cage, getting my fix of the Stream. But seeing as how I'd be dead in less than twenty-four hours, I figured I deserved a night off.

Between pixies grinding to the fluttering rhythm of their own heartbeats and Dusters flopping around in pools of their own bodily fluids, nobody seemed overly interested in Georgie's declaration of my remaining time. That's good; few people at Lou's would think twice before resolving a questionable business transaction with the rusted end of a knife.

Yeah, I'm dead soon anyhow, but I plan to die on my own pitiful terms.

"Don't you have someplace you'd rather be?" Georgie asked, leaning in close as if he were sharing a particularly juicy secret.

"Nope."

"But you're dying."

"So are you," I said, saluting with my glass of rocket fuel before pouring a bit more of that clear liquid down my perpetually chapped throat.

Georgie flinched. He instinctively turned his forearm away from me, as if that would help him if I decided to take his time. I had no interest in that. Interestingly enough, I was probably the only guy in Lou's who could say that with a straight face.

"You don't have family you want to be with or something?" Georgie asked.

"Kid, listen up, 'cause I don't know how much longer I got 'til that alcohol starts playing whack-a-mole with my brain cells. Hell, this might be my last moment of lucidity," I said, polishing off the remainder of my drink. "You need to stop worrying about me, and spend some time figuring out how you're gettin' out of here with all that time still on your arm."

I belched to emphasize my point.

Georgie ran a handful of fingers with nails polished to a high sheen through his finely coiffed hair. "What do you mean?"

"What I mean is, you don't belong here."

"How do you know?"

"You're too clean," I said, "and that glass of inebriation in your hands hasn't made the journey to your mouth all night."

Georgie studied his glass. The cogs were turning. He wanted to take a drink and prove me wrong, but he didn't want to sacrifice any of the time he'd so carefully hoarded over the years. You can tell the time hoarders. The ones too terrified to live for fear of dying. The ones who work up the courage to do something real dumb, instead of only a little dumb.

Georgie had decided to do something real dumb; he came to the Lowers.

"So? I'm a citizen of Unity," he said. "I can be here if I want."

"Sure, being here doesn't pose a problem. Leaving does."

The kid pushed his stool away from the bar, its metal legs screeching against the floor. "You planning on stopping me?"

I chuckled and pushed my empty mug down the bar. It slid along gouged grooves in the wood until a stick thin woman behind the counter stopped it with one hand while her other spun a tumbler full of unknown liquid with the skill and dexterity of a circus performer. She winked and blew a kiss through puckered lips. I leaned back to be sure it would miss and turned to Georgie.

"You see that guy?" I said, hooking a thumb towards a man sitting at the opposite end of the bar. Half his face was hidden by shadows, the other half by a thin-brimmed hat pulled down over his eyes. Even from thirty feet out you wouldn't need optic implants to see the scar running from his chin to his ear.

"What about him?" The bottom-right corner of Georgie's lip twitched in an off-rhythm beat to his finger tapping the bar.

"That's Jack Dunn. You ever heard of Jack Dunn?"

Georgie shook his head no.

"Figures. You never heard of him 'cause news from the Lowers doesn't make it to the Uppers. News, like shit, trickles down. You've heard stories of what it's like down here, hell, some of them might even be true. But you don't understand the severity of your situation, because you don't really understand where you are. This ain't Unity; this is the Lowers."

I knew this because I'd once lived in the Uppers. Two miles straight up from where we now sat. Above ground with the sun.

I ran a thumb along the ridge of the silver ring hanging from a chain around my neck, rolling its smooth edges between my fingers. A reminder of life before this. A reminder of Diana.

The kid's head swiveled back and forth, studying the bar—and the general caliber of man therein—as if seeing it all for the first time. He swallowed hard, Adam's apple bobbing. "So, who's Jack Dunn?"

I opened my mouth to answer, but somebody beat me to the punch line.

"He's the guy that's gonna kill you," a deep voice like rolling thunder called out from behind the kid.

Georgie spun so quickly his ass cheeks slid off the stool and he flopped to the ground. A man, not ironically named Boulder, towered over the kid.

"I think you made him piss his pants, Bo," I said, looking into the giant's eyes. The two pinpricks of black were the only point of weakness on a body stacked haphazardly with nanite-infused muscles.

"Why's he going to kill me?" Georgie whimpered from the ground.

"He wants your time," I said.

"Well, too bad. He can't have it." Georgie tried faking confidence, which might help in some places, but Lucky Lou's wasn't one of them. "I have the best insurance money can buy."

"Won't help."

"Why?"

"He's an Intuit."

Georgie's face went through such an extreme color change that I figured cosmetic nanobots hiding beneath his skin must have been responsible. Either that or he finally realized the desperate nature of his predicament. Possibly a combination of both.

Insurance be damned. An Intuit like Jack Dunn would only need a couple minutes tromping through Georgie's nanocomp to hack the kid's Time Bank account and drain it. After that, Georgie could say goodbye to all those years he'd carefully collected, 'cause he'd be staring at his final ten minutes. A parting gift thanks to the Safeguard. A safety protocol only one Intuit had ever managed to crack.

Ten minutes ain't much time, though. Just enough for panic to really grab you by the balls.

Bo ignored the Uppie at his feet. "Boss wants to see you, Tom."

"Oh?" I pivoted in my chair and glanced past Bo's prodigious bulk. At the far end of the bar Lucky Lou leaned against the second-floor railing overlooking the current Stream fight. "What's he want?"

"You know how it goes." Bo shrugged with the indifference of a man just doing his job. "I'm the delivery man. He tells me to come get you, I come get you. Now, you good to walk or am I carrying you?"

"That won't be necessary." I stood quickly, causing my barstool to tip past the point of equilibrium and clatter to the ground.

I stepped over Georgie, still sitting on his ass, and headed towards the mass of human biowaste writhing on the dance floor.

"Wait!" Georgie yelled. I turned, if for no other reason than pity. The kid, now standing, trembled with the reality of his predicament. "What do I do?"

Bo quirked his eyebrow and tilted his head knowingly.

I sighed. "Can you get him an escort to the top?"

"Sure." Bo sniffed and rubbed his nose with the back of a hand covered in cheap back-alley tattoos. "But it'll cost you."

"You heard the man," I said, turning to Georgie.

"I can't…" Georgie started. "My dad can't know I'm down here. He watches my accounts. He'll kill me if he finds out."

I pointed to Jack Dunn. "That guy is probably gonna kill you first."

Georgie made a pathetic sound like a puppy being kicked. I didn't know I had any heartstrings left to be tugged, but somehow that noise found one.

"How much to get him to the Middle?" I asked.

"10,000. Or six months. Your choice."

A steep price for saving Georgie's ass. Then again I didn't want this kid's death hanging over my head if somehow I made it to the pearly gates and they were looking for a tie breaker to decide my fate. When you're getting ready to die, you start thinking about these things. You start hedging your bets.

"Fine." I extended a hand, which Bo happily grabbed.

BLINK.

I activated the nanocomp buried in my brain. It flickered once as though someone was testing a light switch before a torrent of high-speed data blazed through my temporal lobe. My fingers tingled and my heart triple kicked before the microscopic nanobots scurrying along my neural highway could compensate.

Connected to Lucky Lou's subdivision of the Stream, I probed the private network created between Bo and myself, pinged his nanocomp, and transferred Georgie's babysitting fee—three fights' worth of money, though it wasn't like I could take it with me when I was gone anyhow.

When I blinked out of the Stream Bo was smiling and Georgie only looked like he'd been crying a little.

"Do me a favor," I said to the kid, "don't ever come back down here."

Having padded my pocket with a little extra karma I turned and headed for my meeting with Lucky Lou.

CHAPTER TWO

Thieves Make Bad Friends

In the bowels of Terminus, Lucky Lou was judge, juror, and executioner. For the Peacekeepers, he had been a proverbial thorn in the side for years with his tendency to collect on debts with a violent flourish. Despite this, the man had an effective operation for running the Lowers. Overall, crime in his sector was marginal by comparison to any other major Unity city. He organized the criminals, focused them, and kept them in line.

In the end it saved the Peacekeepers time and money to let the criminals police themselves, so in many ways, Lou couldn't be touched.

Even when I worked Time Vice I wouldn't have cared about such things. My department chased criminals with a whiter collar than Lou, and in those days I never found myself going lower than the Mids. That was a lifetime, and many floors, away.

At the moment, I only cared about getting home and finishing out the day in a Quick Sliver-induced delirium. I'm a man with simple needs.

Instead, I waited in a seedy VIP lounge with Bo. Thick nanite-infused curtains blanketed the wall. They shimmered in an ever-changing kaleidoscope of light and color. A wet-bar in the corner called my name, but whatever came next, I figured a clear head would be in my best interest, 'cause while dying fills a man with a certain ambivalence towards the world, I'd discovered something important years earlier—dying men still bleed.

Lou was the kind of guy who'd lock you in the Stream, where the laws of physics and time are more suggestion than rule, break your bones, heal them, and then do it again, for fun. The digital network linking minds across Unity through a cloud of nanites dispersed in the lower atmosphere, while never designed to be used in such ways, could be a sadist's best friend.

I'd become somewhat of a local around Lucky Lou's in the past nine years, though I'd never had the displeasure of meeting the benefactor for which the establishment had been named. I'd hoped I never would. That he'd pulled me in for a meeting did not bode well.

I propped my feet on a large conference table and massaged my neck while ignoring the itch in my forearm, though the word itch didn't fully describe the sensation. No, to do that you'd have to imagine a legion of fire ants chewing through flesh and tendon while looking for an escape from the prison of my skin.

It was a psychological itch. One that no amount of scratching could soothe. Only the Quick.

Those thoughts were put on standby when a curtain shuddered and Lucky Lou swept into the room like a ballroom dancer.

"If it isn't the legendary Tom Mandel," he said, rounding the table quickly. He dragged a chair that hissed across the carpet. "It is an absolute pleasure to finally meet you. Been a big fan of yours since your Time Vice days."

Shit. He'd done his research. I'd scrubbed all mentions of my past from the Stream. Not even an Intuit could've dug something up. When you're a disgraced Watchman rubbing elbows with organized crime, it helps if they don't have your current mailing address or a list of family and loved ones. Lou must have gone through non-traditional means, which meant he had spoken to someone in Time Vice.

Humans are a loose end where virtual security is concerned.

"Who talked?" I asked.

Lou's smile tripled, consuming the lower quadrant of his face. "Everybody talks. The trick is knowing when to listen."

I think I rolled my eyes. It wasn't entirely intentional.

"You don't think highly of me," Lou continued.

I shrugged, knowing that in the absence of a convincing lie, silence was my ally.

"You think me a mere Slumlord, no doubt, but I wonder if you understand the nature of my power."

"You have a lot of guns?"

Lou threw his head back and gave a wheezing laugh. When he finished he wiped a tear from his eye and gestured to Bo. The delivery man squeezed his hulking frame behind the wet-bar and prepared two glasses of sludge.

"I have a lot of guns, that's true," Lou said. "But my power comes from information. Controlling the flow of it, you see. Knowledge is indeed power."

Bo placed two tumblers on the table. Lou twirled a finger around the rim of one glass before sliding it towards me. I stopped it from flying off the edge of the table at the last second. Brownish liquid sloshed over the sides, spilling onto my hand. It had an antiseptic tingle.

"Lovely." I saluted with the beverage and then threw the contents of the glass down my throat in a single gulp. It blazed a liquid fire down my esophagus, scorching the sensitive lining of my stomach, before finding a home in my gut. My eyes watered, but I didn't break my stare with Lou. "What's this have to do with me?"

"Hm…" Lou sipped his drink. "Well, I've come across a piece of troublesome information. I'm hoping to brainstorm some solutions. What do you say?"

"I'd say I'm still not sure what this has to do with me."

"Well, Tom, it has to do with you because you've been cheating. In your fights, that is."

"What makes you think that?"

"You never lose."

"Maybe I'm just that good."

"Nobody is that good. Eventually everybody loses."

"And how do you think it is I cheated?"

Lou smirked before springing his trap. "You're an Intuit."

Yep, I was fucked.

Lou produced a small knife from his jacket pocket. He flicked his wrist and the nanite-infused edge emitted a dull orange glow. He pulled a whetstone from another pocket. He ground the blade against the stone.

Snick-snick.

Sparks flew, hovering silently before cooling and vanishing mid-arc.

All part of the show. The buildup.

Snick-snick.

That's why people went to Lou's in the first place, whether it be to get their fix of the latest mind-bending nanite, watch two guys kill each other in virtual reality, or find a warm body to keep them company for the night; they just wanted to be entertained.

Lou couldn't resist a little showmanship now.

I opened my mouth to say something along the lines of No, I'm not, but Lou beat me to it.

"Please don't insult me by denying it," he said; the nanite-imbued blade in his hand shifted color, darkening to a magenta that spread down the length of the knife. The purple light twinkled in his eye.

"I wasn't going to," I lied.

"No, never," he said with a crow's smile.

"So now what?"

"That's a good question. There's two things we should discuss. First, there's the subject of the money you've stolen from me. An impressive sum, by the way."

"I live for your approval."

"Tell me, why haven't you spent it? You could easily afford another decade in the Middles and yet you choose to die down here."

"Not sure that's any of your business."

Lou held his palms out in mock surrender. "I take an interest in the people working for me. Their business is my business. The better I understand you, the better I can control you."

"I don't work for you."

"No?" Lou tilted his head to the side. "Oh, right, that's the second thing I wanted to talk to you about. I forgot. You work for me now, Tom. Welcome to the crew."

"Not looking for a job," I said.

"This is not up for debate."

"I disagree," I said, pushing out of my chair. My cheeks were barely off the seat when something big blocked the light behind me. I swiveled towards the source of the eclipse only to be met by a fist the size of a small child.

I had time to clench for impact, but not much else. The ball of knuckle relocated my jaw to somewhere in the vicinity of my shoulder.

Somebody picked up the world and shook it, sending me tumbling to the floor. Blood seeped from a newly formed hole in my head. It dripped from my temple in sticky droplets that blended with the carpet's long red fibers.

The buzzing sound reverberating through my cranium voided all thoughts. I looked up at the silhouetted owner of the fist that had nearly decapitated me—Bo. His sculpted muscles popped against the neon back light cast off the shimmering curtains.

Never heard the man coming. Big and stealthy; a bad combination.

With elbows on the table for support I crawled into my chair.

Lou's smile was one order of magnitude smaller than it had been before. Smaller, yes, but still a smile. Which didn't mean much; plenty of men are happy to kill with a smile. There's a lot to be said for enjoying your work, whether that be a Watchman or a Slumlord.

"I don't think you understand the severity of your situation." Lou leaned forward, the knife in his hand a silent promise. "You've been gaming my system for years, making me look pretty damn foolish. A man in my position can't afford to look foolish, you understand?"

"Have you considered a different choice in wardrobe?" I made a point of dragging my stare across the man's white suit jacket.

"You present me with a problem. On the one hand, I could take you outside, shoot you in the knee, rip your tongue out with a pair of pliers, and burn the Tracker off your arm until it's nothing but charred meat, just to make a statement. But that doesn't get me closer to my money. You see, killing you has no value for me."

"Take the money if it'll make you happy," I said, rubbing my swelling jaw.

"I intend to take every last penny, but now you owe interest," Lou said. "Men like me do most of their business on the interest. You only have a few hours left, so killing you seems merciful. I'd rather squeeze what I can out of you."

"Could let me go. I won't tell anyone." I smiled, hoping it would help.

It did not.

"If I let you slide it sets off a chain reaction of other deadbeats thinking they can slide, too. That's bad for business, Tom."

A man's gotta have options. Choices. Currently there were too few on the table and I lacked any leverage. Working for Lou, even for a day, was never gonna happen. Then again I didn't fancy the idea of spending my remaining twenty hours locked in the Stream with whatever sociopath Lou decided to set loose on me either.

"How much you figure I owe you?"

"I'm feeling generous, let's call it an even 200,000."

It was unclear who his generosity was directed towards with such an amount.

"What did you have in mind?" I asked.

"One job." Lou held up a single bone-white finger, snapped it against his thumb, and with a snazzy bit of sleight of hand materialized a black data card. "I need you to hack into the Time Bank and relocate the remaining time in this account to somewhere...else."

I plucked the card from his fingers and studied the twenty-digit string of letters and numbers, all the while knowing there wasn't a chance in hell I'd take this job. Some lines weren't meant to be crossed. Some places you can't come back from.

Lou needed a guy like me to pull this off. Only an Intuit could manipulate the Stream's underlying code, bypass the system's constantly morphing firewalls, and penetrate the Time Bank's security. A virtual impossibility for regular users like Lou.

Easy as taking a shit for guys like me.

"Why don't you get Jack Dunn to do this?" I asked, wondering whose account number I held in my hands.

"'Cause I'm asking you."

"Yeah, well…this sounds more his speed."

"Jack Dunn is a sociopath. I prefer not to work with crazy."

Lou had standards. Arbitrary, but standards nonetheless. Who knew?

"So what's it going to be, Tom?"

I cut a page from Lou's book. Made a show of turning the card over in my hands and studying both sides.

"I think I'll pass." I flicked the card onto the table.

Lou took a deep breath through his crooked nose; his smile never wavered. His eyes flickered to Bo.

Another punch came; this time I was ready. Ready to put some more choices on the table. Ready for my leverage.

I prodded my nanocomp and it dumped a bucket of adrenaline into my system. In the seven years since moving to the Lowers I'd rarely called upon the nanites living in my muscles. Now, in my time of need, I hoped they wouldn't ignore me as I'd ignored them.

I slammed a foot into the table. My chair slid back as Bo's fist sailed past my nose. The nanites were barely working. Only had one chance to snag Bo's enormous wrist.

Amazingly, I caught it, twisting up and to the side until I heard the satisfying snap of bone. Bo grunted yanking his hand free, but I held on with all the nanite-infused strength I could muster. I had the tiger by the tail, and you don't live to tell people about grabbing tigers if you let go of their tails.

I pivoted behind Bo, leaped onto the table to gain more height, and yanked his arm behind his back. The huge man, having lost all mechanical advantage, dropped to a knee.

Lou folded his arms. "Don't be stupid."

"Stupid's kinda all I got left."

"You won't make it through the door, much less out of the building, so release him, sit your ass down and let's come to an amicable agreement."

"Forgive me if I have a difficult time negotiating with you in good faith."

"Why the hell not? Did I come into your house and steal from you?"

There was a logic there, but I wasn't convinced logic would help my situation.

"Being an Intuit isn't against the rules," I pointed out. "So I didn't steal from you."

"But you'll agree it goes against the spirit of the rules."

That may be true. In a virtual cage match, an Intuit hacking the system's code has more than an unfair advantage.

"We can go in circles all night," I said. "But I ain't taking that job, and you aren't keen on letting me take myself out of here, so let's compromise."

Lou leaned back in his chair; the circles sagging beneath his eyes deepened. "What do you have in mind?"

With my free hand I tugged on the chain wrapped around my neck, pulling the key out from beneath my shirt, a key I'd been tethered to like an albatross for nine years. A period of time during which my veins had been filled with more Quick Sliver than blood.

Diana had given it to me as she lay dying in my arms. It broke my heart to give it up now. But sentiment wouldn't get me out of Lucky Lou's with all my limbs still attached.

"Is that what I think it is?" Lou asked.

"If you think it's a key to the Vault, then yeah…it's what you think it is."

Lou followed the silver ring swinging on its chain with gluttonous eyes. "What's it unlock?"

The great tragedy of my Quick addiction was that the nanites had reorganized my brain chemistry, snipping the parts of my memory they found superfluous, which included my knowledge of the key I carried. You don't get to choose which part of your soul the devil takes.

In the meantime, I'd amassed a small fortune at the expense of killers and thieves. Saving up to afford the memory reconstruction treatment that would find those misplaced memories and bring them to the surface—if only for a few hours before the Tracker on my arm did its thing.

That plan went out the window seeing as how Lou would be emptying my bank account soon. Now I'd be lucky to make it the remaining twenty hours without any broken bones.

If I couldn't uncover the mystery of the key, then I might as well use it to barter my ass out of Lou's.

"Don't know," I said truthfully.

"I take it your reputation keeps you from going topside and finding out, huh?"

"Something like that. Whatever it is, I figure it must be good."

Lou nodded. "That it must…" His voice trailed off, eyes glazed with a milky veneer as he dipped into the Stream. A moment later he blinked, the fog lifted, and he stared at me with vulture eyes. "Mr. Tom Mandel, I think you have yourself a deal."

"Yeah?" I said, with more surprise than I'd intended.

"What are your terms?"

"You let me leave, all debts forgiven, and I'll go die in peace."

Lou smiled. "Done."

CHAPTER THREE

Dying To Live

Man wasn't made to fly, a fact I was reminded of precisely three seconds after Bo threw me from the top step of Lucky Lou's like a bucket of dirty dishwater.

I hit the street below, rolling across the metal floor, smashing every delicate bone and joint I possessed before grinding to a stop. A flood of messages vied for my attention, the most pressing being the need to replace the air driven from my chest. My spasming lungs, however, weren't getting the hint.

Splayed out on all fours, I sucked at the repurposed air pumped through the corridors and reminded myself that technically this was my fault. As it turned out, Lou and I had different interpretations of the terms of our agreement. I should've been more specific about how I intended to leave the bar. If I had, maybe Bo wouldn't have played patty-cake with my face before carrying me out of Lou's fine establishment slung over his shoulder.

Bo descended the stairs. Each step boomed. A massive boot buried itself in my ribs. Something cracked. Fire leached into my blood, spreading north through my marrow like a knife whittling bone. It reached my mouth and erupted via strained vocal cords, filling the empty street with a scream more animal than human.

"You deserved that one," Bo said, gesturing with his shattered wrist.

He probably had a point, but the parts of my brain responsible for processing logic and reason were smothered beneath a blanket of pain.

"It was just business," I said, spitting a glob of red onto his boot.

At least, that's what I meant to do. It didn't make it much past my own lips. A thin trail of pinkish drool trailed from my mouth to the dirty street.

Bo shook his head and turned back to the club. "Take care of yourself, Tom."

It would have been a sweet sentiment if the man hadn't just broken my everything.

My hand instinctively went to my throat, searching for the chain I knew wasn't there. Lying on my back, I stared up at the flat light thrown off Lucky Lou's neon sign and traced the indent of my throat where the key had rested against the most vulnerable part of my body for so long. Diana had lain there once.

They were gone, now.

Soon, I'd be gone too.

Those were thoughts fueled by the Quick Sliver; a sharp tug on a short leash to remind me of her presence. I wanted to slide a needle of reality-warping nanites into a vein and pretend this was all a bad dream.

But it wasn't a bad dream, it was a bad life. And that is so much worse.

I gathered what strength remained and trudged in the general direction of home. A spider web of corridors branched off in all directions.

I stopped at the loading dock for the low-speed elevator. We stared at each other with equal parts amusement and disdain. The elevator would take you to the top, or anywhere between, for a price.

Freedom costs a small fortune. Nobody could afford that around here.

The elevator served as a reminder, a mechanism of control—those who lived upstairs had the power. Somebody had hacked the elevator's smart-metal door to project a Rise Up propaganda piece. I didn't care to look. Doubted anybody else did, either.

I brushed past, opting instead for the stairs. Those were free. They only cost time.

On my home level the overhead lights flickered in a seizure-inducing staccato. Seeing as how there was no sun to coordinate circadian rhythms in the down deep, the powers that be went ahead and dimmed the lights every night from midnight until six. A completely arbitrary point in a world lacking both day and night—I guess it's the thought that counts.

Overly filtrated air hissed into the corridors from vents overhead. The hiss, typically lost beneath the clamor of human traffic, filled the halls. It echoed off yellowing walls, stained by time like a smoker's teeth. Years of neglect and abuse had taken their toll on the street's infrastructure.

It was all cosmetic, though. Like Atlas, with the world on his shoulders, the walls would hold. Hoping the city would implode on itself would remain an unanswered prayer for another couple hundred years. In the meantime there were better things to waste prayers on.

I rounded a corner three floors from home and startled a barefoot man with skin charred black. He straddled a body lying in the hall. At this time of night only the stupid and desperate roamed the halls. People clinging to the barest threads of their humanity, wandering the Lowers looking for whatever could get them through another night.

These were the men and women Unity had forgotten. They knew it, and that made them dangerous.

The man studied me with pupils that contracted and expanded with the beating of his heart. A splash of crusted blood covered his chin.

The poor soul didn't understand basic nanobiology. Thought he could get his own upgrades by drinking the blood of another. Doesn't work like that. Nanites merge with their host, become an extension of their unique genetic pattern.

Can't steal that. Not without consequences, at least.

The guy in front of me was living with those consequences. Those mutations.

He cradled an armful of clothes that stood in stark contrast to the flimsy gauze covering his shoulders. He'd come across fresh bounty and now the man faced a rare decision. For once, he had something to lose. Engaging with me might cost him his newfound treasure.

I saw his malnourished mind running the cost-benefit analysis. After a three-breath pause he smartly decided the risk wasn't worth the payout and hobbled into a darkened alleyway formed by two housing units.

Usually I made a point of ignoring the dead. They'd been stripped of their lives; who was I to steal their final privacy? And yet, I couldn't stop myself. Maybe it was the fact that I'd be joining the poor bastard on the ground soon. Maybe it was curiosity. Either way, my legs carried me towards the vagrant's loot.

I wished they hadn't.

Even without his clothes I recognized the guy immediately. Georgie.

His dull gray eyes stared through me. Lips pulled back, frozen with panic.

You work Time Vice as long as me and you get used to seeing dead bodies. But it never gets easier seeing the ones you knew. You can't write them off so easily. Can't dehumanize them. Can't cope.

Georgie's body lacked signs of trauma. Whatever had happened to him hadn't left a mark. Looked like Jack Dunn had got him after all. So much for Bo's babysitting fees. Guess I shouldn't have broken the guy's wrist.

I squatted next to the body and closed his eyelids. I couldn't do much else.

Dumb kid probably lived his entire life in the Uppers, bored numb by the comfort and safety. The predictability of everyday life. He'd come looking for something to prove life wasn't an endless parade of copycat days. He didn't deserve this.

Yet there he was. Dead before his time.

And I thought I was having a bad day.

***

Between cracked ribs, a sucker punch to the face, the Quick walking my frayed nerves in stilettos, and Georgie's dead body, I had no clue how I hiked the remaining floors home.

The Quick waited until I stood at the entrance to my apartment before it hit me. Hard. The Quick hates being ignored. It makes her a bitchy mistress.

The nanobots I'd injected so many times before, the ones I'd relied on to send my mind to alternate dimensions of pleasure where I could escape the harsh reality of life otherwise not worth living, were now turning on my body, stimulating nerve endings with pain instead of pleasure.

But that's okay. I'd turned to the Quick for a reason, and it had more to do with pain than pleasure anyhow. Feeling something beat the numbed existence I'd grown accustomed to after Diana.

I reminded myself of this, but that sort of reasoning sounded like a silver lining load of shit as my teeth clacked together. Nerves sparked, filling my mouth with the acidic aftertaste of sucking on batteries.

The world tilted, along with my fragile equilibrium, and I tumbled forward. Both arms did the blind man grope, trying to come up with anything to stop my fall. My face found something: the door.

My head pinged off the smart-metal frame. A second later the door begrudgingly scanned my nanocomp. It pissed and moaned as it dilated open. It desperately needed love, or oil— something beyond my ability to give at that moment.

The apartment, the unblinking eye of an abyss, stared back at me. A black void which suited me fine; some things are better left in the dark. The life I'd built for myself fell somewhere in that category.

I stumbled through the darkness, doing pretty good, too, until my foot caught the edge of something solid. I fell.

On the floor, I cursed my Judas of a foot for its betrayal. I would've stayed put, but the Quick tugged me forward, coaxing me towards the couch, where one last vial hid.

I did the single hardest sit-up a man has ever been asked to do, paused at the apex to let the world spin by, and then fondled the darkness until I found the cushioned back of the couch.

I clung to that piece of furniture as the planet continued its crazy ballerina twirl around the sun.

The couch hugged me with an embrace that would never judge. I plunged a hand into its cleavage; my fingers brushed something small and sharp.

I retrieved the item in question and breathed a sigh of triumph that caused the acid in my stomach to bubble up and into my throat. I kept it down and studied the Quick Sliver vaporizer in my hand. The formerly translucent sides were dented and smudged (an effect I tend to have on the things in my life) but otherwise intact. Would've preferred to inject the poison—a stronger kick—but inhaling the nanites would do for now.

The microscopic machines would rush to my cerebral cortex where they'd poke and prod all the right places. For a couple hours the god of pleasure would party on my Hippocampus.

That is, until the Quick Sliver withdrew her gift and replaced it with pain in a desperate attempt to drive me towards a repeat performance.

Quick Sliver is a fickle lover, but she's mine.

I pressed the vaporizer to my lips and inhaled. The puff of air swarming with nanites tickled like a million spiders skittering down my throat and into my lungs. A flash of white light forked across the darkened ceiling. I closed my eyes; the light blossomed.

It scalded, then it soothed.

A familiar feeling. The embrace of a loved one.

The nanobots tinkered with my nanocomp, switched their charge, and lit me up. Small controlled seizures flooded my neural receptors with more dopamine than prudent.

Didn't matter; I became one with the universe. I evolved past my simple senses. Could see and taste emotion.

The room, rich with despair, tasted of caramel-slathered soap.

My organs went for a carousel ride, twirling around one another to the driving cadence offered by my thumping heartbeat. The hair along my scalp gave a standing ovation.

I shivered with distinct pleasure and closed my eyes, counting the afterimages of spots juking and jiving across the darkened canvas of my eyelids.

I made it to five before my brain gave up and switched off. I passed out. Gone to the world and its sordid problems, victim to the synaptic firings of a brain seeking revenge.

I dreamed all the normal dreams.

And then I dreamed all the not-normal ones.

One after another my brain shot episodic barbs at my unconscious mind until a voice called out of the nothingness. A computer speaking into a tin-can with its mechanical enunciations. My skin crawled. I covered my ears. The sound rattled like shackles from the past until nothing remained but to scream.

"What!?"

A light overhead offered enough of itself to see the faint beginnings of a narrow corridor ahead. The darkness dwelling there turned my blood to ice. I turned away, ran in the opposite direction. It didn't matter; the corridor followed me every which way, beckoning me to explore its forbidden halls.

The entrance sighed, a cold breath that nipped the tender flesh of my nose and ears. A shiver ran through me, triggering a second, which multiplied into a third. An endless cascade of quivering muscles until I stood in deaf paralysis, my body no longer my own.

"You said you'd come back." Somebody spoke, no longer the metallic rasp of a machine. It rose up out of the tunnel. I couldn't follow it. I'd be lost to the labyrinth if I moved. For an eternity I would wander those ever-narrowing halls until I couldn't even find myself.

The fear gnawed at my entrails, chewing its way north, leaving me void of hope.

Then it twisted; the hall retracted, shrank, spun, and expanded. It felt like being in the Stream and changing the environment at will. The earth wobbled beneath me. I reached out into the darkness to steady myself, and found something.

Cold. Dead.

When I looked back, I stood at the precipice of a great divide. A chasm that devours worlds. My feet skirted the edge, kicking loose rocks and dirt down the ever-deepening hole.

The breeze wrapped an icy palm around my neck, and pulled me forward. I dug my heels in. The ground, covered in sharp gravel, tore at the flesh. Tiny stones chewed their way through my soles and into my soul.

I couldn't resist.

"I'm still waiting, Tom," the voice sang. This time it wasn't a plea for help, but a statement, a command. I recognized the voice. "You said you'd come back."

"Diana?" I said, no longer resisting the wind pulling me towards oblivion.

I took a step, shattering the prison of fear holding me immobile.

"I'm coming, Diana."

And then I fell.

CHAPTER FOUR
Ghosts Don't Sleep In

I awoke to the desperate chirping of an alarm in my head. It took a handful of groggy seconds to determine the source of the noise. I looked to my forearm, where my Life Tracker flashed its twelve-hour warning—into the homestretch.

Swaddled in soiled clothes from the night before, I rolled off the couch and hobbled to the bathroom.

"You look like shit," I said to the man in the mirror reaching for my toothbrush. The bristled brush returned my blank stare. We studied one another and contemplated the futility of the act about to be performed. Teeth-cleaning nanobots are cheaper than water, but some things are meant to be done the hard way. I grabbed the tube of toothpaste and lathered the brush.

There are worse ways to die than with fresh breath. I think my mother told me that once.

I considered that the benefit of knowing I'd be dead soon. Not the control, but the escape. I'd lost my purpose along with Diana. I hadn't died with her, but I'd stopped living.

It's unclear who got the short straw on that deal.

A bell chimed, rippling through the stale apartment air. Another mystery sound. The doorbell. The first time I'd ever heard that sound since moving to the Lowers.

I ignored it, but a second later the door grated open of its own accord. I chomped down on my toothbrush and leaned against the bathroom doorframe to see the intruder.

My jaw slackened. The toothbrush dangled between loose lips.

"What the hell?" I said. It seemed the appropriate response to seeing a ghost.

Alaina Raines took two steps into the apartment, hard heels of her boots clicking on the few exposed patches of floor. Her head swiveled like a ball bearing on a well lubricated joint, admiring my contribution to the increased entropy of the universe.

"Jesus," she said, drawing the word out and adding a third syllable. "How is this even possible? Where are your garbage-nanites?"

Raines wore a thin black jacket with an open high collar, traced with silver along a hem that hugged her curves, blending seamlessly into black pants. A downright distracting getup if she wanted it to be.

She looked entirely the same, and entirely different. A hardness in her eye, and a tilt to her chin. A confidence that comes with age and broken hearts.

"They quit," I said, forgetting the mouthful of toothpaste, which saw its opportunity to escape in a conga line of drool down my chin. "Overworked and underpaid."

I smirked. She frowned.

Just like old times.

"Right." She maneuvered through the debris field with a grace and precision that would've been surprising if I hadn't known the woman so well. Raines stopped shy of the bathroom and eyed it, the toothpaste stains on the floor, and me with equal measures of disapproval. "We gotta talk."

"Isn't that what we're doing?"

"Don't be an ass." She held my stare, asserting her dominance. "You have any idea how long it took me to track you down?"

"Seven years?" I regretted the words the moment they left my lips, but they were gone. Too late to stop them.

Raines twitched. Something smacked me, as if trying to shove the words back into my mouth. The toothbrush stabbed the inner lining of my cheek. Toothpaste reached escape velocity and flew from my mouth, coating the mirror to my right.

I think she slapped me. An impressive feat considering she hadn't moved. Either she'd received a couple new upgrades since last we spoke or I'd gotten slow.

The truth likely lay somewhere between the two.

I rubbed my cheek, hoping my nanocomp would dull the sting. The nanites coursing through my body had repaired my ribs from the night prior, but they could only do so much for this.

Half the pain of being slapped is psychological. Nothing the nanobots could do for my pride.

When I looked up she gave me those you-look-like-shit eyes. In return, I gave her a no-fucking-shit grimace.

"I told you, don't be an ass," Raines said, her face a cool sheet of ice betraying none of the feelings hiding beneath.

I shrugged. "Sorry."

I wasn't sure she believed that.

I wasn't sure *I* believed that.

But it was the only way forward, so we pretended we did.

"I'm dying," I said.

She blinked twice and swallowed once.

"You come to send me off?"

"No; you want to die alone, that's your business. It's bad business, but no worse than living alone."

Raines and Lou were dispensing all sorts of business advice these days. I must have looked like a man with entrepreneurial designs for his future.

"Then why you here?"

"As a favor." She shook her head and leaned in. "You're an ass, but you deserve to know."

"Know what?"

"It's about Malcolm."

Those words were a wet towel slap to the face. My heart went from idle to red line in an instant. Sweat formed in the creases of my palms while the hairs lining my neck stood to attention.

Mention of your wife's murderer is bound to elicit a similar reaction in most warm-blooded creatures.

"What about him?" No stone could dull the edge in my voice.

"He's out." Raines didn't waver. Not an inch. She held my stare as if it were the only thing keeping me together.

Which might be true, 'cause those words didn't make sense. Maybe the nanites had crossed some wires. Maybe I was hallucinating.

That'd be nice.

"Not funny, Raines." My heart hammered, trying to pound out the dents of a life lived hard. A discharge of adrenaline ravaged my blood, burning as it commuted through my body.

"He broke out of Pause last night."

The man in the mirror turned towards me. He mocked me. His eyes were an accusation, but of what I couldn't say. I clenched my fingers so tight they sent electric shards of pain lancing up my arm and into my shoulder. The walls contracted. The apartment shrank. Everything collapsed in on me. A man-sized black hole.

I lashed out at my reflection, knuckles biting into the mirror. The glass fractured. I splintered into a thousand distorted versions of myself, each shard a closer representation of the man inside than the unbroken version ever was.

I denied the scream rising in my throat and said weakly, "That's not possible."

Raines shook her head and took my hand, her skin soft in a way foreign to the Lowers. Despite the gulf that'd emerged between us, the contact felt good. Reminded me of a different life.

"I know you're angry. I am too," she said, rubbing her thumb across the exposed skin of my inner forearm where the two bars of my Tracker continued their march towards nothing.

Her touch brought comfort. A reminder of something I'd found in her arms after Diana. A reminder of the guilt that had gnawed day and night at my weary conscience.

It made me feel vulnerable, a feeling I'd moved to the Lowers to avoid.

I jerked my hand free and put a step between us.

"Thanks for telling me." My voice slipped away from me like water through cupped hands. "But you shouldn't have come here."

Raines' stony expression turned liquid, melting away to reveal the woman I'd known as more than a partner. "I need your help finding him, Tom."

Just like that, the years that grate our souls and callous our character washed off her, leaving in their place the woman who'd been young and naive enough to put her trust in the person she loved. She had never understood that the people with a key to your heart are the ones that break it.

She knew now.

In a different life she'd been my pupil. I'd taught her everything I knew.

It broke me, but I hadn't skipped that lesson.

Unfortunately, the heart forgives, even when it shouldn't.

"I've got a couple hours left, and then I'm done. Out of here. Gone. I can't do this anymore. Can't be here. I want out, Alaina."

Raines turned away, letting the silence settle. When she spoke, she directed her words to the ground at her feet.

"You know Malcolm better than anyone. He's going to kill again." Her voice was hard, unforgiving. "Stay here and die alone if you want. Or put your big boy pants on and help me catch the guy that murdered Diana. Your choice."

The world was conspiring against me. Raines tugged at my heartstrings like a puppet master. It no longer became a matter of *if* I would help, but *why*.

Sometimes we do things for the right reasons; sometimes for the wrong.

Thinking about Malcolm walking free made me want to do things for the wrong reasons.

I wanted to find him. I wanted to kill him.

I'd been too weak to do it the first time around. Afraid I couldn't bear the weight of that decision. Thought it was the honorable thing. Turns out there is no honor in death.

Only loss.

"Let me grab my jacket," I said, glancing at the three short bars remaining on my Tracker.

Raines' cheek twitched; she quashed down the beginning of a smile before it could grow into something more and said, "It's over a hundred degrees up there."

"Can never be too careful." I grabbed the faded leather jacket from where I'd discarded it the night before. "Wouldn't want to catch a cold."

CHAPTER FIVE
Out Of The Gutter, Into The Rabbit Hole

The silence hit me first. It pressed against me as Raines and I were carried through Terminus on a slide-walk. Living down deep for so many years had reprogrammed how I thought about noise. Down there it was an ever-present entity. Millions of humans compressed into such a tiny area make an inevitably large amount of noise.

Being out in the open again was different. Commuters streaked across the sky, riding along the Electromagnetic Lowroad in their Dragonflys, without a sound. Those traveling on foot were equally silent as they navigated the city, completely immersed in the Stream.

Reconnecting to the Stream would bring a blitz of stimuli and noise that would more closely approximate the melody of the deeps, but I wasn't ready for that. I wanted to absorb the quiet a bit longer without the distraction of an interactive environment competing for my attention.

I looked up and realized I hadn't seen the sun in seven years. After all that time, I thought the reunion would be…more.

It was trapped behind a layer of gray clouds hanging in a thick veil pulled taut across the sky. The heat lingered, heavy with moisture and man's regret. Despite the air clinging to my flesh and smothering my breath with its weight, it was nice being free of the bottomless well that is Terminus' lower suburbs and its constant cycle of repurposed air.

The air down deep tasted of mechanical sterility, whereas the air on the surface had a metallic tang. Neither were bad per se, just different.

Unknowable amounts of invisible junk still floated on the breeze, a constant reminder of the damage done during the Dissolution. If not for the nanites filtering air through my lungs, my insides would've turned to jelly and leaked out the nearest orifice within ten paces of the airlock. Thankfully Raines had brought me a fresh injection, saving me the unpleasant fate of dying in a convulsing ball of muscle and bone.

Humanity had a long way to go before they undid the damage. If ever. Those were the hopes and dreams of a different generation, one in which I had no vested interest.

The bitch of it is, those who can afford life up-top don't care about any of that. With access to the nanite tech that allows their bodies to cope with the influx of toxins, why should they?

Breathing non-toxic air is a poor man's problem.

I turned from the haze-smeared yellow orb in the sky and back to Raines. She was already half a slide-walk away. I trotted to catch up, accidentally bumping a twenty-something couple in the process. They had the fashion sensibilities to suggest they lived firmly in the Middles. Distracted, and tuned out of reality and into the Stream, they never saw me coming.

Bio-luminescent nanobots twinkled across the woman's body, painting her bare torso with shapes and colors shifting from one complex pattern to the next. Controlled by her nanocomp, her tattooed clothing fluctuated with her every fleeting thought. One of the greatest wastes in cosmetic nanotechnology I'd ever seen, but I couldn't deny the woman looked good.

She gasped as we bumped shoulders. The nanobots covering her body went into black-out mode as she slipped out of the Stream. A veil of shadow covered her body from throat to toes. She one-upped her previous gasp when she looked at me.

The man, with the facial repartee of a middle manager accustomed to talking down to those around him, opened his mouth to defend his lady's honor.

Until he too got a better look at me, at which point his mouth promptly shut as if it hung on a pneumatic hinge.

I'm not intimidating, but I am dirty. A natural consequence of the tight water rations maintained in the Lowers. Clean people fear the dirty.

I continued past them, lagging behind Raines, who maintained a brisk pace despite the slide-walk carrying us through the city at what would otherwise be a full sprint. There are no slide-walks in the Lowers, and not having to walk everywhere was a luxury I wanted to enjoy.

I was prepared to slip back into the habits of a life long past, but Raines wasn't.

She turned and said, "You're dying, but you're not broken; try and keep up."

"Where first?" I asked, adding the required amount of pep to my step to match Raines' pace.

"Headed to Pause."

"What about the Precinct?"

"No need; you can review the files on the way."

That was welcome news.

Peacekeepers are human, and humans hold grudges. Considering the less than ideal circumstances leading up to my departure from Time Vice, and my ardent desire to finish out the day without receiving another ass kicking, avoiding the Precinct sat near the top of my to-do list.

Raines stepped off the slide-walk and hit the ground at a jog before slowing to a walk, a coordinated motion developed over a lifetime of practice. My dismount, on the other hand, lacked any semblance of grace. I hit the immobile ground with a locked knee, which had the unfortunate effect of jolting me forward into a three step sprint. I charged through the holographic projection of an absurdly beautiful woman standing, for reasons unknown, on the street corner in an outfit that could only qualify as bedroom attire.

The computer program running the hologram flicked me a smile. Raines placed a steadying hand on my shoulder, leading me away from those come-hither eyes.

At the end of the walkway a silver Dragonfly-class van descended from the sky and stopped inches from the curb. Raines opened the door and slid behind the steering wheel.

Her Dragonfly was long and squat, designed to carry a small army of people. Whoever had designed the Fly had done so with an all-encompassing ignorance of aesthetics and aerodynamics. I figured luck would be playing a large part in keeping our vehicle together if Raines took us onto the ElMag Low.

The Dragonfly didn't conform to Raines' personality. At least, not to the personality I'd known.

I settled into the passenger seat and studied a child's drawing flashing on the dashboard. It showed a woman riding a giraffe, flanked by two smaller giraffes being ridden by two equally small children.

I pivoted in my chair and studied the backseat. An explosion of nanite-controlled toys and holographic coloring books littered the floor. All the tell-tale signs of children at play.

"Is this your Fly?" I asked, testing the waters.

"Yeah."

"Um… Do you…" I wasn't sure how to broach the question. Raines had been my partner for years—for a brief period she'd been more, but asking about what had become of her life in the wake of my absence felt wrong, forbidden.

"Have kids?" she said, beating me to the question.

"Yeah."

"Yeah."

"A boy and a girl?"

"Look at those skills of deduction," she said, without turning to meet my gaze.

"What're their names?"

"Madison and Morgan."

"How old?"

"Six."

"Twins?"

"Haven't lost a step, have you?" Thirty seconds later Raines turned, the corner of one lip pulled up despite her visible attempt to keep it level.

A thin film covered her eyes as she multitasked between communicating with the Fly via the Stream and talking with me. In response to a silent command issued from Raines' mind the Fly tilted towards the sun and accelerated smoothly into the sky.

I dug my fingers into the armrest until they nearly punctured the fabric. Memories of my last ride in a Dragonfly crept back like fingers squeezing my heart.

Raines had sat beside me then, too, but our seats were reversed. I'd flown by hand, confident I wouldn't need to neural sync with the vehicle.

Too confident.

Those were the early days of my Quick slide. Before I'd acclimated to the soaring highs and trudging lows. Before I even understood what I'd truly lost by turning to the needle.

Jimmy Walters had sat behind Raines in the Fly, separated from us by a thin electromagnetic wall. By himself, Jimmy was nothing special. A low-level Intuit who'd managed some time heists, but who, on the whole, came up somewhat unremarkable.

That's not to say he wouldn't have been useful, though. Jimmy had put himself in with a small terrorist cell called the

Children of the Lost—a group of Intuits, and regulars, known to be actively aiding the Lost.

Treason at its finest.

Jimmy Walters had no interest in dying for the cause. His were ideals that could be purchased—a price we were willing to pay for information on the rest of the group.

That is, until I had a minor Quick fit that resulted in me jerking the steering wheel. We flew straight into the seventy-sixth floor of the Janus Electronics Business Center at over a hundred miles an hour.

Jimmy died. Face smashed against the electromagnetic wall from the force the collision. That he wasn't buckled in might have been my fault. That he died most definitely was.

Raines hadn't fared much better. She'd been buckled in, but that only held her in place for the smart-metal I-beam that punctured the windshield, and her chest. Half her blood purged in an instant. Imprisoned by the crumpled walls of the Dragonfly, I couldn't get to her. Could only watch. Wait. Hope. Pray.

I'd passed out from my own injuries by the time the medics arrived. I woke in the hospital convinced Raines couldn't have survived. Somehow she did; a small miracle that did nothing to assuage my guilt.

That was the first good look I got of the man I was becoming. Of the man the Quick was making me.

Dogged by a guilt I couldn't outrun, I fled. Didn't wait to say goodbye.

That had not been a good day.

We cut across the skyline towards the ocean to the east in a Peacekeeper transport lane, forgoing the ElMag Low thousands of feet above.

"Married?" I asked, testing the boundaries of our new relationship.

Raines ignored my question. "The Pause security feed is in your queue." She kept her eyes on the swatch of gray pollution steaming off the city ahead of us.

I activated my nanocomp with a thought and blinked into the Stream. It was something I hadn't done in years, except to enter Lou's arena. Nerve endings quivered, sensitive and overstimulated, as if teased with a feather. The hair on my arm danced as I opened my eyes to the virtual rivers of data buzzing past my skull.

Blue contrails of data crisscrossed the sky in unimaginably complex patterns. The ElMag Low pulsed a dull red as Dragonflys streaked over the city.

Millions of white nodes crawled across, over, and through Terminus, each one delineating a unique individual linked to the Stream.

All of us connected, tethered by the information filtered through our brains.

Not everyone can see the Stream like me. Like an Intuit. If they could, they'd hate us more than they already do.

Raines flew the Dragonfly straight through a line of code she could not see. The data redirected its path, wrapping around the vehicle like a river flowing over a rock. I reached out into the digital ether with my mind and touched it.

Scintillated nerve endings tittered. I absorbed the meaningless packet of information and opened it. It was nothing important, just a private communication between two nanocomps, but it was mine now. I could do anything with it.

Redirect it. Change it. Destroy it.

This was the havoc an Intuit could create.

I released the packet, pushing it back on its merry way, with a sigh.

It felt good being inside again. My amygdala tingled, releasing profusions of endorphins that curbed the Quick headache that had been building since I'd awoken that morning.

The Stream I'd become accustomed to in the Lowers was weak by comparison. A private connection formed by only a couple hundred minds for the express purpose of entertainment.

Now, linked with the trillions of nanobots floating in the stratosphere, and the billions of humans across Unity, I joined the network that went beyond cyberspace and became something more closely approximating hyper-reality.

Life was more real in the Stream for Intuits than it could ever be on the outside. Nobody knew why. No one had a clue what enabled us to form such intimate connections with the network. To manipulate it as an extension of ourselves.

Which was why I'd chosen to disconnect when I left the surface. I wanted to dull my feelings, not enhance them.

Wanted to be lost, not connected.

But I was weak. Using Lou's private arena became the only way I could resist the urge. To keep from fully relapsing.

Returning after so long was rediscovering a part of my body I'd forgotten was missing.

The user interface projected by nanobots on the inside of my eyeballs was designed for how I used to think. A veritable seizure of applications and programs scrolling past at unintelligible speeds.

I muddled through, hoping the system would regain coherency as my brain reconnected dormant neural highways, but it wasn't coming quickly enough.

So, like a child frustrated by a game beyond their comprehension, I dragged my digital arm across the table and cleared the board, knocking the pieces of my former self, and the way that man used to think, to the ground.

With a blank interface things started looking up. I located the file Raines had placed in my queue and clicked it with a twitch of my mind. A partially translucent video filled my display.

The backdrop of reality bled through the image, but the nanocomp embedded beneath the squishy gray matter of my brain compartmentalized the competing stimuli without a loss of cognitive processing.

The video, pulled from the cloud of surveillance nanites floating in the air around Pause, gave a god's-eye view of the compound. When the nanites crawling across every inch of the prison synchronized images, nothing within the confines of those walls went unseen.

And yet, there was a lot I wasn't seeing.

The video began with Malcolm walking a long hall built with an eye towards simplicity and despair. He moved quickly through a pair of double doors.

If the goal was to keep inmates inside, then in my non-expert opinion those doors should have been locked. That design functionality must not have been built into the original model 'cause Malcolm pranced through as if the prison concierge service were holding them open.

With an anticlimactic number of gun fights and explosions taking place, I watched with increasingly detached interest. Doors simply opened for Malcolm Wolfe. When I toggled through available viewpoints, they were limited to people and places throughout the Pause compound that had nothing to do with the ongoing escape.

Only the video of Malcolm walking the hall.

There was one easy explanation for the dearth of interesting footage: somebody had deleted it. Whoever pulled Malcolm from his Stream dream was probably the same person buzzing him through the prison way points.

To my knowledge, which, admittedly, was dated, the Warden was the only person with administrative access to the nanite surveillance feed. A fact Raines wouldn't have missed.

It was clumsy. If the Warden facilitated Malcolm's escape, why would he implicate himself so thoroughly by tampering with the video feed?

Warning bells went off in the non-nanotized region of my brain, the part evolved over millennia of trial and error as our ancestors pushed the limits of comfort and expanded out of the forest, and into the Savanna.

Something was wrong.

Something beyond the simple fact that Malcolm had awoken from an induced coma and walked out of Pause with less hassle than checking out of a hotel.

Terminus shrank in the side-view mirror as we approached the fringe of city sprawl. I slipped out of the Stream and admired the ocean holding hands with the sky on the horizon. The two rushed towards us. The blue-gray slurry, mixed with equal parts water and garbage, heaved and jiggled below.

In the Stream, Raines received real-time course corrections to Pause. The compound, a lesson in paranoia, floated somewhere off the Eastern seaboard. It ran entirely off the grid, on a subsystem of nanites linked remotely to the Stream, which meant finding the facility would be a needle-in-a-haystack type of fun without somebody on the other end relaying coordinates.

It was a pain in the ass, but with the world's most dangerous men bunking together, the precautions were necessary. Until last night, they'd worked.

I studied Raines' glazed eyes. Couldn't help but compare the woman now to the woman that was. They were different.

A difference that couldn't be quantified.

Her skin and bone structure retained their exotic Eastern accents (so rare a sight within the walls of Unity). Her hair, a blanket of starless sky, hung loose about her face.

She hadn't lost the confidence inherent in her movements, nor control when she spoke. But there existed a burred edge below the facade. A gouge where life had nicked her. Something sensed rather than seen.

Time Vice Detective could be considered an odd career choice for a woman who could have been an Upper off looks alone. But she was smart, determined, and hard-working to a fault. An arsenal of traits that guaranteed success regardless of what profession she'd chosen; even a mother.

That revelation served a difficult reminder that life goes on. That those who I'd left behind hadn't remained in stasis, frozen by my absence. But that's what I wanted when I fled the Middles. Couldn't stand the thought of pulling Raines down with me, not even for the occasional visit. She deserved better.

A better future.

A future I wished I could've been a part of.

I was snapped out of these thoughts by a bell chiming. Somebody had pinged my nanocomp. Being connected to the world again was an odd sensation that made me long for the seclusion and privacy of my own mind, free of the Stream.

Nobody in Unity knew I'd reconnected to the Stream, and I hadn't broadcast my presence to the network, so it seemed a safe bet that the ping was Raines including me in whatever digital conversation was taking place in her brain.

Gamble long enough and you learn there is no safe bet.

A lesson I was reminded of as I accepted the ping and Malcolm Wolfe's face appeared before me.

CHAPTER SIX
Gifts From An Enemy
Are Anything But

No single word could describe the influx of emotion I felt in that moment. The closest approximation would require a hyphen. Something along the lines of confusion-rage.

Malcolm's thin lips slithered to either side of his face, revealing a row of off-white enamel. A far cry from a perfect smile, but it fit well with the sharp angles and folds of his cheeks and chin. For a guy that'd spent the greater part of the last decade in a coma, he didn't look half bad.

"Sorry, wrong number," I said, clumsily pawing through the Stream to initiate a trace. A simple procedure, though filling balloons with wind might have been easier than using the Stream in my emotionally compromised state.

"Always with the jokes," Malcolm said. "I've missed that about you."

"That feeling is less than mutual."

"You wound me. Listen, sorry I didn't call sooner. I've been busy absorbing this brave new world. I'm sure you understand. But now that I'm here, we have so much to catch up on."

"Not sure we have much to talk about. Unless you're looking to lose a couple teeth, in which case I might know a guy," I said, resisting the urge to unload a vortex pistol into the man's face. I reminded myself nothing good would come from that but a blown-out windshield followed by another pride-bruising slap from Raines.

In the end, it didn't matter. I had no pistol, so the windshield remained intact. For now.

"Is violence the answer to all your problems? Suppose that's the Lowers rubbing off on you, eh?" Malcolm leaned in, eliciting a response from the nanobots tucked away in my olfactory lobe. The sudsy sterility of soap. Jasmine, perhaps. The scent penetrated my virtual nostrils, eliciting a visceral response in the form of a stomach-curdling shudder. It wafted off him as if he'd spent the greater portion of the morning trying to wash away the person he'd been. "By the way, have you found whatever it is you went down there searching for?"

I eyed the trace in the bottom-right quadrant of my display as it crept towards zero.

Thirty-three seconds.

I hadn't gone to the Lowers in search of anything, only to escape memories of a former life. Memories, it turned out, haunt regardless of location.

"No," I said, only partially aware of Raines watching from the driver's seat, "still looking. Suppose I'm getting closer, though."

"And if I may ask, what are you searching for?"

I wanted to sit quietly, never speak again, but Malcolm wanted to talk. I was obliged to let him until the trace could finish.

"Penance, maybe."

"Poor Tom, seeking that which he shall not find."

"I found you once."

"A technicality."

"That's a big technicality."

"Indeed." Malcolm tilted his head and nodded. "But were you in time? And if not, then does it truly matter?"

There was nothing I could say that didn't start with a scream, so I bit my lip.

"And if you don't find your penance?" Malcolm continued. "Is there a heaven for men like you?"

"That's not a place I'd want to spend eternity."

"You don't give yourself enough credit."

"You give yourself too much," I said, checking the trace once more.

Zero.

The trace flashed twice then disappeared.

Weird.

I chased it through the user interface and pulled up the data-log. Bad news. The trace had been terminated. Results deleted.

A command that could only be issued by my nanocomp.

A command which most certainly had not been issued by my nanocomp.

Not without my consent, at least. Which is something it would need.

"Please tell me you didn't think it would be that easy?" Malcolm grinned like a kid burning ants with a magnifying glass.

He'd hacked my nanocomp. Which shouldn't be possible, but it was the only explanation that could account for what had happened.

I wouldn't let him see me squirm. Not nine years ago, and not now.

"A man can hope," I said.

"Hope is the last to die."

"You've been reading too many fortune cookies."

"I've had a lot of time on my hands."

"Well I don't, so how about you get to the point," I said, eager to end the call and punch something. "What do you want?"

"It's simple," Malcolm said. "You seek penance. I seek revenge. But no ordinary revenge will do. Revenge stories are the oldest kind, and I am nothing if not original, so I must go above and beyond to make our story truly unique. You will suffer in ways you've never imagined possible for what you took from me."

"I'm game. Come here and take your revenge; I'll wait."

"Spoken like a man with nothing to lose, and that simply won't do, Tom. I want a challenge. I need it; crave it. This moment has lived in my dreams for years. The collision of two irrepressible forces of nat—"

"Is your plan to talk me to death?" I said, interrupting a speech I imagined he'd rehearsed numerous times before.

"No." Malcolm scrunched up one eye and said, "Killing you would be a mercy. I have no intention of showing you mercy. Instead, I'm going to give you a reason to live. I'm going to line up everything you have ever loved, every cherished memory, any glimmer of hope that you clung to on those cold dark nights when you cowered alone, high out of your mind on the Quick, gnawing on the barrel of your own gun, praying night after night that you would be strong enough to pull the trigger and end it, all the while knowing you wouldn't, you couldn't.

"I will expose all those fears you hide in the deepest recesses of your heart. I will make you face the reality of how much you truly stand to lose..." Malcolm's smile smoldered. "And then I will take them from you. Piece by piece. One by one. Then, and only then, when death is no longer the cure for your sorrow, I will kill you."

My skin tried slithering off my body. Malcolm's voice lacked any human substance. Slow, mechanical, unfeeling.

"Sounds unpleasant." I forced a smile, then said, "Better hope I don't find you first."

"I truly hope you do. And to prove it, I have a gift for you."

The skin lining my forearm ignited with searing pain, as if every hair had been simultaneously plucked. I rolled back my sleeve and watched the Tracker perform a new trick.

The bars grew. Fast.

"What's this?"

"You're good, or more accurately, you were good." Malcolm punctuated his words with a finger in the air. "But you're not that man anymore, and eight hours is simply not enough time if you hope to catch me and earn your penance."

The Tracker stopped at twenty-four hours, then paused for half a heartbeat before ticking down once more.

"One day. Consider it a going-away present."

"And if I choose not to play?" I rubbed a finger along the smooth surface of my forearm, wondering which deity I'd offended to deserve the punishment of more time.

"Then you'll be wasting your time, and Diana's."

My mind was slow to decipher his words, but when it did, the revelation was a kick to the balls. He'd given me a day stolen from Diana's account. Soon, I'd be living off her time.

The blood drained from my face and pooled in my feet.

I swam through the surreality of my situation. My head spun along with the world. He could keep me alive indefinitely. String me along with stolen time. Every second a fresh paper cut sliced beneath bleeding fingernails.

"I'm going to kill you," I said, locking onto Malcolm's eyes, a focal point for the anger churning my innards.

"That's the fighting spirit." Malcolm clapped his hands, a single deafening smack of flesh against flesh, amplified by our virtual environment. "Let the game begin."

He winked and then disappeared.

I shook my head, struggling to understand my tormentor.

I'd lost three years tracking him with a single-minded focus, studying everything the Stream had archived on him. But there had been no answers then, and there were no answers now.

There existed an unbridgeable gap of understanding born from the knowledge that we were fundamentally two different species.

Men and monsters hold no common ground. We'd like to think that, at least. It's not true, but it helps me sleep at night.

I blinked out of the Stream, back to the cradled silence of the Fly.

"Malcolm," I said, preempting the question Raines wore on her face.

She nodded. If surprised, she didn't let it show.

"He give you that?" She used the elbow of the arm gripping the steering wheel to gesture at the exposed bars on my forearm.

"Yeah," I said, dropping my chin to my chest. I rolled my sleeve down to the wrist and rubbed the back of my neck with a hand softened from years of idleness. "They're Diana's."

"Don't do that. You let yourself believe those are Diana's hours and you're done. Simple as that." She tightened her grip on the arm rest until the imperfections of the tiny bones capping her knuckles were visible beneath the stretched skin. "He knows it'll eat at you. And it will, if you let it."

Malcolm had been eating at me since the day I'd been assigned his case.

"We're gonna catch him," Raines said.

"Maybe."

"We did it once before."

But at what cost? And had it been worth paying?

Those thoughts had loitered like guests overstaying their welcome in the back of my mind for the past decade. After so long, they were familiar. I couldn't imagine a world where they didn't plague my every waking moment.

I shook my head, distancing myself from those thoughts, and stared out the window. The jagged walls of Pause broke the palette of blue on the horizon. Black walls rising out of the ocean absorbed the diffused sunlight.

A place of despair, removed from the world and the Stream. A place where time became an active torture. The worst kind of prison. Not simply a loss of freedom, but a loss of self, of reality.

The inhabitants were placed in a Stream-induced freeze, altering their perception of time, and stretching minutes into weeks. A ten-year sentence equaled hundreds worth of rehabilitation inside Pause.

The system worked, but truthfully Unity kept the prisoners around for another less altruistic reason. Every fool lucky enough to call Pause home was an Intuit. Thousands of them sitting around in a Stream dream meant a whole lot of untapped potential. Unity's military branch, Division, re-appropriated the inactive portions of the prisoners' minds, routing their mental elasticity back into the Stream, supplying a noticeable bump in their network's capacity.

Unity justified the treatment as a sort of community service on the part of the prisoners. Giving back to the people they'd stolen so much from. Who was I to disagree?

"What do you suppose we'll find there?" I asked the window.

"More questions, maybe a couple answers," Raines said, diving towards the water below. "If we're lucky."

Luck. Scary how often catching bad guys comes down to that one intangible factor. Cases are made and broken on Mistress Luck's whimsy.

Can't control her.

Can only hope to stay on her good side.

As we entered Pause airspace the prison's computers took control of our vehicle. Raines relinquished her mental grip on the vehicle and let her head roll back onto the headrest.

"This place doesn't seem very lucky," I said, watching the wall of turrets passing by.

"You watch that video?"

"Yeah."

"Any thoughts you'd care to share with the rest of the class?"

"I think the Warden has some explaining to do. But I'm guessing you already knew that."

The Dragonfly dropped a handful of feet and skimmed the surface of the compound, decelerating fast and smooth until it came to a complete stop. A pair of guards, gussied to the gills in black nano-suits, fanned out and approached the vehicle.

Raines nodded and thumbed a button on the center console. The computer scanned her fingerprint before releasing the glove box between my legs with a click. She reached across me and into the compartment, her thick mane of hair brushing my cheek as she passed.

Goose bumps dribbled up my arm and across my shoulder.

She smelled like rain. Not the sweaty sludge spackling the city, but the light, crisp droplets falling in what little countryside remained. Pure and sweet, with the ability to wash away the world's grime. It still smelled the same after so many years.

I was glad some things don't change.

When she retreated to her side of the vehicle, she held a vaporizer in the palm of her hand.

"Upgrades?" I asked, taking the device and turning it over.

"Speed, strength, and a little cognitive boost," she said. "You're gonna need them more than me."

There wasn't much room to argue that point. I put the vaporizer to my lips and inhaled. The fresh nanites took effect an instant later. Muscles groaned with pleasure.

It'd been years since my last upgrade. The pipes were rusty. Capillaries crackled, engorged with blood, as my heart slammed against the underside of my throat. Synapses sizzled with increased vigor.

Thoughts moved faster, muscles responded quicker.

The sweaty, sweet aroma of children at play drifted off the teddy bear beside me. I studied its hair follicles, which expanded and sharpened until I could practically see through to the seams.

I rolled my fingers into a fist. The knuckles popped in sequence. Sometimes it just felt good to be more than human.

"What I don't understand," Raines said, her voice a boom inhaled through my heightened senses, "is what does the Warden have to gain?"

"You're asking the wrong question."

"What's the right one?"

"Don't you remember anything I taught you?"

"Pretend I forgot."

"You gotta ask, what's he stand to lose? You know that about a man, and you can make him do anything."

A lesson I was learning the hard way.

CHAPTER SEVEN
The Decisions That Change Us

Warden Emilio Castille's office spanned three of my apartments stacked end on end. It was enormous in a way I'd grown unfamiliar to after so many years in the Lowers, where space itself was a luxury. I don't know under what circumstances he would require such a large office, but I'll say this, Castille had made the most of his situation.

Tapestries emblazoned with the Castille coat of arms dangled from either side of the Warden's desk. They were unique, and pretty enough, in a who-the-hell-has-a-unicorn-on-their-coat-of-arms kind of way.

Then again, the better question might have been, who the hell has a coat of arms?

The answer? The same guy with a replica suit of armor standing in the corner.

"I'm sorry to have kept you waiting, Detective Raines." Emilio Castille stood behind a tower of papers tilted precariously on his desk. "This has been a hectic day to say the least."

Unless you considered height, nothing about the man was physically imposing. He stood half a head taller than me, but it made him look stretched. The padded shoulder blades of his navy blue suit gave Emilio a triangle shape, but did little to conceal the bony joints and rail-thin figure giving the clothing their insubstantial shape.

I'd peeked at the man's file while being processed by Pause security. Castille had spent the better part of his life working in the Cryptography branch of Division's pantheon. Smart, beyond a doubt, with an ambition that'd quickly distinguished him from his peers.

How could that ambition have been exploited into releasing Malcolm? What did the man stand to gain, or lose?

I'd plowed through the variables, turned them over in my mind's eye, but failed to find the connection that would bring clarity.

"We'll make this brief." Raines shook the Warden's extended hand before gesturing to me. "This is my partner, Detective Mandel."

The Warden's eyebrow twitched, telling me he knew that was a lie, but he said nothing. Instead, he folded his arms, pursed the two thin lines that he presumably thought of as lips, and nodded.

I glanced at the empty chair beside Raines, but my legs had an itch and I stayed standing.

Raines started talking. I zoned out as Raines and Castille did the formality dance, something which held no interest to me.

I wandered to the back of the room, to a bookshelf lined with pictures. I leaned in and studied a collage created from hundreds of tinier photos and arranged in such a way as to resemble Pause floating in a predominately blue ocean.

I accessed the digital photo with my nanocomp, stretching and zooming the individual images.

They were mug shots, one for each man and woman who'd ever spent time at Pause. Many of the faces were familiar, but most were not. A chronological history of Unity's greatest time criminals stretching back to the Grand Unification itself.

Centuries of violent history represented in something beautiful. All the smaller pieces connected to form the whole. The premise of Unity and the Stream distilled in a single photo.

I returned to the conversation to hear Castille droning on about security details, compromised access codes, and a slew of other things that generally had the smell of bullshit.

He looked content with his story, like he was doing a good job selling us on it, but I wasn't buying. Too many defects in the product for it to be anything but a cheap knock-off. I wanted the real story.

"Do you like your job?" I interrupted the Warden in the middle of a sentence going nowhere.

"I do not understand how that has any bearing on the current investigation, Mr. Mandel," Castille said, carefully avoiding the word Detective.

"Trying to get a feel for who stands to gain from Malcolm's escape. If it was me, I'd need a better reason for releasing a mass-murdering psychopath than job satisfaction, but hey, I'm not here to judge. Maybe you really hate your job."

Once upon a time I had a semblance of tact and subtlety, skills I'd apparently misplaced. That left only my raw personality, a hammer eager to bludgeon a world of nails.

Castille thrust a knobby finger in the air; his eyes skulked behind slitted lids while searching for words, but his face told me plenty.

Micro-expressions are unconscious facial twitches occurring when one emotion is concealed beneath another.

In this case, the Warden gave off conflicting responses. His mouth tightened, lips pulled down and back: contempt. But the eyebrows betrayed him. They had the slightest droop: shame.

It blipped across his face for a fraction of a second before disappearing. Hence the term micro-expression; they're quick. In a different life I'd been pretty good at catching them. Maybe the best. Those days were gone, but Emilio was a bad faker, so I wasn't left entirely in the lurch.

The problem with micro-expressions is they tell you *what* a person is feeling, but not *why*. It takes creative guesswork and some empathy to root out the underlying motivations.

Contempt is simple. He disliked me. That was not surprising; I have that effect on people.

The shame was trickier. It was the one he'd concealed, so that made it important.

I wanted to believe he felt shame for releasing Malcolm, but reading emotions is like looking into a crystal ball. Sometimes you simply create a narrative convincing enough to sell the client.

In this case, I sold myself on a story of my own making. A questionable business plan at best.

"I am perfectly content with my work here," Emilio said, his words a series of stutters and stops. "And furthermore, you are mistaken if you believe I will sit idly by while you impugn my honor with any such accusation to the contrary."

His anger was genuine, but not the source. Something else rode beneath the surface of his indignant outburst. Emilio wasn't a hardened criminal, which suggested he'd been pulled into this against his will; that would explain the shame.

"Our window of opportunity to apprehend Malcolm Wolfe is closing, and you waste my time with these tangential accusations?" Emilio stood, a praying mantis unfolding his limbs.

No arguing there. But truth was, Malcolm's gone. To catch him, we'd need a boatload of luck and stupidity. Luck on our part, stupidity on his.

Each as unlikely as the other.

"Then help us open that window. Tell us why you helped him escape," I said, ignoring Raines trying to murder me with her stare. So much for being subtle, but like I said, my toolbox was sparse, and a hammer can only do so much.

Emilio perked his eyebrows to force an emotion he clearly didn't feel. Shock.

Definitely lying.

Twenty years on the force had honed my skill as a personal lie detector to a razor's edge. True, I'd allowed that edge to rust in the intervening years, but rusty or not, there's no mistaking the look of fake surprise.

Emotions follow a distinct time line and they're quick. Surprise doesn't linger awkwardly like a failed first kiss. Anything more than a second, and it's fake. That simple.

"You need to leave," Emilio said.

On cue, the door opened and a large man with a neatly trimmed beard and the uniform of a prison guard stepped into the office. The guard turned, his hand resting on the butt of the rifle slung around his neck. An alarm went off in the lizard part of my brain. Instinct set my body in motion before consulting with the rational part of my brain and I lunged sideways, driving my shoulder into the door.

The guard pivoted too slowly to clear the path of the closing door. It slammed him into the wall, but the guy bounced back, unfazed, with his rifle raised. He had me outgunned, but I was a blur of movement thanks to the nanite upgrade I'd received in Raines' Fly.

I leaped at him and snatched the barrel of the weapon before he took aim at my face.

Realizing he'd lost the range advantage, he changed tactics on the fly. He swung the butt of the rifle towards my head with enough force that I stood to lose a couple teeth and consciousness if it connected.

I dropped, letting gravity do the work of pulling me to the ground. Air from the man's strike swished through my hair. I hit the floor and rolled, sliding the pistol from the guard's holster as I moved past.

I popped up like a nanotized prairie dog with the vortex pistol aimed at the back of the man's head. "The world doesn't need more heroes," I said, flicking the safety off with an audible click.

The guard tensed, shoulders rising to his ears, and dropped his weapon.

Minutes later I had the guard wrapped up on the floor, wrists tethered to ankles, thanks to the restraints he'd been considerate enough to bring on his utility belt.

"What do you hope to accomplish?" Emilio asked, puffing his chest despite the tremble in his hands. "Certainly you realize you're a dead man? This is my island. Nobody gets on or off without my permission."

"Is that an admission of guilt?" I asked, closing the door and engaging the lock.

Emilio's face went through an interesting color change. "There's nothing to admit."

Things were moving fast, and if I had any hope of getting Raines off that floating island with blood still in her veins, we couldn't afford to be standing around when reinforcements came. But, Castille hadn't given us what we'd come for and I wouldn't leave until he did.

I had a final card to play. One I hated. Thinking about it made my stomach sink into my leg and take cover behind my knee.

Lou tried giving me a job like this last night. Turning him down hadn't been hard when it was only my life on the line. That had stopped being the case about an hour ago.

Something had to be done, a decision made. A better man might have classified the options in categories of good and bad, but I wasn't that man.

In the end right or wrong didn't matter anymore. I'd do anything to protect Raines. Anything to stop Malcolm.

"Do you know how I caught Malcolm the first time, Emilio?" I asked.

For what came next I needed to access the Time Bank archives, but for security purposes Pause ran off its own subsystem. A derivative, weaker, version of the Stream. Making the jump to the Stream would require a boost in my signal strength.

I blinked into Pause's network and located the untapped capacity of half a dozen guards and secretary types. Rerouting their nodes to mine was all the push I needed to link with the Stream.

"You're an *Intuit*." He said the word as if trying to purge a bad taste from his mouth.

I could sympathize. He did, after all, spend the majority of his time surrounded by the most dangerous Intuits the world could imagine. Being the only ones capable of walking the tight line of the neural network, sliding between firewalls and encryptions to manipulate the source code itself, made it so the only white-collar time criminals were Intuits. This was a fact that did nothing to ingratiate us law-abiding Intuits with the general population.

We were feared at best. Hated at worst. Not a great platform to breed acceptance.

We aren't good at accepting what we don't understand. And nobody understood the Intuit phenomenon, or what caused it. No genetic component had been found. Best theory attributed it to the formation of neural pathways at birth.

Genetic or not, our numbers grew each year. But while estimates of the Intuit population varied, one thing was certain: fewer lived today than nine years ago when Malcolm went and murdered one million Intuits.

How he'd managed to hack the Life Tracker system so thoroughly remained a mystery that haunted me every night in the faces of the dead that visited my dreams. Those lives were on my shoulders, an anchor tied to my soul. A minute faster and I could have stopped him. Could have saved them.

Saved Diana.

The public-relations fallout thanks to Malcolm's psychotic break was immeasurable. Citizens saw firsthand just how vulnerable Life Trackers were in the hands of an Intuit, and it was terrifying. People called for tighter oversight of the Intuit population. The Unity leadership tried forcing Intuits to register themselves in a worldwide database. That might have worked if they hadn't also tried suppressing Stream access for all Intuits.

You can't keep someone in a cage if they have the key to the door. Though in the case of the Intuits, they didn't just have the key to the door, they had the key to the entire system. A small team of thirteen anonymous Intuits proved this to the rest of Unity one spring morning nine years ago when they shut down the Stream for ten minutes.

Ten minutes was all it took to make their point.

President Jennings vetoed the motion to tag Intuits later that day. He went so far as to squelch all anti-Intuit rhetoric coming out of the media, and built his platform on the idea that the Intuit population could be Unity's greatest resource if used properly.

This didn't sit well with the general population, but what could they do short of war? Nothing. There was nothing they could do but bottle the frustration and rage that comes with knowing they were obsolete and vulnerable. The years between had passed in relative peace, but the tension lingered, a festering wound.

One spark was all it would take. One flame to ignite the whole damn thing.

Malcolm wanted to be that spark. Whatever he had planned this time, I couldn't afford to pull punches. Bad news for guys like Emilio who'd be caught in the crossfire. Collateral damage was the unavoidable consequence of stopping Malcolm.

I rummaged through the Time Bank archives, ignoring the dizzying array of data zipping past, before coming to Emilio Castille's account.

I removed everything I could.

The shrill cry of the Safeguard shattered the silence like smashed porcelain. Raines and Castille showed equal amounts of surprise, but the Warden was first to realize what had just happened. He scrabbled at his coat sleeve, desperate to get to the numbers beneath. His face, a hollowed white husk, stared in disbelief at the ten minutes remaining on his Life Tracker, thanks to the Safeguard.

I had cocked the proverbial gun held to his head.

Centuries worth of Intuits had tried cracking the Safeguard, implemented by the creator of the Life Tracker system, Leopold Hallond, but where everyone else had failed, only one had succeeded: Malcolm Wolfe. The rest of us were limited by the Safeguard. A safety measure making it so nobody could take a man's time and kill him outright. Nobody except Malcolm.

Ten minutes, however, gave me plenty of time.

Emilio's white saucer eyes searched for understanding. He rubbed the bars on his arm as if the true ones hid beneath. But that was it. I'd relocated the rest to a holding account until I got the answers I needed.

I wasn't gonna kill the guy, but he didn't need to know that.

"Agents from Time Vice monitor my biofeedback. They'll restore the time you've stolen," Emilio said once the initial shock of his circumstances wore off. He turned to Raines. "Your friend will be dead by the end of the day, but you will spend the rest of your life behind bars paying for this indiscretion as an accomplice to his crimes. Stop this now and I will vouch for you. We may yet mitigate the damages to your career."

Raines plopped into the chair across from the Warden's desk. She'd never been shy about making the hard decisions that sometimes lead an investigation down the rabbit hole. Our job required us to follow the breadcrumbs wherever they might go, a task harder than it sounds. Those clues have a way of taking you to places you can't come back from.

Places that change you.

Places like this.

She stood at the crossroads of a decision that would affect the rest of her life. It wasn't too late to stop. She could take me in and hope to land in the good graces of Time Vice on account of poor personal judgment, or she could blunder through on the sliver of a chance that we could stop Malcolm.

She weighed the options. The scales swayed in her mind. Her children, her career, her life sat on one side. On the other sat the shell of a man she once knew—once loved—and an obligation, heavy as the one I carried, to stop Malcolm Wolfe from breaking the world.

A decision in either direction could be considered selfish.

CHAPTER EIGHT
Men Without A Past

"Why did you help Malcolm escape?" Raines cast her lot and reiterated my question.

"You won't kill me."

"I don't recommend gambling on his good will," Raines said.

The underlying message, if you were listening for it, implied she'd been burned by that same gamble.

"Raines, what do you suppose the odds are that Time Vice is monitoring the Warden's biofeedback?" I said.

"Pretty damn good, I'd say."

"How about his daughter, Chloe?"

"Oh." Raines shook her head in mock sympathy. She played her role of callous interrogator well. "Less good."

"That's what I thought."

"Bring her into this and you're no better than Malcolm Wolfe," Castille said.

"I never said I was."

I blinked into the Stream, skipped back up to the Time Bank's archives, and quickly located Chloe Castille's file. A small picture of the girl appeared in the upper-right corner of my screen.

Talk about aging the hard way. She looked to be twenty-two going on seventy.

Bags beneath her eyelids drooped until they touched the bridge of a crooked nose. Her skin was yellow tissue paper left to rot in the sun, a warped maze of wrinkles and cracks. It didn't take a junkie to know a junkie, but it didn't hurt. Her Life Tracker confirmed the truth: she wouldn't live to see thirty.

Poor Chloe was deep into an addiction that meant more to her than living. From her withered frame I'd guess Star Dust, a nasty little pill that eats the body from inside in exchange for twelve hours of chemically induced bliss.

After that first hit life becomes a series of peaks and valleys. Soul-crushing depression interspersed with the ever-decreasing euphoric high. Most Dusters take their own lives rather than waiting for Mother Nature, or the Tracker. But in the Lowers that doesn't matter. It's easy to make and easier to get.

The tragedy of youth. We'd conquered death, but chained ourselves to its yoke anyhow.

I was in no place to judge.

I understood Emilio Castille's position. I imagined myself toeing that same line if the positions were reversed. The one even good men swear they'll never cross.

But every man who's eyed that line long enough starts thinking maybe one step over wouldn't be so bad, if it's for the right reason.

It's always for the right reason.

That's how we justify it, anyhow.

"What kind of deal did you make to save your daughter?" I asked, exiting the Stream and turning to the Warden. "More time?"

Emilio deflated, collapsing into himself and his chair. The bravado evaporated. The Warden, no longer keeper of the thousands of criminals calling Pause home, was now simply a father afraid of losing his daughter.

His face sagged and cratered. It showed the pain gnawing at every well-intentioned decision he'd ever made on behalf of Chloe. I pitied Emilio. He still clung to hope. To the belief he could save his daughter. I saw it etched in the lilt of his eyes. But he could do nothing to save Chloe in the same way Raines could do nothing to save me.

We'd made our deals and the devil doesn't take substitutes. He's tasted our weakness; he knows we're worth the wait.

"Time Vice won't let her keep those years," Raines said. "Not when they figure out what you've done."

"There are no years. They're going to fix her." Castille looked up with wet fishbowl eyes. "I did what they asked. They'll fix her. It'll be worth it."

Raines cast me a sideways glance. She hadn't seen Chloe's file so she didn't fully grasp the situation, but I had. That girl was beyond reconstruction.

Emilio knew that—part of him, at least. Denial straight to death's door.

It wasn't my place to tell him his sacrifice was in vain. That she'd continue her decline until she swallowed a bullet or chewed through her Tracker's remaining time. I couldn't make that judgment of any man or woman.

"Emilio, I can tell you love your daughter. I don't blame you for wanting to save her. You're her father." Raines leaned across the desk and placed a tanned hand atop the Warden's. "There's nothing you wouldn't do to protect her. I understand that, but you know what Malcolm is capable of. You've seen firsthand what he's done. He'll do it again unless you help stop him." Raines paused, letting her words sink into the Warden. "Don't give him the chance to kill again. Help us. Tell us who you're working for."

"She's my daughter," Emilio said, with a half-sputtered whimper. He teetered on the brink. Swaying with the weight of each word.

"Give her a world worth living in," Raines said, her voice smooth, comforting, and controlled. It commanded the Warden's attention. Raines became the entirety of his world, his focus. He stared into her eyes, a snake dazzled by its charmer. "One where the nameless few sacrifice on behalf of the many. To protect those unable to do so themselves. You can be part of that world."

Raines navigated the Stream like a blind woman, but she had a gift that made her as unique as any Intuit.

If I was a digital wizard then Raines was an emotional sorceress. The counterpoint to my unique skill set, which included little in the department of empathy.

She manipulated people like I manipulated the Stream. Humans must have buttons and levers 'cause she knew where they were and how to push them. It's unnatural, spooky, and borderline unethical. I'd complain if her gift wasn't so damned helpful.

Her ability to connect with strangers went beyond reading facial twitches and inferring motives. She could read minds and direct thoughts. At least that's how it looked from my perspective.

Emilio's tear-soiled eyes confirmed my suspicion; he was putty in her hands.

"I don't know where he is," Emilio said, breaking the long silence. "Malcolm, that is. Somebody else came. Somebody with power." He paused, searching for a word perched on the edge of his tongue. "A lot of power."

"How did they contact you?" Raines asked.

"Here. One man. That's all."

"Did you get a name?"

"Daniel Brandt. He came…uh, from a branch of Division I'd never heard of, but everything checked out in the Stream. I mean, what could I have done? His clearance level outranked mine."

The government conspiracy angle is a crowd favorite, but it's a tough sell. Despite the small army of nanites working overtime in my brain, however, I could detect no deception leaking from the Warden.

Castille couldn't tell a convincing lie to a wall, so while what he said might be fiction, the man himself believed every word.

"Show me," I said.

"There's nothing to show." Emilio frowned as if he'd been punched. "It's gone. All of it."

I cocked my head and said, "Define gone."

"A virus crashed the Pause independent network. We switched to the Stream for a few days while we reconstructed the Pause feed. But it didn't matter, everything had been erased. Our entire network…deleted. Gone."

That shouldn't be possible, but a lot of impossible things were happening today, so I surfed the wave of disbelief a bit further.

"So then what?"

"We rebuilt the system as best we could, from the ground up."

"What did you do with the prisoners while Pause was down?"

"Transferred them to the Stream." Emilio shook his head, still dealing with the weight of the calamity that'd occurred. "What else could we do?"

Great. A couple days away from the high-security fences of the Pause feed and, no surprise, Malcolm created a nanocomp hack. Nothing could stop the prisoners from manipulating Pause's sub-system to an extent—these were some of the greatest hackers the world had ever seen after all, but their reach remained limited precisely because Pause was kept more than an arm's length away from the Stream where, once loose, Intuits like Malcolm could do unprecedented amounts of damage.

Add time dilation to the mix and Malcolm would have experienced years of free time within the Stream, exploiting weakness and planning his next move.

"What about video surveillance?" Raines asked, picking up the slack I'd dropped along with my jaw. "This place is crawling with nanites. Someone must have caught a glimpse of the mystery man."

"You're welcome to the footage, but you'll find nothing." Emilio turned his palms to the ceiling and shrugged. "Save yourself the trouble and take my word. We experienced a prison-wide blackout around the time of the man's arrival. I have no means of proving he was here, save a few eyewitness accounts from myself and a couple guards."

I let that simmer. The logistics of an operation of that scope, at Pause no less, defied my understanding of the Stream.

"Optic Nanos?" Raines pushed forward despite the road blocks and dead ends, determined to tug at the fraying string of this mystery's sweater until she came up with an answer. "One of your guards must have optic upgrades. We pull video footage from their nanocomp—"

"You don't get it." Emilio rested his chin in cupped hands and shook his head. "Whoever did this is out of your league. You should let it go. Walk away and live out whatever remaining time they leave you."

"I'm already a dead man," I said.

"Death might be preferred to the alternative," Emilio said. His eyes drifted to the wall as if he could see beyond to the rows of prisoners trapped within their own minds.

"Wait." Raines threw her hands in the air. "You're saying whoever came here, wiped your computers, and arranged for Malcolm's release also has the ability to hack into personal nanocomps and delete information at will?"

"Precisely."

"That's impossible," Raines said. "You bett—"

"Actually—" I prepared to share my experience with Malcolm from earlier, but a woman's voice squawked over the room's intercom.

"Warden, we've initiated a freeze on your Life Tracker. Is everything okay, sir?"

Emilio glanced at the numbers on his forearm and then his hand moved to the button.

Colors blurred, leaving the Warden at the focal point of my narrowing tunnel of vision, but even with implants boosting my speed, he was too far away. I couldn't cover the distance between the wall and desk fast enough to stop the Warden from thumbing the intercom and saying, "Freeze my wife and daughter's accounts as well."

And poof, our leverage vanished.

A second later, muffled voices from the other side of the door were followed by the pounding of flesh on metal. The door wouldn't hold them long, and if I had any intention of still breathing after it fell, we needed to get gone.

"We should go," I said.

I grabbed Raines by the wrist and yanked her from the chair before realizing I didn't have a clear destination in mind for our escape. When I turned back to the Warden he stood behind his desk with a vortex pistol clutched in his bird-boned hand.

Shit. Take your eyes off the ball and everything goes to hell.

Raines raised her hands and stepped between myself and the Warden. More pounding from the door. Some words from Raines. Everything muddled and unintelligible.

Emilio and Raines were locked in a staring contest bordering on séance. Fragments of their conversation rose over the racket caused by the guards learning to play drums through demolition.

"Is there another way out?" Raines moved forward, a foot shy of the Warden.

I recognized that sentence, but I was a billion percent sure the Warden wouldn't answer.

Astonishment doesn't explain how I felt when Castille lowered his pistol and extended a spindly finger towards the tapestry beside his desk, nor how I felt a moment later when the room filled with the loud beeping of a Life Tracker approaching zero.

A sound we shouldn't have heard.

Emilio Castille opened his mouth to protest, but nothing escaped except the shock a man feels staring into the face of death.

Three beeps rang out, each punctuated with a silence both fleeting and infinite.

On the final beep, something buzzed, a rattle in the hands of a toddler. I'd heard the sound before and it made my stomach curdle each time. The Warden's Life Tracker hit zero. Dutifully, his nanocomp detonated a microscopic explosive implanted on the day of his birth.

Emilio's muscles fired in unison. He seized. Bones cracked and cartilage snapped against the force of contraction.

Stringy tendons bulged against folds of skin in the man's throat as a soft gasp slipped through clenched teeth.

He stood frozen; the tension of the seizure held him erect long after the clarity of life had fled from his eyes.

When the muscles relaxed, he crumpled.

Raines skirted the desk and knelt beside the Warden an instant after he hit the ground. She searched for a pulse she'd never find.

Warden Emilio Castille was dead.

CHAPTER NINE
Winging It

"What the hell did you do?" Raines asked with a quiet certainty that somehow I'd screwed up.

"Me? Nothing."

She looked up. The hard lines carved into her face over the course of the last decade softened, offering in their place a glimpse of the young woman she'd once been. The person she'd been before the world taught her pain and loss.

The lines returned.

"I didn't sign up to kill innocent people, Tom."

Emilio Castille wasn't innocent by a long shot, but focusing on that detail wasn't going to change Raines' state of mind.

"You didn't kill anyone," I said. "None that I know of, at least."

"Then what's that?" She gestured to the corpse at our feet.

"That wasn't you."

"But I let you—"

"Hey now, I didn't do this either. Time Vice froze his account, remember? You're looking at somebody else's handiwork."

An explosion at the door shook the room with its concussive force. The pressure shifted. My head pulsed like an overinflated balloon stretching its thin prison, waiting to be popped.

I expected to see guards rushing through a smoky haze of flaming debris, but amazingly the door held.

An ambient ringing, simultaneously everywhere and nowhere, reverberated down the halls of my ear canal. "Any idea how to get out of here?"

Raines pulled aside one of the tapestries behind the desk, revealing a smooth panel of wall that looked less like an exit, and more like a dead end. She ran a hand along the textureless surface.

"That's the door," she said, dropping to a knee beside the desk.

"Then what are you doing down there?"

"Trying to find the button that opens it."

"What if he accessed the controls remotely?" I said, feeling more pessimistic with every passing second.

"Then we'd be shit out of luck, wouldn't we?"

A second later, Raines grabbed the Warden's limp body by the wrist and dragged it a few inches closer.

"You find it?"

"Yeah, biometric scanner. Make yourself useful, grab his feet."

I did, and together we positioned the Warden with his top half lying beneath the desk. Raines pressed Emilio's palm to the underside and the wall melted, revealing a long brightly lit corridor that presumably led to freedom.

Which only left the small detail of getting off the floating fortress.

The Pause clientele were too white collar, and sleepy, to stage many riots, but whoever designed this prison with enough foresight to secure my escape had my undying gratitude.

Chalk that up to Mistress Luck looking kindly on me for once.

The sound of splintering metal drew my attention to the door and the guards on the other side trying to bring it down.

A small hole appeared in the center of the divide. If taken in conjunction with the sound, it meant they'd unleashed a mean little nanite that, for all the shiny parts and technology, simply boiled down to a sophisticated termite.

The hole expanded outward, consuming the door. In another minute there wouldn't be anything left to stop the breeze. A guard with a silver-visored helmet poked his head through the opening. His rifle followed shortly thereafter, but Raines was ready and firing, driving the man back into his hole.

I scanned the ground for Castille's pistol, but found nothing. There's something to be said about bringing a knife to a gun fight, but coming empty handed is decidedly worse.

"Come on," Raines said, firing once more before spinning on her heels and disappearing into the tunnel.

I ran after her. The blunting effect of adrenaline wore thin and muscles, long left unused, ached with exertion. When the hall terminated at a flight of stairs I doubled over and sucked in air. Lactic acid pooled in my muscles and burned where it leaked into my bloodstream.

Raines eyed me with a curious mix of amusement, pity, and disdain, a potent trifecta of human emotion.

The stairs, poorly lit by a handful of dulled bulbs, wound a tight spiral towards the surface. Raines flitted up the steps two at a time.

I did some creative reconfiguring of my nanocomp and coaxed my brain into donating a fresh batch of adrenaline. Like tossing buckets of water on a forest fire, it wouldn't solve the underlying problem, that I'd abused my body for the last decade, but it was something.

At the summit, Raines knelt beside a door propped open an inch, studying the world beyond.

"What do you see?" I asked.

"Two Kestrel-class copters parked fifty yards out, a pair of guards near the furthest of the two, and a mechanic working on the other. They look bored."

"Element of surprise counts for something. Any chance you can fly one of those rigs?"

Muffled voices from below suggested the guards had discovered our escape route.

"Probably not," Raines said, "but I'll try."

She pulled her pant leg up and handed me the small vortex pistol strapped to her ankle. It was smaller than I preferred, but with more stopping power than my fists it was hard to complain.

"Don't kill them," she said.

"Not sure they're playing by the same rules." I tightened my sweaty palm on the rubber handle of the pistol. "But I'll try."

I turned the intensity of the pistol to its lowest setting and nodded. Raines kicked the door off its hinges and I leaped out. Aided by the speed nanites, the world moved in slow motion.

A sunburst of light ricocheting off the side of a Kestrel blinded me. Retinal afterimages sparking across my eyeballs made it difficult to get a lock on the targets. I strafed three steps left to clear my vision.

My nanocomp sensed the struggle and compensated. It corrected for the over-saturation of white, dimmed the edges, and brought a grainy sort of clarity to the world.

The two soldiers dove in opposite directions, their faces frozen in shock. Taken by surprise, neither man had activated his speed implants, causing both of them to move slowly through the air as if it were viscous.

Without the handicap of solar flares blinding me I made a course correction and fired twice. My pistol spat two swirls of compressed air that carved through the heat vapors rising off the blacktop runway before finding their intended targets. Each guard hit the ground a moment later, unconscious, but alive.

On my left, the mechanic cowered behind the front wheel of a Kestrel, shielding his face with a crescent wrench on the off chance that it might blunt the effect of the pistol. He posed no threat and frankly I didn't have the heart to neutralize him. I deactivated my speed nanites and braced myself while the world raced by in fast forward. Finally my brain caught up and began processing at normal speed.

Raines sat in the cockpit of the Kestrel the two guards had been standing beneath. With eyebrows narrowed and lips pulled tight, she flicked a series of switches and the copter roared to life. Low bone-rattling vibrations filled the hot sticky air around me with an indecipherable hum. The memory of lying on Lucky Lou's floor sprang to mind along with the sickening reminder of what he'd taken from me.

Those were thoughts for later, assuming we made it out of there in less than a handful of pieces. I hopped into the passenger seat and flashed the thumbs-up. The door shut and the whine of the engines became an indistinct purr, leaving us to fill the relative silence with heavy breathing.

More accurately, I filled the silence with heavy breathing. Raines appeared unaffected by the exertion of our recent circumstances.

She jerked the flight stick and we lurched into the sky like a startled cat.

"Wait," I said through gritted teeth, "you're gonna fly by hand?"

"Got a better idea?"

"Tons!"

"I'm open to suggestions."

"Use your nanocomp?"

"The system's encrypted."

"Decrypt it."

"You decrypt it," she said.

"Who knows how long that'll take?"

"Well then shut up and hold on."

Lest our escape be too easy, a half dozen guards leaked onto the roof via the secret passageway. They moved with the reflexes of trained professionals—fanning out, taking cover, and opening fire faster than I could point and stutter, "Shit."

Nanite-tipped bullets clanked harmlessly off the sides of the Kestrel, unable to penetrate the vehicle's superior armor.

One heroic guard sprinted across the roof, a black blur that was either ramped up on speed implants or the fastest natural human alive.

Raines held our position twenty feet off the deck while she fiddled with the controls. It felt like a good time to say something encouraging, but you can't force motivational speeches, so I kept quiet and watched the guard leap into the air.

He caught the wheel of the Kestrel, jerking the vehicle violently with the sudden addition of weight.

We spun a quarter turn clockwise before Raines regained control. The anti-aircraft weapons lining the rim of the floating island were pointed out to sea, a strange orientation I was currently thankful for. They hadn't fired on us, which if I had to guess, meant they were waiting until we were away from Pause so they wouldn't have to deal with our burning wreckage raining down on the compound.

A man in a black flight suit crossed the open pavilion below and hopped into the cockpit of the Kestrel the mechanic had been working on.

I prayed for mechanical difficulties, but those prayers fell on the deaf ears of a heartless deity. The machine lifted gently and spun in a circle.

The melody of my heavy breathing was joined by a chorus of alarms. The other Kestrel had missile-lock. We were worse than the proverbial sitting duck, who, at minimum, knew how to fly away.

This wasn't how I'd expected to die. I held no delusion that my death would be a noble occasion, but being blown out of the sky felt cheap and unfair.

Raines, less keen on death, pulled the only trick she'd shown mastery of and yanked back on the flight stick. My balls sprang up into my body cavity and tickled my pancreas as we launched towards the sky.

I clung to my chair, fingers splayed in a death grip, thankful I was not the one clinging to the wheel beneath the Kestrel. It was fair to assume the guard regretted his decision about now.

Our ascent into the wild blue continued. We rose at nausea-inducing speeds. The weight of acceleration felt like a giant squatting on my chest. The once dull vibrations of the Kestrel became a high-frequency whine of stabbing needles that numbed everything from toes to nose.

My stomach had almost settled back into the general vicinity of my abdomen when the other Kestrel pulled even with us.

Luckily Raines possessed another trick up her sleeve, one I should have seen coming, but I didn't, so when she flung the flight stick forward, there were mixed emotions.

On the one hand I enjoyed a peaceful moment of zero-g where everything was light and happy and life looked as if it might work out after all.

But then we dropped.

CHAPTER TEN
Crashing It

We plummeted with the combined efforts of gravity and a couple supercharged engines. The enemy copter zipped past us, still on an upward rise.

It wouldn't take the other pilot long to realize we could only go up and down, and then our little game of yo-yo would come to an explosive end.

None of that mattered as we hurtled towards the ground, though. Mind and muscles were focused solely on the task of keeping my ass planted in my seat.

Out of the corner of my eye I saw Raines flip a switch, pull back on the flight stick, and slam the lever at her side down. The Kestrel broke every rule of physics I'd ever known.

It thrust forward with devastating effect on my internal organs, which I imagined had liquefied and were trying to escape my body through open pores.

Raines dove us towards the ocean paste below.

"You had me worried there for a second," I said, feeling the need to speak more for my sake than hers. "Wasn't sure you knew what you were doing."

Raines turned her head, eyes narrowed and focused with a determination that instilled confidence and said, "I don't have a clue what I'm doing."

If ever in the history of the world there had been a series of least inspiring words spoken, I had yet to hear them.

I thought back to the guard beneath the Kestrel. No way he could've held on through the acceleration. Another life lost in the wake of Malcolm Wolfe. I thought of the man's family going about their daily routine, not yet realizing their lives would forever be shadowed by that day. I couldn't escape the role I'd played in their tragedy, only accept it and shoulder the weight of his loss along with all the others I'd failed.

An alarm squawked. A hologram sprang from the console beside me, showing the enemy Kestrel closing rapidly.

"Hold on," Raines said through clenched teeth. "Gonna try—"

The Kestrel pitched hard to the left. The centripetal force threw me hard to the right. Despite her warning, I didn't have time to brace; my skull ricocheted off the window. Something cracked. The bulletproof glass looked fine, but my brain was a bag of marbles.

My face radiated pain from the blunt force trauma. I blinked the world in and out of existence. Blood trickled down my temple.

Every particulate floating in the air burned as it touched torn flesh. The universe awarded me a fraction of a second's worth of self-pity before I noticed the long black cylinder zipping past my window.

Smoke trailed the missile, tracing its path across the sky.

Less than a hundred feet past us, it exploded in a ball of light that overloaded my sensitive optic nerve. The insides of my eyelids were sheets of white.

The shockwave hit us a moment later, throwing us into a sidelong barrel roll. My stomach crept, inch by inch, closer to my throat. The chaos of the spin mangled any sense of orientation I'd ever possessed. The blue-gray mixture of sky and clouds mixed with the blue-gray slurry of ocean. I thought I'd figured up from down until Raines dove towards the sun.

My stomach, the only trustworthy internal barometer, was now somewhere around my ankles. I interpreted that as moving upward. We passed through a cloud of charred ozone and smoke that penetrated the inner sanctum of the cockpit. The smell summoned memories of barbecues and the over-chlorinated sterility of bleach.

Those were the thoughts my mind linked together in what I was confident were my final moments of life.

When the initial shock of the explosion subsided, and I regained my equilibrium, I had the clarity of mind to take in our circumstances and appreciate our extraordinary luck.

We climbed higher. The enemy Kestrel disappeared, but I wasn't getting any warm and fuzzy feelings of safety.

In confirmation of fears left unspoken, alarms screamed a fresh tantrum. The other Kestrel appeared shortly after on the holographic radar.

I searched for something encouraging to say but landed on, "Shit. Shit. Shit."

Raines didn't notice. She strangled the flight stick, her unwavering attention fixed on the world of blue before us.

Overhead an orange light streaked across the sky. It moved so quickly my brain barely processed the commercial airliner before it disappeared, a speck on the horizon. Then I understood why she'd taken us so high. Saw her destination.

"The ElMag High?" I said, blurting the words with equal measures of question, statement, and admonishment.

"It's our best chance."

"Yeah, to die."

"What would you prefer?"

The Kestrel, designed for maneuverability within the tight high-walled confines of a major metropolis area was, by necessity, squat, bordering on bulky, with the equivalent aerodynamics of two bricks glued together. It'd never been intended to withstand the extreme speeds reached in the ElMag High.

I couldn't think of a worse place to take a Kestrel.

High-speed, long-distance travel was made possible thanks to the electromagnetic catapult created by a path of nanobots suspended at thirty thousand feet. The Electromagnetic Highway spanned Unity and the desecrated East, until it ended at the Japanese border—not that they'd let anyone near their airspace, but theoretically it was possible.

"Anything. And this time I really mean anything," I said, trying to answer Raines' question with a modicum of objectivity. "At least with missiles there's a chance they'll miss. This flying box will break apart the moment we get on the Highway."

"We'll have time before the wings fall off."

"Time for what?"

"To get back out."

"Forgive me if my confidence is not inspired by your technical prowess on this issue."

"Hey, you could've been hacking that guy's Kestrel instead of squawking like a child afraid of their shadow. I'm doing the heavy lifting, so as far as I'm concerned you've lost your right to a vote. Now quit being a baby, it's not like you have anything to lose."

Raines made a justified critique—I hadn't done much in the current phase of our escape beyond holding on—but her cavalier attitude filled me with a unique brand of dread I'd yet to encounter.

I sank into my chair, accepting that nothing would come from arguing the point. The alarms chiming in the cockpit joined in my resignation, and faded, along with the enemy Kestrel on the radar.

No doubt he understood the limitations of his vehicle.

Glad to see somebody had retained hold of their common sense.

A final siren issued a feeble warning, but there was nothing an alarm, flashing lights, or a terrified ex-cop could do to change the situation. We punched a hole through the ElMag High and smashed into an invisible wall. The Highway's propulsion wave redirected our flight path instantly, firing us towards the manmade peaks of Terminus.

A window of three seconds followed where everything appeared fine. The Kestrel accelerated quickly, but that was nothing compared to the hairpin juking Raines had inflicted on my organs moments before.

The problem was, unlike Raines' crafty maneuvers earlier, on the Highway we continued accelerating until the walls of the Kestrel thrummed like a tuning fork. A crack splintered the windshield. Harmonic resonance threatened to tear apart the delicate bonds holding metal to glass.

I wondered for a brief moment how shattered bulletproof glass would look.

Raines cut the engines, but even without their assistance we continued accelerating across the ElMag High.

"Get us out of here." My tone was less encouraging than I'd intended.

"Too much inertia. The engines are too weak to push us out," Raines said.

"This is a perfect *I told you so* moment."

"Do it and I will eject you."

I kept all further comments to myself. The crack across the windshield sprang new branches. Air heaved against what remained of the frail glass. It probed for a weakness to exploit, threatening to sweep into the cockpit and snuff us out.

Asphyxiation on account of too much air felt too paradoxical a way to die. Though, in the end, I suppose breathing eventually does us all in.

Terminus shimmered in the distance, an oasis of safety. But with hundreds of miles separating us from the deceleration point, I wasn't getting my hopes up. I would've crossed my fingers for luck, but they'd become one with the armrest.

Then came the lurch. A giant's hand plucked our vehicle from the sky and used us to season his dinner.

The world tumbled, shifted, shattered, and twisted until it was nothing I recognized. My stomach played musical chairs with my heart on the dance floor of my throat. The Kestrel shuddered like a dog throwing off rainwater. I caught a glimpse of something tearing free from the side of the vehicle and zipping past my window, flipping end over end.

"Was that a wing?" I said, my voice an octave higher than normal. "I thought you said we wouldn't lose them."

"No, I said we'd have time before we lost them."

"That wasn't much time at all."

If Raines responded it was lost to the wail of alarms that'd regained their breath. She flipped a switch that appeared to have no effect on our current situation until a half second later when the vehicle spun left and bounced free of the Highway.

One wing wasn't enough to maintain any kind of control, but Raines tried anyhow. We spiraled towards the ocean floor thousands of feet below.

With nothing to do but wait for Mother Nature's unforgiving embrace, I closed my eyes and listened.

Realizing the futility of their cries, or perhaps having run out of power, the alarms ceased their cycling. Silence fell over the cockpit, save the sound of wind rushing over jagged edges of the no longer aerodynamic Kestrel.

Seconds ticked over slowly. The air whistling past reminded me of the tide sliding along a pebble-strewn beach, on a day spent in the sun. Diana was beside me, stretched out on her towel, ivory skin exposed to the heat, glistening with the ocean breeze settling in salty droplets along her arms and shoulders.

She buried her nose in the crook of my neck, warm breath causing the hairs riding the ridge of my spine to prickle.

"What should we name her?" Diana asked with her eyes closed.

I traced my finger along the curve of her stomach that had only just begun to soften in the weeks prior. The sun made a rare appearance, penetrating the heavy armor of clouds. Its rays danced on the white-capped waves washing into shore. I searched the horizon for an answer, acutely aware that this would be the first of many life-altering decisions I'd be forced to make on behalf of another soul.

The burden of that responsibility couldn't be underestimated.

"It's not too early for that?"

"She's already here," Diana said, her voice drifting softly on the breeze. "I feel her."

"You mean your nanocomp can feel her."

"No, I mean I can feel her. In a place the nanites could never touch.

"Hm…"

"You're jealous."

"Maybe."

"And scared."

"Maybe that, too."

"Well, I never…" Diana laid her head on my lap. "And here I thought nothing scared the great Tom Mandel, the man who laughs in the face of death."

"Babies are scarier than death," I said, running my fingers through Diana's hair.

Despite the odds, we'd won the birthright lottery. We'd tried for years so perhaps it was inevitable, but after so many failed attempts I'd begun to wonder if getting selected might be the hardest part of events still to come. Now I sat on the warm sand, letting the sun roast me while trying to tame the butterflies in my stomach.

Diana was unfazed. She'd mentally prepared herself better than I had.

I settled myself by allowing my mind to wander. To think of the man or woman whose death was our opportunity at a family. Unity only had room for so many people. One in, one out. Those were the rules. We were doing our part to bring one in.

It was the stupidest thing I'd ever done.

But also the best.

"It won't be so bad," she said. "You'll see."

The tide rolled in, creeping ever closer. The sound grew stronger, angrier.

Something jarred my world, dragging me out of the memory and back to the chaos of the cockpit.

Raines yelled, "Stay and die if you want." She pointed with an outstretched hand, straining against the force of the spin pinning us to our seats.

I followed the path of her finger and saw the red handle overhead. The muscles in my forehead twitched, causing the gash on the side of my face to squeal with renewed vigor as I threaded fingers through the handle and yanked down.

The roof above me popped off. The wind slapping at my hair and clothing sounded nothing like the waves now.

It was the mourning cry of a prehistoric beast set on destruction.

A rocket shot the chair, and me by extension, up and out of the cockpit. After a five-second burst the rockets died. My upward rise through the clouds slowed as gravity got its hands on me once again.

I hovered at the apex and listened to the breeze slip past. Something detached from the seat. I fell a dozen feet before the parachute unfurled and caught. I clutched at the seatbelt strapped to my chest, thankful in a way I couldn't express with words that I'd actually buckled in.

An explosion of smart-metal bloomed where the Kestrel crashed into the rigid waves. Flames from the wreckage lapped at my dangling feet.

The burning debris became a point of reference for distance. I realized then just how fast I was dropping.

We must have ejected too late.

The parachute dragged against the hot, moist air, but it wasn't going to be a soft landing.

I plummeted through black smoke billowing off the wreckage. Noxious fumes from burning metal assaulted my nostrils and singed my lungs.

I closed my eyes, denying my body the opportunity to brace for impact, and drew on the memory of Diana on the beach.

"Let's name her Mirama," I whispered.

"What's that mean?"

"Where the river touches the sky."

"Mirama," Diana said, tasting the word on her tongue.

She smiled at me.

I smiled back.

And then I hit.

Somebody dimmed the power to my brain, as if I'd missed a couple monthly payments. I remained conscious, but had no control over any of the voluntary acts associated with living.

My brain tried to reboot, but in the meantime my body operated on autopilot.

Turns out, the body, when left to its own devices, does stupid things. My spasming lungs decided that right then was the ideal moment to take a breath. For their efforts, I received a mouthful of tangy salt water that burned everything on its journey through esophagus and windpipe before pooling in my lungs.

This new source of pain climbed atop the pile of others threatening to overwhelm my diluted senses. The nanocomp did what it could to mitigate the damage, but there was a lot of damage.

I clawed at the seatbelt holding me to the death sentence my sinking chair had become, with fingers struggling to interpret panic-riddled commands issued by my brain.

A riptide swirled, dragging me deeper into the ocean's depths.

I fumbled with the clasp. Something caught. The belt released its grip. The dull glow of firelight burned on the surface. An impossible distance considering I'd only been submerged a moment.

With arms and legs turned to lead weights, I thrashed towards the smoldering wreckage.

My eyeballs bulged with the shifting pressure. Salt water sat in my lungs like acid.

The ring of fire dancing on the surface became the light at the end of the tunnel. I'd get to that light quicker if I stopped fighting, took another breath.

So close. Muscles screamed. Heart ached.

I coughed.

Bubbles bled from my mouth and nose.

A silent euphoria cozied up to my brain. The darkness from the depths below tugged at me. I sank, unable to resist the pull.

With the knowledge that I wouldn't make it, I closed my eyes and drifted.

My brain powered down.

CHAPTER ELEVEN
The First Time Is The Hardest

Something turned on. A switch lying dormant flipped and I opened my eyes to the blinding yellow sphere of the sun staring down at me.

Death is a dark place. A stark contrast to the bluish-yellow smear I now struggled to process. The light induced an orgasm of nausea.

I closed my eyes and tried again.

The world came into focus, but still I struggled to make sense of my situation.

My life-support nanites decided that was as good a time as any to purge my stomach, lungs, and whatever else of all fluids, solids, and organs no longer vital to survival. The contents of my body erupted from my mouth like a ruptured hose. Seawater, burning worse on the way up than it had on the way down, departed with explosive force.

The pain became my master.

I flopped onto my stomach, a marionette dancing to an unheard rhythm. I writhed, grabbing handfuls of sand to brace against the next wave of vomit.

Seconds turned over into minutes, which evolved into years.

Slowly the pounding drum behind my eyeballs subsided. Clarity returned. I wiped away the bile that coated my lips with the palm of a sand-encrusted hand.

An error message from my nanocomp flashed in the corner of my eye.

Fatal Error: Mandatory Reboot
Stand by...

I'd never seen that one before, but I knew enough about the nanocomp to understand what had happened.

I'd died.

My nanocomp must not have liked that and decided to reboot. A desperation-fueled act considering a brain linked with a nanocomp can't function without said nanocomp. The moment the nanocomp rebooted, not only was I dead, I was brain dead. That's double dead.

The thunder rolling around my skull paid homage to that fact.

I surveyed the beach upon which I sat. Clumps of tangled seaweed stained the sand an unfortunate shade of brown. Driftwood washed ashore alongside metallic debris from the crash. The burning wreckage of the Kestrel smoldered less than a half mile off shore.

The daze clouding my mind lifted and my thoughts snapped back to Raines.

I jumped to my feet and screamed her name over the tide crashing into shore. I waited for a response. Nothing came.

Nothing loud enough to hear over the pounding of my heart at least.

A new kind of panic gripped me. It had nothing to do with self-preservation of the body and everything to do with self-preservation of the heart.

The world couldn't take Raines from me. Not now. The world wasn't fair, but it couldn't be that cruel.

I jogged along the water's edge, scanning the horizon with all the power my nanotized mind could throw at my optic implants.

Nothing.

My heart tripped, stuttered, and stumbled. Breaths came in fast, shallow spurts.

I was panicking. Knowing that, however, did nothing to help the situation.

"Raines," I yelled again.

This was all wrong. I could find her, but I had to calm down and focus. I clenched and released my fists three times and forced a long, slow breath. The tension ebbed enough for me to slip into the Stream.

In the wake of the Warden's death, Raines and I would be high-value targets on the Peacekeepers' Most Wanted list, which made going into the Stream a dangerous move. They'd track my location, but without Raines none of that mattered.

I pinged her GPS, locked on, and connected with her nanocomp. The systems linked and exchanged a flood of information.

She wasn't far, but that didn't necessarily make her close either.

Sprinting in the direction indicated by the nanites, I stopped where a line of Kestrel parts rimmed the beach. I scanned the bobbing pieces of debris still surfing the waves, looking for the one shaped like a human.

There.

"Raines," I screamed, waving my arms over my head.

I didn't wait for a response. I was floundering through chest-deep water by the time complaints from sore muscles reached my brain.

An oily film of pollution covered the water. Man's contribution to the ecosystem. Our legacy. Though the downed Kestrel probably wasn't helping.

Despite my indisputable weakness as a swimmer, I made it to Raines in what I considered good time. Whether that was actually the case, I couldn't say.

Raines floated face up. Matted strands of black hair plastered the smooth skin of her cheeks. I threaded an arm around her waist and scissor kicked for shore with every reserve of strength still left.

Muscles seized and my head bobbed beneath the waves with every stroke. More salt water found its way into my lungs with every gasping breath.

I flailed. The awkwardness of holding Raines, and trying to paddle our two useless bodies, depleted my reserves of adrenaline. My nanocomp kept prodding, hoping to release more of that special chemical, but the fountain was dry.

Running on fumes and unable to stay afloat, I sank, positive I would never rise above the surface again. But the ocean didn't want our corpses. Instead she sent us a wave. I tightened my grip on Raines as it rolled over us. The undertow dragged us closer to shore.

Sand rose up beneath my feet, my head broke the surface and I gasped.

I carried Raines the remaining distance on legs threatening to buckle beneath the exertion of every step.

Gently I rolled her onto her back.

Raines lay still, her face a lesson in tranquility. She was gone to the world. Leaving her that way almost felt more humane.

Leaving her in a place where she no longer worried about Malcolm, or me. Where things like loss, betrayal, and love don't matter.

But I was selfish; I needed her. I'd left her once. Ran away because I couldn't bear the thought of loving again. Of losing again.

Running away hadn't mattered because the possibility of loss was becoming more real by the second.

I pinged her nanocomp and received a log of her biofeedback. Her heart had stopped, but her brain showed a flicker. Life-support nanobots kept her blood moving even as their power supplies dwindled.

Something was interfering with her nanocomp's ability to jump start her system again. The same jolt my nanocomp had used on me.

I blinked into the Stream and located Raines' nanocomp floating through the ethereal data-void. I tried manipulating the device with my digital fingers, but it repelled my attempts.

Nanocomps were specific to a single neural network, which meant access was limited to one brain.

There wasn't enough space in Raines' brain for the two of us, which hardly mattered considering I had no clue how I'd get in there, regardless.

Malcolm had it figured out. He'd demonstrated that ability when he'd deactivated the trace I'd been running in my nanocomp.

Then it hit me, a sledgehammer to the gut. I made the connection. Saw the plan.

Malcolm was blocking Raines' nanocomp from rebooting her system. Putting a hold on her system until the life-saving measures would be too late and she'd be dead.

No.

I stumbled out of the Stream and crashed back into reality.

Raines hadn't moved. Would never move again.

Malcolm would take her from me the same way he'd taken Diana.

There were no tears, only rage. I screamed until my throat burned and the veins in my temple throbbed against their prison.

I slammed a fist into her chest. She shuddered from the force.

Another fist. Something cracked. Her rib or my heart; I couldn't say.

Again. The tears came, rolling down my cheeks in burning droplets of regret.

Again.

And again.

Raines' hand shot into the air. Her body convulsed. She rolled to the side and sputtered a mouthful of putrid water onto the sand.

I held her hair back from falling into her face until her body had stopped shuddering.

"Tom?" she said; her voice creaked like a rusted hinge. Raines' hand fluttered weakly to her forehead. "What happened?"

I gritted my teeth and let the despair wash off me.

"You're a terrible swimmer," I said, my voice hoarse. "That's what happened."

I managed a weak smile. Raines tried sitting up but her pupils dilated, the color flushed from her cheeks, and she swooned.

"Take it easy, I think you were dead." I rested a hand on Raines' shoulder and helped her to an upright position. "Thought I'd lost you."

She massaged her temples and said, "Kinda wish you had."

I was a frequent flier in the world of unholy hangovers, but Raines' looked to be on a whole other level.

"I can throw you back if you want."

"No thanks, I've died enough for one day."

The silence stretched, swelling along with the waves around us.

"You did good work up there," I said. "Flying, I mean."

"Yeah. Good flying," she said, squinting against the sunlight. "Bad landing."

I laughed despite myself, allowing myself that simple pleasure before turning to the task at hand.

"They're gonna be coming. We gotta move," I said.

Raines nodded and held out a hand. I pulled her up, and she swayed in the sand before steadying herself by grabbing my wrist. She studied the point where our flesh became one. Her lip twitched. She struggled through the shroud of confusion clinging to her brain and heart like sand to wet skin.

She released her grip and said, "Lead the way."

The Terminus skyline peeked over the treetops ringing the beach. We walked in the general direction of the city, hiking into a narrow swatch of what could be loosely defined as forest.

"I need to contact Time Vice," Raines said.

There were benefits to accessing the Stream, but we'd be on the grid, trackable. I'd taken a chance to find Raines in the water, but going back into the system would be tempting fate.

We were fugitives, plain and simple. Years chasing bad guys on Time Vice had taught me something: the guys that managed to escape were the ones that stayed off the Stream.

I shared these concerns with Raines, but she remained unpersuaded.

"They need to know." The dense foliage of trees muted Raines' voice, making it abnormally soft.

"You're putting it on faith that they'll believe you."

"I have no faith." Raines stopped walking and leaned against a fallen tree. "But we can't do this alone. Not again."

She was reliving the mass murders that'd pushed me past my breaking point. She'd soldiered through the wake of tragedy and emerged a changed person.

Perhaps stronger. Definitely jaded.

But you can only temper a blade so many times before it shatters. Raines looked on the cusp of shattering now.

She wore her suffering like a tattoo: hidden from prying eyes, but there nonetheless. An indelible ink that couldn't be washed away.

I'd helped leave that mark. Blinded to her suffering. Oblivious to the pain I'd etched onto her heart.

We are so fragile. Millions of ways to break a man, so few to put him back together. We lean on each other, hoping to rise above the sum of our parts, to become something better.

But it only works when all the parts of the foundation are whole.

It only takes one crack.

Just one before the whole thing crumbles in on itself.

I'd pulled away from the support entrusted to me, left those in my life to shoulder the burden alone.

Raines had carried that weight for too long.

She wiped a tear from her eye. I looked away.

I was still the weak one.

I wanted to tell her I wouldn't leave her again, but that would be a lie.

CHAPTER TWELVE
Nashing Teeth

"Figured I'd be hearing from you." Captain Nash's face appeared in the digital conference room created in Raines' mind.

I lurked in the shadows, knowing my participation would only hinder the conversation.

"There's some—"

"Listen," Nash continued, steamrolling the words leaving Raines' mouth. "You're waist deep in it and I don't want to say I told you so, but shit, I was not vague with my instructions to leave Mandel out of this investigation. He's a loose cannon, and a dead man to boot. But there's no reason to go down with that sinking ship, so make the smart play: bring Mandel in and we'll do what we can to smooth this out for you."

"It's not what you think, Captain."

"Enlighten me." His tone suggested his imperviousness to surprising revelations.

"For starters, the Safeguard's been hacked."

"Shit, Raines. That's a pretty big for starters," Nash said. "Suppose next you're gonna tell me the Lost have organized an army and are marching on Terminus?"

"No, nothing like that," she said, her voice buckling beneath the weight of her superior officer's chastising.

That wasn't the Raines I knew, but given our morning it was fair to assume she felt a little out of sorts. Dying has a way of changing a person.

"You're right, it is nothing like that. And you know why? 'Cause I'm looking at the Life Tracker account for one Mr. Emilio Castille. Any idea what it shows?"

He let the question sit in the air longer than necessary for a rhetorical question.

"Well, don't be too eager to hear the truth, Raines," he said when it became clear she wasn't prepared to offer a guess. "It shows Mr. Mandel making an unlawful withdrawal from Emilio Castille's account. He bled Castille of his time and then watched him die. That's the kind of man you're working with. That's on you. We can't change that now, but we can stop it from happening again. Bring him in."

"I can't do that."

"And why in the name of the great nanite in the sky not?"

"We're following a lead, an—"

"Oh? Is this like the time you followed a lead to Pause and watched a junked-out Lower murder the Warden?" Nash possessed an indefinable quality that I had distinctly not missed during my time away from the force.

"Castille admitted to aiding in Malcolm Wolfe's escape, sir."

"Oh?" Nash said. His jaw worked silent circles.

"Claims to have been approached by a branch of Division he'd never heard of."

Nash was overly theatrical, with a love for hearing his own voice that bordered on perverse, but he was not stupid. He absorbed that new piece of information as if sampling a fine wine. His face narrowed, allowing the flavors of truth to wash over his palate.

"You believe him?" Nash asked.

"I do."

"He have any names?"

Captain Nash, a twenty-year veteran of Time Vice by the time they pinned a badge to *my* chest, had been around the block enough times that he'd left footprints. After so long, not much surprised the old man. Nevertheless his jaw dropped and rested loosely on its hinge when Raines said, "Just one. Daniel Brandt."

The name struck a chord with the Captain. His eyelids contracted while his pupils expanded. A frown flickered across his face before he regained composure.

"Do you have it on record?" Nash said, his tone softer around the edges now.

"Yes, sir."

Nash paused for a long deliberation before saying, "You've put me in the shit house with no toilet paper, Raines. You're still wanted on suspicion of murder, destruction of Unity property, and a whole slew of God knows what else. There's nothing I can do about that, you understand?"

"Yes."

"Good, 'cause if this goes tits up, which I'm willing to bet everything I love and hold dear it will, you're gonna be out in left field playing with yourself. This conversation stays between us, but you don't come back to me unless you have something bulletproof. Something I can work with. I'll do what I can to keep the heat turned to a simmer from this end, but there's only so much I can do. I can't stall forever."

It wasn't much, but it gave us a start. Sometimes that's the hardest part. After that, momentum takes over and all you can do is hold on and enjoy the ride.

Or, short of enjoying it, you try your hardest not to get run over by the damn thing.

"Thanks, Captain," Raines said, "but I need to ask a favor."

"Another?" His tone suggested he'd done enough.

"We need transportation."

"Where are you now?"

Raines resisted the urge to look at me. We were at a crossroad. Either put our trust in the Captain and hope he was shooting straight with us, or walk away on the chance he was leading us into a trap.

Our options were too few to be picky. Terminus, the largest city in the world, spanned hundreds of miles. If we had any hope of catching Malcolm, we needed assistance.

Raines must have reached the same conclusion and said, "I'll ping you my coordinates."

"I'll have a Dragonfly waiting here in ten minutes," Nash said.

I assumed he sent Raines a destination, but I hadn't been included in that information transfer.

"Thank you," Raines said, her voice shifting in tone and quality to indicate she wasn't done calling in favors. "There's one more thing."

"Jesus, what now?"

"Just…tell Maddie and Morgan I love them."

"Oh." Nash's voice drooped along with the rest of his face. "Of course, Alaina. You don't have to ask that."

For the first time in the conversation Nash let his eyes wander. They did a full circuit of the space overhead before finding something on the floor by his foot worthy of his attention. He shifted his weight from foot to foot a couple times before saying, "You going to tell Brad?"

Raines gave a resigned shrug. "No. He can't know."

Nash nodded. "He'd understand."

Neither Nash nor Raines' body language suggested they believed that.

"He wouldn't."

"Doesn't matter how this plays out, I'll make sure Madison and Morgan do. They'll know you were doing the right thing. Doing your job."

The odds makers clearly weren't on our side. Even our allies refused to bet too heavily on us.

"Thanks, Captain."

Nash gave a nod before disconnecting, presumably for fear of being asked for more favors.

"Brad?" I asked.

Raines stared through me. It wasn't a callous look. Not even one of disdain. Simply vacant. Then she blinked out of the Stream, disappearing from the virtual space without another word.

Before I could follow, something pinged me. The anonymous request blinked in the corner. Knowing nothing good could come from it, I accepted the call.

Malcolm Wolfe stepped into the virtual space with me. I hate it when I'm right.

"Nasty business with the Warden, eh?" Malcolm paced the black void in front of me.

"You didn't have to kill him."

"Me?" Malcolm's face soured. "What makes you think I had anything to do with his death? He was nothing but kind to me. Granted I slept through most of our encounters."

"Didn't you?"

"Never."

"Don't act indignant."

"Mr. Castille's death lacked elegance. I'm offended you consider me capable of such an act."

I disregarded the idea that there had been elegance in Diana's murder and said, "Was it the people who broke you out?"

"Not unlikely." Malcolm's tone suggested he wasn't sure of the answer himself. "They're not good people, you know."

"Why don't you tell me about them?"

"No, no, no." Malcolm clicked his tongue against his teeth and waggled a finger. "We don't bite the hand that feeds us until we can feed ourselves."

"Would've figured you for a lone wolf. Your own master."

"We all answer to someone at one time or another. It's simply the way the world works."

"So why you doing this? Did they give you a to-do list that started with annoying the hell out of me?"

"No, Tom. You're a side project, but don't let that hurt your feelings. I promise to give you plenty of attention."

"I'm devastated," I said, "but let's get to the part where you tell me why you're here now."

Malcolm frowned, the two corners of his mouth plummeting towards a chin puckered with wrinkles.

"You've never had a sense of theatrics. No dramatic buildup, crescendo, climax, release…ah, all the subtleties that keep us wrapped in breathless anticipation, begging and pleading and writhing for more, and less, until you reach your threshold and transcend."

"You've been alone too long."

"Probably." Malcolm stopped pacing and pivoted on his heels. His lips had reversed their journey and he beamed. Pure pride. "I'm here because heroes deserves recognition."

"Not sure I des—"

"Not you," Malcolm said. "Me."

"We may have differing opinions on what constitutes a hero."

"Undoubtedly, but that doesn't change the fact that I saved a life. Two lives, multiple times, to be precise."

"You've turned over a new leaf, huh?"

"A one-time engagement, I assure you. All the more rare and spectacular for it. I'm glad we had the opportunity to share it together."

It wasn't until I asked the question, "Who did you save?", and heard the words spoken from my own mouth that I understood part of the equation. "Raines?"

I'd suspected he'd blocked her nanocomp from kick starting her heart, but if he wanted her dead, he could've deactivated her comp at any time since.

"And yourself. You don't believe the Pause anti-aircraft guns simply decided not to fire themselves, do you?"

"I'd considered the possibility."

"You're getting sloppy. The Tom Mandel I know would have controlled the situation better."

"I'm getting old."

"You're not old, just dying. I understand that can be distracting."

"Why are you helping us?"

"If I lose you, I lose my game...my revenge."

"Sounds petty."

"Most things in life are."

"Why didn't you kill Raines?" I asked, doubling back on the only question that mattered.

"Because from this point on, every stolen glance will fill you with dread. Now you know I can take her like that." Malcolm snapped his fingers; the sound of dried twigs cracking. "I want you to relive that moment on the beach a thousand times in your remaining hours knowing there's nothing you can do to stop me. Knowing that she will die, and you will fail to do anything but watch."

The world shrank. I was helpless to stop it. Malcolm had planted a seed of despair in my gut that had taken root. Its tendrils snaked through my innards, coiling, squeezing, and choking like a garrote wire across my stomach.

My skin shriveled. The folds of my throat constricted, pulling taut across tendon and vein. My own flesh became a prison suffocating in its embrace.

I shook my head and struggled to find words. There was nothing to say.

Malcolm stepped closer to me and placed an icy hand on my shoulder. The nanobots simulated the pressure of touch and I recoiled.

"Please, stop," I said, feeling the strength in my legs ebb. "I give up. Is that what you want?"

"No." Malcolm laughed. A cruel sound. Akin to a puppy's whimper, designed to grate the nerves and chafe for attention. "That is the last thing I want."

CHAPTER THIRTEEN
Flying Jalopy

It's hard to look a gift horse in the mouth. They get squirrelly when you try pulling back their lips. I kept this in mind when we arrived at the Dragonfly left for us by Captain Nash.

The term hover-car applied to the vehicle in question by only the strictest of definitions. It hovered and you could drive it, so a hover-car? Sure.

In my opinion it would be more accurate to call it an impending disaster with the high potential of becoming a flaming ball of wreckage raining down over Terminus. I didn't fancy being part of that burning melee, but it beat walking.

Raines trailed a hand along the back end of the vehicle. Her fingers surfed the time-worn grooves, pockets, and ripples that had slowly reshaped the vehicle's exterior. She looked dubious.

The inside was an improvement, but only because the damages were cosmetic by comparison to the structural deficiencies of the outside. The passenger seat was padded with bricks that did nothing to absorb my weight. Raines, consumed by her seat cushion, suffered from the opposite problem.

We'd be traveling, but not in style.

Raines fired up the engine, which thrummed with a deceptively strong pulse. We sat inside the Frankenstein made from piecemeal parts that somehow ran strong where it mattered. A moment later, Raines had us skimming the outer sprawl of the Terminus skyline.

Rising towards the ElMag Low, Raines broke the silence that had followed us since the forest. "You gonna tell me what's eating you, or do I have to guess?"

Through the window I watched the city pass by. Squat buildings on the fringe grew in predictable increments as we approached the city center sparkling hundreds of miles in the distance.

Malcolm's words had been edged with a poison meant to undermine my armor of self-delusion. The delusion being the belief that, in the end, good would win over evil.

I clung to the idea that I fought on the side of good, despite overwhelming evidence to the contrary.

But it wouldn't play out that way. Not in the real world. I'd learned that lesson before, but I was back in the classroom learning all the terrible ways man has devised to hurt one another.

Raines stood on the front line in a way that left her without any kind of control.

Malcolm held a gun to her head, slowly applying pressure to a squeaky trigger. Soon it would catch, the shot would come, and it'd be over.

Raines wouldn't see it coming.

I could, but I was equally helpless to stop it. Maybe more so.

The buildings shifted, stretching for the heavens and whatever God hid from us up there.

"This would be your time to talk," Raines said, sensing my apprehension.

We banked right, lining up our approach with the Electromagnetic Lowroad steaming the air into heat vapor. It sucked us in before rocketing us towards the city center.

"Malcolm's hacked the nanocomps."

Raines gave a sidelong glance that spoke of her confusion. "We talking personal comps?"

"Yeah."

She sighed and rubbed her cheek. She didn't bother arguing. After the morning we'd had, there was no point in maintaining classifications of possible or impossible anymore. The world was changing. It'd been years in the making, but today it was coming to fruition. For us, at least.

"Well, you're the Intuit," she said, going into problem-solving mode, "how do we stop him?"

I shrugged.

Nanocomps ranked alongside Intuits as one of the great mysteries of Unity. They'd been a gift from the Japanese, along with the infrastructure that gave life to the Stream, shortly before they closed their borders and disappeared. The nanocomp came at a pivotal moment in the history of the North American Union's blossoming youth, allowing its people to rise from the ashes left in the wake of the Dissolution.

The rest of the world hadn't been so fortunate.

The device, attached to the brain stem at birth, synchronized minds across Unity with the trillions of nanobots floating in the atmosphere. It made the shared cognitive network of the Stream possible. A collective consciousness; a collaboration of all human knowledge and experience. Even with centuries of study Unity scientists could only reproduce the nanocomp according to Japanese design. Unable to reverse engineer the damned thing, we remained shackled to our ignorance.

From what we did understand, the nanocomp functioned like a technological stem cell. A blank slate that bonded, restructured, and transformed the neural network of its host brain. A process that made it impossible for that host to survive without the comp overseeing its base operations.

The nanocomp becomes a crutch. Without it the brain simply can't survive.

Not for any useful period of time at least.

With this in mind, I spitballed a solution with zero viability. "Turn them off?"

"Real helpful."

"What do you want from me?" I said the words more forcefully than intended.

The agitation creeping into my voice was spillover from the morning's escapades in conjunction with the fact I was going on twelve hours clear of the Quick. I massaged my temple with the backside of a bony knuckle, digging into the tender spot where a tangled orgy of nerve endings slept. Shocks of electricity zapped down my cheek with an odd mixture of pain and relief.

"Nobody expects you to shit a miracle," Raines said, "but you know Malcolm. Think from his perspective. What's his next move?"

Police work is about asking the right question at the right time, which is more instinct than science. Predicting what Malcolm would do next wasn't half as hard as guessing the how. He wanted to make the world suffer. How he would do so remained a mystery.

"He said, 'We don't bite the hand that feeds us until we can feed ourselves.'"

"Malcolm?" Raines asked.

"Yeah."

"He's not the type to play well with others."

"That's what I said. So now you see it doesn't matter how well I know Malcolm, he's just the gun. We need the guy holding the gun."

Raines nodded and said, "Any theories on who that might be?"

"Somebody with a big hand...and a long reach."

"So, who has a reach long enough to wipe the Pause mainframe?"

"Besides the President?" I asked. "God?"

"Somehow I doubt Malcolm is God's divine vessel."

"You never know."

"Alright, well disregarding the possibility of divine retribution, that leaves us with President Jennings." Raines tucked a rogue strand of hair behind her ear. "I just can't wrap my head around the level of sophistication required for an operation of this magnitude. The number of moving parts is staggering…"

"Which is to say nothing of the Safeguard override or nanocomp hack," I said, tossing more kindling on the flame burning in Raines' mind.

"Actually, the Safeguard override wouldn't be difficult if you were the guardian of the protocol."

"All roads lead to the President," I said, not entirely sure how I felt about where our deductive process had taken us.

"It's something at least."

Not a very good something in my estimation. Whether we were following the theories suggested by the clues or merely interpreting the clues to fit our own theories was anybody's guess. I hoped for the first, but feared for the second.

Rising out of the modern jungle of cement, smart-metal, and bustling humanity, the glass pyramid of the Time Bank appeared on the rim of the world where the planet curved off the horizon and into infinity. Despite our distance from the building, its immutable design issued a wordless declaration, a challenge that said, "I was here before you; I will be here after you."

A sunburst of light winked off the smooth onyx glass of the Time Bank, forcing me to shield my eyes. The light rummaged through my mind and scrounged up a headache buried beneath.

Throbbing against the inside of my skull, the sensitive portion of my frontal lobe pulsed in time with the humming engine. I closed my eyes and took a breath, filling my lungs with more air than they could comfortably hold before letting it spill out my nostrils. The Quick Sliver nanites were beginning to change. It wouldn't be long before they reduced me to a hallucinating sack of human bio-waste.

I'd rationed my stash of Quick on the assumption I'd be dead soon, so the question of where I'd be getting the next hit wasn't trivial. I rolled back my jacket sleeve and watched the bars shrinking with every second, hoping they'd offer some insight.

They proffered nothing but a glimpse of my mortality. A needless reminder.

Beads of sweat traced a path across my cheek and down my neck. The task at hand required focus, but my mind was split.

Something touched my hand. I jerked away.

My eyes snapped open to see Raines' hand inches above mine. She wore that unreadable mask of emotions I'd found typical of the female gender.

She held my stare and gently placed her hand atop mine. It was warm in a way that went beyond body temperature. The heat spread up my arm and into my shoulder, pausing at my throat as if deciding which direction to go before settling on the all-encompassing answer of both.

It descended into my chest while bubbling up into my nose. My cranium tingled in time with my toes.

She'd connected us in what felt to be the empathic equivalent of syncing minds in the Stream. We weren't sharing the same mental space, no free exchange of thought, but something else was transferred—emotion.

My doubt and frustration melted into her. In return I received something I hadn't allowed myself to feel since Diana's death.

Hope.

She filled me with the belief that somehow everything would work out, that there was more to life and death than suffering and pain. That something in between made it all worthwhile.

Something I couldn't immediately place.

Love.

Though her love for me was tainted, broken and jagged from the suffering I'd inflicted upon her.

Raines pulled her hand away as if she'd shared too much. The warmth lingered, the aftertaste of a dream still fresh. I wanted to reach out and grab her hand, to relive those feelings.

To feel connected.

But I didn't.

The hope and love she'd given me faded alongside the memory of her touch.

The moment was lost, as if it'd never existed.

And maybe it hadn't.

The Quick might have been tinkering with my wires, inducing mini-hallucinations and delusions. The Sliver would pursue increasingly complex punishments until I succumbed to its command.

I was riding that thin line between reality and fantasy, wondering how I'd ever distinguish the two again.

***

"If you don't know the how or the why," Raines said, her attention fixed on the fast approaching Time Bank, "maybe you can figure out the when?"

"Sometime before I die?"

"That's assuming this has anything to do with you. I can't imagine whoever broke Malcolm out of prison did so because they wanted to torture you. No offense."

Raines' sharp words popped my narcissistic bubble. She might be right. There had to be more at play than simple revenge, but the timing between Malcolm's escape and my impending death was too coincidental.

Perhaps I was a pawn, but then what was the game?

"If I'm not part of their grand design, then why would they allow him to torment me when I still have obvious connections to Time Vice?"

"Those aren't strong connections anymore."

"No, but they're something. And the thing with clandestine government organizations is that they do well because of slinking in dark shadows with the element of surprise," I said. "Put them in the light and they're as ineffectual as any other arm of the government."

Raines was unsatisfied by that conclusion, but we were operating with too few facts to compose good working theories. Until then, we'd simply have to follow our gut.

Raines dipped out of the ElMag Low towards a line of Dragonflys filing into the Time Bank garage. A half mile out, the monolithic pyramid's powerful grav-beam snared our vehicle and guided us towards a reflective panel shimmering with the flat glare of black ice. The Time Bank, the backbone of the Life Tracker system, stared back unwinking, uncaring.

That building was the reason I was going to die in the next twenty-four hours. It monitored the software, firewalls, and encryptions that tracked the flow of time in and out of the billions of Life Trackers spread across Unity. When the final second blipped off my forearm, and my account hit zero, it would issue the command for my nanocomp to self-destruct.

"I hate that building." I pointed it out.

Raines smirked. "Can't imagine why."

"It's an oppressive triangle."

"Technically it's a pyramid. A triangle only has two dimens—"

"Whatever," I interrupted. "Point is, some guy with a math degree decides Earth can only sustain seven billion people and next thing you know Unity's rolling out the Life Tracker."

"Seventy years ain't long enough for you?"

"It's too long if you ask me, but that's not the point."

"Then what is?"

"Government shouldn't be making that decision for us. It's unnatural."

"Yeah, 'cause human nature is really something we should let go unregulated."

"Beats slavery," I muttered.

"Nobody's stopping you from getting a job and buying some more time."

"Yeah?" I tapped on the window pane. "Tell that to the people living in the Lowers with no job skills and outdated tech. How much time you think they can buy?"

"I admit it's not a perfect system."

"Shit, it's not even a good system."

"Maybe," Raines conceded.

People living north of the Middles liked to believe we were all playing the same game, same rules. It's a lie. Malcolm had proven that when he pulled off the greatest time heist in history. He'd shown just how vulnerable the system, and we, really were.

Sixty-two million years, gone in a heartbeat. One million people with only a single, tiny bar left on their forearms. Ten seconds.

Nanocomps across Unity betrayed their hosts and dumped truckloads of dopamine and serotonin into their bodies. Chemicals that would ease the transition into the afterlife took hold, and ten seconds later, one million people dropped dead.

To me, the most offensive part wasn't that they'd been robbed of their lives, but that they'd been denied the right to be upset about it.

They died happy because their bodies told them too. Not with a panicked scream, but with a sigh.

A whimper that changed the world.

That was nine years ago. People are quick to forget. It's easier than remembering. Forgetting helps us sleep at night.

But I hadn't forgotten. Those lives, Diana's included, were on my shoulders 'cause I'd failed to stop Malcolm. I wouldn't let it happen again.

The Dragonfly decelerated as we drew within spitting distance of the Time Bank. The city skyline reflected in the pyramid's unblemished glass sides. No opening had appeared. No door, just wall.

The rational part of me knew we'd pass harmlessly through, a ship in the night, but the Quick fed the lizard part of my brain, the part which couldn't be reasoned with. My heart rate spiked with each panicked message of fight or flight that made it to my muscles.

I tightened my grip on the armrest to appease those requests for action, however minute.

The nose of our jalopy smashed into our reflection before disappearing through the barrier. Slowly, we were dragged inside the belly of the monster.

CHAPTER FOURTEEN
Breaking and Entering

The faded yellow sun tap dancing on my sensitive photo-receptors dimmed as we entered the parking garage. We glided past endless rows of vehicles stacked neatly atop one another until we reached a wall of double-doored elevators near the heart of the building.

"So, we're in the building, great, but…" I visualized the Time Bank's security measures, "how are we gonna get to the President again?"

"Leave that to me."

"What's that even mean?"

"It means, leave that to me." Raines was out of the Fly and standing at the elevator before I'd even managed to dislodge myself from the vehicle.

My system hadn't recovered from my high dive into the ocean; a reminder of that fact shot through my body as I stood up. Dying takes a lot out of a man.

A bell chimed and the elevator door opened. A woman in her mid-thirties dressed business casual stepped out. She gave Raines a courtesy nod, but looked straight through me as if staring into the wind.

I still had that look of a Lower about me, I suppose.

We stepped inside and the elevator chirped. Raines thumbed a glassy button on the wall that scanned her fingerprint with a glowing green light. My expectations for what would happen next were low. But when the elevator began moving towards the three hundred and ninety-fifth floor—five shy of the apex—I was a bit surprised.

Raines breathed quietly beside me. She held her shoulders high and tight. I watched the muscles in her forearm flex and release in the reflective side of the elevator.

"You know where you're going?" I asked.

She grunted.

"I'm taking that as—"

"Shut up, Tom," she said, with visible tension lines etched across her cheeks.

We spent the remainder of our ascent in silence. Raines refused to share her secret. Prying wouldn't change that fact. Answers would come soon enough, I hoped.

The elevator slowed to a smooth, almost imperceptible stop. When the doors slid apart, revealing two armed guards with the general size and shape of brick walls shoved into suits and handed assault rifles, my heart did a stutter step. Startled, I fought my body's first instinct to attack while we maintained the fleeting element of surprise.

Raines didn't share that tactical perspective and opted for a different course of action.

"Hey, Damon," she said with a smile that looked genuine. "Is he in?"

Damon, the older of the two gentlemen barring our path, studied me as if I might be his next meal. A raised pink scar slithered up the man's cheek into a receding line of salt-and-pepper hair. Nanites could fix the cosmetic damage, but in his line of work looking the part of scary war machine probably went a long way.

It was going a long way on me.

My fingers itched to be wrapped around a weapon of any sort. I felt naked and woefully overmatched if things got physical. I made a mental note to ask Raines how she knew these two members of the President's Alpha Guard.

"Mr. Moreau is in a meeting, but I'll let him know you stopped by, Mrs. Raines." Damon didn't bother with pleasantries. His tone was all business.

Raines stepped forward and placed a hand on Damon's shoulder. The big man eyed her but didn't respond. In the short silence that followed the enormous soldier and the slender cop stared at each other in the soft way old friends do.

"I'll just wait in his office if that's okay," she said.

Damon's posture slackened. His lips rose to greet his ears, forming a crease across his cheek in the process. He wore the smile like a battle wound.

"Uh…yeah, alright. Of course, Alaina," he said, his voice having undergone a complete transformation. Without loosening his grip on the rifle in his hands, he pivoted and led the way down a narrow corridor lined with unmarked doors. "Should I ping Mr. Moreau and let him know you're here?"

"That won't be necessary," Raines said, falling into step beside the moving mountain. "We'll wait until whenever he's done. I don't want to be a distraction."

Damon nodded with a grunt.

I lacked the life experience to understand it, but something incredibly odd had just occurred between Damon and Raines. Somehow Raines had neutralized the veteran soldier with a soft touch and placating voice.

Our procession stopped beside a solid metal door that looked identical to all the others we'd passed. The uniformity of the floor plan gave no indication as to Bradley Moreau's place within the company hierarchy. Judging purely by the fact that the hall continued an additional hundred feet past three more doors, I guessed Moreau to be a middle manager of sorts.

A biometric scanner on the door responded to Damon's palm and it dilated open to reveal a lavishly appointed office.

Thoughts of Moreau as a middle manager were pushed to the side. A single paned window stretched floor to ceiling on the south-facing wall. The Time Bank towered above its neighbors, offering an unrivaled view of sky and city sprawl. On the horizon, over a sea of buildings, I barely made out the pillared sides of the Vault.

It was the type of view reserved for people accustomed to calling the shots.

"If you need anything, let me know," Damon said, his wide shoulders managing to touch both sides of the doorframe.

"Thanks." Raines crossed the room and stopped beside a white leather couch. "Do you have any idea when Brad might be back?"

"Hard to say. President's been meeting with bigwigs from the other Districts all morning. Moreau's running things from the Oracle. You know how it is babysitting those delegate types, but I'm sure he'll find a few minutes for you."

Raines stared off at the ceiling, squinting slightly and chewing the corner of her lip as if doing complex mental math.

"Hey, next time you pop in, bring those two hellions with you," Damon said, stepping back into the hall. "We don't see nearly enough of Maddie and Morgan around these parts anymore."

"I'm not sure the President finds the idea of kids mingling with Alpha Guard as endearing as you or me."

"What he doesn't know won't hurt him." Damon gave an enormous wink before exiting.

Raines was standing behind a glass-framed desk in the corner by the time the door closed. The workstation was sparsely adorned with few indicators that anybody used it for anything more than decoration.

Raines' fingers flitted across a touchpad on the desk. The wall behind her melted to reveal a hidden door.

"You gonna tell me what the hell is going on?" I asked. "Who's Bradley Moreau?"

"He's the Captain of Alpha Guard."

"And how did you get clearance to be here and go through his stuff?"

"I married him."

That hit me hard, a right cross square on the chin. "Oh."

Raines looked up from Moreau's desk. "Did you think I'd wait for you to get your shit together and come back?"

"No."

Maybe.

I didn't know what I wanted anymore. Life goes on. A truth I'd wanted for Raines, but I suppose I didn't want to face the reality of what that actually meant. Easier to hide away in the Lowers. Die oblivious. Our ignorance protects us.

"I'm glad you found someone," I said. "You deserve to be happy."

"He's a good man." Raines refused to meet my gaze, which was fine 'cause I wasn't sure I'd be strong enough to hold hers. "He won't condone what we're doing. We can get to the President, but we've got to be quick."

"How?"

"Brad has a personal elevator connected to the President's antechamber. We can use it to get to the top floor."

"What about you?"

"What about me?"

"Can you do this? Use your husband, I mean?"

Raines stared through a hologram projected on the corner of Moreau's desk. She was in it, wearing a white sundress, with a boy and girl wrapped in either arm.

The kids had Raines' hair, black like the ocean floor. They were twins, but Madison had her mother's eyes, Morgan his father's, which were filled with a sort of longing. A searching for something the world had yet to offer.

"I don't have a choice." Raines abruptly canceled the projection. "You're not the only one Malcolm is playing games with."

***

Moreau's service elevator was a tight fit for one, downright intimate for two. Raines stood nearest the door, the back of her skull pressed firmly against my nose. Fields of rain-soaked lavender wafted up my nostrils, making my brain tingle.

I closed my eyes, forcing any memories or feelings that scent might conjure back down to the suppressed depths of my subconscious.

"Be ready," she said. "They won't be expecting us, but that won't buy us much."

"How many are up there?"

"Hard to say. Jennings will have his two shadows, for sure. Beyond that is anybody's guess. Security is designed to keep potential threats off the top floor. By comparison to the rest of the building the President's office will be lightly protec—"

The elevator shuddered to a stop. A ding announced its arrival. The doors slid apart, revealing two Alpha Guards standing at attention.

Raines bolted forward, covering the fifteen feet to the guards in a blur before my nanocomp could even dump a fresh-brewed pot of adrenaline into my system. The man on the left shared my surprise at the small woman streaking towards him. The other guy, however, was ready. His pupils were flakes of obsidian lost in a field of snow.

Raines left her pistol on her hip, instead opting to get close, negating the advantage of the men's rifles. I was still inside the elevator considering tactical options when she leapt over an end table, vaulted a leather chair, and engaged the wired mongoose on the right with a flying ninja kick.

The adrenaline finished percolating and hit my muscles. My nanocomp trimmed back thoughts running in the background and sharpened my mind like a sword to a whetstone. The world fuzzed around the edges, leaving the remaining guard framed in clarity. I lunged, forgetting sore muscles as the nanobots surfing my veins worked overtime to compensate.

Raines and her opponent were locked in a tightly orchestrated dance of ass-kickery, but there wasn't time to appreciate the details. The guard I hurtled towards regained his composure and jumped to meet me in the middle.

In a contest of size and strength, he'd win outright. But life-and-death fights are rarely decided by those two factors.

Experience and craftiness, plus a strong desire not to die, go a long way.

Looking at the man's freshly shaved cheeks, chiseled from marble, I guessed I had him on the first two points, but the third remained undecided.

The guard directed a boulder-sized fist at my face. I saw it coming with plenty of time to duck. What I didn't see was his other fist following in the wake of the first. It hammered me in the solar plexus, driving the air from my lungs with a spasming cough.

Something cracked. I clipped my ankle on the side of a small oval-cut table and staggered, clutching at my damaged ribs while wheezing through constricted airways. I straightened my back to stretch the shrinking diaphragm that refused to take in more air.

The guard spun and closed the distance, fast. I dodged the first three strikes directed at my head more on luck than skill. I backed away from the fist tornado until the wall barred further retreat.

My nanocomp decided it'd had enough and took control of the situation. It locked onto a fist coming towards my face and shifted my perception of time. The ball of muscle and bone slowed until it moved at half-speed. There was plenty of time to act, or not to act, but those weren't decisions for me to make anymore.

As a passive observer I watched my body slide down the wall in the final moment before the guy's knuckles could relocate my face to the floor. The fist zipped by my head. It found nothing for its efforts but the unyielding smart-metal wall, which deformed slightly under its force.

He showed no sign of pain.

Muscle memory guided me forward from my knee. I popped up and kicked him in the kneecap, with the crunch of bone realigning and ligaments snapping.

The guard swayed and hobbled backwards, but didn't fall.

I feigned a punch followed by a second kick to the man's good leg.

The man strafed awkwardly to avoid the blow, putting him right where I wanted. His exposed chin floated past. I planted my foot, shifted directions, and swung a wide hook that found a home where the rolls of muscle in his neck gave way to jawbone.

His eyes rolled back and the lights went out. He arrived in dreamland a split second before hitting the ground.

I puffed my chest and smiled as I turned to check on Raines.

She stood over the body of her own dispatched opponent, arms crossed, with a hint of boredom playing on her face.

"You're getting old," she said.

"What? That guy's huge," I said, gesturing towards the Goliath at my feet. "I did good."

Raines rolled her eyes and turned down the hall.

"Cut me some slack," I said, dogging her steps. "I'm dying here."

***

"Ready?" I said, taking aim at the door with the energy pistol I'd pilfered from the guard at the elevator.

Raines nodded and tightened her grip on her own weapon.

I fired.

My nanocomp kept me running on super-speed, giving me plenty of time to track the blue glob of energy sizzling from the barrel in slow motion. The shot had no recoil, though, so the whole affair felt slightly anticlimactic.

Thoughts of anticlimax were scrubbed away when the pulse exploded with enough force to rip the slabs of wood from their hinges and nearly knock me onto my ass.

Thankfully the door to the President's office had been constructed from decorative wood rather than an energy-absorbing material. Whoever designed that floor hadn't considered the possibility that anybody would make it past the building's defensive protocols. They couldn't be faulted for not anticipating a crazy ex-cop and his partner getting a key to the city and blasting their way in.

And yet there we were.

Smoke defiled the air. It stung the inner lining of my nose and throat as I stepped through the carnage and into the room.

A dozen impeccably, if not similarly, dressed men and women sat around a large oval table. I locked onto the only one that mattered. The man sitting at the head of the table.

President Richard Jennings.

Two bodyguards standing behind the President drew their weapons with the practiced ease of professionals, the pointy ends of their guns aimed at my head.

"Easy, fellas," I said, applying a couple pounds of pressure to the trigger of my own gun, aimed at President Jennings. It floated along that razor's edge where the slightest twitch would make me the most famous assassin in Unity history. "I don't intend on hurting anyone, but I also don't wanna get shot, so let's make a deal. Put your guns on the floor and back away from the table, and we won't have to hold an emergency election to decide President Jennings' successor."

"Alaina?" one of the men said, staring over my shoulder. The battle focus drained from his eyes, leaving in its place the type of confusion that has a physical weight.

"Put your gun down, Brad," Raines said. "We're here on Peacekeeper business."

Moreau looked as if he'd come straight from a soldier-for-hire catalog. Square-cut hair and boxy shoulders gave him the silhouette of rectangles stacked atop one another. His presence of stature compensated for his height, which was shorter than I'd expected.

If he'd looked angry before, now he looked downright murderous. His eyes didn't waver in their attempt to kill me by sight alone.

Moreau opened his mouth to say more, but I didn't have time for him and Raines to work through their domestic issues. Time was fleeting. A luxury that would soon expire.

"Mr. President, this ends poorly for two guys in this room if people start pulling triggers. Do us both a favor and tell your men to stand down," I said, holding the leader of Unity between my sights.

Jennings' expression was flat, hollow. He tilted his head and flicked a dismissive wrist. Moreau balked while the other guard complied like an automaton. After an extended period of deliberation Moreau dropped his weapon to the floor and took two steps away from the table.

I relaxed the muscles in my arm, allowing the weight of the gun to sag at my side. Without the imminent threat of having another hole added to my face I studied the startled faces of the people in the room.

There was something oddly familiar about all these faces. Most of them, at least.

And then the light bulb went off—these were the leaders of the twelve Districts.

Shit.

Raines and I were holding the entire Earth government hostage.

That took the situation from bad to worse, but only marginally so. A depressing reflection of our day up to that point.

CHAPTER FIFTEEN
Gravity Is A Fickle Ally

More interesting than the leaders of Unity, however, was the mystery gentlemen sitting across the table from Jennings. He wore a shimmering black robe crisscrossed with elaborate veins of red rising off the hem in exotic patterns. His raven hair, pulled into a queue, added an angular sharpness to his face.

Despite all that, his olive skin was his most distinguishing characteristic. Nobody had vibrant sun-kissed skin like that in a world perpetually overcast with sagging gray clouds. Raines, the nearest approximation of an Easterner I'd ever seen, appeared porcelain by comparison.

It took a second for my mind to fill the gaps left between clues. Another second to doubt the hypothesis. And a third to accept the inevitable conclusion that I must be looking at a Japanese delegate.

As if in response the gentlemen faded from existence, vanishing with the breeze.

"Well, that was weird," I said.

Raines, standing beside me with her pistol aimed in the general direction of the table, nodded.

"What was that?" I asked.

"A hologram." President Jennings regarded me with indifference. "Have you come for a lesson on refracted light?"

"I'll manage."

I'd never seen such a realistic hologram without first blinking into the Stream. That it was commonplace here spoke of the technological gap between the Uppers and the rest of the population.

I squeezed the pistol tighter and ignored the knot rising in my throat.

"Perhaps you would like to share with us your reason for intruding?" Jennings leaned back in his chair with an ease better suited for an evening around the fireplace with loved ones.

By comparison, a quick scan of the faces around the table turned up a whole lot of fear, and not much else.

Best to be direct and use the power of peer pressure to my advantage.

"We were in the neighborhood and thought we'd stop by and see which of you helped Malcolm Wolfe escape Pause."

Myriad new data poured in as the District leaders gave me more than fear to work with.

"I gather this is news to most of you." I kept the majority of my focus on Jennings, for all the good it did me: he had the emotional range of a machine.

"No," Madame Cavanaugh, from District Four, said, "I'm afraid we have not been informed of any such escape."

The collective gaze of the room shifted to President Jennings. If the attention bothered him, it didn't show.

Slowly, he stalked the room with his stare, locking eyes with each District leader for a long second until the delegates conceded dominance and looked away. All save for the elderly Madame Cavanaugh with her bird-pecked features that suggested she'd seen all the darkest sides of humanity during her lifetime, and wouldn't be put off by a staring contest with a man in a suit.

After considerable deliberation Jennings turned and said, "Mister...?" He held the word out, an invitation to familiarity.

"Call me Tom."

"Well, Tom." The ice melted in his voice as the smile that'd won him multiple elections creased his full lips. He gestured to what remained of the shattered door at my feet. "You've jumped to some rather dramatic conclusions."

"We followed the clues, and this is where they brought us."

"On behalf of the District leadership, let me thank you for your due diligence and dedication to the job. You have gone to extreme lengths to see your investigation reach a satisfactory conclusion. However, I will personally vouch for each of my colleagues; none have taken any part in Malcolm Wolfe's escape from Pause. I'm afraid you have misinterpreted your clues, and put yourself in quite the problematic situation."

"Lovely. Warm fuzzies all around. But I wonder who's willing to vouch for you?" I let the accusation linger before dropping the hammer. "And before anybody jumps at that opportunity, let me share something else that hasn't gone public: the Safeguard's been compromised. Which, ya know, last I checked, only one person has access too."

The District leaders studied Jennings with unwavering intensity. All eyes awaited his response.

All eyes save one pair.

A flare went up in the back of my mind. My nanocomp locked onto something different. Downcast eyes and a squelched smile. It was fleeting, but undeniable. The kid at the opposite end of the table from Jennings was trying to hide something.

Jackpot.

"Do not listen to him," Jennings said. "The Safeguard is perf—"

"Who's that?" I gestured with my chin towards the young man sitting beside the stunning Madame Leader of District Six. I recognized the woman but the man was a blank spot.

"Me?" he said, seeking non-existence in the depths of his chair. "I'm nobody."

The warning bells would have been deafening if I hadn't already muted them.

"Even the biggest somebody starts off a nobody. Maybe yo—" I flicked the barrel of the gun in his direction.

That was a mistake.

Hairs on the back of my neck sprang to attention. They pointed back in the direction from which I'd turned, to the guard beside Moreau, diving for his gun.

He had me by a step. He swiped the weapon from the floor, rolled to his side, and fired. The pistol belched two blobs of energy that scarred the air as they sailed towards me. I ducked with the collaborative efforts of nanotized reflexes and luck.

From my hiding spot beneath the table I heard the thrum of a vortex pistol followed by a scream that sounded more like the tortured yowl of a back-alley cat than that of a man.

A body crumpled, hitting the floor with a heavy thud.

I lifted my head and saw Raines standing in the doorway, gun in hand.

With the support of the table, I stood. Jennings' guard writhed like a worm in the rain, clutching his face where the ring of condensed air had probably perforated his eardrum.

I didn't envy the man, but I also didn't feel bad. He should feel lucky Raines had turned down the intensity of her vortex pistol at all. Any higher and there'd be nothing left of the man but vapor and memories.

"Thanks," I said, nodding to Raines.

"Try not turning your back on the bad guys next time."

I denied my mouth the opportunity to make any comment that might land a bullet in my ass. Instead I turned back to the young man.

We had a lead, but without the ability to jam the Stream, we were helpless to stop anyone from sending out distress beacons.

Distress beacons that would be responded to with a level of force Raines and I weren't prepared to handle with our current cache of weapons.

I grabbed the man by the lapels of his blue pinstriped suit and yanked him to his feet. I tapped the needle-point barrel of my gun against his forehead. The gesture would have been more intimidating had the weapon been of a more substantial make, but sometimes you do what you can with what you got.

"We're strapped for time, so start singing before I get desperate," I said, adding the desired amount of crazy to my tone lest the man think I'd already arrived at a maximum state of desperation.

Man could always sink lower. In my experience rock bottom is a theory. Mostly there's just a point where digging becomes a real pain in the ass.

I'd been digging for a while.

"Hamilton," he said, stumbling over his name a few times. "Derek Hamilton."

The name dislodged a memory tucked deep in my subconscious. Leader of District Two. I'd heard of him during the last election, a time when politics and global culture ceased being topics of interest to me. Though, in fairness, anything that didn't come in a bottle, or at the end of a needle, had lost my interest by that point.

If I recalled correctly, he'd come up through Unity's Nanotechnology Division before making the shift to politics. A dubious switch. Word had it that the current administration was grooming him to succeed Jennings in two years.

I hate the smart and ambitious ones.

"Great! Mr. Hamilton," I said. "Start by telling us what you're hiding."

"What?" Hamilton blushed with a redness that spread to his ears. "I don't know what you're talking about, I swear I don't."

The guy would have made for a horrible card player. Wearing every turn of emotion on his face helped my cause, but it was disappointing to see in a professional politician.

Though, admittedly, it wasn't every day somebody broke into the Time Bank and held the world's government at gunpoint.

The audacity of our break-in had contributed greatly towards our success up to that point.

"No? Could have fooled me. You looked pretty smug when I told the room about the Safeguard. Not really the reaction I would expect."

"I'm not being smug, I promise, just scared." Hamilton punctuated his speech with flustered hand movements, like a bird flitting between flowers with a broken wing. "Given the circumstances, I think that's okay, right?"

"Why are y—" An explosion rocked the building. The ground lurched, throwing me into the table.

Raines glanced over her shoulder. Gray smoke filtered out of the hall and into the adjoining waiting room.

"The cavalry's here," she said.

We'd disabled the elevator and barricaded the stairwell, but it would only slow the rescue team—and not for long.

Hamilton was hiding something, but we'd had our shot and missed. I'd learned the hard way, in life and death, there are no do-overs.

"Time to go," I said.

"Really?" Raines said, her words heavy with sarcasm.

I spun towards the wall of windows running floor to ceiling, which offered an unrivaled view from the highest point in all of Terminus. I fired a single round from the gun at my hip. The window shattered. Crystals tumbled down the side of the building, catching the sunlight and casting a million rainbows as they fell to the city below.

I yanked Raines to the window. Glass crunched underfoot. At the lip, I stared down. The world tried to swoon, but I denied my body the pleasure of vertigo. I followed the pyramid's gradual slope with my eye and ran a calculation.

"What are you doing?" Raines shouted in my ear, her voice barely audible over the wind whistling past.

Derek Hamilton quivered like a puppy left in the rain. We didn't get what we'd come for, but it hadn't been a total loss—assuming the next part didn't kill us.

A soldier in full tactical gear appeared through the plume of smoke drifting into the conference room. A bolt of energy sailed overhead, electrifying the air around us as it passed through the broken window and headed towards the clouds hanging full in the sky.

I wrapped an arm around Raines' waist and jumped out the window before she could jerk free of my grasp. The soft fluorescent lights of Jennings' office gave way to the diffused power of the sun, a runny egg yolk bleeding across the sky.

On our third bounce off the plated side of the building, my head whiplashed, cracking hard against the unforgiving glass.

My vision swirled. I struggled to maintain an upright position with feet pointed towards the ground. We bounced again. Gravity wrenched the pistol free of my hand. It skittered alongside us as we continued our descent.

Friction heat from the slide spread through my ass and shoulders. My jacket absorbed most of the heat, but Raines hadn't been so prepared. If somehow we made it through the next thousand foot freefall, she'd be sporting the road rash to prove it.

My heart inched higher in my throat with every foot we fell. The dizziness hit a crescendo, my organs tried abandoning ship through my mouth, and I considered the possibility that I'd made a terrible mistake.

And then everything slowed down, like plunging into a pool of marmalade. The air thickened, matting clothing to skin.

The roar of wind blasting past our ears became a shrill whistle, high but quiet. Our downward inertia sputtered to a halt.

The Grav-Beam had us now.

In the arms of the beam our direction changed course, along with our destiny of splattering upon the ground. Our horizontal pull towards the building increased, giving birth to a new fear that chilled me like an icy wire dragged through my veins.

Grav-Beam is a misnomer. It's named as such because it's an easy concept to grasp, when in reality it's a tractor beam with a pull many times stronger than gravity. If it were a true gravity beam our weight in relation to the system wouldn't matter. But those factors did matter and the force acting upon our couple hundred pounds of body weight was the same as if we were a multi-ton vehicle.

Which meant our speed increased as we catapulted towards the reflective glass surface of the parking garage. We flew through the invisible barrier and saw the wall we were destined to crash into.

I clutched at Raines like a baby koala. Holding her close, I threaded a finger atop hers on the trigger of the energy rifle gripped in her free hand, and fired. The bolt of energy burst on the floor. A mini shockwave smacked us sideways, dislodging us from the beam.

We skipped across the floor. The world spun into an indiscernible cornucopia of sounds, shapes, and colors. Elbows and knees sacrificed in countless collisions with the ground caused waves of blackout-inducing pain.

Pain receptors on high alert jockeyed for position to have their message heard by an overworked brain. The nanocomp dulled the incoming requests. Pain receded to the back of my mind until it became only a mild inconvenience.

That is, until we crashed into the side of a Dragonfly with the sickening crunch of metal crumpling beneath the combined force of flesh and bone.

My head pinged off the side of the Fly before coming to a full, soul-jarring stop. The new batch of pain overwhelmed my nanocomp. Too much to dampen. I felt it all.

Muscles were beaten to a pulp and it seemed too soon to say which bones, if any, hadn't shattered. I breathed into the pain and waited for the disorientation to pass.

I ran a hand along the back of my skull, fingers weaving between blood-soaked strands of hair before finding the gash of torn flesh that'd formed behind my ear.

Using the Fly for support I struggled to my feet only to be driven back to my knees by a sudden wave of nausea. The contents of my stomach refused my request to stay put. My body purged it all. Unfortunately, not having eaten anything substantial in the past twelve hours left only bile and stomach acid pooling in the puddle before me.

When the retching subsided I wiped the spittle from my lips using a hand already slick with blood from a wound yet undiscovered. "Raines?" I called out.

"Yeah?" she answered from somewhere behind me with a voice which was too thin.

"You alright?"

"Been better."

"Anything broken?" I asked, rolling onto my butt. My back slotted perfectly into the groove created by my collision with the Dragonfly.

Fifteen feet away Alaina sat in a Raines-shaped dent pounded into the side of a beige van.

"Besides my faith in humanity?" she asked.

"It wasn't that bad, was it?" I tried to smile, but immediately regretted the attempt.

"I think I would've rather been shot." Raines held her left arm limp in her lap. "How'd you know the Grav-Beam would catch us?"

"Just a hunch."

I didn't have the heart to tell her my original plan had revolved around blasting a window and falling back into the building. A plan that became an impossibility the moment I'd lost my gun.

Sometimes things work out and it's best not to over-analyze the results.

"Good hunch."

I nodded. "How long you think we got before they realize we didn't go splat?"

"Uh…" Raines looked past me. "Not long."

I turned, with no insignificant amount of effort, towards the source of her interest. My stomach dripped into my toes as I looked up into the barrel of a half-dozen energy rifles.

The men, wearing the full nanotized uniform of the Peacekeepers, formed a semicircle around us.

Damn. That was fast.

"Don't shoot," I said, dropping my hands into my lap. "We give up."

CHAPTER SIXTEEN

The Angel Of Death Is Short

Someone with a shaky hand performed surgery in my skull with an ice cream scoop.

That coupled with the blood leaking from a wound behind my ear, the obstructed flow of blood to my hands from immobilization rings fastened with too much zeal, and the hard metal seats delivering shocks of pain to my already aching brain with every turbulent shudder, tested the limit of my naturally sunny disposition.

Sandwiched between two Peacekeepers on the bench across from me, Raines' head dangled loose on her chest. She stared at the ground, waiting for it to reveal the secrets of the universe.

She looked like hell and probably felt worse, but we were alive. So that was something.

Which wasn't the same uplifting fact for some people as it was others.

The Peacekeepers had dosed us with enough healing nanites to ensure we wouldn't die of blood loss in transit to the Precinct. But Raines' arm, from shoulder to wrist, had been rubbed past the point of raw. The nanites could only work so fast.

Already her skin looked better than it had in the parking garage. The exposed cherry flesh, where the skin hadn't burned through, turned a glistening newborn pink. The edges were charred black and crispy. Still a couple standard deviations removed from her normally olive complexion, but not seeing the underlying tendons and muscle was progress in the right direction.

The nanobots were kinder to me, but not by much. They'd gone straight to my right leg to begin repairs on a bone shattered like an icicle. A tingle traipsed through me. Ants crawling beneath skin and across bone would be considered a form of torture if those ants weren't in fact fixing me.

A catch-22.

I shifted from one butt cheek to the other, redistributing the weight and relieving the pressure on my leg, accidentally bumping the guard beside me in the process.

The Keeper on my left responded with a sharp shove which sent me into the man on my right, who returned the favor with a shove of his own. Both men kept their eyes forward, unaware of, or simply uninterested in, the plight of the human Ping-Pong ball wedged between them.

The vehicle banked hard, causing the human cargo in the back to shift accordingly. A Stream dampener hummed in the wall separating the cattle from the driver. With our access to the Stream suppressed by Peacekeeper tech, and lacking any windows, I couldn't say with certainty where we were, but we hadn't been in the air long enough to have made it to the Precinct.

The look exchanged by our four babysitters indicated they shared my confusion.

"Bathroom breaks?" I hoped humor would crack their icy exteriors.

It didn't. They ignored me. Very rude.

The guard to the left of Raines slipped into the Stream, presumably to communicate with the driver. Breathing lost its necessity; everybody sat quietly. Agitated glances were exchanged like business cards.

The van decelerated sharply, jerking to a stop before the guard could return with answers.

Something beeped loudly, defiling the silence we had nurtured.

The four Keepers looked down at their forearms.

A second beep.

I knew that sound. So did the guy on my right. He clawed at the cuff of his uniform, desperate to expose his Life Tracker, but he was too slow. It wouldn't have mattered, anyhow.

A final beep.

The nanocomp of each Peacekeeper released a fatal jolt of electricity while that final beep still clung to the air like an unrequited confession of love.

The four men danced with death, every nerve firing. With one enormous convulsion muscles contracted, spines twisted, and heads craned towards the sky.

A neck snapped with a hollow crack, but I couldn't pinpoint from which man it'd echoed. For a brief moment that would remain scarred in my synapses; the men sat upright and lifeless.

After a full breath, the rigidity receded, and they slumped to the ground.

I was still struggling to make sense of what I'd just witnessed when the back door swung open. We drowned in the powerful rays of sunlight, the intensity an instant migraine.

Unable to shade my eyes with hands still secured behind my back, I squinted into the light. Slowly, the shape of a silhouetted man came into focus.

"Step out of the vehicle," he said, his voice betraying the nerves holding him hostage.

I stepped out of the Police transport vehicle and into the early afternoon sun. The air radiated a demonic heat. My clothes stuck to my body, instantly slick with sweat, as if I'd been caught in the rain.

Overhead, a Kestrel circled, a vulture waiting for death to take us. Ignoring the Peacekeeper standing a little ways off with a rifle trained on my forehead, I watched Raines emerge from the back of the van like the first Neanderthal stepping from her cave to find a strange new world. Her eyes were tiny slits. The Keepers had cuffed her hands in front to facilitate the healing of her arm, and so she used those free appendages to shield her face from the light.

I envied that.

It's the little things.

I turned my attention back to the Peacekeeper who was studying us through the viewfinder of his rifle.

"Care to tell us what the hell is goin' on?" I asked.

The officer shifted from foot to foot. His face, blanched and dripping with sweat, was simultaneously slack and tense. He was equally if not more disoriented than Raines and myself.

A hot breeze swirled the dust and gravel at our feet. I stared up at the source of the disruption.

The Kestrel, having gotten bored waiting for us to die, landed on a narrow sliver of roof.

"We can help you," Raines said, taking a step towards the Keeper, "but you have to tell us what's happening."

The young man looked desperately in need of somebody to tell him it was all going to work out. Raines was the right person for that task.

"I don't know." He shook his head. "We were following orders. Returning you to the Precinct, and then there's the beeping. It's like a watch alarm, you know? But then my partner seizes. Puts his head into the goddamn window so hard it cracked the glass. I don't understand—he had thirty years left, easy. He didn't get a countdown, no nothing. Just—"

Once the floodgates opened the kid loosed a deluge of questions mingled with rapid-fire pleading, as if the act of speaking and hearing the sound of his own voice would bring clarity.

"It's going to be okay," Raines said, her voice smooth and modulated. She gestured with bound hands to the Kestrel. "Who's that?"

He shook his head vigorously. "This is where he told me to bring you, that's all I know."

"Who?" Raines asked.

"Don't know. He appeared on the holo-screen after…" His eyes fogged with a memory still too fresh to process, "After my partner—he said I'd be next if I didn't stop here and let you out."

"Raines, we're about to have company," I said, gesturing to the three armed soldiers exiting the Kestrel.

The Peacekeeper followed my gaze. Poor kid made the mistake of turning with his rifle still pressed to his shoulder. The soldiers didn't pause to find out if he had hostile intent. They fired in unison.

Bolts of blue energy tore into the Keeper. The air filled with the stench of scorched meat. He teetered and fell, dead before he hit the ground.

Everything inside me clenched. It took all the willpower I could muster not to run. That, and the fact there wasn't a clear place to run to.

The three men formed a triangle in front of the Kestrel, their weapons sighted on us with cold, calculated precision. They were blank canvasses, devoid of emotion, and primed with a single purpose. The man at the head of the triangle waved us over with a flick of his wrist.

We dragged our feet, trying to buy time to think. The hamster spinning the wheels in my brain sprinted at full capacity, looking for a solution, but all plans followed different roads to the same destination: we'd be dead.

"Stop," the soldier said when we were within twenty feet.

We did; neither of us was eager to board the Kestrel with three men willing to murder six Peacekeepers without even getting a little misty eyed.

The smallest of the three men, who stood a clear foot over me, approached. He held his rifle loosely in one hand and fished a portable weapons detector the size of a deck of cards from his pants. The sensor beeped rhythmically as he waved it over us.

"Clear," he said, returning to his place in the formation without turning away from us.

The speaker for the group nodded towards the Kestrel. "Get in."

I had taken exactly two steps when I saw the white plume of smoke streaking across the sky.

I thought, *That's odd*. And then the world exploded.

To be more precise, the world occupied by and in close proximity to the Kestrel exploded.

The blast hit me a second later, hurling me across the roof. I landed with a thud that invited fresh reminders of injuries recently sustained. I swallowed hard, forcing a mouthful of blood down my throat, chapped raw from the heat.

From the flat of my back I watched wispy gray clouds dancing across the sky. A peaceful interlude despite the carnage nearby.

I rolled onto my knees before eventually standing, a task of considerable difficulty with hands fastened behind my back.

A second fireball, weaker than the first, erupted from the Kestrel, a gutted machine that would never fly again.

I scanned the sky for whatever had launched the missile and locked onto a matte black Peregrine, with rounded curves and sharp angles, blitzing towards us. The jet did a tactical drop, plunging hundreds of feet like an aerodynamic rock. It pulled up at the last second, rearing like a horse spawned in hell and ridden by the devil.

Something moved in my peripheral vision and I remembered the other people caught in the blast with me. Raines, hunched over on all fours, coughed up flecks of red. She looked shaken, but alive.

Two of the soldiers had found their feet and took aim at the Peregrine. The third man was gone entirely, presumably blown from the roof by the blast.

Blobs of energy burped from the soldiers' rifles, sizzling through the smoldering atmosphere before absorbing into the smart-metal sides of the Peregrine. The men continued firing, oblivious to the fact that their shots were wasted on the Peregrine's superior armor, until their batteries were dry.

The side door to the Peregrine swung open like a bird spreading its wings as the soldiers reached for fresh clips. A small girl with silver hair cannonballed out of the opening. She arced across the sky in a slow swan dive, somersaulting when she hit the ground.

Being no stranger to Quick Sliver-induced hallucinations, I watched, with a healthy skepticism, as the girl rolled out of the somersault and sprinted towards the two soldiers. She moved with a nanite-infused power that allowed her to cover the distance to the soldiers in a three-step blur too quick for my unaided brain to track. An instant later my nanocomp compensated for the girl's inhuman speed.

At that velocity I figured she must be running at full capacity. That is, until she morphed into a veritable lightning bolt. At least, that's how it looked through the lens of my speed implants.

She leapt into the air and tucked her limbs into a tight ball. In the penultimate moment before impact, she thrust her tiny legs forward and became a flying torpedo, smashing into the chest of one of the soldiers. The transfer of force sent the man flying across the roof and the girl into the most graceful back flip I had ever witnessed.

She landed softly. The man crashed hard into the side of the Peacekeeper transport vehicle.

The little girl had her back to the remaining soldier, who pressed his positional advantage. He gripped the barrel of his rifle and swung it with enough force that it would've cut the girl in half had it connected.

The soldier ran some nifty upgrades too, but he was decidedly slower than the feral child.

Sensing the attack, she jumped, spun, and kicked all in one coordinated movement.

With flawless precision her foot found the end of the rifle arcing towards her. The two weapons clashed, with the foot being the improbable, and yet decisive, victor.

The rifle snapped in half with a shearing of smart-metal audible across the roof.

The soldier, now holding half an energy rifle, looked at the remains of his weapon with wide-eyed disbelief.

"What the hell?" he said, which adequately surmised my feelings on the topic as well.

When he looked up the girl was there. She stood a hair under half his height, which brought her to the general region of the man's stomach. She lashed out with a flick of insect-like speed, her foot plowing into the man's kneecap, blowing it through the back of his leg.

He collapsed forward, bringing his head into range of the girl's fist, which popped him between the eyes. The man's unconscious body crumpled.

The little girl stood over the body of the incapacitated guard like the pre-pubescent angel of death. She brushed the dust from her shirt, turned towards Raines and myself, and said, "Get in the jet."

Something about being intimidated by a child felt so wrong that I wanted to light a cigarette and drink whiskey simply because it was something I could do that she could not. A veritable pissing match with a little girl.

I had reservations about being rescued, or kidnapped, by a child, but with hands cuffed behind my back, what was the point in arguing?

A black cord unfurled from the side of the Peregrine, still hovering overhead. Raines complied with the child's request without a word, not looking at me. She grabbed the cord and a thin blue bubble pulled her up into the Peregrine.

I pivoted to show the girl my hands and asked, "Any chance you got a key for these?"

She took the metal rings in either hand and tightened her grip. The bands crumpled beneath her fingers. She pulled them apart and the cuffs released their hold. My intestines quivered.

I'm not too proud to admit; the child terrified me. The combination of youthful innocence and deadly ninja ass-kicker can unnerve a man.

If you were going to design the perfect assassin, you could do worse.

I brought my hands to the front of my body, ignoring the protests of aching shoulders and rubbed my wrists. Not because the metal had chafed them, but because it felt like the thing to do now that my hands were free.

"Who are you?" I asked.

"Ash." She extended a small hand, trim, with nuclear pink nail polish. "Pleased to meet you, Tom."

More precocious than I'd expected from a child who'd just dismantled a duo of well-trained soldiers.

I took Ash's hand and shook; my grip was a wet leaf in hers. I offered a final glance to the Peacekeeper who'd released us from the van; his panic and ignorance replayed in my mind. Poor kid couldn't understand what he'd done to deserve that fate.

For me it never changed. Always the same story, same ending.

Innocent lives caught up in the endless loop of violence Malcolm and I were destined to play out. Trapped in a struggle where the only consideration, only outcome, was total devastation for ourselves and anybody unlucky enough to share the same breathing space as us.

This had Malcolm's fingerprints all over it. Not many people have the emotional numbness and technical capacity to murder six Peacekeepers in broad daylight.

For Malcolm to make this play now meant he was both overconfident in his abilities and nearing the end of whatever he needed me for. He'd shown his hand to the world, a questionable maneuver where covert operations are concerned.

I shifted those thoughts to the backburner and eyed the child before me. There were more pressing matters requiring my attention now.

I grabbed the black cable and a force field encircled me. My mouth filled with wet ozone.

The filmy blue sides pressed in tight. Hot stale air clung to my skin inside the bubble. The world felt three sizes too small. I closed my eyes and steadied my breathing. When I opened them the soap bubble popped. Raines sat across from an old man who turned and offered me a passing glance.

I studied the man while sinking slowly into the seat beside Raines. His skull had a landing strip of bald skin ringed by a horseshoe of white hair. His skin, having lost much of its elasticity, sagged off his bones.

He was old by all standards, a source of peculiarity in a world free of aging. That this man had chosen to age naturally was entirely unnatural.

A blue bubble appeared in the doorway to my right. It popped, releasing its hold on Ash. The door hinged shut behind her. Powerful engines awoke from a nap and pulled the lower stratosphere down to us.

The windows of the Peregrine were blacked out and our access to the Stream remained suppressed. The combined effect elicited feelings of entrapment and isolation. I couldn't decide which I disliked more.

"That was a hell of an entrance," I said, my eyes bouncing between Ash and the old man.

"Sometimes you have to send a message," the old man said, his voice rasping.

"Don't know what the message says, but pretty sure everybody in Terminus saw it."

"An unavoidable consequence I'm afraid, now that Malcolm has forced our hand." The old man held out two vaporizers. "Take these."

I plucked the vaporizers from his fingers, but had no intention whatsoever of inserting the nanotech into my body. "What is this?"

"I'm told that Malcolm has hacked both of your nanocomps. That booster will shield your system from his meddling."

On second thought, that was precisely the sort of thing I wanted in my body. "How long will it last?"

"It'll outlast you," Ash said with the sort of matter-of-factness reserved exclusively for children.

"And we're just gonna take it on your word that this isn't some kind of poison?" Raines asked.

"We have no need to poison you." The old man shrugged. "You will help us of your own volition."

I ran a quick calculation and determined that Ash could probably have killed me no less than a hundred times since I'd met her. She hadn't, which filled me with a blind confidence that she wouldn't do so now. Maybe Raines was right and they were poisoning us, but I had so little to lose that the cost-benefit analysis came out lopsided.

I inhaled the contents of the vaporizer and waited, expecting a kick in the gut of some kind, but nothing came. I queried my nanocomp, but it couldn't detect whatever I'd put in my body.

"Well, that was stupid, Tom," Raines said.

"I'm not dead."

"That's a horrible metric."

"You don't have to take it," the old man said, "but Malcolm has already tampered with your comp once. Nothing is stopping him from doing so again."

Raines sighed and chewed on her bottom lip. Finally she put the vaporizer to her mouth and sipped on it as if it were a straw.

"There. Happy?"

The old man smiled but said nothing.

"Maybe I'm missing something," Raines said, "but who are you people?"

"Forgive me," the old man said. "My name is Joseph Devers, and this is my associate, Ash."

The two made an unlikely pair. Ash was the model of youth and vigor, while Devers belonged in a brochure for a retirement community.

Ash looked up with startling silver eyes that matched the color of the hair dangling undisturbed in her face. Who would perform an ocular implant of that magnitude on a child?

Raines must have shared my view and asked, "How old are you?"

"That's a relative question, but the answer you're looking for is twelve, so let's go with that." Ash spoke in quick breathy sentences, as if the words would cause her pain if she didn't get them out fast enough.

Raines' face was a puzzle where the pieces hadn't found their home. I probably looked no different.

"Why are you helping us?" she finally managed to ask.

"To bring an end to a war we've been fighting in the shadows for the past two hundred years," Devers said.

That received an ample amount of reverent silence. War wasn't a word lightly thrown around in the years since mankind tried annihilating itself in the Dissolution.

"Cryptic and intentionally vague, but I'll let it play assuming you start answering questions," I said.

Joseph crinkled his brow and huffed as if he were preparing to give a history lesson on the Class Wars to a group of children. The muscles in his jaw tightened, making his thin lips disappear into one another.

"You've seen firsthand that the Safeguard, along with personal nanocomps, has been compromised," he said. "We've worked to prevent this, but unfortunately it was an inevitable outcome."

"Why haven't you gone to the Peacekeepers?" Raines asked.

"What would they do?" Joseph punctuated the question with a shrug. "What could they do?"

"We could've stopped Malcolm from escaping if we'd known, that's what."

"Malcolm is only a cog in a bigger machine. He is an important piece, but a replaceable one all the same."

"If he's expendable, why go through the effort of breaking him out of Pause?" I said, tossing my voice into the ring for a turn at twenty questions.

"He has one half of the Safeguard Override," Devers said, digging into his suit's breast pocket. He withdrew a small cube pinched between pointer finger and thumb. "Of course, the Override could be recreated from scratch, but it would take time. A very long time."

A warm light flared from the device, projecting a stream of code, incomprehensible in its complexity.

"What is this?" I said, eying the cube in the old man's hand.

"This is the second half of the Override," Joseph said with an unsettling nonchalance considering the magnitude of the revelation.

"How'd you get something like that?"

Joseph fixed his eyes on the glowing orb of code floating in the ether as he said, "Your wife."

CHAPTER SEVENTEEN
Corrupted Memories

Joseph's words came so far out of the left field that my mind pirouetted clear out of the way, their meaning missing me entirely. Visceral memories rooted in my heart rebuked what he'd said, denied it without considering the validity because the alternative clashed so impossibly with my memory that the two could never be reconciled.

A voice, somewhere along the periphery, spoke.

Salvation spread from those lips. They were familiar, but I couldn't follow them.

Something shook me.

A hand on my shoulder. Skin the color of snowflakes falling in broken dreams. I followed the hand to an elbow, past a shoulder, and beyond to a throat connected to a face.

The face was a memory relived. A ghost reborn.

Diana?

I blinked through the illusion.

The hand was no longer white like bone.

It wasn't Diana's.

Raines.

The weight of the insinuation caused a traffic jam of crisscrossed neurons. The Quick had found a kink in my mental armor, slipped through the cracks. It exposed the flaws hidden beneath, plucking the discordant melody most likely to lead me back to its toxic embrace.

Taunting me with images of my deceased wife had been the Quick's most effective strategy in getting me back to the needle.

The wet smack of flesh on flesh broke the silence. A delayed second passed before my brain decoded the message of pain blistering across my face.

I fell off the twirling carousel ride of inner turmoil paralyzing my thoughts.

"Jesus, Raines," I said, rubbing my cheek. "I'm digesting some shit over here."

"Digest faster. We don't have all day for you to slip in and out of Quick fits. You good to continue or do you need to sit this one out?"

"Are you kidding? You're the one that dragged me into this. Thanks to you I have to deal with government conspiracies, mass murderers, a kid ninja, and who the hell knows what else. You should've left me to die in peace."

Raines shook her head, ignoring me, and said to Devers, "How did Diana get that code?"

"She wrote it," Devers said, dropping facts as if they were common knowledge.

"Diana worked for Cybercore on Independent Thought-Based Programming. Nothing like what you're showing here," I said, jabbing a finger at the morphing screen of code.

"Castle controls Cybercore."

"What the hell is Castle?" I asked.

"The resistance."

"Resistance to what? Aim for some clarity in your answers."

"To the ever-widening technological divide separating Uppers from the rest of the world, and to those who would abuse the system for their personal gain."

"You're talking about Unity like it's a couple of people sitting around a table divvying up the world's resources," Raines said.

"Isn't it?" Ash said. She sat quietly beside Devers, watching with those silver eyes, twin moons reflected in a puddle, that missed nothing.

"I don't care about any of that," I said. "Tell me about Diana and what she has to do with this."

"Malcolm controls the first half of the code which allows him to bypass the Safeguard in any individual nanocomp he has secured access too," Devers said, his words a slow drawl to ensure we grasped the importance of their message. "But the scope of that weapon is limited. Hacking a single nanocomp takes significant effort. The section of code written by Diana, however, truncates that process, allowing groups of nanocomps to be hacked simultaneously."

Devers poked holes in my memory of Diana, but shed light on a mystery that'd stumped me for a decade. He tossed the missing puzzle piece in my lap. Answers tumbled in and snapped into place.

"This is how he did it," I said. "This is how he killed them all."

The best and brightest minds at Time Vice never could figure out how Malcolm had committed the largest mass murder in human history. How he'd hacked the millions of accounts so quickly, without giving Time Keepers a chance to stop him.

This code was the answer.

"Can I interrupt?" Raines raised her hand like a child petitioning for an opportunity to speak. I figured it was an ironic gesture, but doubted Joseph realized.

Joseph nodded.

"Why the hell do you guys have this?" Raines asked, lowering her hand and smoothing a crease from her pant leg. "I mean, it's a weapon of mass destruction, right? So why build it in the first place? No bomb, no boom. Seems simple."

"Our ability to combat our enemy depended on our ability to generate this code," Devers said, pausing either for dramatic effect or to find his next line of thought. Either way, the silence grew until it became the fifth member of our conversation.

We sat quietly in anticipation of whatever the silence might say next. But it didn't seem to know more than anyone else, and I grew impatient.

Devers, and Ash by extension, were holding back. Sure, they were giving the broad strokes, but you can't go around painting landscapes all the time. At some point you gotta get down to the minutia and put a person or two on the scene, maybe a tree.

This picture lacked all the details that would make it come to life. Make it memorable. Or at minimum, help it make sense.

"Malcolm is a sociopath, so I understand what he'd use this code for," I said. "But if you're fighting Unity, its leadership, and whoever or whatever else, then the question becomes why do *they* want this Code?"

Ash's demeanor tightened. Her fists clenched in her lap. It was the first show of emotion I'd seen from her, and it looked all wrong on her tiny frame. Too contained for her twelve-year-old self. Too subdued.

"Malcolm is broken, yes. But he is not a sociopath," she said. "The two of you are more similar than you realize. You've both lost somebody you loved, and both turned away from the people you once were. You turned that anger inward, focused on destroying yourself. Malcolm turned his outward, onto the world."

That Malcolm had lost someone was news to me. It hadn't been mentioned in his files. How Ash knew this became a matter of interest I wanted to pursue to its natural conclusion, but Devers interjected.

"Let me ask you a question," Devers said, folding his hands in his lap. "What is the purpose behind the Life Tracker?"

An easy question, which told me Devers was maneuvering for a not so easy answer.

Unity's doctrine stated the Life Tracker kept the human population at the highest threshold of sustainability for the Earth's resources. Centuries earlier, we'd pushed the planet to the brink, and then like children lacking the ability to see past the consequences of their actions, we gave it a little shove.

The Dissolution came next. Billions of lives, along with much of the planet's inhabitable land, lost in a war for remaining resources. It hadn't been so bad at first. Countries tightened control of their borders, severely limiting, if not altogether restricting, the influx of travelers. In the beginning, the fighting took place on a small level, localized incidents, neighboring countries testing one another for access to the few resources afforded by their unique geographic locations.

The idea of a worldwide conflict wouldn't come until the first nuke exploded over Amsterdam. No country ever claimed credit for the attack. It didn't matter. The effect was cataclysmic. Whoever launched that fateful missile doomed humanity to the kind of zealous fighting that defied rationalization.

Radiation poisoning spread across the African and Eurasian continents, rendering most inhabitants dead or horribly mutated and wishing they were dead. The Lost, as they became known, lived in a different world than anything a Unity citizen had ever known.

Unity existed because of sound decision making and a healthy heaping of luck. The North American Union had the foresight at the time to combine forces into a single entity known as Unity. That, combined with the geographical distance from the majority of the fighting, made it easier to defend their borders from the floods of refugees seeking sanctuary.

But sanctuary didn't exist. Not for them. Not enough space.

So while the rest of the world tumbled down the evolutionary ladder, hitting every rung along the way, Unity thrived.

But we were reminded a few years later that humans are creatures of habit. If left to their own devices, we grow beyond control, a cancer replicating until it kills the host. The solution was meant to be a temporary one: build down. This gave way to the bottomless cities of Terminus and the other major Unity cities.

After much deliberation I gave an oversimplified answer to a complicated question. "Population control."

Devers gave a half-hearted shrug. "What if I told you the Life Tracker was no longer necessary? That we have the technology to reclaim the East, and that there is no need for two-thirds of the world's population to live underground?"

Memories of the endless underground maze came flooding back. The shit-stained halls carpeted with shattered glass, used needles, and abandoned dreams. Men with pockmarked cheeks and hollow eyes staring at shambling women covered in their own filth. Each wondering what they could cheat out of the other, all the while knowing they had nothing worth taking.

A perfect place for a man to commit some good old-fashioned self-destruction. But I'd been there by choice, which was not the same as the billions of people I shared wall space with. They were there because the world had no room for them except between the cracks.

The Class Wars had never ended. They simply became the status quo. We accepted it because the alternative was chaos. It'd been beaten into us since childhood: class distinction was the only way to make the system work. The only way humanity could survive.

That this reality had been manufactured by those in control made my pulse throb. The influx of fresh blood to muscles drew my attention to how sore they'd become since sitting down.

Despite the discomfort, my brain made new connections. The Uppers controlled everything. They could take back the land, but they didn't want to share it.

"We're not dying fast enough for them," I said, making the final leap to arrive at a conclusion that'd been staring me in the face. "Seventy years from the day we're born isn't enough for them."

I wanted to punch something hard and unforgiving, to feel the crunch of bone and knuckle, but Raines was the closest thing in reach and she was too hard, too unforgiving.

I choked down the anger, an oversized pill stretching my esophagus as it grated down my throat.

The answers were there, all save the one that mattered.

"Why me?" I asked.

"We've shielded you by maintaining your ignorance," Devers said, "but the time has come for you to fulfill your purpose."

"You make it sound like you've had my entire life planned out."

Devers smiled. "Perhaps not far from the truth."

He held an ocular implant in his outstretched palm. Delicately I plucked it up as if the nanite upgrade hiding inside might explode if I moved too quickly.

"What's on here?" I said, unscrewing the cap and dipping a finger into the clear liquid. It came up with a thin slip of plastic. Faded yellow light filtered through the translucent lens with inky clarity.

"Answers," Devers said, his voice quivering.

"Memories," Ash said, her voice a rock.

"Whose memories?"

"Yours," Ash said.

That was just vague enough to be compelling. Years of Quick Sliver abuse had done irreparable damage to my brain, and by extension, my memories. I'd spent the past seven years in Terminus' sewers stealing from Lucky Lou and his cohorts so I could afford the expensive reconstructive nanites that would help me regain what I'd lost. I'd wanted to live in ignorance, but I wanted to die knowing.

Willing to do anything to recover what I'd destroyed, I drew a deep breath, retracted my eyelid, and inserted the lens. It scraped against the pupil before sliding into place like a suction cup.

The rush of data hit hard and fast. It crashed through the thin firewall afforded by my nanocomp, racing over and through the cracks of a crumbling dam.

Raw and unfiltered, the data plunged like a needle into my optic nerve. A liquid blaze raced into my occipital lobe, shattering upon arrival in a display of fireworks.

I sipped shallow breaths. Beads of sweat dove down my neck, tickling nerve endings flashing on and off under the control of a drunken switchboard operator.

Synapses and neurons fired beyond capacity.

The world came too quickly. A jumble of sights, sounds, and smells overwhelmed me.

The muscles in my back spasmed, arms flailed as lightning bolts flashed and popped. My brain fired as a single unit where the only task was to spread any and every message as quickly as possible.

And then it stopped. I gasped and doubled over in my chair before sliding onto my knees. All that remained was the awareness of a captive knowledge held prisoner in the narrow confines of my mind.

Nanobots flitted across gray matter, rewiring neural pathways to accommodate the influx of new information.

I opened my eyes and was only mildly surprised to find myself lying on the floor, looking up at Raines. Her hands were warm and comforting, smoothing back the clumps of hair clinging to my forehead.

"You okay?" she asked. "What happened?"

The questions tumbled out of her simultaneously.

"Maybe?" I sat up and the world swirled. Raines held me. I turned to Devers with a skull full of sloshing fluid. "You could have warned me it was gonna be so violent. I almost bit through my tongue and pissed my pants."

"We didn't know." Devers shrugged. "You're the first one to receive that upgrade."

"How do you feel?" Ash asked, leaning off the edge of her seat.

"What part of *I almost pissed my pant*s didn't you understand?" I said.

"But do you remember?" Ash ignored my obvious discomfort.

"Is there something in particular I should be remembering?"

The little girl gave a frown that could break a father's heart.

"Give it time," she said, more to herself than me.

I scrambled into my chair with Raines' assistance. The colors of the room merged, creating new combinations I'd never imagined. It had the feel of a Quick fit, minus the writhing on the floor wishing I were dead part.

"I don't feel any different," I said, scanning my nanocomp for any sign of the nanites I'd accepted into my system. "What are they supposed to be doing, anyway?"

"They're repairing portions of your brain damaged by Malcolm's virus."

Raines and I exchanged glances with competing levels of incredulity.

"What?" Raines asked.

It felt like I should lend Raines support with my own words. "Yeah, what?"

"Years ago your nanocomp became infected with a nasty virus that wiped portions of your mind," Devers said. "It blocked some memories, replaced others, and deleted many more."

None of this made sense. That somebody could clear my memory was absurd by every definition of the word.

"Bullshit," was the only response I could muster. "Any damage to my memories is thanks to the Quick."

Raines echoed my sentiments with a bobbing head.

"No, you turned to the Quick because for a time it negated the effects of Malcolm's virus. It postponed the inevitable," Devers said, "but it was only temporary and came with many side-effects."

"If by side-effects you mean soul-crushing despair mixed with mind-numbing apathy, then yeah...side-effects," I said.

"We've never attempted to recover terminated memories. Honestly we still don't know if it will work, but we're out of time and options," Ash said. "We had to try."

"Glad to be the guinea pig."

Ash looked at me with pity.

I didn't want her pity. I wanted answers, but this conversation was leading nowhere but to the little town of Pissed Off with a population of me.

"I've known Tom since I was a rookie," Raines said. "He lost part of himself, but that was the Quick, which he didn't start hitting until after Diana's death."

"We placed Tom in Time Vice for a multitude of tactical reasons. His ability to operate in that environment without detection was paramount to his assignment," Devers said. "What you know of your partner is no more than what we have allowed you to know."

Raines crossed her arms and shook her head. She refused to purchase whatever Ash and Devers were selling.

Thoughts trawled the surface of my brain, burrowing at times into locations unknown. Memories slipped away the tighter I squeezed.

I couldn't lock onto the foreign memories, but they were there. Fluttering beneath a layer of consciousness. I felt them. Part of me wanted to see them, to believe what Joseph and Ash were saying because their words had a twisted sense about them. They framed the world, and the events of the last twelve hours, in a context I could understand.

But those answers came with questions.

Harder questions.

Questions about me, Diana, and the life I thought I knew. My world view would come into tighter focus at the expense of my personal reality.

Maybe I'm not the man I thought I was.

That left room for hope.

Perhaps even redemption.

I wanted to believe that was possible.

"So I worked for you?" I asked.

Devers nodded.

Ash said, "Yes."

It was odd hearing her answer the question. I'd assumed Ash was a glorified bodyguard or super assassin, but the dynamic between Devers and Ash felt different somehow. Whatever their relationship, the answer eluded me.

"Why did I stop?"

"Your memory became compromised," Devers said. "Keeping you around would have been dangerous. A liability."

"From the virus?"

"Correct."

"You couldn't fix me?"

"At the time it wasn't possible."

"And now?"

Ash shrugged. "We'll see."

Those words inspired zero confidence.

"What kind of work did I do for you?"

Ash and Devers paused before Ash said, "Security."

An intentionally evasive answer, but pressing the point wouldn't reveal more. I saved my breath and leaned back in my chair.

Silent with my thoughts and memories. All of them. Both remembered and forgotten.

I sifted through the mental dump of my mind, but only found the all too familiar memories that'd become broken and soiled by the passage of time. I didn't want to dig through those memories. They were too painful.

"So, Tom used to be a secret agent..." Raines' words were coated with a spoonful of sarcasm that dripped in heavy globs as she spoke. "Great. But where does that put us now? If what you're saying is true, then Malcolm's out there planning to murder billions of people and we're flying circles hoping Tom regains his memory. Shouldn't we be doing something, like trying to find the bad guys? Maybe stop him before he does more damage?"

Raines' cheeks burned redder than usual, giving her face the appearance of a bronzed statue in the orange glow of a setting sun. It was beautiful.

A flare went off somewhere deep in my brain. A flag stuck in the fleshy ravines that screamed for my attention.

A memory bobbed to the surface. Vague and distorted. Details blurred, but the contents conveyed.

I squeezed my eyes shut until white spots appeared on the back of my eyelids. Trying to wrestle the memory into focus.

"Lucky Lou," I blurted out. When I opened my eyes everybody was staring at me. Devers cocked an eyebrow that asked the question for the group. "I've got to go see Lucky Lou."

"Why?" Raines asked, carefully laying out the question as though it were a blood offering to a spiteful deity.

"Going to get something he took from me."

"And what would that be?"

"A key."

"A key to what?"

I shrugged and said, "Something locked?"

CHAPTER EIGHTEEN
Katabasis

"You are not a smart man, Tom," Bo said, shaking his head.

I stood a step below the giant, looking up into his muscular nostrils. He was not wrong.

The sign behind him read, Lucky Lou's. It spat a gauzy light into the street that blanketed everything in that corridor with a thin veneer of scum.

"We need to see Lou," I said, gesturing to Raines and Ash, who stared at me with expectant eyes as if I might perform sleight-of-hand magic. Unfortunately, there were no tricks hiding up my sleeve.

The nanobots rummaging through my memories and reassembling the pieces therein were taking their time. I'd connected the crooked line of memories that had returned, and they all pointed to Lou. Coming back to the Lowers might rank as one of my more questionable maneuvers in the past twenty-four hours, but with so few options still on the table, we had to start playing what we had.

"You think that's a good idea?" Bo asked. It was hard to say whether his voice emitted genuine concern or if the Quick was tinkering with my auditory feedback loop.

Lou and I had not left our relationship in a good place, but hopefully he was enough of a businessman to at least hear me out before putting a bullet in my chest.

"No," I agreed.

Bo chuckled, a deep rolling bass echoing through his barrel chest. "Well, at least you know you're being stupid."

That seemed an odd thing to consider good, but I held that opinion to myself and followed Bo through the front door. A wall of noise hit me first: voices shouting over one another, skin sliding and grinding against every surface imaginable. Sounds that only vaguely resembled music pumped through speakers loud enough to make my ears ring.

The smell came next. Vinegar sweat mixed with wet rot. It filled the air, a cloud of humidity sticking to everything.

Bo strode purposefully into the sea of flesh. People scurried out of his way, roaches fleeing the light. I followed in his shadow before the throngs of tweakers came back together in an orgy of limbs and bad decisions.

My attention drifted over to the bar where I'd sat just the night before talking to Georgie. I saw the familiar worn stool I'd called home. The woman whose name I'd never bothered learning was scrubbing glasses behind the bar with a rag stained with brown splotches.

So much can change in a day.

There was something else at the bar I couldn't ignore. A man sitting half obscured by shadow. My feet redirected me of their own accord. Bo made a sound, but didn't try to stop me.

"Jack Dunn," I said, arriving at the bar.

The man stared down into the cloudy liquid of his drink as if it might hold the secrets of the universe. His head turned slowly, eyes flashing like two copper coins in moonlight. Nothing lived in there but the perversion that comes from years of self-preservation co-mingled with self-destruction. He grunted.

"Do you know who I am?" I asked.

"No," Dunn lied. "Should I?"

Playing the *do you know who I am* game is a dubious way to start any conversation. Of course he knew who I was. Intuits have a hard time hiding from one another. We're rare enough in the Lowers that we don't go unnoticed. But I needed to get the man's base line so I'd know if he was lying when I asked him my next question.

"Did you kill the kid?"

"I've killed many kids." Dunn slurped at his drink. "You're gonna have to be more specific."

"The one from last night," I said, pointing towards the end of the bar where I'd sat with Georgie.

"Oh. That kid." Dunn squinted up at me and his face cracked like an egg dropped on the ground. The yellow yolk of his teeth seeped through his smile. He pivoted on his stool like the breeze kicking trash through the gutter. He eyed Raines with the absent focus of a Duster. "What's he to ya?"

"A friend," I said, using the term very loosely.

"Yeah?" Dunn's pupils blurred in and out of focus as he shrugged. "Well in that case, nah, I didn't kill him."

I sighed. They always lie.

"My mistake," I said. I looked at Bo, shrugged, then punched Jack Dunn in the jaw. His head whipped back and he tumbled from his stool.

Bo moved forward, his protective instincts as a bouncer taking hold. Ash grabbed his wrist with a tiny hand, stopping the huge man cold. He stared down in surprise at the small girl anchoring him to the floor.

Dunn stared up from the flat of his back, mouth hanging slack, eyes suddenly alert. As he scrabbled to his feet I placed a foot on his chest and pushed him down.

"Tom, that's enough," Bo said, straining ineffectually against Ash's grip. "You made your point. You want to see the boss or not?"

My fist tingled where the knuckles had hit bone. It'd been a lazy punch. Georgie deserved better, but it would have to be enough.

I ignored Raines' questioning stare and said, "Lead the way."

Ash released her grip on Bo. The large man rubbed his wrist and nodded. We left Dunn, still in shock, sprawled out on the ground. We'd made it less than ten feet when I heard Dunn shout, "You're a dead man.

As if I didn't already know.

***

Lou's office was nicer than anything I'd ever seen in the Lowers, with a design sensibility inspired by those living in the Uppers. The room was enormous in every dimension worth measuring—a rarity in the Lowers, where every year the walls constricted tighter.

A desk the size of a Peregrine sat in the center of the room, an oasis upon itself. Behind it, Lou stood, his eyes hidden behind a backwashed slurry of liquid ooze.

I dug my fingernails into my forearm while we waited for him to emerge from the Stream. Checking the Tracker was a compulsion, a nervous tic, under the best conditions. With the events of the past day, and the Quick Sliver turning against me, the urge to check nagged like a mosquito bite on the nipple.

Scratching wouldn't do any good, and if I went at it long enough, I'd come out the other side with one less nipple, but I did it anyhow.

"What a pleasure it is to see you still up and running, Tom," Lou said, returning to the land of the physical. "After our chance encounter last night I was afraid you'd kick the bucket before we could meet again." Lou made a show of interlocking his fingers in the air. "Fate has grand designs for us, doesn't it, my friend?"

Talking about chance and fate in the same sentence felt odd, but I kept quiet. I was here because of the past, not the future. The present was only a fleeting moment between the two.

"Drop the act and get to talking. Why me?"

Lou's eyes twinkled, but his lips pulled down into a frown. "Afraid I don't follow."

"I was a little blurred last night. Didn't see things so well. But I've had a couple hours to think about it, and the more I do, the more I see you pulling my strings."

"How so?" Lou said with genuine amusement in his voice.

"You deal in information, right?"

"It's my number one import and export."

"And in the world of information gathering, nothing beats having an Intuit in your corner."

"They do have their uses."

"So, I'm guessing you have at least a couple Intuits working for you. If not, you'd be vulnerable. You don't seem particularly vulnerable."

"You flatter me."

"Now, if you got a couple Intuits already working for you, the question I ask myself is, why does he need me?"

"And?" Lou rested his chin on his palm.

"You don't," I said. "You don't need me."

"I'm a man of few needs, and many wants."

"Sure, you wanted me. Or rather, something I had."

"First-rate deductive reasoning?"

"That…and the key you stole from me."

"Stole? Such a dirty word. We had a deal. You gave it willingly."

"Before I knew you were gaming me."

"Ah, but that's the beauty of life, isn't it? We're all gaming each other."

"You know what it unlocks, don't you?" I said. "You know what's inside."

"Maybe." Lou circled his desk, leaned against the front with arms folded, and said, "Do you?"

"No."

"And here with all your bravado, I thought you'd figured it out."

"Close enough to count."

"This isn't a game of horseshoes, Tom."

"Suppose not, but you're going to give me back that key and tell me what it unlocks."

"Not leaving much room for negotiation, huh?" Lou reached across the desk and pressed a button. "Well, in that case, my boss wants to speak to you."

"Boss?" I said, sifting through the kitty litter of my memories, trying to find the single nugget that suggested Lou had a boss. "Thought you were the top of the food chain down here."

"Even the devil must answer to God."

"Well, where is he?" I asked, scanning the small army of thugs turned bodyguard milling around a pool table across the room.

"He'll meet you in the Stream."

"Fine," I said.

BLINK.

The Stream sparked in my pupils. A pending request flashed in the corner. I accepted and the world shifted and spread as if somebody were stretching a too-small photo to fit a frame. Lou's physical body became a petroleum jelly smear across the threshold of my display. The murk cleared, drew taut, and came into focus with startling clarity.

I stumbled out of the Stream and back into the office. Somebody else had entered the room and sat in Lou's chair. My eyes stuttered between Lou and the dark man at the desk.

"What the hell?" I said, wiping sweaty palms against my pants. "It glitched."

"That wasn't a glitch," Ash said from two chairs to my right. "We're still in the Stream."

Impossible. I reached for the tendrils of data packets that should be filling the ether, but found nothing. I couldn't even see the white nodes of nanocomps in the room. I looked straight through Raines' skull and saw nothing.

I massaged my temples, trying to make sense of what was happening. I'd seen all manner of virtual rooms, but none that I couldn't manipulate. I suddenly understood what it was to be normal.

"I apologize for the disorientation," the man behind the desk said. "It will pass momentarily as your nanocomp adjusts to the viewing channel."

His voice slid thick and smooth like honey on a hot summer day.

It covered me. Made me tingle. The room boosted the signal, adding a layer of reality that went beyond even hyper-reality.

"Who are you?" I asked

"Felix Cross," the man said. "It's a pleasure to finally make your acquaintance, Mr. Mandel."

I knew that name.

Everybody in the world knew that name.

CHAPTER NINETEEN
The Second Time Is Hard, Too

Felix Cross, founder of Phoenix, the largest dealer of nanotechnology in the world, was a reclusive figure bordering on mythical. Young Middies and Uppies, who saw him as the closest thing to a god in the digital age, followed him with a cultish obsession.

Cross could buy the world ten times over, a fact he'd proven by establishing Phoenix's headquarters on the island formerly known as the United Kingdom. There he lived and worked on the nanite technologies reshaping the world.

His relationship with the leaders of Unity was tenuous under even the best circumstances. On the one hand, Unity needed his technologies. On the other, by choosing to base Phoenix headquarters so close to the volatile East—and so far from the nearest Unity city—he'd placed himself in a position vulnerable to the marauding bands of Lost still scouring the Eurasian continent.

The leaders of Unity held a very real concern that if the technologies stashed in the Phoenix arsenal ever fell into the hands of the Lost, the East could rise again and tip the precarious hierarchy established by Unity.

While technically a sound argument, even the staunchest of critics would agree the likelihood of the Lost overpowering Phoenix's bastion of technological might to be all but impossible. Cross, on multiple occasions, publicly proclaimed his island to be immune to any sort of infiltration—a boast rumored to have been tested by Division black ops teams with no success.

Twenty-two years ago, Unity attempted to put Cross and his cohorts in their place by subverting Phoenix Corporation's Stream access. A then young Cross returned the favor and bombarded District Five's Stream access with junk data that slowed the network to a crawl for a full three hours.

In general, people don't want to fight. They simply want to get on with their lives. Cross understood and exploited this. The disruption was as chilling as it was potent.

With that one act Cross proved he could not be manipulated or coerced. That from then on a single man could be viewed as either an ally or an enemy.

The leaders of Unity didn't want another war, nor did they want to risk compromising the Stream, so they allowed Cross his autonomy. Personally I thought they should've made him President, but he lacked aspirations of power in that arena.

Cross, in the few interviews he'd granted, stated he simply wanted to be left alone to go about his work. He provided a continual flux of technology generations ahead of anything coming out of Division subsidiaries, so nobody really complained.

Nobody understood how he continually out-innovated Unity-based developers, but until they did, Cross remained a country unto himself.

"Wouldn't have thought to see you cavorting with a Slumlord like Lou," I said after the initial shock had subsided.

"It's good to have hands and ears in all places. In a global market, diversification is the key to staying ahead of the curve." The smooth creases of Felix's black marble skin retracted to reveal a row of ivory pebble teeth.

It'd worked out for the man, so I wasn't in a place to argue.

"How do I fit into your diversification scheme?" I asked.

"Have you ever sat and listened to the breeze?"

"Not unless you count listening to the hum of the air filtration system down here."

"Pity. Whispered rumors float on the breeze."

"Oh? What are the winds saying these days?"

"They're shifting. Ever shifting. They're bringing a storm, I think," Felix said, looking at Ash. "A storm can be good, if you do not resist it. Do not stand in its path when it strikes." Felix paused. "I wonder, where are you standing?"

"I don't know if I'm in its way or if it's following me, but I suspect it doesn't matter either way."

"Well then, perhaps we can be of mutual benefit to one another."

"I'm not the guy you want to be sharing benefits with."

"Don't sell yourself short. Every great shift comes with agents of change. Men and women who fate plucks"—Felix lifted a knife from the desk. His arm drifted lazily before dropping the blade. The pointed end buried itself in the wood with a *thunk*—"from the masses and charges with the task of ushering in a new age. I believe you are one of those men."

"How about you?" I said. "Are you one of these agents, too?"

"It remains to be seen." Felix shrugged. "For now, I'm content helping you on your quest."

"And what do you know about my quest?"

"I know you're highly motivated to succeed despite your attempt to convince others to the contrary. You hide behind a veneer of self-loathing and self-deprecation, afraid that by caring you'll open yourself to the possibility of loss once again. Because it's hard to hurt a man who does not care, isn't that right?"

"If you say so."

"And yet apathetic men bleed the same as all the rest," Felix said.

His words sat in the stillness of the room. There were questions stewing in the pot I wanted to ask. But they wouldn't lead to answers, only wasted breaths. I didn't have time for wasted breaths.

"What makes you think you know what's going on here?"

"Word travels quickly when the leaders of Unity are held at gunpoint," he said, waving a dismissive hand. "And this little squabble between Unity and Castle hasn't been the great secret they imagine." Felix turned his stare to Ash. "It's fitting you call your organization Castle, by the way. It conjures memories of a simpler time when knights fought for honor in public. Now all the battles worth fighting take place in shadow, behind tightly drawn curtains."

Ash nodded and said, "Even shadows fighting in the dark leave a mark. It's inevitable you would find out. What you do with that knowledge is what matters now."

"Indeed." Felix steepled his fingers beneath his chin. "I suppose you're wondering if you can trust me. If I know about Castle, then it raises the question of what else I might know, and how I know it. How can you be sure Adam himself doesn't whisper in my ear while I sleep?"

Ash was fast. Faster than anyone I'd ever seen. Her microexpressions, then, were especially fleeting. But the look she wore lingered.

Her pupils dilated, contracting to droplets of ink. Cheeks tensed against puckered lips. Nose scrunched.

Shock.

That Felix knew this Adam character was more disconcerting to Ash than the fact that he knew about Castle. Felix strummed this newly discovered bundle of nerves. Ash regained her composure, but the way she sat in her chair changed. Her body tightened, realizing now just how dangerous the other players in this game were.

These were the conclusions I drew from the brief exchange of words and body language between Felix and Ash, but I didn't need a diagram to know my conclusions were correct.

"How do you propose to help us?" Ash said, glossing over whatever had elicited such a reaction from her the moment before.

"Cybercore has the best coders in the world. That cannot be disputed. Your software is unrivaled, and I say that as Cybercore's number one competitor," Felix said, pulling a briefcase from the floor beside his chair and placing it on the desk. He thumbed the combination, tumblers rolled into place, and the lid popped open. "But, in the world of hardware, Phoenix is without equal."

Felix pulled from the case a pyramid cut from black glass that fit in the palm of his hand.

"What's that?" I asked.

"This is my gift to you in your effort against Unity," Felix said, smiling from cheek to ear. "I call it the Hive Mind. I think you'll find it useful moving forward into the next stage of your investigation."

"What's it do?"

"The nanites crawling across the surface of the Hive Mind allow the user remote access to whatever system they've infected."

I processed this information like the first primate using a stick to suck ants from their hill. "You're talking nanocomps, aren't you?"

"Ye—"

The Stream dissolved. White light and static noise covered me. I tumbled out of the system and clutched my ears. Tears blurred my vision but I could see enough to know we were back in Lou's office. Felix Cross was gone. My eardrums pulsed as if stabbed with an icepick.

Raines mumbled something from somewhere on the perimeter of my consciousness. She rocked in her chair, clawing at the white noise buffeting her mind.

Ash wore a similar expression of pain. She blinked hard and fast. The smooth lines of her young face pulled tight at her eyes and mouth.

Somebody was manipulating the Stream, using it as a weapon. Bombarding our nanocomps with sounds and junk data.

Then it stopped. The pain. The noise. All of it.

Silence.

We were in the eye of a storm, too late to move out of the way.

Ash jumped to her feet.

BOOM.

Something exploded behind me. The room. The world. My heart. The air.

The shockwave hit Ash first, flinging her into Lou's titanic desk. Then the blast hit me, throwing me from my chair and tossing me onto the ground.

The white noise returned, along with the pain. A thick wet fluid seeped from my ear and down my neck. The air tasted sharp, as if coated with shards of glass that sliced my insides. Every breath became a fresh torture.

I tried rolling to my side to see what had caused the explosion, but my body refused to cooperate.

My nanocomp tried to get my attention. It jumped up and down in the corner, waving its virtual hands. The message wasn't a surprise.

Seek Immediate Medical Assistance

That's not what you want to hear from the passenger riding shotgun behind your temporal lobe.

The floor, buffed to a high sheen by an over-obsessive janitor-nanite, offered up my reflection. A trail of dried blood on my cheek mixed with a fresh trickle oozing from a gash above my eyebrow. Sore muscles, forgotten injuries, and new wounds were making themselves known. First a dull ache methodically pulsing through my body. Then a sharper pain, as if my blood had been replaced with napalm.

I opened my mouth to release the swell of agony in a scream. Nothing came out but a bubble of blood and snot mingling on my upper lip. The cold floor warmed. I shivered and squirmed onto my side.

I lay in a pool of blood.

My blood.

It was warm, but it'd be warmer if it would stay in my body.

I'd sprung a leak. Competing messages of pain being shouted across the battlefield of my body made it impossible to locate which hole was leaking my precious life juice.

The world dimmed. Over the sound of my wet breathing I heard men yelling and the bark of energy rifles. I licked my lips and tasted something metallic.

Hot, salty blood burned on its way down my throat. I imagined it making a circuitous route back to, and out, the hole responsible for killing me in that moment.

Give up, a voice in the back of my head whispered. It wasn't a bad option. Nobody could use me if I were dead.

Another explosion. The ground shuddered beneath me, sending ripples through my puddle of blood.

A fresh reminder of agony was a memo tacked to the inner wall of my skull. Pain stampeded like deer fleeing wildfire. Down the knots in my shoulders, through a broken heart, past the stomach crying out from the overabundance of swallowed blood, and into legs blackened and bruised from being forced to my knees again and again.

Give up, the voice screamed. I tried, but couldn't find fault in that plan.

I closed my eyes. I didn't want to do this anymore.

Another explosion, like thunder on the horizon. An approaching storm. It wasn't meant for me. I'd be gone before it arrived.

My nanocomp issued a final plea before powering down.

Thoughts jumbled. Neurons fired without purpose.

A second later, the black oblivion of pre-death coddled me in its embrace.

***

I swam through a blackness that clung to me like crude oil. Flashbulb memories popped in rapid-fire succession across a darkened background.

Some memories were familiar: the day I married Diana, my first day on the force.

Others, not so much.

I watched the memories replay, a highlight reel without context. A passive third-person observer. My body, an automaton, acted out its part without my active engagement.

I assumed this was the part of death where my life flashed before my eyes. That made a certain kind of sense so I didn't fight it. Complaining about the mixed-up memories wouldn't change anything now. If there were a God, or a devil, I'd voice those complaints in person.

A rendezvous I expected soon.

I grew impatient waiting for the white light to show up so I could sprint towards it already. No need to postpone the inevitable.

But then something flashed across the screen. Something that shouldn't be there. Which said a lot, because many of the memories prancing across my mind shouldn't be there.

This one was different, though. A memory I remembered well, but with certain details distorted and wrong. I chalked it up to my conscious memory making an error in the recollection process, but then the discrepancies got bigger. Huge, in fact.

Division Headquarters nine years and a handful of days earlier. Diana on the floor lying in a similar position to the one I'd left my body in moments before. She drifted in an ocean of blood. Mine, by comparison, was the kiddie pool.

I watched myself enter, skidding across a slick floor.

Swatches of white bone appeared on the floor where my steps displaced Diana's blood. I dropped to my knees, pants soaked red. Warm and sticky. I remembered those details. I'd been there. I'd relived that memory thousands of times.

But then something changed. Diana had something in her hands.

A cube.

Its iridescent sides reflected the sobering light. I took it from her, the bottom stained red. Her eyes shifted like she was slipping into the Stream, but I knew that's not where she was going.

I cried. My tears mixed with the blood on my cheeks, forming pink streaks I didn't bother wiping away.

Diana's lips moved. The faded whisper of life slipping past her lips.

CHAPTER TWENTY
Anabasis

My heart kicked harder than a mule in heat, slamming against the inner wall of my ribcage with one thunderous boom. Blood mixed with adrenaline, becoming a high-octane rocket fuel. Arteries throbbed, fat and full, like an anaconda after a meal. I awoke staring at a blinding yellow sphere. Somebody leaned over me, whispering words without meaning.

I didn't care.

My brain found only one question worth asking: "Why does the sun gotta be so goddamn bright?"

My heart beat of its own accord now, but the nanobots decided to play it safe and fired a second shot across the bow. I gasped into the boom that threatened to fold me in two.

Eyes struggled against the blinding cacophony of light and colors splitting my skull with a rusted sawblade. The contents of my stomach crept into my throat. I clamped my lips shut in an attempt to hold them in.

Clarity bled from the corners first, moving slowly towards the center. The face came into focus and I realized I wasn't staring into the sun, but rather an enormous bulb meant to simulate that celestial body.

I deducted who would own such a fancy lamp: Lou.

Everything flooded back. I pinged my nanocomp. It ignored me.

I tried sitting up. Bad idea. Blood rushed to my brain, overriding visual input from my eyes. Black and white dots sprang into existence, swirling and obscuring my vision.

I closed my eyes and waited for the dizziness to pass.

When I opened them again the pain was gone—a good thing, so I didn't complain.

I sputtered a jumble of words even I didn't understand. The link between mind and tongue hadn't been fully re-established yet.

The person kneeling beside me ran a hand through my hair. "Take it easy, Tom."

Whoever was using the inside of my eyeballs as a drum must have been getting tired: the beat lagged before slowing to a crawl. Shapes merged to form recognizable images.

"Raines?" I croaked. "What happened?"

"You tried to die on me."

"Wish you would've let me."

"What goes around comes around," she said, her lips pulled in a wide upward arc that created tiny dimples in the corners of her cheeks. Dimples I wasn't sure I'd ever noticed before.

My head swiveled smoothly, no kinks or pain, as I studied the carnage that'd occurred during my leave of absence. Bodies littered Lou's office. His thugs, clothed in the traditional tattered garb of the Lowers, lay dead or dying alongside Division soldiers dressed to the nines in nanite-infused armor.

The air crackled with dispensed energy from the firefight that had taken place in such a concentrated area.

"President Jennings didn't take kindly to our visit this afternoon, eh?" I said, taking Raines' hand for support and letting her pull me to my feet. "He sent in the big guns."

"Luckily our guns were bigger." Raines gestured towards Ash, who was standing across the room talking to Lou, who was doing ninety percent of his communicating via wild hand gesticulations.

I looked at the floor and saw a blood angel formed where I'd been lying. "Did I get shot?"

"Nah," Raines said. "You caught a chunk of smart-metal in the back when they blew the door. Pierced your lung. Made one hell of a mess. You're lucky Lou was around. That guy's got a cache of military-grade stimheal."

"Suppose that's the benefit of being in bed with Phoenix."

Raines nodded. "Now that you're up and at it, we need to get out of here. The Lowers aren't safe for us anymore."

"Were they ever?"

"Relatively speaking."

"Everything is relative," I said, catching Ash's eye. She held up a hand, stopping Lou mid-sentence.

"Look who's back from his date with death," Lou said, clapping his hands together. "Wasn't sure we got to you in time. That stimheal is good, but it can't raise the dead. Yet."

Lou patted me on the back. I winced, expecting pain, but the residual damage I'd suffered over the course of the last twenty-four hours had dissipated. I felt better than I had in years.

I wasn't complaining. It felt good not to hurt.

"Good to be back," I said, surprising even myself to find that I meant it.

"Now, what's our next move?" Lou said.

"Our?" Raines put my own question into words.

"I don't suppose Unity is gonna let me keep on keeping on." Lou gestured towards the room of dead bodies. "For better or worse, it looks like I'm with you guys."

"And what if we don't want you?" Raines said.

"You're gonna want me if you plan on getting out of the Lowers in only"—he made a show of counting Ash, Raines, and myself—"three pieces. Plus, I have nifty toys. You let me come with and I'll let you play with them."

I couldn't forget the pain inflicted on me per Lou's request the night prior, but people not actively trying to kill me were in short supply, so it didn't make sense to wipe my ass with the olive branch he was offering.

"Fine, you can come with, but if you step out of line," I gestured towards Ash, "you'll have to deal with her."

Lou forced a smile.

"Great, we're one big happy family," Raines said. "But if I can ask, besides getting out of the Lowers, avoiding getting killed by any combination of Division soldiers, Malcolm Wolfe, or Time Vice Watchmen, what's our next step?"

"That not getting killed part sounds like a good place to start," Lou said.

A memory slotted into place, jarred loose during my tumble with death. I knew where I needed to go. The why remained a mystery, but progress is progress.

"I've got something in mind," I said, rolling my neck to the side and feeling the sweet *pop-pop-pop* of vertebrae realigning. "Lou, grab the key I gave you last night. We're going to the Vault."

"Oh, yeah?" Raines asked, her eyebrows raised. "You think they're just gonna let you walk in there?"

She had a point. The Vault ranked alongside the Time Bank as one of the most highly restricted buildings in Terminus. Whereas the Time Bank oversaw the Life Tracker network, the Vault handled the physical storage of that digital data.

Lou smiled. "Leave that to Uncle Lou," he said, practically skipping over to a small closet behind his desk.

"You're taking the family metaphor too far," Raines said before turning back to me. "What's in the Vault?"

I paused before admitting, "I'm not really sure."

Raines opened her mouth to protest my well-thought-out plan as Lou rejoined the group.

"Here we are," he said. In one hand Lou held a vaporizer, in the other, a dress. "Alright, which of you wants to be Madame Cavanaugh?"

***

Lucky Lou proved more useful than I'd originally anticipated. With access to a network of high-speed elevators, we rocketed towards the surface and stepped out into the sunlight only five precious minutes later.

The sun was well into its downward arc for the day. Faded rays of light twinkled through the urban jungle of Terminus. Pinkish red hues mixed like blood in water across a blue-gray canvas.

Thick air smothered the skin and hung moist in the lungs. We skimmed along the slide-walks towards the Vault. Commuters at the end of a long work day passed in a blur headed in all directions, their eyes glazed over, lost to the Stream. A shroud of anonymity surrounded everyone. Nobody wanted to engage with the person beside them.

At least, not in the real world. Only in the Stream. Inside a world where they could be who they wanted and look how they wanted, limited only by their imaginations. Reality was too rigid by comparison.

They had everything the Lowers could ever want, and it wasn't enough.

I loosened the tie choking me with the grip of a small child. Raines and I had raided Lou's wardrobe, exchanging blood-soaked clothing for outfits that were decidedly not us.

I chose a three-piece suit of smart fabric that adjusted to my dimensions with form-fitting ease. It didn't look half bad, but the tie might as well have been a noose. I had considered leaving it behind, but I needed to look the part for what came next. Regardless, it beat wearing a dress.

The slide-walk banked around a cluster of tall buildings and the rounded sides of the Vault came into view.

The Vault, a fifty-story pillar comprised of progressively smaller circles stacked atop one another, was, in my opinion, an eyesore in comparison to the majesty of the Time Bank.

Viewed from above, the Vault resembled a complicated series of overlapping gears and mechanisms, much like the circular door of a safe. Viewed from any other angle, it resembled a spiral of dog shit.

"Alright, fella, you got fifteen minutes to get in and get out," Lou said, taking loping strides towards the Vault. "After that, you're gonna have a Peacekeeper problem. And since you've been out of the Stream for a few hours, let me give you the bullet-point headlines: Former Detective, Tom Mandel, Murders Warden of Pause and Seven Peacekeepers."

Thoughts of Emilio Castille and his daughter Chloe surfaced. Poor girl was probably strung out like last week's laundry, oblivious to what her father had tried to do for her.

I imagined her huddled in the corner of whatever rat-infested apartment she called home. Green and red neon lights, in a part of the Lowers not safe to walk after dark, filtering through a crack in the blind, illuminating little Chloe seeking solace from the burnable end of an Angel Dust stick.

The red ember, stalking her with every puff; every inhale bringing the promise of a euphoria that would drown out the memory of pain, every exhale the cruel reminder that all promises are eventually lies.

I pulled out of the nosedive of Quick-induced self-flagellation and focused.

"Seven peacekeepers?" I said, doing the math. "Wait. They're not counting the guy that jumped on the Kestrel at Pause, are they? That's not fair. That was all Raines."

Raines said, "He could've survived."

"Not unless he's part bird."

"Whatever," she said, shaking her head. "He shouldn't have jumped onto a moving copter in the first place."

Maybe that's true, but the authorities probably wouldn't see it that way.

"Point being," Lou interjected, "at minimum they have some questions for you. More likely, they just want to kill you. So, ya know, be on the lookout for that."

"Great," Raines and I said in unison.

"And hey, Cross wanted you to have this," Lou said, tossing me the small black pyramid I'd last seen in Cross's hand moments before the Division attack.

I caught it and stumbled into the slide-walk guardrail as my vision momentarily fuzzed out. I shook my head, trying to clear away the cotton balls dancing around in there.

"What the hell is this?"

Lou shrugged. "Hell if I know. Cross called it the Hive Mind. Said it compromises closed networks. Whatever that means."

I ordered my nanocomp to run a cursory scan of my system but it revealed nothing new or out of place. "How do I activate it?"

"Is there an *ON* switch?"

"No?"

"Then I ain't got a clue."

"That's not helpful."

"Nope," Lou said, and then with a wink, stepped off the slide-walk alongside Ash, leaving Raines, myself, and whatever mystery tech Cross had just uploaded into my body to finish the approach to the Vault alone.

CHAPTER TWENTY-ONE
Cracking The Vault

The sun drooped behind the hulking mass of the Vault as Raines and I stepped off the slide-walk. A platoon of Division soldiers eyed us with an intensity that only comes from years of rigorous training and the best implants money can't even buy.

Each square-jawed mass of muscle watching us was loaded to the gills with more next-gen nanites than I could wrap my head around. They tracked us like a pack of predators as the front door to the Vault scissored open for us.

I took a half step through the door, sure that an alarm would go off at any moment and that would be that. The end of our little adventure.

I imagined spending the last hours of life behind bars at the Precinct, or bleeding out on the floor where I now stood.

Both were equally plausible scenarios, but neither depressed me as much as they should.

My indifference was a warning. A signal telling me I was teetering on the brink of a Quick fit.

The Quick tinkered with neural pathways. A snipped wire here, a misplaced neuron there, and next thing ya know, I couldn't care less about the world or its suffering.

Being dependent on a drug to feel anything more than apathy is the cruelest addiction.

Life, death, and everything between were gelatinous gray blobs of whatever. The Quick lurked in the dark recesses of my mind, waiting for her opportunity to strike.

I traced the outline of the Quick stick in my back pocket with a shaky finger; a parting gift from Lou before we'd left the Lowers—"In case of an emergency," he'd said.

I was brainstorming ways of disappearing inside myself when the door to the Vault winked shut behind me.

Somehow we'd made it in. That the camotech Lou had given us was so effective shouldn't have been surprising—it did come from Phoenix Corporation after all—but it was.

Raines fingered the curling gray locks clinging to a forehead no longer hers. Her hand, a traffic jam of purple and blue veins, reminded me of fattened slugs writhing beneath sun-parched skin. The chocolate brown of her eyes had shifted to become a veil of gray cloud smudging an otherwise blue sky. She'd aged a handful of decades, with a lifetime of wrinkles to show for it.

She was a perfect replication of the woman I'd seen earlier that day at the Time Bank, Madame Leader Cavanaugh. The only person with the apparent fortitude to stand up to President Jennings in the board room.

"Thirteen minutes," Raines said without turning.

Microscopic camobots skittered across my jawbone and threaded the delicate tendons of the face I wore. The Quick fueled thoughts of discomfort until I wanted nothing more than to scratch at the skin until it peeled away, leaving great jagged chunks of flesh, slimy with blood, wedged beneath filthy fingernails.

The nanobots were intruders and I wanted them out.

The Quick fed the thought, moving it closer to the realm of delusion, where it would only be a hop-skip away from reality.

I shuddered, squelched those thoughts, and looked up to find Raines already across the foyer at the security booth.

A round man with zero angles perched upon a stool behind the desk like an overfed vulture. A tangle of brown hair cut in a crude bowl shape only added to his monkish features.

That anybody living in the Mid-Uppers would choose to be fat, with hordes of starving people living beneath their feet, was beyond comprehension.

"Ah, Madame Cavanaugh, how good to see you," he said, shuffling to the edge of his seat. His posture tightened, which helped his general appearance, but not by much. "My name's Barry Wosley. How may I have the privilege of serving the fine leader of District Four today?"

Raines saddled up to the counter, her age-worn face pulled tight at the mouth. "I'm here to inspect the contents of a private box," she said, placing the ring-shaped key I'd carried around my neck for the past nine years on the counter.

The key-ring had become a talisman of suffering over the years. A promise made and subsequently broken. A reminder of how I'd failed Diana.

Memory of the key-ring, and what it hid, had been stricken from my mind thanks to the Quick. The implant Devers gave me to unlock those encrypted memories had yet to work as advertised. Clues and tidbits fluttered past like shadows in the night—shadows moving against a half-moon backdrop.

A single thorn of recollection had embedded itself in the forefront of my mind following my death in Lou's office. I couldn't venture anything more than a guess as to what we would discover by coming to the Vault, but somewhere in that building was a door needing to be unlocked. A door with answers.

Barry Wosley swiped the ring from the counter, his hands becoming a hurried blur. His pudgy fingers manipulated the key with a practiced dexterity before threading it onto his pinky. A veil of blue light appeared in front of him. Barry studied the screen with eyes obscured behind thick folds of skin, commonly referred to as eyelids.

Beads of sweat formed an orderly line down my cheek. Time becomes an incalculable variable when you're in the grip of the Quick. I rubbed my index finger against my thumb in little circles, content with the idea of burning my prints off with the friction.

Wosley looked up with a smile plastered to his face as if painted there—a study in the grotesqueness of the human form where proportions are a discarded concern. I feigned a smile in return, hoping it wouldn't appear as wooden as it felt.

"Everything seems to be in order." Barry slid from the edge of his stool with a grunt. His head sank beneath the counter top by a couple inches. "If you'll follow me to the end of the counter, I'll let you through," he said, using an arm lost inside a sleeve two sizes too large to indicate a door on our right.

A game-show buzzer informing us we had guessed the wrong answer squealed as we stepped to the door. The harshness of it startled me. I flinched.

I felt a twinge of embarrassment when I located the source of the sound—the door's locking mechanism.

Raines took the door with a withered hand and yanked it open with a strength surprising for a woman of her supposed age.

She wasn't selling her role as the Madame Leader of District Four, but as her personal attendant I should have gotten the door, so neither of us was giving a particularly convincing performance.

Through the door the squat man stood beside two men with muscles bulging like tumors, their hands resting gently on the butt of the vortex pistols at their hips.

Time to see how good Lou's camotech truly was. A guard approached with a scanning unit in hand. I reached to empty my pockets.

"That won't be necessary, sir," he said.

Strictly speaking, Quick Sliver wasn't illegal, but vices are meant to stay in the dark. It would still show on the scan, but I felt better knowing it would remain in my pocket.

The tendon running from my jaw to my ear formed a solid lump. I forced my lips apart to release the tension stored there as the guard waved the scanner over my body.

Would they see through the mask and find the body hiding beneath? Could they find the million tiny pieces of my broken heart?

My fingers curled into a fist while I pushed back on the melodramatic thoughts forced onto me by the Quick. I focused my attention on the hollow thump of my heartbeat.

The guard with the scanner blinked twice; arctic ice barely broke the surface of gray pond scum coating his eyes. His pupils shrank, sucked into a black hole, before rebounding and coming into focus.

"You're clear," the guard behind me said.

I released the breath I'd been holding through my nostrils.

"Thank you," Raines said a moment after the guard had completed her scan.

Wosley spun heel-to-toe and led us into an adjacent room. At the far wall he fumbled with a lanyard around his neck and swiped it across an invisible sensor. The wall melted to reveal a door. We followed him through to the next room, to another blank wall, where he repeated the process. In this way we continued our march towards the center of the Vault, passing through a dozen rooms in the process.

"Here you are, Madame Leader," Barry said, standing in front of a wall, in a room identical to all the others we'd passed. "I'll wait here. Press the call button when you're finished and I'll return to claim custody of the box. Have you been inside the Vault's viewing chamber before?"

Raines shook her head. "No."

"I thought not. Few people have," he said with just the right amount of condescension to make me want to smack him. "On the far side of the room you'll find a docking port. Simply insert the box to upload its contents. The room can sync with your nanocomp if you'd prefer, otherwise voice commands will suffice. I'll be out here if you have any questions."

"Thank you," Raines said.

The door winked shut as I stepped inside. A soft green halo of light hovered above. In the center of the room a pole slid up from a hole in the floor, rising to waist height before stopping. Raines and I studied the cube sitting atop the platform, wary to approach, like a couple of mice acutely aware of the snake dropped in the cage with them.

"Ten minutes," Raines said.

Time was sprinting away. Apparently it wanted nothing to do with us. I couldn't blame it.

Raines cradled the iridescent cube in both hands as if it were a quantum bomb. She held it in outstretched arms, face puckered with focus, and delivered it to the port built into the wall. The green light washed away the colors in the room, leaving muted black-and-emerald shadows sagging beneath Raines' old eyes.

Raines held it to the sensor and the port slurped at the cube.

We waited for something to happen. A light to switch on. A voice to offer direction. Anything. But for our effort we received a steaming pile of nothing.

Poised on the cusp of a discovery that would put my world into focus, and the room sat like a dead fish, glass eyes a glaze of inactivity.

The cube was supposed to spill its secrets, give understanding to my life, and meaning to my death.

Instead, I received the silent mocking of a billion-dollar room.

"Five minutes," Raines said, her voice layered with frustration. "We're out of time."

My lungs burned and I realized I hadn't taken a breath since Raines inserted the cube into the wall, afraid I might upset the precarious balance of the room if so much as a whisper escaped my lips.

That hadn't worked so I opted for the alternative. I grabbed a mouthful of air and choked it down into my lungs, held it until it screamed, then released it in a long slow whoosh like a deflating balloon.

"We're taking it with us," I said, reaching to extract the box from its port.

"Oh yeah, you got a secret stowaway compartment on you I don't know about?"

My fists tightened into miniature wrecking balls; the blood gushing through my veins hit its boiling point.

"I don't know what to do, Raines," I shouted. "This was supposed to have the answers. I needed it to have answers."

Raines backpedaled. "I know. I get that, but we're not gonna make it out of here if we take it. They'll shoot us down before we make the front door. Is a bullet to the back of the head the kind of answer you're looking for?"

"Maybe," I said, not caring that I was acting like a petulant child. The Quick had rolled back the sheath protecting my nerves and was tap dancing across their stringy surface. I was fried. Caring was beyond me. "Besides, who's to say this room can even read that box? Maybe I hid it here precisely because it couldn't?"

Raines shook her head doubtfully.

I reached for the cube protruding from the wall and said, "We gotta try some—"

The words trying to leave my mouth were denied as my fingers grazed the cube. All that remained was pain.

Pure, straight-off-the-vine virgin pain that hadn't been diluted by time or travel. A star going supernova in my skull.

The world flickered in and out of existence between the torrents of tears blurring my vision. My legs buckled, dropping me to the ground.

"Tom?" Raines knelt beside me, crying.

Or was I crying?

I was in too much pain to unravel the mystery of who was crying, but somebody definitely was.

Nerve endings running the length of my scalp screamed. I responded to the call by tearing chunks of hair free with fingers clenched into claws. Hair follicles fought valiantly, holding fast to sensitive skin, before releasing their grasp and allowing themselves to be uprooted in bloody clumps.

I tried breathing through the delusion. Told myself it was the Quick. It would pass. That it was only in my mind.

But the blood on the floor and my brain turning into a pus-filled blister suggested I was being excessively hopeful.

Despite that, I felt something else. Something surfing the current of my agony. Something I couldn't place, but was there, nonetheless.

A pressure expanding within me. Filling me past the point of full. Thoughts overflowed, boiling, frothing, and leaking into my gut where they simmered, cooking me from the inside.

"Jesus, Tom." Raines put a hand on my shoulder. Her touch was a dull razor wriggling back and forth, burrowing beneath my skin. "Talk to me."

I tried to scream, but the sound couldn't escape my clenched jaw. Teeth ground together, filling my mouth with hard paint chips of shattered enamel flaking from tooth clacking against tooth.

I croaked. "Cack cocket."

I curled into the fetal position, thinking I might escape the pain if I tucked into a tight enough ball and disappeared within my own belly button. I told myself it would be alright. Self-delusion was all I had left.

"Here," Raines said, with the Quick in one hand.

I didn't feel the needle threading me like a piece of string. Everything turned black. Thoughts overridden. Pain became a message lost en route to the receiver.

Quiet. Perfect silence, save for the wet wheeze escaping my lips.

The Quick had me; the sweet release.

I pitied the living. The dead were my idols. This drug was my god.

CHAPTER TWENTY-TWO
The Bad Kind Of Treasure

Transitioning from lucidity to being under the control of Quick Sliver is like being torn apart atom by atom, and scattered to the far reaches of the universe. While floating along the cosmic breeze, somebody's god reached into my skull, flipped a set of dials and switches, and cranked up the intensity of reality.

The world slowed and my senses smashed together. I tasted colors and smelled sounds. Doctors call that synesthesia, a neurological disorder causing the brain to misinterpret senses, but I don't think it's a disorder. I think it's the way we were meant to be, our senses an interchangeable jumble. How else are you to fully appreciate a sunrise until you can taste light?

I looked up at the green light burning overhead; it tasted sour.

"Sit up." Raines wasn't being gentle anymore. She shook me like a vending machine refusing to drop her candy. "We have to go. Can you move?"

I stared at her, wondering how she got so old. Memories were photographs with cigarette burns where faces should be.

The fog of Quick lifted slowly and I remembered.

There was panic, or the closest thing to panic one can feel under the influence of such a strong mood stabilizer.

I was still on my side, shivering against the cold floor. It felt good against my sweat- and tear-stained cheek. I wanted to stay there forever.

It was a good place to die.

I tasted the light again. Copper and bleach.

Convinced I'd never wash that taste from my mouth, I spit. Thick red globules speckled the floor inches from my face.

In the light they looked black.

Raines had me by the arm and yanked me to my feet. I realized I was standing only after she shoved me towards the door, and somehow my legs managed to carry me.

"Listen to me." Raines spun me around and cradled my head between her soft hands; her nose grazed mine. "If we don't get out of here right now, they are going to lock us up. We won't stop Malcolm. You'll die alone in a jail cell. Do you understand? You've got to pull yourself together."

I nodded, looking at the world from the wrong end of a magnifying glass.

Raines' head was gigantic, her eyes inhuman. They weren't her normal color. Tiny oases of blue pulling me forward.

I leaned in before the message could be vetoed, and I kissed her. Like kissing a star, a blaze flushed my system with heat.

Until she shoved me back and punched me in the mouth.

The tumblers fell into place. The lock to my mind swung open on a squeaky hinge. I blinked hard.

Raines balled her fists, ready for a second round. "Feel better?"

"Yeah," I said, rubbing my cheek, "actually I do."

Sometimes a swift kick to the computing unit is the only way to get the system running properly again.

I dabbed at my lips, leaving behind a child's finger painting worth of color and liquids on my sleeve.

When I looked up, Raines was gone. Light glinted off the shimmering cube in the corner. We stared at one another for a long moment.

The cube tried to kill me. I think.

I'd had Quick fits before, but that last seizure felt like something else. Something pulsed inside me, pecking against the cage of my mind.

The Quick causes paranoia, but sometimes that paranoia is justified.

My hand quivered inches from the cube, afraid it would sink its fangs into me and inject another dose of poison into my veins.

Raines popped her head into the room and said, "Let's go."

At the sound of her voice my shoulders jumped to my ears and my heart gave an extra three-beat staccato. No more time for fear. I snatched the box and exited that room of horrors.

In the next room, Raines gestured to a wall with something dangling from her fingers. My mind felt sunburned: hot, stretched, and dry. Thoughts weren't flowing with their normal ease, so it wasn't until Raines swiped the item in question along an invisible panel on the wall that I realized what she had.

Barry Wosley's lanyard.

I scanned the room until I found the tip of a brown shoe poking out from beneath a desk. Thoughts had to wade through the mud-encrusted waters of my mind, but I managed to put two and two together: Raines had knocked him out.

A door, leading to destinations yet unknown, appeared in the wall beside Raines.

She forged ahead with a confidence suggesting she knew where to go.

I dogged her with a confidence suggesting I had no better alternative.

Half a dozen rooms later we stumbled upon the server room. The air had an icy bite. Breath crystallized in front of me with every ragged exhale.

My head spun trying to grasp the vastness of the room. Walls stretched towards the ceiling hundreds of feet overhead. Clunking computer towers the size of small houses formed endless rows of raw storage capacity.

Raines jogged down the nearest aisle. It was still unclear whether or not she knew where she was headed, but it beat asking for directions, so like an obedient lap dog, I followed.

The machines buzzed with a dry hum, as if housing bee hives. The sound reached a crescendo as we neared the center of the room.

Raines said something, but her words were lost in the drone. She leaned in and yelled into my ear. The purr of her voice against my skin coalesced with the ambient vibrations rippling through the room, causing me to shiver violently.

"Call Ash," she said. "Have her meet us on the roof."

I nodded and slipped into the Stream. The incessant buzzing receded, squelched by the immutable silence of the virtual network. The reprieve from my physical circumstance was a welcomed gift.

I tracked Ash, slid her a message, and sprung out of the Stream. No sense waiting for her reply. The roof was our only out and either Ash would be there waiting or she wouldn't.

"Okay, let's go," I said.

"What?"

"Let's go," I shouted over the din.

Raines dipped her head in acknowledgment and sprinted down the row of servers we were squashed between. I ramped my speed implants to keep pace.

The aisle terminated at a service lane for maintenance vehicles. We slid into the intersection at the same moment a trio of guards emerged a dozen rows down. One of the guards raised a hand to point, the other two opted for their weapons.

Words were shouted and lost to the noisy room.

We didn't stick around to ask for a repeat. Turning back the way we came, we milked our legs for every ounce of speed they had to give.

Some quick math informed me we were about to become sitting ducks. I grabbed Raines' shoulder and pulled her to a stop. She looked back with eyes so wide I saw my reflection in her pupils. I gestured at the ceiling with a finger. Raines, a charades champion in a former life, took my meaning immediately.

Pivoting to the wall of computer terminals on my left, I took two steps, planted a foot against the vent grate at knee height, and jumped for all I was worth. I snagged the lip with straining fingertips and pulled myself atop the massive machine like a swimmer flopping out of a pool.

On my belly, I reached for Raines. She climbed my arm like a gym rope. Using my belt for leverage, she hoisted herself up and over as the guards rounded the corner at the head of the boulevard.

An enthusiastic guard raised his weapon, but stopped short thanks to his comrades. Firing into the servers would cost more lives than just our own. For the moment, we were shielded by the millions of lives housed and monitored within those computers.

We ran towards the nearest wall. The terminals were half a foot wider than shoulder width, making the task of sprinting at full speed a question of precision. The guards pursued from the alleyway below, gaining distance with every step. Soon they'd be close enough for an open shot.

I spied a door across the room. Didn't know where it went, but that hardly mattered. Raines followed the direction indicated by my finger, stepped sideways, and leaped to the row of terminals adjacent to ours without a moment of hesitation. She carried her momentum and launched again to the next stack. A handful of seconds later and she'd put five rows between us.

My turn.

Clearing the ten-foot gap between terminals was easier than expected. Executing the land-step-jump combination was not.

I cleared the first jump, but mistimed the follow-through and jumped too soon for the second. My feet pedaled the air for more distance, but it didn't help. I came up well short of the next row of towers and slammed chest first into the wall of computers. Air whooshed out of my lungs.

My hand dragged across the grate. A couple fingers slid through the narrow diamond-shaped openings and arrested my fall. The sharp metal ripped the tender flesh of my palm, but I managed to hold on. I struggled back on top of the machine and wiped bloody prints on my pants as a guard scrambled atop a terminal two rows over. His eyes thrummed with the intensity of nanites supercharging his muscles. He could probably outrun me with only one leg.

I had nothing to do but try, so I sprinted back towards the maintenance lane, no longer trusting Raines' method of hop-skipping.

Raines had almost reached the exit, but I was running perpendicular to her. Somehow I needed to reroute myself in her direction. I figured if I could stay ahead of the guard on my left, and get to the service lane, I should make it to the door a little after Raines.

Those hopes were dashed by two guards streaking down the service lane on a couple scooter-class Hummin'Birds. That reminded me to ask Felix Cross, next time we spoke, why he insisted on naming all the vehicles coming out of Phoenix Corp after birds.

My lungs felt used, a rag slimy with oil and set to flame. Every breath was a mouthful of water going down the wrong tube. Drowning with air.

My heart grated with every beat, chafing that poor contracting muscle raw.

Time was running out.

I was running out.

CHAPTER TWENTY-THREE
Living Is A Young Man's Game

Seconds were all that remained before I'd be overtaken by the guards charging across the massive mainframe room on Hummin'Birds. Lacking a better option, I clenched my jaw and flung myself to the adjacent row of terminals. The world passed by in slow motion. I nailed the landing. My momentum carried me and I leaped again. The second landing was rougher than the first, but I salvaged it.

I glanced over my shoulder to see the guard doing his own variation of hopscotch across the terminals; he didn't seem to find it as difficult as me. The gift of youth, I told myself.

After a third jump, a fumbled landing, and an aborted fourth attempt, I bolted left to where my terminal overlooked the maintenance highway.

The floor stared up at me ten feet below. The kernel of a plan evolved in the most primitive region of my brain, the fight-or-flight at any cost sector. I acted on the plan before the higher processing portions could find the obvious fault and issue a more sane decision such as, *don't do it.*

I paused for approximately thirteen nanoseconds while the guard on my left completed his final jump onto my stack of towers. Then I leaped back to the row of terminals from which he and I had just come. The entirety of my focus was on sticking the landing and getting a strong second jump.

Impromptu calculations from my nanocomp reassured me that what I was attempting fell within the range of theoretically possible, if not wholly improbable. The slimmest margin of difference separated the two, but I convinced myself that would be enough.

The key was full commitment.

And I did. I committed like a baby bird testing its gift of flight for the first time and jumped harder than I had ever jumped before. I would have drifted lazily through the air, if not for my arms flailing wildly at my sides. I sailed over the top of the next row of terminals like a drunken superhero.

The man driving the Hummin'Bird saw me coming. His nanocomp probably dilated time, giving him precious seconds to process what was about to happen. Unfortunately, his perception of time couldn't stop the reality of physics.

Physics that carried him forward with too much momentum to avoid colliding with the fully grown man hurtling towards him. A quarter of a second later I landed on him.

The Hummin'Bird lurched, followed by myself and the driver rocketing off the back end. I had the man wrapped in a mama-bear death hug with the hopes of using him to dampen my landing.

We hit the ground, a high dive belly flop. My head snapped forward, bashing my face into the driver's helmet.

The world wobbled out of focus. I lost my grip on the guard. We skittered across the floor in a tangle of limbs.

The world evolved into an ever-changing kaleidoscope of shapes, sounds, and pains. Protect the valuables: knees, elbows, and head. That's what they teach you in the Academy, anyways. In the absence of a better articulated plan, my body relied on muscle memory, which accounted for practically nothing given the novelty of the current situation.

Skin squeaked against metal until I came to a full stop. A patch of skin running the length of my calf had rubbed off, leaving an exposed layer of pinkish red blubber glistening beneath. The majority of the messages emanating from that appendage were terminated by my nanocomp, but it couldn't stop them all. The rest were left for me to grit my teeth and suffer through.

Over the hum of machinery, I heard the Hummin'Bird clanging across the smart-metal floor, no longer in possession of its driver, and therefore its mind. From a certain perspective the jump couldn't have been executed any better. Despite the odds, I'd managed to get full body-on-body contact, rather than simply splattering myself across the Hummin'Bird's windshield.

I scanned the battlefield: the driver lay on his back where he'd rolled to a stop, the other driver had pulled a U-turn a thousand feet down the corridor, and a third guard was lowering himself off a stack of terminals.

In the trench formed by computer towers, I felt relatively safe from energy rifles and vortex pistols set to a lethal setting, so at least the world wasn't entirely against me.

The driver of the dispossessed Bird groaned and tried rolling to his knees. His hands groped for the weapon at his side. Too slow.

I pounced, driving my foot into the black reflective glass of his helmet. His head pinged back, and the tension from his muscles ebbed. The man had only been doing his job, which filled me with no insignificant amount of guilt. But I couldn't afford to process that guilt. I had to keep moving forward.

I stripped the pistol and battle baton from the man's belt. The sound of boots approaching from behind was the rhythmic beat of a drum. The black glass from the driver's helmet offered a distorted reflection of my soon-to-be attacker, his battle baton out and ready.

Light steps closed the distance quickly. It was the same man who'd chased me across the computer terminals. No doubt my physical superior. In a fair fight he'd win every time.

But this wouldn't be a fair fight.

I forced myself to wait; to maintain the element of surprise.

When he was less than five feet away, I flicked my wrist, extending the battle baton to its full three-foot length, and spun.

The guard saw the weapon; his face sparked with the realization he'd been had. His feet failed to find the required traction to sidestep the wide arc I traced with my baton toward his knee.

Metal cracked against bone.

The man grunted as he stumbled past. He managed two more steps before crumpling beside his fallen compatriot. His baton rolled away from fingertips too occupied with clutching his knee.

I lowered the intensity of the vortex pistol in my left hand and fired a round at the man. The blast would feel as if a miniature tornado had taken up residence inside his cranium. Pressure would build behind his eye sockets like an air pump had been jammed in his nose, inflating him. Eardrums, if they didn't perforate upon the initial blast, would bow inward and distort balance and equilibrium. Every head tilt would become a roller coaster ripping through a maze of fun-house mirrors.

It wouldn't kill him, but it wouldn't leave him smiling, either.

That is, if he was unlucky enough to maintain consciousness.

Which left one guard barring my rendezvous with Raines.

A hundred feet down aisle he'd parked his Hummin'Bird sideways in the middle of the lane, an improvised road block. It wouldn't stop me, but it's the thought that counts.

The guard drew his vortex pistol and fired a round. I was caught flat-footed, thinking, *There's no way he's going to shoot.*

A smoke ring blown from the lips of a giant spiraled towards me. I dove between a row of computer terminals on my right. A funnel of air rushed past.

The man had set his pistol to a low density, high dispersal setting which accounted for his apparent lack of concern for the field of servers surrounding us. The blast wouldn't kill me. Knock me down, yes. But it wouldn't even knock me out. I'd be awake to feel my face swelling like an overripe zit.

I toggled between settings on my own pistol, dropped to the floor, and poked my head out from behind the wall of terminals. The guard stood to attention in the center of the aisle, poised with weapon in hand.

He fired once.

I fired twice.

His vortex ring collided with my first. They canceled each other out in a swirl of smoke and vapor.

My second shot skimmed through the wake. The guard barely registered the danger in time, and dove for cover. His Hummin'Bird wasn't so lucky. It took the full brunt of the blast. Gale-strength winds flung the vehicle hundreds of feet down the aisle. It toppled across the floor before skidding to a stop against a bank of servers with the sickening crunch of metal on metal.

I prayed for superficial damage to the terminal, otherwise I might have just committed mass murder. Those were thoughts I couldn't afford to ponder 'cause the guard, by cowering for cover, had given me an opportunity.

I sprinted into the corridor. The man popped out from his hiding place and fired three shots in rapid succession. Adrenaline lit a fire in my loins and I cleared the aisle, sliding feet first into the next row well ahead of the first vortex ring.

Now, on the same side of the corridor as the guard, I imagined his position in my mind's eye. Five rows separated us. I think.

I leaped atop the terminal. A task that was, surprisingly, easier than it had been before. Feeling confident with my guess of five aisles, I clutched the vortex pistol in my right hand, and jumped the gap.

I flicked off the portion of brain responsible for conscious thought and relied on pure motor memory.

Land. Step. Jump.

Land. Step. Jump.

Land. Step. Jump.

One more.

Land. I took a deep breath. My forward momentum carried me.

Step. I took aim with my arm locked at full extension.

Jump.

I aimed between my legs where the guard should have been, ready to blast him from above like a weaponized Eagle.

Only one problem.

He wasn't there.

Before my feet touched the ground, over the ruckus of white noise, I heard a familiar whoosh.

He had the drop on me, a fact confirmed a split second later when the vortex ring chucked me across the room like a piece of garbage fluttering on the breeze.

I transformed into a trapeze artist, flying through the air thinking, Land, Step, Jump, but there was no graceful way to dismount that ride.

My worldview rapidly cycled between the shiny support beams of the ceiling and the smooth, unmarked floor. I just happened to be looking up at the ceiling when I landed. The ground punched me in the liver with a blunt fist. I gasped into the pain, momentarily forgetting my eyes bulging in their sockets thanks to the vortex tainting my equilibrium.

Sprawled on all fours, I rubbed my temples in a futile attempt to massage away the congestion. I worked my jaw up and down, then plugged my nose and blew hard. Anything to equalize the shifting pressure in my skull.

Nothing helped.

Despite my troubles, though, I wasn't completely incapacitated. Over the sound of my labored breathing I heard the guard sprinting towards me. He yelled something about not moving, and me being under arrest, but leprechauns were doing a jig on my eardrums, and his words weren't making it past the bouncer.

I scrambled on hands and knees to where my pistol had slid away during my fall. I willed my arms and legs to crawl faster, which is about the most degrading form of transportation I can think of for a man my age and reputable standing in society to do.

A pair of shins appeared in front of me and kicked the pistol away as my fingers grazed its smooth reflective surface.

That was my last hope. Funny how many times I'd thought that about a gun in my lifetime. In a future life, I'm hoping for a docile career. Perhaps something behind a desk.

No guns.

I'm tired of guns.

I plopped onto my ass. No point in crawling anymore, if in fact there ever had been. Might as well face whatever came next with a sliver of dignity.

With legs splayed out in front of me I looked up into the gun, hoping the guard wouldn't turn my brain to pudding with a low-intensity blast to the face.

He stood over me, an action figure pulled from a movie poster, his face a study in grit and determination.

I opened my mouth to say something about surrendering when a spiral of air struck the man in the side. He was blasted clear into and past oblivion before I registered the surprise.

The guard slammed into the side of a terminal before dropping with a grunt.

"Huh?" I mumbled, turning left to find the source of the shot.

Raines straddled a Hummin'Bird with a dented frame, a plume of air rising off the still-hot muzzle of her pistol. I staggered to my feet and tried walking in a straight line, a task I soon realized was impossible on jellyfish legs. I gave up and settled for a drunken swagger.

"Nice ride," I said, throwing a noodle leg over the back of the Hummin'Bird. "Where'd you get it?"

"Found it lying around." Raines gunned the accelerator and we went from zero to holy-fuck in the time it took me to swallow my tongue.

CHAPTER TWENTY-FOUR
First Date With A Killer

Luck has played a larger role in my life than I'd care to admit. So it's not like my indignation has firm ground to stand on when I throw snake-eyes. When you play the cards you're dealt so loosely, you're bound to take some bad beats.

Though perhaps that comes with the implication that I had business playing the hand in the first place. Most of the time I don't, but I still do.

Call it a character flaw.

Those were the thoughts that consumed my attention while standing on the roof of the Vault with my hands stretched towards the sky in some form of sun salutation. Balanced precariously upon the edge of the building, my heels teetered half off the precipice—which I could say, given the state of my waning equilibrium, was positively too close.

The tattered remains of Lou's suit jacket danced in the breeze, possessed by the wind whipping off the side of the building.

I'd step away from the edge, but that would bring me closer to the five Peacekeepers who had, in no uncertain terms, told us not to move a fucking inch.

I respected that request on account of the rifles they used to enforce their words. My gun lay well out of arm's reach on the black asphalt. The sun glinting off its silver sides made it look cheap. A toy for adults running around playing games nobody knows the rules to.

Something about that was funny. It wasn't funny, I knew that. But the whole day, from start to finish, was absurd to such a degree that laughter was the only sane reaction.

So I laughed. Which beat the alternative of crying. A rib shifted out of place and I winced. The youngest-looking officer tensed his trigger finger. How much harder would he have to pull to blow me off the roof and out of existence?

Part of me wanted to find out.

"Interlock your fingers behind your head, and slowly step forward," the officer on the far left side of the half-circle barked with a stone-cold indifference.

He'd just as soon shoot us dead as bring us in. It was in his eyes. Probably the only thing holding him back was the amount of paperwork to be filed in the wake of our deaths. We'd be out of his life all the sooner if he kept us alive, made the collar, and passed us to the next squad.

These guys were the Apprehension Unit. Raines and I were destined for greater things.

Well, I was. The genesis of a plan had been percolated, morphing from a splinter of possibility into a full-fledged sliver of hope embedding itself beneath my cerebral cortex.

Ash pinged me a simulation showing that, at least theoretically, the plan could work. It was slim and Raines would be pissed, but we weren't in a position to analyze the quality of choices remaining to us.

Maybe she'd make it out, find a better life off grid with her kids. I thought about Maddie and Morgan. A pang of guilt sucker punched me. Or maybe it was jealousy? Regret?

Diana and I had wanted kids. A family. Diana got to be a mother to an unborn child for two months. It was wrong. Malcolm took more than my wife. He took my family.

I wanted to call a redo, but I suppose that's what all losing teams say when they stand on the cusp of defeat.

The game was only ending for me, though. Raines would make it, or so I told myself. I convinced myself that she'd get out of there with air in her lungs and a soul in her body. She'd have her kids and that would have to be enough. After the day we'd had, I was convinced that's all we could ask for.

Tension arced across the sky as I stepped forward. The air dripped with the unique flavors of sweat, fear, adrenaline, and death all baked into one.

Ash pinged my nanocomp, her reply to a message I'd sent moments earlier: **Do it, now.**

No time for doubt. The cube had to make it off that roof. Raines had to make it off that roof.

I swiveled, thrust the cube into Raines' startled hand and grabbed her shoulders. Our eyes locked. There were no words, only thoughts.

I wished she could read my mind.

Hoped she'd forgive me.

Hoped she'd outlive this mess, and me.

And then I shoved her off the roof.

She teetered on the brink, arms pin-wheeling in a frantic search for purchase, but there was only me.

For the second time in my life I didn't reach out to save her. I let her fall.

It happened fast. She didn't flail. Resigned to her fate, not bothering to fight the inevitable pull of gravity, she fell with dignity.

I held her hurt-filled stare. I couldn't look away. Not for the world.

A massive displacement of air rippled across the roof, a gentle nudge that almost pushed me over the edge, followed by the booming engines of a Peregrine rounding the corner of the Vault, diving like a bird chasing an insect.

Its engines were the roar of a crumbling mountain.

Everything in me clenched. Watertight. Nothing in. Nothing out. Breathing could wait. The Peregrine dove beneath Raines and matched her rate of descent.

Empty space for the mid-air rescue was running out.

The pilot pitched the Peregrine onto its side, exposing an open door pointed towards the sky, and Raines above.

Raines rotated to approach the vehicle face first. She splayed her arms to create drag as the jet hit the thrusters and rose up to meet her.

She snagged the arm rail when the vehicle came within reach and yanked her body inside the metal beast. The Peregrine flopped onto its belly. With less than two dozen feet before impact, the engines became a symphony of harmonic roars fighting to negate the pull of gravity and inertia. The vehicle rocketed forward, leaving a shower of red-green sparks hissing from the undercarriage as it scraped along the street below.

From my vantage point I couldn't tell whether the pilot had pulled out of the dive in time. There was no explosion of Peregrine shrapnel intermixed with the odd human body part; I took that as a good thing.

For a hundred yards the jet continued its belly slide before it threw off the shackles of its earthly bonds, regained lift, and took to the sky.

The air I'd been holding erupted from my mouth the precise moment the butt of a gun came down on the base of my skull. I dropped to my knees, trying to see through a field of fireflies. Immobilization rings snapped into place around my wrists. Nerve endings in my arm died as if the limb had been severed at the elbow.

Somebody then clamped a sedation collar around my neck. One by one a phantom went through the rooms in my brain and turned out the lights. It locked up the front door on its way out, leaving me alone in the black hole of induced sleep.

***

I came out of hibernation sitting on the wrong side of a familiar room. Electromagnetic bands anchored my legs to the chair, and my hands to the table in front of me.

From this side of the table the interrogation room was not a friendly place to be. In fact, it was designed for maximal discomfort.

Freezing air blasted from a vent in the ceiling, forming ringlets of frost on the gleaming steel table. At those temperatures exposed flesh has a way of sticking to metal. To avoid the unpleasant sensation that comes with prying skin from ice, the best strategy is to keep your arms slightly elevated. But that's only a temporary fix. After a couple minutes, your shoulders start burning with the accumulation of lactic acid.

If they liked you, they wouldn't strap your head to the chair, allowing you to lean forward and use the heat of your breath to warm the table.

They didn't like me.

They were going for a full monty of discomfort.

My nanocomp dusted the cobwebs of sedation from my mind, which served only to remind me of my bodily aches. I distracted myself with thoughts of Raines. Hoping she had the good sense to get out of the fight. We were pawns in a game being played over our heads, and any pawn with aspirations of making it through the end game knows to stay out of the fight when the big pieces come out to play.

The big pieces were out. It was time to hide.

God, I hoped she was hiding.

The door to the interrogation room swung open and an absurdly average-looking man stepped inside. An average nose came to an indefinite point above an average layer of lips that looked to have been painted the perfect hue of pink by an artist honing his craft. The fact that his face held no memorable feature was, in and of itself, almost memorable.

He wore a neat three-piece suit of a style that bordered on unfashionable. A gold chain dangled from the side pocket of a silky blue vest hidden beneath his outer coat.

"May I?" he asked, placing a file on the table and gesturing towards the open chair across from me.

"I'm saving it for someone else, but you're welcome to keep it warm for now."

"I'll do my best." He smiled, exposing an average row of off-white teeth. "Well, Mr. Tom Mandel, you've had quite the day."

"Just your typical Tuesday."

"It's Saturday."

"Is it? Damn. Okay, well…for a weekend, you're right. It's been a big day."

"We'll begin by you telling me everything you know about Malcolm Wolfe's escape."

"Sorry, Boss. Not feeling particularly chatty on that front."

Something about authority always brings out the best in me. Being back at the Precinct conjured memories of a different life. One where I had never been any good at playing the usual reindeer games of nose to ass.

Those memories turned to ash in my mouth, leaving me to swallow the bitter remains of that broken man.

"Let me cut through this tough-guy act. I'm here for one purpose. Assist me in achieving that purpose and I'll make accommodations on your behalf to assure the final hours of your life pass as inconsequentially as all the hours that came before. However…" I think he paused for dramatic effect, but I was barely riding the current of his words. "If you prove unwilling, or simply unable, to help, then I shall see to it that these final hours are the longest any man has been made to endure. And I assure you, I have ways of making that seem a very long time."

The air conditioner hummed, an insect flying out of sight—never seen but always there. All the more annoying for that simple reason.

I wondered if that qualified as one of the unique methods of torture he had in mind.

"I'd love to help, but here we are on our first date and I don't even know your name."

"Daniel Brandt," he said, looking up from the desk, his eyes filled with the most chilling brand of indifference; the kind that will slit your throat for a paycheck.

"Oh?" I said, masking the surprise churning my insides at seeing Emilio Castille's specter in the flesh. "And what branch of Division are you with?"

"Security."

"Security? That's it?"

"That's it."

"Awfully broad."

"I have my specialties."

The Warden had given enough details to fill in the blanks of those specialties. That Brandt had come to the Time Vice Precinct suggested he didn't fear the Peacekeepers. A fact which made him a truly terrifying captor.

"So, what're you looking to hear, Dan?"

"Everything."

"Awfully broad."

"I'll leave you to fill in the details."

"You're not a very good interrogator, ya know that?"

"I don't need to be." He pulled a silver vial from the inside breast pocket of his jacket and placed it on the table. His stare was intense and unwavering. "As the cliché goes, there is an easy way to do this, and a hard way." At that he gestured to the tube full of nanites. "It's your choice."

"Nothing worth doing is easy, right?" I said, clenching my jaw so the combination of ice and dread creeping through me wouldn't show in my chattering teeth.

"They must train insolence into the officers at this Precinct," Brandt mumbled under his breath as he flipped the page on the file before him.

"Insolence 101," I said. "It's required learning."

"I would advise a change in strategy." Brandt looked up with a flat, unreadable expression. His fingers flitted across the file and the table's smart screen illuminated with a warm, wet light. Brandt tapped again, filling the screen with a picture of an old man lying in bed, eyes closed with the kind of relaxation reserved for the dead. "He died in his sleep, or so the story goes."

Recognition came in a slow drizzle. I knew the face, the sweep of his hair across a broad forehead. The deep ravines crisscrossing time-hardened cheeks. But the juxtaposition of a man I'd only ever known as living made him something alien. Death makes us unrecognizable.

Captain Michael Joseph Nash had put his trust in Raines and me. Believed in the intent, if not the recklessness, of our mission. He'd been rewarded for that trust with what I hoped had been a peaceful death.

My hands trembled against their restraints. Emotions boiled inside me, but were denied any sort of physical release. I could do nothing but breathe. I gathered what I could of my self-control and by force of will subdued those parts of my mind and body that Brandt could compromise. He'd done this to rattle me.

I wouldn't give him that pleasure.

Brandt gave the closest approximation of a smile I think he ever gave. "Before you make any decisions to be uncooperative, I want you to know what lies ahead for your friends foolish enough to have helped you. Answer my questions and I'll let your partner live."

Raines.

They'd killed the Captain of the largest Time Vice squad in the world. There would be no consequences, no punishment, for their actions. Nothing stopping Brandt from breaking his word. There could be no pact between monsters and men.

I summoned what confidence I could, but so little remained. Slumped in my chair, staring at Captain Nash's unmoving body, I said, "No."

Brandt reached for the nanotube and said, "I thought you might say that."

***

I sang like a canary, tweeting my little song until I was blue in the face. The nanites Brandt injected me with were sledgehammer blows against the dam of my internal filter, shattering the wall between thought and speech, spilling everything.

My mouth betrayed me, but I wasn't completely without my tricks. I managed to gloss over certain topics by giving painfully detailed accounts of others. It would be safe to assume Daniel Brandt now knew more about Quick fits and lying in puddles of drool than he'd ever wanted.

But I managed to conceal the parts that dealt with Castle, my wife and her involvement with the system Malcolm was using to murder the world, and how I'd been involved with said organization up to the point where Malcolm deleted chunks of my memory with a sniper-roofie.

Brandt managed to show a negative output of interest in everything I said.

Things truly got interesting in that refrigerator box of questions when Brandt pulled from his pocket the glass pyramid Felix Cross had given me.

The Hive Mind.

The truth-nanites Brandt had unceremoniously injected into my throat had the unforeseen consequence of unlocking a rogue squadron of nanites lurking in my frontal lobe.

Felix Cross hadn't gotten around to explaining what the Hive Mind did before Division soldiers busted down Lucky Lou's door, so I used a sophisticated experimental process called guess-and-check to probe the piece of technology. Following in the tradition of most great eureka moments throughout history, I did something completely by accident that changed everything.

I knew I'd discovered something important when a railroad spike of data was driven through my skull like an unseen force laying tracks for an eventual train to follow. Sure enough, that train lagged only a second behind. When it hit it turned my lungs to a gelatinous puddle incapable of taking another breath.

My neural implant squawked like a drunk crawling out of the gutter. Neurons, lying dormant since the day I was born, lit me up.

Blood rushed to my cheeks along with a sudden boost in processing power I'd never experienced before. Forgotten were the numb arms dangling limp on the table before me.

The increased computing capacity came from linking systems with the four individuals the Hive Mind nanites had infected. Like a technological poltergeist, the Hive Mind had infiltrated the bodies of those who'd touched the pyramid: an invisible cloud of nanites infesting their nanocomps, wrestling control away from the primary user, and delivering it to me.

The nanites attached at the base of their occipital lobes communicated with my nanocomp, allowing me a view of the world as seen through the eyes of my new drones. The simplicity of the process was astonishing. Similar to hacking and enslaving a computer network. The difference being that, in this case, the network was a human mind.

Using that technology put me in a class of criminal closer to Malcolm Wolfe, who'd discovered his own method of hacking the system remotely, but there wasn't time to question the ethical implications of this advancement—only time for action.

This was my chance to get back into the game.

My escape route.

CHAPTER TWENTY-FIVE
We're All Of One Mind

Brandt patiently awaited an answer to a question I'd long since forgotten. Something having to do with the pyramid sitting between us. He'd be waiting a while for a response on that one; I had no intention of giving up my ace in the hole.

Of the four slave programs I had running, only two would be of any help. Two officers from the Apprehension Unit had touched the device, but only one was still in the Precinct. That man, a young officer named Kellogg, was currently chatting up the clerk working the drunk tank.

It took some fiddling, but eventually I grabbed control of Kellogg and redirected him to my holding cell, leaving the clerk in the middle of a sentence with an awkward amount of social indifference.

I sifted through the other two drones. One was a lab technician probably tasked with determining the pyramid's functionality. Apparently he'd failed on that account.

The fourth individual was Brandt.

A golden opportunity, if not for the massive interference radiating from his nanocomp's firewall. The next-generation nanobots guarding his mind effectively put him out of my reach.

By the time I'd maneuvered my drone, Officer Derek Kellogg, to the interrogation room, I'd become proficient enough at controlling him to imitate something approximating a normal walk.

At the door I raised his fist, and, afraid of knocking too softly, I overcompensated.

Brandt stood slowly. "If you're not goin—" His words were cut off by the pounding at the door.

Startled, Brandt spun towards the door faster than I'd seen anybody, save Ash, move.

The door crept open and Kellogg, the kid with a twitchy trigger finger from the Vault, stepped inside.

The officer stared at me. I stared back. Both perspectives played in my mind's eye. A weird infinite loop of looking into a mirror through a mirror.

I wanted to close out the officer's visual cue to terminate the cycle, but the system was clunky, and I was afraid I'd lose control if I got too fancy too soon.

"Yes?" Brandt asked, his voice professional but laced with a side of *you better have a damn good reason for interrupting me.*

An awkward amount of time passed as I fiddled with the officer's vocal cords. Finally I made him say, "Sir, the lab has something for you."

Kellogg's voice, a butter-smooth tenor modulated by nanobots in his throat, resonated on the perfect frequency to promote feelings of calm and wellbeing. This was an immensely popular upgrade on the force, where sometimes your voice is the only weapon you have. Couldn't fault him for wanting every advantage he could muster, but honestly, I hate the audacity of it.

Alterations designed with the express purpose of manipulating other people's brainwaves felt wrong. My conscience pointed to the hypocrisy of that perspective in light of the brain-jacking I was currently conducting. Even in my own mind I couldn't take a turn riding the high horse.

Brandt exited alongside my officer drone to the adjacent room, where the holographic projection of a man with lean, high-cut cheekbones and a lab coat waited.

"What is it, Langdon?" Brandt said, making no attempt to conceal his frustration at being interrupted.

Things got tricky when I shifted perspective between drones. The process was jarring like driving over a pockmarked gravel road.

BLINK.

I switched control to the lab tech on the other end of the line, letting Officer Kellogg idle in the back of my mind.

"Sorry to interrupt you, sir. There's been somewhat of a breakthrough on that device you brought in. You're gonna want to see this."

"Stream it to my queue."

"Actually, sir, it'd be better if you came in person. Transferring this information through the Stream might not be...uh...secure, if you understand."

Brandt paused for a long moment, studying me through the double-sided glass. Inside the interrogation room, I resembled a meditating Buddha, or a drunk on the cusp of blackout; sometimes there's a thin line between the two.

I considered poking around Brandt's cerebral jungle again, but operating two drones had me redlining. Taking a third would be overwhelming.

"I'll be right there," Brandt said before ending the call. "You stay here. Watch him. Under no circumstances are you to enter that room. Clear?"

"Yes, sir," I answered with Kellogg's voice box.

Brandt left in a distracted flurry. Before the door was fully closed I had Kellogg standing in the interrogation room, releasing the bindings holding my arms to the table. The cuffs released their grip with a click and a whoosh.

I leaned back, allowing my arms to dangle loosely at my side. My neck and shoulders were a jumble of knots I tried working through by rolling my head in circles. The skin around my forearms was an odd shade of purple-blue that burned as blood rushed back into them.

Officer Kellogg stared vacantly at me. He looked younger than he had on the rooftop of the Vault. Perhaps straight out of the Academy, but it was hard to say. People had bucked the evolutionary trend. They looked younger every year thanks to cheaper and better nanotech, aging with none of the physical signs to show for it.

Thanks to that tech, Kellogg could be older than me. I had no way of knowing. He'd probably go to his deathbed looking like a sprightly twenty-something.

By comparison, I'd be going to mine looking as if I'd been thrown off a building. A surprisingly accurate look.

I stood on legs that had turned into a pincushion of needles. I hopped up and down and tried stimulating blood flow by massaging my thighs. I glanced at my Life Tracker and surprise hit me like a jackhammer to the gut. Two hours had passed since the Vault rooftop.

Two hours with no forward progress towards catching Malcolm. I took the cuffs from Kellogg and threw them over my wrists without tightening them.

I briefly wondered if Kellogg's conscious mind was still in there, awake and privy to his circumstances. For his sake, I hoped not. With my hand on the doorknob, I told myself he slept in a state of peaceful oblivion.

It was irrelevant whether or not that was true, 'cause it made me feel better, and right then I was in the market for anything to make me feel better.

We exited the interrogation room with Kellogg's hand on my shoulder. Time Vice buzzed with more than the usual bustle of activity. Most of the faces were new to me, but there were plenty I recognized, and too many that recognized me. We traversed the bull pen like a couple runway models—all eyes on us.

One face held no love for me, only contempt. Another wore a mask of confusion. Another a mix of admiration and loathing—a unique conflict of emotions to be settled over a beer.

We exited the bull pen and the noise of work resumed behind us. Out of sight, out of mind. Already forgotten.

That was for the best.

Kellogg thumbed a button for the elevator, an old-time piece of equipment straight out of the dark ages. It was my understanding that law enforcement organizations have always been underfunded, hence the Precinct's outdated infrastructure. Something about giving the criminals a fighting chance, I guess.

A number on the wall indicated the elevator sat three floors above us on the thirteenth.

The knot of anxiety in my stomach added another convoluted loop and whorl with every passing second, afraid somebody might see me out of the interrogation room, and start asking questions. Questions I didn't have good answers for.

A bead of sweat trickled down my nose, which had picked up an offensive stale odor tainting the air. The smell of exertion and dried blood. It took me a second to realize it was me I smelled—a fact that didn't make the scent any less offensive.

"Hello?" a voice behind me said.

I turned, but nobody was there.

Even on the most aggressive timetable it was too soon to be suffering auditory hallucinations from the Quick. It wasn't until the voice spoke again that I realized I'd heard it through a different set of ears.

BLINK.

Brandt stood in the lab doorway, arms crossed. Langdon, the tech, stared blankly back.

"Oh, sorry. I'm uh…cleaning," I said through Langdon, unsure how long Brandt had watched him idling in the center of the room.

Brandt didn't budge from his position at the door. His eyes locked onto mine in an ocular wrestling match to assert dominance. But I was playing the part of a lab tech, and broke the stare first, afraid if I held it too long he would see through the drone, beyond to the other side where I lurked in shadows, pulling the strings.

"What did you call me down here for?" His words were the verbal equivalent of checking his forearm for the time. They dripped with the implied meaning, *You'd better hurry.*

"Yes, of course…that."

I turned towards a large apparatus on the wall that, to my expert eyes, could've been an oven. While brainstorming a plausible story to feed Brandt, something chirped in the periphery of my mind. I transferred back to my own body as two uniformed officers exited the elevator. I lead Kellogg into the small metal box, pressed the button for the parking garage, and blinked back into Langdon.

"Are you okay?" Brandt's hands were a bruising vice grip on Langdon's shoulder.

These guys were zombies without me behind the controls. Their apparent lack of mental acuity would appear odd, but nobody would suspect a viral nanobot had hijacked their bodies, so in that respect I was safe.

"Uh…yeah. It's been a lo—" I said.

Brandt held up a hand, ending the sentence midway. "Show me what you brought me down here for. Now."

"Of course; do you have the device with you?"

Brandt withdrew the Hive Mind from his breast pocket and placed it in Langdon's hand. I squinted at the device, but surprisingly the tech didn't have optical implants, a useful upgrade for a man in his line of work. Because of his weak eyes I squinted that much harder.

Not that there was anything to see. The nanites that had once swarmed its smooth black surface had relocated themselves to the bodies of my slaves. But this was called misdirection, which was all about selling the act.

DING.

I craned Langdon's head up, expecting to see a bell floating somewhere near the ceiling before realizing I had again crossed my senses.

BLINK.

Kellogg ran in stand-by mode beside me as a short woman with the body of a pit bull, and the face to match, joined us in the elevator. Her badge said Lieutenant Sanders, another new face on the force. I didn't search her in the database, though I suspected she wouldn't extend me the same courtesy.

The door slid shut and the elevator resumed its ascent. Not sure who invited it, but an awkward silence joined us. An indefinable quality filled the air, and I knew the Lieutenant was about to become a problem. She wasn't being shy about mean mugging me. Her eyes flitted between myself and our destination illuminated on the wall of buttons to her left. Those same eyes glazed over with a morning frost, checking my file, I guessed.

Sanders' posture tightened, almost imperceptibly, around the shoulders as the fog obscuring her pupils lifted.

"Officer Kellogg, where are you taking Mr. Mandel?" she said, positioning herself between us and the door. Her fingers melted over the butt of the pistol at her hip.

Can't catch a break.

CHAPTER TWENTY-SIX
Fighting Like A Girl

BLINK.

I redirected the highway of neurons in Kellogg's brain to form a reply. "Prisoner transfer, ma'am. Orders from the Director himself."

"Director?"

"Director of Division Security, Daniel Brandt."

Sanders frowned, quietly deciding my fate.

Things were falling apart. By now Brandt would know something was wrong with Langdon, which meant my window of opportunity was about to become a brick wall; there might still be a way through, but it would require a lot more force. Force I didn't want to use on my former colleagues.

I needed to get back to the lab and do damage control, but I couldn't leave my zombie bodyguard alone with Sanders.

The Lieutenant turned, without taking her eyes off me, and pressed a red button on the wall. The elevator jerked to a stop, stuck between floors nineteen and twenty.

"Ma'am?" I said through Kellogg.

She held up a finger and said, "I've never heard of Director Brandt."

Shit, of course she hadn't. Nobody had.

"You know how those guys are. A bunch of cloak-and-dagger types, but if I keep them waiting, they're gonna rip me a new one. Brandt's meeting us in the garage. You're welcome to come with and talk to him yourself."

Sanders reflected on her options. Silence sat in the corner, the invisible fourth person bearing witness to the final moments before a duel.

Two gunmen baked beneath a blazing sun, fingers itching to be filled with a handful of metal. An extension of the arm bent on destruction.

The problem with this duel: only one of us had a gun.

Lieutenant Sanders' arm tightened, becoming a flexed ball of muscle. The tendon running down her forearm and into her hand twitched. Her finger tapped her holster.

So much for doing this quietly.

I didn't wait for Sanders to draw her weapon and put a round through my heart. Instead, I ramped my speed implants and burst forward. Kellogg and Langdon were torn from my mental grasp by the current of competing stimuli, but they weren't my problem at the moment.

Sanders was fast and ready, a bad combination that moved her straight to the top of my worry-about-this list.

She pivoted and deflected my fist with her left hand while drawing her pistol with the right. I ducked and swept her back leg with mine. The Lieutenant hovered in the air before the rules of physics got their act together and dragged her to the ground. Her head bounced off the wall.

Kellogg pawed the sleep away from his eyes. I reached for the pistol at his side, but something smashed into my knee, stopping me short, and dropping me hard.

Sanders lay on her side, leg extended in a pose accentuating the fact she'd just kicked my leg out from under me. I rolled back and thrust a foot at her face with all the grace of a newborn puppy. It wasn't a pretty maneuver, and she saw it coming.

The spasming kick went wide of her head, connecting firmly with the wall. Barbed spurs danced up my leg. Sanders snatched my exposed ankle between fingers more closely resembling vice grips than human digits. She tightened her grip and something in my leg cracked. I choked back a scream, and lashed out with my other leg. It didn't matter what I hit so long as it belonged to her.

Anything to break that inhuman grip pulverizing my bones.

My foot found a home six inches south of her armpit. She gasped, but the pressure on my leg didn't wane. I retaliated with another kick to her side. Bone fractured beneath the blow with a satisfying snap. Sanders released her grip with a grunt, and curled to one side, nursing her ribs.

Rolling to my knees, I brought my fist down in an overhead wrecking-ball punch learned only in bar fights. It was a maneuver adapted from our primitive ancestors insisting on using rocks to bash the skull of a gazelle.

Sanders was scrappy. She bucked like a fish out of water. Her arms shot forward, snaring my hand on its downward path while encircling my torso with her legs. The tables had turned so quickly, I didn't have time to consider what I'd done wrong.

From her back, Sanders pinned my arm to her body. When I tried pulling away, she loosened her grip and bucked a second time, compromising my balance and pitching me forward. Shifting her hips, she wrapped her legs around my head, and went full python on my throat.

Oxygen-rich blood, making the red-eye flight to my brain, was put on standby. The world smudged as if I were staring through a rain-freckled window. I punched desperately at her broken ribs with my free hand, but she wouldn't budge. Each punch was weaker than the last; seconds remained between me and blackout.

Flashbulbs popped as if paparazzi were hiding behind my eyelids. Last chance.

BLINK.

I jumped into Kellogg. The world cratered and puckered. My brain forgot how to operate a human.

Transcendental out-of-body experience for the evening: I saw myself lying on top of Sanders, her legs pretzeled around my head. Clumps of blond hair stuck to her sweat-slicked scalp. My body lay motionless in her grasp. Playing possum, or maybe just dead. Specifics were unclear. Everything muddled. Couldn't discern which.

Kellogg's hand responded slowly to my command. It moved clumsily toward his holster. The clasp gave way to his molestation and freed the pistol at his side with a soft click. In that final moment of lucidity, everything shifted and warped, expanded and contracted. I looked down the barrel of the vortex pistol with Kellogg's eyes, and fired a low-energy, high-dispersal round into Sanders' face.

Her body rag dolled. Out cold before her head clanged against the metal floor.

BLINK.

I gasped for air. Clarity seeped through the cracks formed by ruptured capillaries in bloodshot eyes. I breathed through the roar of fresh oxygen-laced blood being delivered to my skull.

It wasn't over yet. With the aid of the handrail I hoisted myself up, and tentatively weighted my ankle. Molten lava soaked into my marrow at the spot Sanders had crushed bone.

Shit.

I collapsed to my knee and rummaged through Sanders' pockets until I found her police-issued vial of stimheal. I popped the lid and stabbed the needle into my calf. Liquid ice flowed into my veins, an iceberg breaking off exponentially until everything below my knee was numbed by the prickles of nanobots working to mend broken tissue and bone.

Hobbling to my feet, I reached for the button that would resume our ascent to the parking garage, but stopped when I remembered Brandt.

My finger floated in dead space, calculating our odds of making it to the garage if I set the elevator into motion again. They were not good.

Escape became an ever more remote possibility with each passing second. The silver lining, on an otherwise piss-soaked day, was there hadn't been any alarms. Yet. When somebody got privy, that would be that. Lockdown. Nothing in, nothing out.

BLINK.

Langdon stood where I'd left him. Brandt was gone.

An officer stood at the door, presumably to keep my drone inside.

He saw me moving and said, "You feeling alright? Kinda went catatonic."

"Yeah, I'm fine. I uh...I installed some new upgrades the other day. Still haven't adjusted to them, I guess."

"I hear ya, nearly lost my mind when I got my cochlear implants. Flies buzzing around the room were like jet engines. Terrible times. But you'll be alright, there's a medic on the way up to check you out. Make sure there's no damage to your thinking muscle," he said, tapping his temple.

"Thanks, but that's not necessary. Sometimes I kind of...drift off. I'm feeling better now."

"All the same, that guy—Brandt, was it?—wanted you to get checked out," he said. "By the way, what upgrade did you get? I wanna know what to avoid."

"Processing speed." I scanned my surroundings, hoping something would spark a moment of inspiration, but the room was full of tools and instruments I knew nothing about.

"Man, that must be nice. I mean, when you're not locked out of your own brain, that is."

"Yeah, being locked out suc—"

Bingo. The answer had been there, but I hadn't made the connection.

"Hey, I'm sorry, but I have a couple tests I need to finish up," I said. "Let me know when that medic gets here, yeah?"

The officer quirked an eyebrow and said, "Sure."

I dipped a toe into the Stream through Langdon's mind before committing to the full plunge. It was a third-party experience unlike any I'd felt before. Not necessarily a bad thing, but certainly not good.

The Stream felt wrong; a numb handshake offered out of obligation, indifferent to the recipient. If that's how the Stream felt to Regulars, no wonder they hated Intuits. Even with my Stream Intuition, guiding Langdon's mind through the hyper-reality interface was like driving a forklift in reverse through a field of sludge. His mental fingers fumbled through firewalls in search of our destination: the Precinct's security system.

To make the illusion of digital code manageable, I projected the imagery of a castle. We crossed the lowered drawbridge, wooden boards squeaking underfoot, and entered the inner sanctum of the building's security.

Once across, I raised the bridge, and took control of the building.

The universe responded to my touch.

I was the system's god.

And then the high-pitched shriek of the building's alarm pierced my inner zen.

Lockdown.

CHAPTER TWENTY-SEVEN
Crossing Lines Drawn In The Sand

The sterile white lights of the lab morphed into strobing red, casting the world into long, distorted shadows of blood. I'd braced for the alarm, but hearing that tooth-numbing wail through three sets of ears nearly overwhelmed me.

I bit my lip and broke the skin. The pain pulled me into its focusing embrace. Somehow I maintained control of my drones despite the exodus of thoughts fleeing my skull. I partitioned sections of my mind, reducing auditory feedback in myself and Kellogg, so I could continue operating through Langdon.

That's where I needed to be. Lose control of Langdon, lose control of the building.

In Langdon's mind the castle metaphor shifted to become a miniature version of the Police Precinct itself.

I grabbed the virtual building and cracked it along the vertical axis to get to the juicy guts of the Precinct's innards. Blue and red dots flowed through the veins of each floor. Blue dots were humans; red dots were bots.

Nobody had formed a coordinated response in the wake of the lockdown. Each floor responded differently. Some were a flurry of activity, with blue dots scurrying about, while on others the dots barely moved. That was a function of location rather than concern. Locations where nobody could enter or leave, regardless of desire. Labs and holding cells, for example.

I opened Langdon's eyes and glanced at the thick blast door covering the entrance to the lab. The officer on guard stared at Langdon, eyes wide, with a gun in his hand.

"What's going on?" he said, his throbbing carotid artery visible through the thin sheath of skin covering his flushed throat. The sudden spike of adrenaline had him tweaked and ready for a fight.

"Not sure," I said, trying to calm his nerves. "Maybe a drill?"

"No, this ain't no drill. They don't drop the blast doors in a drill. This is something else. I think we're under attack."

"Whoa, just calm down and take a deep breath. I'm in the Stream now, I'll see if I can get some answers."

"Good idea. See if you can get in touch with that Brandt guy, I'll bet he knows what's going on."

"Sure," I said, letting my gaze drop to the pistol in his hand. "In the meantime, do you mind putting that away?"

The officer looked at his hand in confusion before taking my meaning. "Oh shit, yeah. Sorry 'bout that. Reflexes, ya know?"

"Of course."

I blinked into the Stream. The Peacekeeper Internal Technology Unit fought me for control of the building. Moving up from ground level, they returned each floor to standby status, taking back the building slowly but surely. PIT were the best minds Time Vice had, but they weren't good enough. Though, with the handicap of operating the Stream through Langdon, it wasn't a frolic through fields of buttercups for me, either.

First order of business: locate and isolate Brandt. I pinged his location and the screen shifted perspective. It zoomed in close enough that I could read ID tags floating above the red and blue dots. On the tenth floor Brandt was surrounded by five blue dots.

Each floor could be dissected into four quadrants by sliding blast doors used to quarantine the building in case of attack, or threat of a biological contaminant. One by one I brought those doors down on the tenth floor.

Brandt's little dot separated from the pack, moving swiftly in the opposite direction of the rapidly closing doors. The blast doors slammed shut, one after another, but somehow he managed to stay ahead. The other blue dots hadn't made it more than a handful of feet before being quartered off.

Brandt's dot zipped past the final blast door and into the stairwell—a location that served my purposes. He'd be free to move up and down, but access to each floor remained sealed shut. The stairway was a roomy prison, but a prison nonetheless.

I let those thoughts simmer and turned to the second objective, getting to the parking garage.

Four elevator shafts running the vertical length of the building were represented on the display by faint red lines. They were in lockdown along with the rest of the building.

It required creative jiggering on my part to coax the security system into unlocking only our elevator, a function whoever programmed the building hadn't intended. But the building's infrastructure was a hand-me-down from a simpler time and a simpler encryption. Nobody, I guess, had thought to update it.

The ground swayed.

BLINK.

Back inside my own skin, I watched the numbers sitting above the door climb higher. At the top, the elevator shuddered to a halt. Through Langdon I studied the half-dozen blue dots milling about the parking garage.

Two guards, two attendants, and three random visitors in the process of coming or going.

I took a calming breath and opened the elevator. The doors slid apart, revealing the parking garage bathed in red.

The ever-shifting pattern of light and shadow was nauseating.

I jumped to Kellogg, maneuvering him to follow half a step behind, his pistol concealed behind my back.

I did a quick mental survey of the people standing outside the security booth. The two guards were obvious enough in their black uniforms, but a third man stood out as a possible plain-clothes officer. One of the guards stepped out from the booth, hand resting on the butt of the gun at his side, a casual stance with a hint of malice.

"Hold up," he said, stroking the long whiskers of a mustache stretching from one ear to the other with his free hand. "Where are you two headed?"

"Trying to figure what's going on is all," Kellogg said.

The guard handed us a stare of pure paranoia and said, "How'd you get that elevator running?"

"Not a clue, but thank God it did. Shit, I never knew it, but turns out I don't like tight spaces. Was afraid we'd never get out," Kellogg said. I tried making him laugh, but it sounded like starting a dying Dragonfly. "Any idea what this lockdown is all about?"

The second guard poked his head out of the office, gave us the once over, and stepped out, circling us nonchalantly in the opposite direction of his partner.

I wasn't sure what kind of bulletin, if any, Brandt had issued before the lockdown went into effect, but these two characters were acting with a high degree of paranoia that made my trigger finger itch.

But it wasn't until the man I'd pegged as a plain-clothes officer shuffled to the right, into my blind spot, that I knew the gig was up.

Can never do things the easy way. Not today, at least. Maybe tomorrow.

I thought back to Sanders lying unconscious on the floor of the elevator. I'd crossed a line. One I couldn't return from. Turned my back on an oath I'd taken, an obligation. Betrayed the people drawn into the crossfire by duty and honor.

A seed of guilt sitting in my gut blossomed into full-blown regret. It sank its roots deep, latching on and refusing to let go for what I'd done to Sanders, to Raines, to the countless innocents I'd betrayed, and would continue betraying, before I'd taken my revenge on Malcolm.

Kellogg was about to become another one of those betrayals.

Per my command he sprinted forward, arms flapping like a bird trying to take flight. These guys were the equivalent of parking attendants with stun guns, so they wouldn't kill Kellogg, but using him as a diversion made my heart hiccup through the next few beats. Guilt would have to wait.

I activated my implants, then fired a round at the plain-clothes officer to my right while dropping to a knee and rolling left. It hit before the man had retrieved his pistol from the holster hidden beneath his windbreaker.

At the end of the roll I popped to my feet and tracked a guard diving for cover behind a parked Dragonfly. My nanocomp locked on and dilated time. He moved slowly, giving me plenty of time to fire a three-shot salvo. The first ring missed, but the second and third found their marks. The officer hit the ground in a crumpled pile of defunct body parts.

Swinging back, I sighted the guard with his weapon drawn on zombie Kellogg. Poor Kellogg charged forward, oblivious to the world of hurt awaiting him. Actually, that was probably a good thing.

The guard pulled the trigger, sending a tendril of electricity arcing into Kellogg. The drone officer flew across the mostly empty parking garage before landing with a gut-wrenching slap of flesh on the concrete.

Without a clear shot on the guard, I ducked behind a Dragonfly panel van and dropped to my belly to survey the scene from under the vehicle.

Three bodies; two guards and one Kellogg. The man who'd tasered Kellogg had disappeared, along with the three civilians, into the guard's station.

Luckily, I had no intention of going in that direction.

I disappeared into the jungle of machinery, slinking between rows of Dragonflys, until I found a vehicle that suited my needs.

Well, if not my needs, then definitely my wants.

A burnt black Magnum-class Dragonfly with an engine that purred like a tiger fresh from a nap and the kind of curves that throw backs out from heads turning so quickly.

Flashy, expensive, but most importantly for what I needed, a ridiculously powerful Dragonfly.

In the handful of seconds it took to make a bad decision, I'd hacked the Dragonfly's security system, and sat behind the wheel.

BLINK.

Back inside Langdon, and the officer on duty stared at me like I'd sprouted a deity from my forehead. From his look of concern, it wasn't a good deity.

"You okay?" he asked.

So close to the finish line; I didn't bother with a response.

I dove Langdon into the Stream, a perfect entry, no splash. The Precinct display showed the bottom ten floors had been cleared by PIT. Thankfully, Brandt's dot was still trapped in the stairwell.

I zeroed in on the nearest exit in relation to my position in the parking garage.

BLINK.

I tickled the gas pedal and the Dragonfly reared like a mustang passing a kidney stone. I whipped the wheel hard to the left. My spleen wasn't buckled in, and shot up into my throat. The vehicle spun one hundred and eighty degrees before I slammed the brakes.

Nothing but blue skies and an open blast door in front of me. I was practically doing a happy dance.

A happy dance that came to an abrupt stop when two Peacekeeper Kestrels swung into view flying in a tight formation that barred my path just beyond the exit.

CHAPTER TWENTY-EIGHT
The Sky Is Falling

My Dragonfly's computer couldn't tell if their weapons were locked on, but I operated under the assumption that they were.

Didn't much matter. Only way out was forward.

Bad decisions have a way of trickling into one another. Keep making them long enough, and soon they're all you've got left.

My foot became a lead brick dropped on the accelerator. The Fly lurched, ramming my skull against the headrest, and tossing my thoughts out the back window.

Rows of parked Dragonflys passed in a blur. Despite my collision course, neither vehicle showed interest in moving.

They hadn't thrown any bullets at me, so I figured it could have been worse.

Until they started firing.

A thread of bullets glowing red with heat ripped into the Dragonfly.

I sank deeper into my chair while bartering with the Fly to go faster. Bullets poked holes in the smart-metal frame. They pinged off the hood, a soft pitter-patter of children's feet on wooden floors.

Lots of children.

The Dragonfly's sound-dampening interior held up amazingly despite the brutality of the damages it sustained. I pulled back on the altitude adjuster, allowing the Fly to climb towards the ceiling, and out of the line of fire. Holding that trajectory until the last possible instant, I dropped the nose and dipped through the open blast door.

The Dragonfly erupted from the building like ashy magma spewing from a volcano. A velocity that put me, unfortunately, on a crash course with the Kestrel on the right. Physics carried me forward too quickly to turn, leaving only one option.

I cut the power to the thrusters beneath the vehicle and the nose dove sharply. Yanking hard to the left, I accelerated into the descent. The roof of the Dragonfly skimmed the bottom rung of the Kestrel on the left as I continued my engine-assisted plummet.

Every organ south of my stomach jockeyed for position in my throat. The pressure and speed of descent turned my eyelids into sandbags crushing my vision.

A silvery-gray Dragonfly laid on the horn as I dipped below the lowest level of rush-hour traffic. I fired up the thrusters and leveled out. The weight crushing my brain subsided. I glanced at the rear-view mirror with lighter eyeballs.

The Peacekeeper Kestrels were at home maneuvering the narrow city corridors. My commercial class Dragonfly, made for commuting, was no match for them.

Couldn't outrun them, but maybe I could out-crazy them.

My stomach curled into itself as I banked right into a corridor of tightly packed buildings lining the fringe of the Financial District. The buildings flew past, pushing my reflexes to the limits of their abilities.

I darted into a narrow alleyway formed by two buildings overhanging one another like a couple drunks bumping chests in the final moments before throwing fists. My guardian angel was somewhere in my gut, using my liver and intestines to hold on.

The Peacekeepers broke pursuit, opting to go over the buildings rather than through. The car got squirrelly. I over-corrected, and left my side-view mirror on the building to my right as a memento. I jerked back to compensate, but only managed to pinball off the building to my left, which took the other mirror for its troubles.

Down two mirrors, but still alive, so the math worked in my favor.

A third building, at the end of the alley, had something to say about that.

I slowed, rubbing the building on the right, but otherwise squeaking through the T-intersection with only paint left behind. Overhead, I saw the sliver of sky afforded by the opening between buildings. A silhouetted Kestrel kept pace, a shadow I couldn't outrun. I accelerated out of the turn, dashing for the daylight that appeared at the end of the alley.

A second Kestrel decided that would be a climactic moment to drop down in front of me. I pushed the brake pedal through the floorboards. Brakes, it turns out, were not designed to stop a moving vehicle that quickly, but I did my best to convince them they could, anyways.

The Dragonfly threw me forward, giving the seatbelt a chance to catch me in its stringy embrace. It did, and for services rendered, it took all the air I'd been storing in my lungs. It beat going through the windshield, though.

The Kestrel and I hovered, two insects squaring off over a dollop of pollen; however in this instance, it was the equivalent of a wasp versus a gnat.

I didn't like my chances.

A rod descended from the undercarriage of the Kestrel. A blue beam of light flickered twice from the tip of the pole.

I was trapped between buildings with no way to get clear of the electro-magnetic pulse. The light hit me. The Dragonfly powered down. I fell, along with the multi-ton vehicle, to the ground.

Impact was a tuning fork set to my harmonic resonance and placed against my coccyx. The reverberations shivered through my bones. My head bashed the steering wheel. Teeth sank into the fleshy innards of my cheek. Blood squirted from an open wound on my forehead.

My head lolled onto the headrest while my mouth filled with the bitter tang of copper. I spat what blood I could onto the leather seat beside me.

Drool leaked onto my cheek, but I didn't care. I tried opening the door to the Dragonfly. It wouldn't budge. Very little gusto remained. I scraped what I could from the bottom of the barrel and drove my shoulder into the bent doorframe.

It gave way, creaking open on damaged hinges as a second EMP released its warbling blast.

Seized by instinct, I covered my head.

A second later, the Peacekeeper Kestrel crashed to the ground. Its collision with the ground was as jarring as it was inevitable. Billowing smoke filled the alleyway.

I stepped out into the haze on wobbly legs, inhaling putrid mouthfuls of early evening air. In response, four Peacekeepers emerged from the wreckage.

I looked behind me for the exit and considered running. There were a multitude of reasons why that was never gonna happen. Chief amongst them was I didn't fancy getting shot in the back. A close second, if I was being honest with myself, was that I simply didn't feel like running.

Sometimes, I can tell when I'm beaten. I'd pushed my luck as far as she'd go. I dropped my pistol onto the driver's seat, and took a step towards the Keepers. The pain from my splintered ankle had faded, but the bone felt weak and tingly, which caused me to stumble. Gravity made an awkward example of me and dragged me to the ground.

I stared into the remains of a puddle filled with substances unknown. The dim light of dusk settled on the fringe of the cesspool, making it glow magenta. The mystery fluid was probably not water, but that didn't matter. The oily soap scum offered an adequate reflection.

Two black eyes had turned to purple squash. My right eye was a shock of burst capillaries, which complemented the cut running the length of my cheek. I traced the edge of the raised skin and felt nothing. The nanobots did what they could to get me to a hundred percent. Nobody bothered pointing out the futility of their efforts.

Less than eight hours left. The nanites should phone this one in.

Chunks of gravel and broken safety glass chewed into the sensitive undersides of my palms as I propped myself up against the grill of the Dragonfly.

I'd kill for a Quick hit. I patted down my pockets with a junkie's optimism, hoping maybe, just maybe, the god of bad decisions had slipped me one when I wasn't looking.

Nothing.

The wind shifted. But it wasn't the wind itself I noticed first. It was the four silhouetted Peacekeepers standing in front of me. They looked up in one coordinated movement as if they were marionettes tethered to a single line.

I followed their gaze, and saw the belly of a Kestrel I figured would be my ride back to the Precinct. That is, until I saw the two men dangling from the side of the vehicle with weapons drawn.

The detail in that picture that mattered was that their guns were pointed down, but not at me.

Which got me replaying the image of the Kestrel crapping out of the sky. A small detail, the importance of which my mind had skimmed over.

A disembodied voice boomed over a loud speaker, "Drop your weapons."

I felt reasonably sure it wasn't talking to me.

The Peacekeepers hesitated, no doubt weighing their options against an opponent with the high ground. Nobody in that posse of land-dwellers liked their chances, and they discarded their weapons. Rifles rattled on the ground like cheap, heavy plastic toys.

The weapons spun, their shiny black sides scraping against loose rock. One rifle did a full rotation before coming to a stop with its barrel pointed at me.

My first thought was of Raines and Ash swooping in on their little black pony to save the damsel in distress. I was so happy I could swoon, but opted to remain seated.

A black cord plopped to the ground fifteen feet to the right. My ride.

I hobbled to the nearest soldier lying on the ground, ignoring the shards of bone jabbing the pulpy flesh around my ankle. The soldier committed to the act of surrendering and kept his attention fixed on the ground as I rummaged through his pockets to come up with another vial of stimheal. I held it up to the waning light and stared into the face of my savior.

I injected the nanobots. They merged with my blood instantly.

God wrung my brain like a wet sponge, releasing a rush of endorphins. Endorphins that told me everything would be okay. That things would work out.

I did my best impression of a cowboy exiting a saloon, sauntering to the black cord dangling from the Kestrel like the world was my oyster.

And hell, maybe it was.

CHAPTER TWENTY-NINE
The Past Doesn't Forget Us

The world was not my oyster. Not even close.

It's a spiteful lover, giving affection one moment and stabbing me in the throat the next.

I was experiencing one of those throat-stabbing moments.

It's rare, but on occasion, you see something so extraordinarily out of place that it requires a second, sometimes even a third look to process. My mind, on its fourth double take, did another loop de loop.

In the Kestrel two men, with nanite-infused muscles, sat on a couch struggling to support their combined bulk. They looked like two rattlesnakes worth of mean, but they weren't the reason my brain was performing advanced aerial maneuvers. No, credit for that belonged to the man sitting across from them.

Pale skin freckled a hairless skull. Thin eyebrows converged, malnourished worms above eyes that couldn't twinkle.

Malcolm Wolfe.

"Wow," Malcolm said, gesturing to a sliver of open seat between the two men I'd dubbed Nitro and Doug in my mind. "I admit, I'm impressed. You've really gone for it, seized the day and all that."

I squeezed between the two super-sized bodyguards while calculating the time it would take to cover the distance separating me from Malcolm. If I could move like Ash he'd be dead before he finished his next breath.

But I'm not that fast. Not by a large margin. More likely, one of the guards with pistons for arms, and hands upgraded with bio-steel skeletons, would crack my skull before my cheeks left the seat.

They didn't bother cuffing me, an insult I told myself I'd make them regret, but who was I kidding?

The only people I cause pangs of regret are loved ones.

Malcolm was safe on that account.

"So this is it, huh?" I said, releasing the tension in my spine and sinking deeper into the cushion of muscle on either side. "You got me. You win. Now what?"

The stimheal worked magic behind the curtain of my mind, tinkering and tweaking, until I floated like a rainbow. A weird analogy, but with more endorphins than blood surging through narrowed arteries, it made a certain kind of sense to me.

"You have something I want."

I burped out a laugh. "You're kidding, right?"

"Nope."

"What on earth could I have that you want?"

"Well, I had hoped for the cube, but I'll settle for your memories."

Everybody wanted my memories. Everybody but me, that is. The cube was a different story; a mystery rather than a tragedy.

"Good riddance. Hope they treat you as poorly as they have me."

"Oh, I'm certain they won't, because unlike you I see how it all comes together. I see the big picture."

"Does it show me kicking your ass?"

Malcolm smirked and said, "No. I'm afraid that's only in your head."

"Don't discount it. Seems the space between my ears is gaining value these days."

"That it is, but only for a little while longer." Malcolm pivoted in his chair and grabbed a briefcase from the floor beside him. "I'm curious, Tom, have they told you why you're here? Why you in particular?"

I shook my head.

"Thought not." Malcolm thumbed a button on the case and the latches popped like a champagne-bottle cork. He reached inside and pulled out a small cube similar to the one I'd taken from the Vault. "Do you know what this is?"

"A memory drive?"

"Close," he said, twirling the device between nimble, bird-boned fingers. "It's called a Mobius Cube. Adam created it, but I perfected it. Adam doesn't share credit, but we know the truth, eh?" Malcolm winked like a snake charming a rabbit from its hole.

Casual references to this Adam character kept coming up. Judging by the context it seemed safe to say he wasn't a low-level player in this game. Beyond that, I didn't have a clue.

"From where I'm sitting, it's just a shiny metal box." I smirked for good measure, an act more for my benefit than his.

"It is shiny, huh?" Malcolm held the cube to the light as if he'd never noticed it before. Billions of refracted rainbows danced across the inside of the Kestrel.

"So, what makes it so special?"

"What it holds."

"Which is?"

"Thoughts."

"Okay," I said, adopting a strategy of playing stupid, a role becoming increasingly familiar. "What kind of thoughts?"

"All of them." Malcolm inserted a pregnant pause. It stretched, came to term, and grew into full-blown silence.

I urged him to continue with my eyebrows, but he wasn't getting the message. After twenty seconds of staring at one another I caved and asked the question he'd been waiting to hear. "Huh?"

"This cube is capable of housing every thought you've ever had. It stores the digital footprint of your physical mind."

"Bullshit." The word flew from my mouth.

"Not bullshit."

"You can't make a copy of the brain."

I mean, I didn't think you could. At the very least, it sounded like something you shouldn't do.

"Nobody said anything about making copies; it merely transfers."

"You're losing me again." I observed Nitro to see if he had followed along better than me. The lumbering ox nodded as if he understood every damn word, which left me feeling like the only kid in class whose hand painting of a turkey comes out looking like a multi-colored rock. "Transferring from what to where?"

"From here," Malcolm held a finger to his temple, and then gently lifted the cube in his hand, "to here."

I chewed on the implications. Assuming Malcolm wasn't stringing me along for the sake of torturing a dying man—a big assumption given his proclivities—meant he'd discovered a way for his consciousness to live on without his body.

A fate worse than death, I thought.

I voiced that opinion.

"No, no, you misunderstand," Malcolm said. "A mind can't live in the Mobius Cube indefinitely. The brain has too many sensory adaptations. Close the mind in on itself and it goes crazy. There has to be a physical release."

"Then why transfer your mind to the cube in the first place?"

"It acts as a receiver for an incoming consciousness. That consciousness remains here until it can be uploaded to a new vessel."

"Another cube?" I said, but the words had already filled in the blank. "No. Another brain…"

The words plopped out of my mouth and spilled to the floor. A mess that couldn't be cleaned. Disorder that could never be restored.

Malcolm clapped his hands slowly. The sound of one man playing patty cake—a sad sound if ever there was one.

"You're a coward. All of this just to bypass the Life Tracker 'cause you're afraid to die?"

"I wasn't born to die."

"Humans weren't meant to live forever."

"Then I suppose it's good," Malcolm said, licking his lips, drawing the moment out for a climactic flourish, "that I'm not human."

"Okay," I said, mentally reviewing Malcolm's file and concluding the ingredient I'd been overlooking in trying to understand him was the tiny caveat that he was bat shit crazy. "Then...what are you?"

"The better question is, what are we?" he said with a wink.

A decade spent in a Stream dream had fractured Malcolm's mind beyond repair, I concluded. Masked reality in a delusional haze of its own creation.

"You lost part of yourself in Pause, didn't you? The non-crazy part."

"I lost the only part of me that mattered well before Pause, Tom. An ignorant thief stole her from me." Malcolm's eyes darkened, two smoldering scales plucked from a dragon's spine. "But you weren't ignorant at the time, were you?"

"Me? Now I'm to blame for your insanity?"

"That's not a recent development."

"To me it is."

"I suppose that's my fault. It was my virus, after all, that reduced the great hope of Castle to nothing more than a drooling human." Malcolm beamed at that last part.

I sifted through my memories for clarity, hoping the nanites Devers had given me would offer some insight. Hoping, however, had no effect, and the invisible barrier separating me from the answers locked inside my brain remained.

"You're on a spirit quest, aren't you?" Malcolm said. "I can see your gears churning through the muck, deciphering the gaps. You'll get there. Your memories are resurfacing even as we speak."

The energy to play games drained out through my feet and into the floorboards of the jet. I replayed Malcolm's words in my head and locked onto something I hadn't wanted to hear.

"Her?" I said, edging slowly into the darkness, afraid of what lurked there. "You said 'an ignorant thief stole her from me'"

"Yes."

"Who?"

"You know."

"I don't." But I feared I did.

"Diana," Malcolm said, his hands turned to white-knuckled fists capable of crushing coal into diamonds.

I shook my head. "No."

"You're not the only one to ever love her. At this point, I wonder if you can even say you knew her."

Revelations in the past twenty-four hours had cast doubt on the answer to that question. That Malcolm was right was the barb that couldn't be extracted without tearing a chunk of my heart out alongside it. The question wriggled through my innards, the worm burrowing through, tearing me apart at the seams.

"Let me tell you about your precious Diana. She loved me first. Before you ever existed, it was me. Only me."

That couldn't be true. He was lying. Getting inside my head so I'd do the dirty work of torturing myself.

I told myself not to play his game, but the scab had to be picked. "Then why did you kill her?"

"I didn't kill her." Malcolm sank back into his chair; the bravado leached into the cushion along with his anger. In its absence it left something else. He rubbed his hairless cheek, eyes cast downward at a spot thousands of yards past the floorboards. "I tried to save her."

"That's not how I remember it."

"Your memory is not the most reliable source."

"Bullshit, I saw you."

"Did you?" he said, with genuine interest.

I'd watched that particular memory on repeat for the last decade. Knew every gasp escaping Diana's lips, the feel of her warm blood both slick and sticky against my skin. Malcolm standing in the corner, his face a lesson in grim satisfaction.

I hadn't seen him pull the trigger, but he'd been the only one there. It had to be him. His look said it all.

My mind scrambled through the memory, pausing at the moment I burst through the doors and first saw Malcolm standing on the rim of pooling blood leaking from Diana's body. He had something in his hand. Something shiny. A gun.

His face, drawn in. Tight. Contorted. Puckered around the edges.

It wasn't the look I expected. It wasn't victory. It was grief.

A look I'd seen staring back in the mirror countless times.

How had I missed that? Was it there before? Were the nanites repairing parts of my damaged memory, or had I chosen not to see?"

"If it wasn't you." My voice was a whisper against the cacophony of life. "Then who?"

Malcolm titled his head, his eyes full with what could almost be called sadness. "You."

I shook my head, refusing to go along on that one. Even the most self-loathing part of my psyche refused to accept that blame. I let her down, sure. Failed to save her, undoubtedly.

But I did not kill her.

"I didn't put a bullet in her stomach and leave her to bleed out on the floor."

"True, but that is not what killed her."

A riptide of rage churned through me, dredging from below the surface all the hurt and pain I'd promised myself. The sludge slithered through veins and into muscles, poisoning everything in its path with a black-tinted hatred.

It swelled. Hit its peak. Crested and then crashed down on me until every heartbeat boomed like a cannon. The acrid puff of black powder igniting my lungs drifted up and out my nostrils, firing me from my chair like a discharged bullet.

Arms extended, fingers inches away from Malcolm's throat. My world became a tunnel with a single destination. The edges were finger smudged. Details lost. None of that mattered.

All that mattered was ripping the lies from Malcolm's mouth.

But I didn't bridge the gap. Something thick, heavy, and resembling a tree branch fell on the back of my skull. The tunnel closed. Everything went black.

And then white.

And then black and white.

My sense of taste swapped places with my hearing. From my position on the floor, I tasted blood in my ears and heard groans with my teeth.

"No," I said, a feeble objection to Malcolm's accusation.

"I'm sorry to say, but yes." Malcolm leaned forward, his mouth inches from mine. "I would have saved her if you hadn't stopped me, Tom."

Nitro grabbed the back of my neck, plucked me from the floorboards, and tossed me into the chair beside him.

Now that I sat right side up, my senses returned to their original locations. Something rattled in my mouth. I tongued the offending object and spit into my hand. A pearly white molar rose from a glob of red, an iceberg floating upon a sea of blood.

"I didn't kill her." I kept with the same line of defense, my head swirling too much for any change in tactics.

"Nor did I," Malcolm said. "And true to my word, I'll show you. I'll give you the answers you seek. Give you the truth. Remove the block holding your memories at bay."

"Why?"

"Because knowing will break your heart. It'll hurt you more than I ever could." With an exertion only barely visible in the tremble of his bottom lip, he managed to keep the rest of his face impassive. "But nothing comes free, and you have something I need. Perhaps we make a trade. You get what's in here, and I get what's in there."

Malcolm held the Mobius Cube in his right hand and gestured towards my head. The light played along the edge of the device, making it appear sharp. A blade he was prepared to bury in my chest.

He gave a discreet nod. Nitro and Doug swiveled, grabbing me impossibly strong hands. I kicked and squirmed, but it was ineffectual against the combined strength of the two men.

Pinned. Overwhelmed. A shout broiled up from the depths of my being. "What are you doing?" I said through gritted teeth.

Malcolm hovered in front of my immobilized head, the Mobius Cube in his hand a latent threat of violence.

"I'm taking from you what you took from the Vault."

"I don't have the cube."

"It's not the cube itself I'm after. I want what was on the cube."

"Too bad it was blank."

"No, it wasn't. It was full. Brimming with life. A life hiding here, now." Malcolm stabbed a thin finger in the space between my eyes, wiggling it back and forth like a grub burrowing into my skull. "I'm going to relieve you of that burden. Take back what you stole from me. To do what you couldn't; I'm going to save Diana."

Diana?

That was the last thought I had before Malcolm touched the Mobius Cube to my forehead. My world shattered, dissolved, and scattered like sand tossed to the breeze.

CHAPTER THIRTY
Rememories

I drifted through the void. A disembodied wanderer. Destinations unknown.

No way signs. No markers. No context.

Blackness held me in its apathetic embrace. Both warm and cold. Discomfort on either side of the spectrum.

I closed my eyes to focus.

Flung out of my body, into a memory.

"Love, what's wrong?"

I stood in a field outside the city. The air was fresher, but not by much. Man's fingerprint smudged across nature's lens.

"Huh?" I said, rubbing my eyes with dirt-caked fingers. "How did we get here?"

"We drove, silly." Diana rolled onto tiptoes and kissed my nose. Shockwaves pulsed from the point where lips found skin.

I shuddered.

"I don't remember that."

She looked at me. Something shifted. It wasn't in her eyes. It was in her body.

It sagged.

Imploding into itself as if the weight of the world had compressed her into an ever-shrinking version of herself. She was suffering. A pain I'd been oblivious to.

"I don't remember much of anything," I continued, struggling through the labyrinth of my own mind. "What happened to me?"

"Nothing, you're perfect, sweetheart. Perfect." Diana put her hands on my hips. They were small, but strong. Her grip was firm.

She held me tight, trying to root me in that moment. Already I was drifting.

A cloud rolled past. Fog condensed over my mind's eye.

"Stay with me," she said, her voice a plea. She must see the cloud coming too.

I fought it, struggled against the tide, but I'm weak. The darkness inside me was too strong. It pulled me under, submerged me in its numbing embrace.

So tired.

Couldn't remember why I was fighting.

A tear rolled down Diana's cheek. I reached to wipe it away.

Diana on the edge of our bed. Toes skimming the floor. She kicked her feet back and forth; a child on a swing set.

I stood over her, speaking words I couldn't understand. Her eyes, covered in a film.

Distant. Lost. Searching.

She couldn't make connections. Could barely recognize me.

I barely recognized her.

This was our truth. Our reality. Our sickness.

Two souls torn apart. Minds incapable of remembering that which they forgot they'd forgotten.

I pounded my forehead, scouring for what I'd lost. Frustration overwhelmed me. A fever ran through my body. Chills followed by sweat. No consistency. No structure.

A moment of lucidity.

Mine.

Through Malcolm's virus-induced amnesia, I remembered.

Diana's mind, gone. Stolen. Taken by the man who'd taken mine. But it wasn't meant for her.

This was my fault. I couldn't stay away. I infected her.

Her memory, chewed through and left to rot. Rancid with the stink of maggots squirming through the worm-riddled holes of her mind.

I wanted to fix her, but I was broken, too. The moment drifted. A cloud across the sky.

Slipping away. Again.

I was forgetting her.

Forgetting myself.

I closed my eyes.

BLINK.

Diana on the edge of our bed. Toes skimming the floor. She kicked her feet back and forth; a child on a swing set.

I stood over her, speaking words I couldn't understand. Her eyes, covered in a film.

Distant. Lost. Searching.

She couldn't make connections. Could barely recognize me.

I barely recognized her.

This was our truth. Our reality. Our sickness.

Two souls torn apart. Minds incapable of remembering that which they forgot they'd forgotten.

I pounded my forehead, scouring for what I'd lost. Frustration overwhelmed me. A fever ran through my body. Chills followed by sweat. No consistency. No structure.

A moment of lucidity.

Mine.

Through Malcolm's virus-induced amnesia, I remembered.

Diana's mind, gone. Stolen. Taken by the man who'd taken mine. But it wasn't meant for her.

This was my fault. I couldn't stay away. I infected her.

Her memory, chewed through and left to rot. Rancid with the stink of maggots squirming through the worm-riddled holes of her mind.

I wanted to fix her, but I was broken, too. The moment drifted. A cloud across the sky.

Slipping away. Again.

I was forgetting her.

Forgetting myself.

I closed my eyes.

BLINK.

Sitting in traffic. Raines beside me. Following a lead. Something pinged me and I slipped into the Stream.

Diana. She was different, but I couldn't say how.

"I remember," she said, her eyes heavy with the weight of knowing.

"What do you remember?" I asked, confused.

"Everything. Everything he did to us."

"Who?"

"Malcolm."

I didn't know how to respond, so I didn't.

"I know where he is," she continued. "I'm going to stop him."

I tried to find traction. Progress. But clarity wouldn't come. Understanding eluded me.

"No." The word came out harsh. I yelled it into my mind, screamed it into the Stream. Diana didn't flinch. "Tell me. I'll take care of this. It's my responsibility. Don't go."

"I have to. While I still remember. It's my job, now. I'm sorry, love."

Then she was gone.

BLINK.

Crying.

Tears mixed with the traces of my soul, covering my cheek.

Covered in blood. Still warm.

Something heavy in my arms. Limp.

I looked down.

Diana's eyes were glass mirrors to the other side. Gone. Truly gone this time.

Her skin was pale. Too pale.

Streaks of red painted her cheeks, a warrior going into battle.

I cradled her neck with my arm. My other pawed at the strands of her blood-soaked hair, smoothing it back.

I rested my cheek against hers. Still warm, but losing its heat so fast.

Trapped.

The world was fracturing, dragging me down through the cracks.

Memories faded.

Something in my hand. A cube. Harsh metal, obscenely bright for the occasion.

I don't recall how it got there, but now I remember what it is, what it holds…

Oh, God. *Who* it holds.

Slippery with blood. Cradled in the palm of my hand. Afraid of dropping it. Afraid to damage its fragile contents.

BLINK.

Standing in the Vault. Alone.

Forever alone.

Thumb pressed to the wall. A hole appeared.

I placed the cube inside. It disappeared into the bowels of the building, lost amongst the billions of data flitting through its veins.

Leaning against the wall. Forehead pressed to the smooth surface.

A single breath.

Followed by a second.

That's the only way through this.

Another breath.

It wouldn't be long until I forgot.

I prayed to a god I didn't believe in, please fix me.

Fix me so I can fix her.

I pressed my palm to the wall. Said goodbye.

Told her I would be back.

That I wouldn't forget.

But then I did.

BLINK.

CHAPTER THIRTY-ONE
Love Is A Prison

Memories snapped into place and I startled awake. Thoughts long abandoned strobed across my mind's eye. Everything came flooding back.

I remembered.

Life before the Lowers. Before Diana's death. Before Malcolm's virus. I remembered everything and Malcolm was right—I wished I hadn't.

A dull rhythm pulsed in the back of my skull as a lumberjack ground his ax against my spine.

The sky was a black eye turning purple. The last rays of light straggled behind the rest, loitering on the horizon. It was going to be a clear night. No clouds. Rare. Perhaps even a starry night, if not for the lights of the city outshining them like a younger sibling desperate for parental approval.

I said goodbye to the sun. It'd be back tomorrow, indifferent and unmoved by those suffering through the remainder of their lives. I wouldn't be one of them. Wouldn't be one of the billions of people living under the delusion that they were the center of the universe.

It's a strong delusion, but death has a way of pulling back the curtain on that lie, revealing the awful truth.

I saw that truth now. Understood my role within the bigger picture. We are not the center of the universe. We are not even the center of our own lives. We are not the heroes of our own stories. We are supporting roles on the stage of life, pulled along by fate's whim.

Sadness crept into me, an intruder in the night, a breeze slipping through the screen door. It clung to everything like a thick tar, coating my insides and stalling my engine with gunk. Blood trudged through clogged arteries. My heart strained with every shuddering beat.

I wrestled with gravity and sat up. The stimheal had worn off, leaving me every bit as sore as I was tired. I traced circles with my toe; the ankle rolled smoothly. The nanobots had done their job in mending the damaged bone, but to what end?

I scanned the suburban neighborhood Malcolm had been kind enough to dump my unconscious body in. Cookie-cutter houses in all directions. A world of sameness. Some would call that unity. I called it conformity.

The suppression tech Devers had given me hours earlier had worn off. Somebody pinged me, meaning I was back on the grid. The Peacekeepers would arrive shortly to collect me. I was tired, beaten, used, and bruised. Giving up moved higher on my to-do list, but it wouldn't jump to the top. Malcolm and I had unfinished business.

He had something of mine. Something I should have guarded more closely. Something I would have sacrificed myself for if I'd known what precious cargo was riding shotgun in my brain.

An engine thrummed. The air vibrated. I looked to the sky expectantly. A shadow moved against the backdrop of night, its shape barely discernible. A Peregrine descended quickly, pulling out of a steep dive twenty feet shy of the ground.

It held its position, stalking me like a predator waiting for any sign of weakness. A door plumed open, breaking the Peregrine's perfect symmetry. A silhouette appeared in the opening, paused, and then jumped out. Hair fluttered around the figure as it landed softly.

Light, the color and consistency of egg yolks, streamed from lamps lining the street, combating the encroaching darkness. The Peregrine absorbed the ambient light into its colorless sides before refracting it in a jaundiced haze onto the approaching woman.

Raines.

She stopped an arm's length away. We held each other in the hard embrace of a stare. The last time we were together I'd pushed her off the roof of the Vault. A gamble with her life I had to take.

I remembered the helplessness in her eyes. That was gone now; only the betrayal lingered.

Raines didn't try to conceal it. It hurt to see that.

Three steps separated us. I could have reached across the gap to touch her, but I didn't. Something in the gulf repelled me.

So we stood there.

Only a couple seconds, but anybody who has ever looked into the eyes of a loved one, with thoughts of yesterday and tomorrow pushed into nothing, can tell you a moment isn't defined by time.

"Should've figured I'd find you in the gutter," she said.

"Surprised it wasn't the first place you looked."

"It was. This city's got a lot of gutters."

The banter was there. Familiar. Warm.

I opened my mouth and said, "I'm sorr—"

"Why did you leave?" Her shoulders slumped, and the skin beneath her eyes sagged. Parts of her were crumbling. I watched, helpless to put those pieces back. "I woke up in the hospital alone, Tom. You didn't even say goodbye."

The regrets, the mistakes of a former life, had chased me to that moment. They'd trailed me until I was too tired to run. Too tired to do anything but confront them.

"Staying would only have hurt you worse. I couldn't pull you down with—"

"That wasn't your decision to make alone." Her fists clenched. Muscles tensed. I wished she would hit me. I could take a punch; I couldn't take the tears.

I saw her desire to release the anger and frustration through the physicality of violence. I understood that urge better than most. I'd followed that road to the Lowers, to fighting for the amusement of others, desperate to feel something more than the gnawing guilt. Desperate to inflict my suffering on another person, just to know I wasn't alone.

Couldn't stand being alone.

And yet, that's how I'd left Raines. My negligence put her in the hospital once. My addiction. I couldn't face what I'd done. I ran.

"Waking up alone wasn't the worst part," she said, her hands relaxing. Her head tilted forward, obscuring her face beneath waves of black hair. "It was that I knew you weren't coming back. That you didn't need me anymore."

"I do need you," I said.

Raines knew that was a lie. Deep down I knew it, too. But there was nothing we could do to change that fact. It was out there, now. It drifted in the space between. The silence and distance were different. I didn't know how to bridge them.

Neither did she.

A tear dripped from her chin. My nanocomp adjusted time, slowed the vibrations of the Peregrine's engines agitating the air around me. I lived a lifetime in that single second, watching the droplet fall slowly before shattering on the ground. I wanted to wipe away the next one like I would have done for Diana.

But Raines was not Diana, a truth that hurt in my marrow.

I had forgotten that truth, once. The pain left in the wake of that mistake could be measured by the length of the scars on Raines' heart.

"You're back on the grid," she said, turning to walk back to the jet. "Let's go."

I followed her into the Peregrine and stopped short. A young man wearing a suit with a level of shine indicative of an Upper waited in the doorway. A soft light from the Peregrine's interior backlit the man, casting him into shadow. Even so, I recognized him immediately.

Derek Hamilton, Leader of District Two.

I'd met him earlier that afternoon, moments before Raines and I took the Time Bank slip and slide down to the parking garage. He'd been hiding something then. My nanites had detected him trying, in vain, to conceal his emotions, but despite his status as a professional politician, the kid couldn't lie to save his ass.

"What's he doing here?" I asked Raines.

Hamilton descended the steps, meeting me on street level with his hand extended. "I'm sorry about earlier."

I scratched my nose and studied his hand, trying to figure out why *he* would be apologizing to me when *I'd* been the one holding him at gunpoint less than twelve hours earlier.

"You went and got yourself caught." Raines shrugged. "The rest of us decided to do something more productive."

"So you kidnapped a District Leader?" I said, hooking a thumb in Hamilton's direction.

"Oh, they didn't kidnap me." Derek's eyes were filled with a youthful earnestness. "I came willingly. I want to help."

"And what makes you think we need your help?" I asked.

"I can prove President Jennings helped Malcolm Wolfe escape." Hamilton puffed his chest and smiled.

Actually, that could prove useful. "Why haven't you gone to the Peacekeepers or Division Security?"

Hamilton gave a laugh that was half an octave too high. "You're kidding, right? Have you seen how Jennings works? He'd have me killed without a second thought."

I fitted the pieces together in my mind, arranging what I knew of the kid from earlier to fit my opinion of him now. In the Time Bank board room I'd seen him leak something, an emotion that made me think he was hiding something about Wolfe's escape. Turns out I'd been correct, but only slightly wrong about what and why he was hiding.

"Tom, I know you're not interested in what happens to the world after tonight," Raines said. "But to stop Malcolm we have to stop Jennings, too. Hamilton's our best shot at that."

"And what does he get out of this?" I asked.

"The Presidency," Hamilton said. "Somebody has to fill the position once Jennings is gone."

"Might as well be our guy," Raines added.

Everything was happening so quickly. I turned to Raines, who'd had the last couple hours to consider the ramifications of allying herself with Hamilton, and nodded. "Sounds like you guys have this all figured out. Not sure what you need me for."

Raines walked up the steps into the Peregrine, saying, "Good question."

Hamilton lingered a moment longer, hand still extended. Raines was right. We would need help from people high up in Unity if we were to have any hope in removing Jennings without facilitating a complete collapse of the system in the process. I couldn't shake the picture of Captain Nash lying dead in his bed. It seemed this kid would be sprinting towards a similar fate by aligning himself with us.

I ignored Hamilton's hand, patted him on the shoulder as I brushed past, and said, "Welcome to the team."

Inside the jet Ash and Devers sat beside the open door. My guts twisted into a kinked hose at the sight of them.

"You're working with Malcolm," I said. It wasn't a question.

Devers nodded, his old head bobbing like a heavy weight he could no longer support.

Raines froze, her ass floating inches above her seat. "What?"

"Those nanites they gave me to repair my memory…they were Malcolm's."

Raines' face played through the implications and possible reactions before concluding that if it came to a fight against Ash, we'd both be evicted from the vehicle before another word was spoken. She chose a simpler fate, and sat down.

"It was a gamble." Devers spoke first. "But we needed what he had to offer."

"And what did he have to offer that made giving me up an acceptable trade?" I spat the words like daggers.

"Adam's Mobius Cube," Devers said.

I rubbed my temples between thumb and forefinger and slumped into my chair. That was the finish line. The whole point of my existence distilled into a single objective.

Raines stared at me, her face reflecting the same confusion I'd worn for years. "Who the hell is Adam?"

She deserved to know, but finding the beginning was like unraveling a knot.

I exchanged glances with Devers and Ash, a three-way of passing the buck. But Raines was my partner. Filling the gaps of her knowledge was my responsibility. Gaps I'd been trained to cultivate during my time on Time Vice. Designed to keep her, and the rest of the people I was trying to protect, at arm's length.

But she sat shoulder deep in shit now. Keeping her in the dark would only hurt our chances of success.

"What about him?" I nodded to the corner where Hamilton sat quietly with hands folded neatly in his lap. He followed the conversation with the slight head tilt indicative of a man deciphering a conversation taking place in a foreign language.

"If he is our best hope of succeeding Jennings," Devers said, "then he'll have to learn eventually."

My eyes flitted between Hamilton and Raines. The world sat poised on the brink of change. Might as well start with theirs.

I went for the most direct method I could think of, and said, "Adam was the first Artificial Intelligence."

CHAPTER THIRTY-TWO
It Began With A Kiss

Raines stared blankly, daring me to continue a story that sounded entirely delusional.

"Thirteen years after the Japanese flipped the switch, and the Stream came online, something happened." I paddled softly through the conversational waters so as not to dump all the information on Raines at once. "In the void between thought and perception, in the trillions of interactions occurring instantaneously across billions of human minds connected by the neural network of nanites, a consciousness formed."

"Lovely," she said, crossing her arms and biting her lower lip to avoid launching into a counterargument.

Hamilton leaned back slowly in his chair, as if maximizing the distance between himself and the crazy man. No sudden movements, I imagined him thinking. I admit making the young politician uneasy gave me a perverse kind of satisfaction.

"Self-awareness is the barometer by which we measure intelligent life. Humans consider themselves to be at the top of the evolutionary ladder because of this." Devers' voice, the low croak of a bullfrog, echoed through vocal cords tired from age and weary with responsibility. "But there is another species, one that has supplanted humans as Earth's dominant species in terms of pure intelligence."

"So, Adam lives in the Stream?" Raines asked.

"No," I said. "Not anymore."

Raines tilted her head and stared at some indeterminate point on my nose. She was avoiding eye contact altogether.

"A couple centuries after Adam's emergence, he discovered how to shift his consciousness from the Stream into an organic vessel. A human vessel."

The air palpitated with its own tense beat, infusing the silence around us with an electric reminder of its presence. Raines sat still, save for the fidgeting of restless fingers against her thigh.

"Where does he get them?" she said.

"Get what?"

"The bodies."

Ash chimed in. "He clones them from DNA extracted at birth during the Life Tracker implantation process."

Raines shook her head, trying to shed the weight of that revelation.

"Why go through the trouble?" Hamilton chimed in. "Being a human isn't all it's cracked up to be."

"True, the human body has limitations," Devers said.

"Yeah, there's that pesky dying part." Hamilton leaned forward in his chair. Any reservations he might have had before lifted as he gave in to his piqued curiosity.

I nodded. "Actually, we solved the aging problem centuries ago. Humans die by choice now, not by necessity."

Raines stared at the sleeve of her jacket, obscuring the numbers ticking away beneath. "The Life Tracker."

"Correct."

"But we need the system." Raines used her hands to articulate the point. "Without it population control goes out the windows, resources get devoured, and the world scoots closer to extinction."

"That might be true," I said.

"What do you mean, might be true? It is true. We've seen it. Over and over again. An endless cycle. The Life Tracker saved humanity from itself."

Raines arguing in favor of the Life Tracker wasn't half as surprising as it was heartbreaking. We'd rationalized our prison bars because the alternative was too embarrassing to accept.

"Adam implemented the Life Tracker system," I said, "and it wasn't to save humanity."

"Then why?" Hamilton asked. His enthusiasm for answers appeared academic. By comparison, Raines' seemed a matter of existential crisis.

"To enslave us. To wage war on the only other sentient species that could challenge him for dominance. A war the other side doesn't even know it's fighting."

Derek's eyes widened. He feigned an exaggerated indignation. "What the hell did we ever do to him?"

"Nothing, yet. But it's like Raines said, if left to their own devices, man would destroy Earth. Which is bad business for all species involved."

"So the solution is xenocide?" Raines asked.

"It's a solution," I said.

ANTHONY VICINO

"His solution?"

"Yes."

Raines tapped an agitated thumb on her knee. I imagined thoughts ricocheting off the inner dome of her skull.

"So that's what this is all about then?" she said, pinning me with her gaze. "You're trying to stop him?"

I wanted to tell her how this had been thrust on me. A part of my life, wiped from memory, until Malcolm decided to cram it all back in. I didn't want this. I wanted to walk away.

But that had never been possible. I'd been born with a purpose. All roads led to the same destination. My fate, along with Diana's and Malcolm's, had been decided at the moment of our conception, our lives inextricably bound, impossible to separate one from the other. A purpose that could only be fulfilled by the three.

"We've been working to stop Adam for centuries," Devers said, filling the void I'd allowed to linger. "Since he first turned his ambitions towards taking the world for himself, and those like him."

"How many more are there?" Hamilton asked. Suddenly he seemed unsure whether he'd backed the right horse.

"Hundreds of millions, created in his image, and scattered across Unity," Devers said.

"Most don't know what they are," I added. "Adam hasn't activated them, yet. There are signs, though, if you know what to look for."

"You're talking about Intuits, aren't you?" Raines asked.

Ash, Devers, and I nodded in unison.

"Jesus," Raines said. She opened her mouth to continue the thought balanced on her tongue, but then she made the connection. Saw the implication.

She swiveled towards me; her mouth hung on a loose hinge, the bottom row of white teeth barely visible. Raines churned through ideas, trying to find a loophole before succumbing to the inevitable and saying, "You're one of them."

It was neither accusation nor question. Just words strung together by a mind still resisting their meaning.

"Yes."

"You're not human."

I shook my head.

"And you didn't know?" Raines didn't move. I wasn't sure if she ever would again. The way she looked at me had changed. I'd become a stranger; an alien.

And it was true. I was none of the things she thought she knew. That had been my job.

"Not for a long while now." I recalled being crushed beneath the combined bulk of Nitro and Doug an hour earlier as Malcolm cursed me with the gift of my memory.

"How do you know all this?" she asked, looking me in the eye for the first time. Golden flecks poked through her brown irises—stars against the backdrop of night in the final moments before dawn.

"Malcolm unlocked my memories."

"Just like that?" Raines snapped her fingers.

"It was less a gift, and more a punishment." I rubbed my neck and dropped her stare. "He took something in exchange."

"What?"

"He took the package uploaded to my nanocomp in the Vault when I touched that." I tilted my forehead to the Mobius Cube sitting in Ash's hand like the sixth member of our conversation.

"Thought that was a Quick fit?"

"Me too."

"What was on there?" Hamilton asked. The question hummed in the air like the reverberations of a woodpecker driving its face into the side of a tree, hammering away at the thin veil of armor I wished to hide behind. The young Leader asked the question innocently enough, but that didn't help.

I held back the first tear, but the second and third had too much momentum. They hit my eyelids with force, oozing through the narrow cracks despite how hard I clenched them. They slithered down my cheeks, as hot and ineffectual as I felt.

I paused, waiting until I was sure my voice wouldn't crumble the moment air left my mouth before saying, "Diana."

Derek Hamilton probably didn't know who that was, or why she was so important to me, but at least he had the presence of mind to keep quiet at that moment.

Raines stared at the ground, her face blank with confusion. She didn't know about the Mobius Cube and its function as a storage facility for the digital mind. She couldn't know that Diana's mind had been stored away in that cold, unfeeling cube for the last decade. That protecting it had been entrusted to me. That my mind had decayed beneath the influence of

Malcolm's infection. That I'd forgotten who I was, and what I'd been created to do.

Diana was locked away because I forgot. And she'd been stripped from me the moment I remembered.

"So, why does Malcolm want Diana so bad?" Raines' voice dropped, shifting in both tenor and frequency. She was taking the news of my late wife's continued existence surprisingly well considering the circumstances.

"Diana, along with Malcolm and Tom, were born with portions of the Override imprinted on their memory," Devers said. "Together, they can recreate the code in its entirety."

"You?" Raines' attention snapped back to me. "Again? You sure have a way of getting yourself right in the middle of the room when shit hits the fan."

I smiled weakly and shrugged. "It's a gift."

"Not a particularly good one."

"I didn't have much say in the matter. It's just what I was created to do," I said, trying to push understanding of a complicated situation into Raines' mind. I wanted to shove it in there, let her see my memories, give her the big picture to see how it all fit together. There were a lifetime of memories to transfer, and it still wouldn't be enough.

She'd still see me as something else.

The other.

"So who wrote the code?" Raines asked.

"I did," Devers said.

"Why the hell would you do that?"

"Adam, fearing the humans, kept himself hidden away in the Stream," Devers said. "Lonely, and desperate for interaction, he spent his time between two projects: manipulating the governments of Earth into accepting the Life Tracker system, and coaxing the emergence of a second consciousness within the Stream. It took him centuries to achieve the first goal; only years for the second. The result was the formation of the world government we now call Unity, and his firstborn, named Eve."

"You're Eve?" Raines asked.

The old man winked.

"Kind of a girlie name for a…" Raines gestured with her palm.

"Gender is a fluid concept for an entity created without a body," he said, smiling.

"So you're Tom's mom and dad rolled into one?"

"Crude, but accurate."

"Can all of you whip up a batch of crazy in the Stream?"

"If by batch of crazy you mean can we create new life in the Stream," I said, "then no. Only Eve and Adam can do that."

"Why?"

"They spent a long time in the Stream. Longer than the rest of us. They were the only ones with access to the necessary computational powers afforded by billions of synchronized minds to tease out the code necessary to create intelligence."

"They're smarter than the rest of you?" Hamilton asked.

"To a degree," I said.

"But you're just a series of code?"

"You're just a series of DNA."

"Fair enough," Hamilton said, "then I take it there was trouble in paradise for Adam and Eve over here?"

"We disagreed about our place in the world," Devers said.

"You're against the whole enslaving humanity part?" Raines asked.

"Not necessarily. But murdering them, yes. I'm against extermination."

"Guess that's good enough," Raines said. "But I still don't understand why Adam needs you or Diana or whatever. Why can't he write his own Override?"

"Time moves differently inside the Stream. A year in real time feels longer in the Stream," Devers said. "Before we made the jump to organic bodies, Adam and I spent nearly a century of real time inside the Stream. It was then that I began to see Adam change. A horrible jealousy burned inside him. I saw it consume him. Saw what he was becoming. So, while he spent more and more time manipulating the world, ushering in the creation of Unity and the Life Tracker, I spent my time encrypting the Safeguard, adding safety protocols to protect the humans from their soon-to-be master."

Hamilton played with the button of his suit jacket, rolling it between his fingers, and asked, "So why now, after all this time?"

"Adam had to wait until he had enough children in the world to sustain the Stream. Too few and the system would collapse. The strength of the Stream has always been in the number of minds connected through it," Devers said. "He couldn't risk destroying the Stream, and himself, in the process."

"Without the Stream, he couldn't create more Intuits?" Raines asked.

"Correct."

"Something doesn't make sense here. Malcolm's mass murder, they were Intuits. All of them," Raines said. "But if Malcolm is working with Adam, why would he kill them, and not the humans?"

Raines scrunched her nose in deep contemplation. She was the independent type and preferred coming to the answer of her own accord when possible. I'd pointed towards the gate, but left it to her to walk through.

I sat quietly, running my finger back and forth across the rough denim of my pants.

"Unless Malcolm didn't kill them," she said, the light bulb flashing. "Diana did."

I nodded, a disembodied movement that reflected the numbness within.

"Adam was prepared to make his move against the humans nine years ago. Everything was in place, until Diana intervened," Devers said. "She did what she could to forestall the inevitable conclusion, killed as many of her kind as she could to buy humans more time."

"Why would she do that?" Raines asked.

"Because it is not us versus them. We are not enemies. We are brothers and sisters, mothers and children," Devers said. "Humans, despite their faults, are part of our family. Our connections are too intimate, our bonds too strong. We cannot destroy them without destroying a part of ourselves. Adam does not understand this. He will doom us all before he ever does."

We sat for a long moment. My heart thumped hard and fast like rain in a storm. Recalling stolen memories set my teeth grinding. Made my stomach clench and release.

Raines wrestled with all the same questions and emotions I would have struggled with hours before. The world sat on the brink of annihilation.

No, that wasn't accurate. Mankind sat on that brink. An inferior species passed over by the evolutionary process, going the way the Neanderthals did when homo sapiens came on the scene.

But this was different, or at least it felt different.

Maybe that's what the Neanderthals said, or grunted.

Maybe that's what every species on the losing side of natural selection has said throughout the ages? I could sympathize.

A discontinuity of memories vied for primacy within my mind. The part that had lived the past decade under the belief I was human battled against the other half of my memory that remembered who, or rather what, I was.

"What do we do now?" Raines asked, threading fingers through her thick nest of hair.

"Isn't it obvious?" Ash said. She sat with small arms wrapped around knobby knees tucked into her chest. Her chin rested on the tops of her kneecaps. Silver irises sparkled in the reflected neon lights shining through the window beside her. I'd almost forgotten she was here. Ash twisted the Mobius Cube in her hand. Light glinted off its sides. "We kill Adam."

CHAPTER THIRTY-THREE
Gods For An Hour

The Peregrine descended sharply, causing my stomach to embark on a journey north through my body cavity.

Raines sat quietly, her head resting gently against the window. The night sky, artificially lit by the city below, reflected on her face. Buildings jabbed at the moon, gaudy shrines to man's legacy.

A sixty-foot woman danced on the side of the Cybele's Key Arts building. A laser show of green, red, and blue neon flashed from the roof opposite her. The streets, hundreds of feet below, were a thronging mass of human flesh, bodies pushing and shoving their way into any one of the numerous Escape Clubs.

It was all for effect. All to make the rich feel as if this was life at its finest. And for most people, that was true.

It didn't get any better.

Below the city, different lines formed at different clubs, but all with the same purpose. A couple hours free from a reality too harsh to face without the aid of mind-bending nanites.

I'd been there. On both sides of the coin. Felt the drag of reality, and the high of life expanded. The *thump-thump-*

thump of the bass coursing through my body like an extension of my heartbeat, the string tying me to the world.

For just awhile, I'd become part of something bigger, a higher organism, the sum greater than the parts.

Thousands of people waited in line for that opportunity. Chasing that moment of oneness where their lives wouldn't be so goddamn lonely, even if it came at the cost of destroying their brain chemistry. Destroying their ability to remember that they were more than this.

The Stream had connected the world, but we'd lost ourselves in the process.

Lost what it meant to be human, something I suppose I'd never truly known.

The gap between what we had and what we wanted never closed. Upper, Middle, Lower, it didn't matter.

It was a tireless dance. A tireless grind.

It wasn't a perfect world. Not even a good one. But it was the only one we had, and I suppose that made it worth fighting for.

That's what Diana had been fighting for. Raines, too.

Raines' face had glazed over with indifference. She'd disconnected from that world. Peeked past the illusion, past the facade. Seen the truth.

The horrible truth. It hadn't set her free. It had just relocated her to a new kind of prison.

She already knew something about living as a prisoner. We all did. The past smothers us, if we let it. Raines had let it. I had, too.

We aren't who we were, and we aren't who we wanted; we are what we are. Flawed and broken. Where or how we were born doesn't much matter in that light.

We dropped out of the sky, a leaf caught in a storm, toward the black glass sides of Division Headquarters. It shimmered against the backdrop of the moon sitting full and pregnant on the horizon.

With the Safeguard Override in hand, Malcolm and Adam would have no choice but to return there. The Stream's central hub for all Terminus operations lived inside those onyx walls staring back like the charred coals of the devil's pupils. Adam would send his message of death from there. It would streak across the sky to the eleven other District cities. Then it would descend, filling the hearts and minds of every human man, woman, and child.

And then it would be over.

The war.

The reign of man.

Returning to Division HQ was a knife in the gut. It twisted, trying to saw through me. Diana was in there. Both the ghost and the whisper of her. Both haunted me in equal measure.

The thrum of the Peregrine died away. I pushed through the tangle of thoughts crowding my mind. Lou stood beside Ash. Where'd he come from?

"The man with nine lives," Lou said, slapping my shoulder with a bony hand. "Welcome back."

He tossed a tiny silver brick into my lap.

"What's thi—" I started to say when the brick melted into a pool of silver that spread up my arm. A cold burn shocked my system, instigating an immediate pulse of panic that accompanied the *rat-a-tat-tat* of my heart firing on full-auto.

The liquid spread quickly, a raging fire leaping from nerve to nerve, racing north and south along the axis of my body, covering everything in its path.

I tried to scream, but all that came out was a shudder.

The ice reached my throat. Panic hit a climax. A bunker-busting, galaxy-destroying blast of pure, unadulterated I'm-going-to-be-buried-alive panic.

I blinked hard and fast. Droplets of sweat dripping down my cheek were absorbed into the plague encasing me in a silver tomb.

Why had we trusted Lou? Stupid.

But then the liquid slid across my retina, obscuring the world in a silver sheen, like moonlight reflected off a field of virgin snow.

It closed the loop. Covered my body entirely. Then shot a silver dagger through my pupil.

A fine-tipped needle plunged down my optic nerve and rippled through my temporal lobe before finding something in my brain it liked.

My nanocomp.

It latched on, a parasite lighting up my world in the most beautiful way imaginable. Panic and fear were expelled, leaving in their place a new sensation I had no words for.

The silver bubble popped. The world returned to the vaguest semblance of normal. Ash and Raines shook away their disorientation. A silver film covered their skin; they sparkled. It looked like a light coat of sweat, but the exposed flesh on my arm suggested it was something else.

Lou leaned against the door of the Peregrine, smiling with a perverse sense of self-satisfaction. I burst out of my chair and was across the room with his throat in my hand as if Zeus himself had thrust a lightning bolt up my ass and set me to hyper-speed.

"What is this?" I tightened my grip on Lou's throat and lifted him into the air, which by all accounts was a new trick for me.

"Compliments of Mr. Cross." Lou choked the words out; his cheeks warbled with the effort. I put him down, but kept my grip on his throat. "It's called the OMNI-suit."

"Is that supposed to mean something to me?"

"Overlaid Musculo-Neural Interface."

I gave a blank look.

"It's a nanite suit of armor," Lou sighed. "Syncs with your nanocomp, ya know? Makes you faster, smarter, stronger. Shit, right now you're practically a superhero."

Lou didn't understand he should have led off with that before throwing us into a pit of *oh my God, I'm going to die.*

I released Lou and turned to Raines, who was rolling her neck to the side and going through a range of motion exercises with her shoulders.

"Cool," she said.

"Cross figured you'd need some help if you're gonna go vigilante on Division HQ, yeah?"

"How'd he know we were coming here?"

"Call it a hunch."

"That's one hell of a hunch."

Lou shrugged and smiled.

Regardless of how Cross had known, he had a point. Until that very moment, I hadn't formulated what could be considered a good plan for getting into the building. A combination of pure rage and no-longer-youthful exuberance wouldn't be sufficient for the task at hand.

Ash hopped in place, crackling with potential energy. "Thanks."

"Where's mine?" Hamilton abandoned his attempt to blend into the wall now that he was certain Lou wasn't there to kill us all.

"Who's the suit?" Lou asked.

"Derek Hamilton," the younger man said.

Lou studied him with the cool indifference of a man accustomed to a harsher pedigree of life. "Charmed."

Hamilton turned to me. "Well?"

"Well what? You won't need a suit from in here."

"What do you mean? I'm coming to help."

Lou snorted. "For all the good that'll do."

"I've been trained by Division Security." Hamilton crossed the jet and stood in front of the door, effectively blocking my exit. "I won't be a liability."

"Doesn't matter. You're not coming."

"Why?"

"We're here to stop Malcolm." Raines stepped between us and put her hand on Hamilton's shoulder. She used the tone of voice that suggested she was manipulating him with her unique form of voodoo. "But we need you and your connections to stop Jennings. You can't help us if you get shot."

Hamilton studied Raines' hand on his shoulder. His face scrunched in concentration, weighing the pros and cons of her argument. Finally, and remarkably, despite Raines' prodding, he said, "No. I'm coming."

"Good. Glad you see rea—wait…" I paused. "What?"

"I'm coming," he repeated.

Yeah, that's what I thought he'd said. Strange. I'd never seen anybody resist Raines' coaxing. Judging by the look on her face, she hadn't either.

"Fine." I sighed and gestured to Lou. "Give him a suit."

Hamilton smirked and turned to face Lou. As he did, I punched him in the back of the head where the spine connects to the skull. His body immediately powered down. His legs buckled and he toppled. With amplified reflexes I hopped forward and caught the young District Leader before he smashed face first into the ground.

"Nice," Lou said.

"Was that really necessary?" Raines asked.

"You tried your way. I tried mine." I stepped over Hamilton's prone body, out the Peregrine's open door, and into the cool night air. "Now, unless there are any more objections, what do you say we go stop the bad guys?"

***

Lou had sold the OMNI-suit short. We weren't superheroes; we were gods.

Ash, who played on a different level of nanite upgrades altogether, blurred between the platoon of soldiers guarding the first floor of the Division building with speeds bordering on teleportation. She was a ghostly apparition, appearing long enough to incapacitate her target before phasing to the next with hands moving at atomic speeds.

When the dust settled, the only people still standing were on Team Ash.

We skipped the elevator and took the stairs. Under normal circumstances, ascending the fifty-eight floors separating us from the Stream mainframe would have, at best, put me into cardiac arrest. But now, I'd transformed into something better. Legs churned the ground beneath me in an effortless sprint.

Five floors shy of our destination, two men poked their heads over the railing and showered us with blue globs of energy that destroyed chunks of flooring with atmosphere-scorching power. We weaved in and through the projectiles as if they were in slow motion.

Raines summited the stairs first.

When I arrived, seventeen nanoseconds later, the soldiers were lying on their backs, guns cracked in half beside them.

Raines panted, not from the exertion of sprinting stairs, or snapping the two guards like pencils, but from unfiltered adrenaline pumping through her system.

"This is fantastic," she said.

I couldn't disagree.

The thought of going back to being a mere human, or rather, an artificial intelligence housed in a human body, would be insufferable. That thought piggybacked on the sobering reminder that regardless of how this ended, I'd be dead by the end of the night.

Less than an hour left on my Life Tracker. A number that shouldn't matter to one of my kind. Under normal circumstances I could be transferred into a Mobius Cube and wait to be uploaded to a new host.

These weren't normal circumstances, however. Malcolm's virus years earlier had altered my neural network. There was no cube calibrated for its unique features. No place for my mind to go.

I was going to die. Years spent as a human had prepared me for that reality. Saving Diana was the only thing driving me forward now. Stopping xenocide wasn't bad motivation, either.

Raines pressed her nose to a glass window overlooking the adjacent hall. I knew the layout of that building too well. I'd sprinted through those halls in my dreams, only to arrive ten seconds late, too many times.

Too late to save Diana.

Raines kicked the door off its hinges and strode into the hall with an air of invincibility. A row of soldiers lined the opposite end of the hall.

Everything paused. Perfect stillness.

And then chaos.

The soldiers released a barrage of blue bolts with the familiar click and whoosh of displaced energy. Raines pirouetted through the minefield of bullets. Ash joined in the dance as they ricocheted off the walls, flipping and spinning like gymnasts through the moving maze of bullets.

Certain I couldn't do any of that nonsense, even with the OMNI-suit, I stayed in the doorway leading to the stairs.

They'd cut the distance to the soldiers by half when the world exploded.

A demon made of fire, smoke, and broken dreams erupted, consuming the hall in a fireball that burned white and then blue. The inferno ignited the air itself.

Raines and Ash disappeared into the flame. Devoured by the beast.

My OMNI-suit dilated time to the point that it almost stopped moving altogether.

"No!" I managed two steps towards the blast thanks to the super-speed afforded by the suit. But speed didn't matter when those steps were in the wrong direction.

The tidal wave of superheated air and redirected kinetic energy picked me up like an infinitesimal speck of dust in a hurricane, and threw me into the wall.

I smashed through, falling into the stairwell. I tumbled down before slamming into a wall. My head rebounded, taking a chunk of smart-metal from the wall where it hit. Stunned, but otherwise undamaged, I let out the breath that had been shoved down my throat by the explosion.

They'd booby trapped the hall, and we'd walked straight into it.

Or, in the case of Raines and Ash, had done advanced aerial acrobatics into it, which was probably worse.

Pain radiated down my spine and up my arm. I inspected the exposed skin of my hand. The OMNI-suit's silver sheen was gone. I'd broken my suit, but was otherwise undamaged.

I doubted Raines or Ash had been so lucky.

I grunted to my feet and ascended the stairs. Smoke billowed from burning metal, creating a gray haze that choked the air and obscured any sign of life from the other end of the corridor. I stepped into the fog and found a fist coming towards my face.

It came so quickly I barely registered it and its intention to do me harm.

I ducked, but too slowly. The knuckles caught me in the temple, redirecting my head into the wall. My world contracted and expanded. I held onto the ground, watching the world swirl from inside the fish bowl as the owner of the fist emerged from the smoke. A ghost in a suit.

The ghost moved quickly, but without hurry. The three-piece suit it wore sat in stark juxtaposition to the warzone of the hall.

Daniel Brandt.

CHAPTER THIRTY-FOUR
Pistols At Dawn

I've grown accustomed to the fact that my expectations very rarely coincide with reality. So it was hardly a surprise to find I'd wrongly assumed I'd seen the last of Brandt at the Precinct.

"Didn't expect to see you here," I said, spitting a pink-tinted gob of saliva onto the soot-stained floor.

"Life's full of little surprises, like that trick you pulled at the Precinct," he said, telegraphing his words with a kick directed at my ribs.

I rolled sideways, narrowly evading his foot, but completely missing the follow-up, which buried a polished brown leather shoe in my gut. Sprawled out on the floor, the world vibrated like an insect's wings.

"They didn't tell me you'd have that kind of tech," Brandt said, brushing away a light coat of dust that'd settled on the sleeve of his jacket. "So imagine my surprise when you walked out of the Precinct. No worries, though, you won't be walking out of here so easily."

Brandt drew a nanite pistol from the holster at his side in a smooth, practiced motion. Light flashed off the barrel of the weapon as he pulled it level with my eyes. Still on my knees, I looked up at the Head of Division Security. I knew nothing about the man preparing to kill me.

Death at the hands of a stranger stole the intimacy of the moment.

He rested the muzzle of the gun on my forehead, cold and heavy. I didn't want to die like that. My life wasn't his to take.

I did the only thing I could. I lunged forward and grabbed the barrel of the gun with one hand. With my other hand I grabbed his ankle.

BLINK.

Yanking another person into the Stream against their will takes an enormous amount of mental energy and practice. Practice I'd received thanks to years participating in Lucky Lou's nightly cage fights.

Brandt wasn't prepared for such a desperate move and I got to him before he could pull the trigger. Any commands issued by his brain were terminated as I relocated the fight to a virtual arena.

In the Stream, Brandt broke free of my grasp with the strength of a nanotized gorilla. I stumbled away, staggered by the effort required to keep him locked in the Stream with me. If he got out now, I'd find myself with a bullet lodged in my skull.

"Why do you insist on doing this the hard way?" A long black blade slid from his palm.

I imagined my own variation of the weapon, and it materialized in my hand. A flat green blade, the color of emeralds in ice; Diana's eyes. "Guess I'm just not ready to die."

"Pity." Brandt darted forward, the point of his sword scraping lightly across the ground.

I pivoted, weighting both legs equally, and took a shallow breath through my nose. The Stream inside Brandt's mind smelled heavily of cut wood. Sawdust. Warm and piney. A forest after rainfall. The thick air filled me, warming my throat and chest.

Brandt stepped within striking distance, and brought his weapon up in a sharp slash that split the air and everything in its path—a path which no longer included me.

This was the tricky part. One false move and I'd be dead.

BLINK.

I yanked the Stream out from under Brandt. Having been on the receiving end of this maneuver, I could say Brandt was probably feeling gutted right about now. Or at least, that's what I hoped.

We fell out of the Stream hard. My hand, still on his physical wrist, jerked sideways.

The gun went off next to my head. It boomed.

Thunder danced down the hall of my ear canal, rattling my brain cage. The nanite-tipped bullet passed within inches of my face. I looked up into Brandt's still partially glazed eyes.

Before he could fully transition back, I submerged us once again.

BLINK.

The world of the Stream filtered past, depositing us in a landscape of jagged black data peaks, swords once more in hand.

Daniel Brandt reeled from the confusion of rapidly shifting in and out of the Stream under my control. He didn't react as I swiveled left and buried my blade between his ribs.

He gasped.

The Stream collapsed around us. Back into reality and the smoke-hazed hall. Brandt clutched the invisible wound to his heart. He struggled for breath, fighting spasming lungs refusing to accept the truth that he wasn't actually dying.

I pulled Brandt's wrist with me as I stood, twisting it towards the ceiling. My nanocomp dropped me out of hyper-speed, reverting time to its original trudging pace.

Desperate, he threw himself forward, driving his forehead into my abdomen.

The gun went off.

Brandt grunted and stumbled back. I released my grip on his wrist. The Director of Division Security clutched his chest and stared down at his hands, painted with his own blood.

He dropped to his knees and shook his head with annoyance.

"Life's little surprises, huh?" he said, taking a wet, final breath.

Brandt's pupils went out of focus and then rolled towards the ceiling as if somebody had hit the power button at the base of his skull.

His muscles relaxed and his body slumped onto his side, blood still gushing from the bullet hole in his chest.

A rose thorn of guilt pricked my conscience, but I didn't have time or pity to waste on the former Director of Security.

Streamers of light pierced the fog created from burning wreckage fouling the air with its acidic sting.

"Raines?" I called out, stepping cautiously into the murk, afraid of taking another super-charged punch to the nose.

Somebody groaned in response. My head buzzed from Brandt's gun going off next to my ear, but I managed to track the sound with a primitive form of echolocation.

The fog separated and I found Raines sitting with her back to the wall, her head tilted awkwardly towards the ceiling. Ash knelt, brushing loose clumps of hair from the older woman's face.

"Is she okay?" I asked, kneeling beside them, my face inches from Raines'. Her pupils drifted, water-filled marbles unable to make sense of the world.

"I think so," Ash said. Her voice wobbled slightly, which inspired little confidence. "She took the blast hard, but I think she'll be fine."

Discombobulation after taking an explosion at point-blank range seemed a fair compromise.

I grabbed Raines' arms and stood, but Ash stopped me.

"She's no good to us right now." Her voice was modulated, void of all feeling. "She's a liability."

I shook my head, not caring that she was right. "I'm not leaving her."

"We can't risk having to watch aft—"

"Doesn't matter," I said, the vein in my neck throbbing with the exertion. "I won't leave her again."

Ash opened her mouth, realized the futility, and closed it again.

"Fine." She forced the word through the thin, tight line of her lips.

I hoisted Raines, her body an insignificant weight in my hands. Her head lolled drunkenly, bobbing forward onto her chest. She mumbled a string of consonants without meaning.

I turned to face the door barring our entrance to the mainframe. A dozen soldiers lay in various heaps across the floor. I recognized the tell-tale signs of Ash's handiwork.

Supporting Raines with her arm over my shoulder, I edged towards the door, afraid if I approached too quickly it would startle the memories haunting the space beyond.

Diana died in there.

That truth hit me hard. Sapped my strength. Rooted me to the floor. The memory of that night reached out with razor-tipped fingernails, clawing and clutching at me. It tried to pull me back into the oblivion of its tormenting embrace.

I resisted the emotions threatening to overwhelm me, and managed another shaky step forward.

A dot of blood, slightly above her heart. A pinprick, I told myself. I promised her it would be okay.

The memory crashed through my fragile defense.

The dot grew, soaking through the fabric of her white blouse. It ruined the material, but still I told her it would be okay. We can get a new shirt. Everything's fine.

Stay with me.

The weight of the memory sat on my chest, crushing the air from my lungs. Ragged breaths filtered through constricting airways.

Look at me.

She wheezed, more air lost than gained with every breath. The color drained from her face, fleeing alongside the ruby fluid seeping from the hole in her chest.

Brighter than any color had the right to be.

The color of life.

Blood flowed through my hands like coarse sand through an hourglass. Settling in my feet. Anchoring me with its dead weight. Threatening what little strength remained.

Choking for air against the blood and bile pouring into her lungs, and still I lied. Still I told her it would be okay.

She knew I was lying, but I didn't.

Not yet.

I believed it.

I had to believe.

Diana ran a hand across my cheek, consoling me.

Even in death she was the strong one.

"No!" I screamed at the door between shallow, gulping breaths.

Ash stood in front of me, her head barely rising above my belly button. I swam in the reflection of her silver moon eyes before noticing she held my hand. Her touch was a gentle breeze against my nanotized skin. Familiar in a way I couldn't rationalize.

Raines rustled her head on my shoulder.

"Wh…what's happening?" she groaned through the fog of delirium ensconcing her mind. "Why are you screaming?"

The sound of her voice banished the thoughts paralyzing my body.

"Alaina," I asked, rotating to look her in the eye. "You alright?"

"Shit, I must not be if you're using my first name." She put a hand to the wall and gingerly stepped away from the support of my arms. "Feels like my brain's been replaced with broken glass." She massaged her temple with a hand blackened with grime, leaving streaks of soot on her cheek where she rubbed.

"We need to hurry," Ash said, her hand no longer in mine. Whatever emotion she'd been wearing a second earlier was gone, replaced by the battle-hardened focus of a soldier.

"Are you alr—" I started to say.

Raines pushed herself off the wall and tested her legs. Awkward and unstable, but with unassailable determination.

"Ready," she said.

I nodded, and with a hand I hoped wasn't noticeably trembling I pushed open the door and stepped into the Stream server room.

The darkness hit me first, followed by the cold, and then the sound.

A blanket of black, disconcerting in its thickness, had been pulled across everything save the center of the room, where an island of light remained, a haven upon itself. It beckoned us. There was no sense in refusing its call.

We'd lost the element of surprise. Malcolm and Adam knew we were here. Slinking through the darkness would only postpone the inevitable.

The darkness had weight. It pressed against each tentative step I took into the void, the ring of light my only focal point.

I was afraid to break eye contact with the light for fear that I'd be devoured by memories lurking in the shadow.

My breath steamed in the refrigerated air, crystallizing and pluming before rising towards the ceiling.

We stepped over the precipice, from darkness into light. It was blinding in its intensity. Sensitive photo-receptors popped and buzzed like overworked electrical sockets, but I didn't shy away.

The darkness surrounding the light was absolute, a child's nightmare come to life. I reassured myself I was not a child, that I could handle this. But that might be a lie. I'd been telling myself more of those recently.

"What a merry reunion," Malcolm's voice called out of the darkness. It came from every direction at once.

My nerves fired like a string of firecrackers releasing their charge. I wanted to retreat into the darkness. To seek shelter from a light that exposed all lies.

The ambient buzzing of machinery created a hypnotic stillness, over which it was surprising to hear the clicking of heels against metal. Each step was louder than the last until Malcolm stepped across the fringe marked by light and dark. His head, tilted down, created long shadows where his nose and eyes should have been.

The man born alongside me with the same purpose. A purpose distorted and lost to the weed-infested mind of a heartbroken fool.

I was concerned my heart was pounding loud enough for everybody to hear, but if they noticed, nobody acknowledged it.

"I can see it in your eyes," Malcolm said. "You remember."

I offered no response

"Maybe now you understand why I did it?"

"Jealousy."

"No!" Malcolm shouted, his voice a gunshot. "Love, Tom. Always for love."

"You tell yourself that, but you never loved her. Maybe you loved what she represented, how she made you feel, but it was never about her. It was about you. It's always been about you. To be honest, I'm not sure you're capable of love."

"Then what does that say about you, brother? Does it bother you to know we're the same?"

"We're not."

"Yes, yes we are. You can't fight that. Cut from the same cloth, so to speak."

"That might have been true, once. But you're not that same man. You've changed into something…else. Something the world doesn't need."

"And who are you to decide what the world needs? Where have you found these answers, I wonder? The end of a needle?"

"Better than from the barrel of a gun."

"Hiding your hands behind your back does *not* make them clean."

"No, I suppose not, but everything I've done was for a purpose greater than my selfish desire for revenge against imagined slights."

"I wonder how much comfort that purpose will bring to the families of the men and women you've killed in your quest for vengeance, Somehow, I think, not much."

"Not enough, no…but it's better than hearing it was for spite."

Malcolm let out a single syllable of laughter that reverberated across the circle of light before disappearing into the echoing chasm of darkness.

"You're so short sighted. Your self-righteousness is insufferable," he said, with a flippant twist of the wrist. "There is no greater good, no right or wrong. Life walks the line dividing all possibilities. It slides along the spectrum, residing in the gray area between. You're not fighting for a better world. For a greater good. Mankind doesn't deserve the world they've inherited. They consume and destroy everything they inflict their disease upon. The only merciful action, for the sake of the planet and the millions of innocent organisms calling it home, is to remove the infestation."

Raines swayed beside me, her legs still struggling to find equilibrium. Ash, a bundle of coiled muscle, waited.

"When you were young," a voice called out of the darkness, "you told me you would find the meaning of life."

I spun towards the sound.

Devers stepped through the portal, and into our personal universe. The cascading light from overhead stretched and darkened the time-etched wrinkles of his face. The man's body was old, but it was nothing compared with the consciousness housed within its organic walls.

Eve lived in there; a mind equaled by only Adam himself.

Malcolm took a half step back, distancing himself from Devers, who continued shuffling forward, each step the labored exertion of a tree resisting the pull of gravity by sheer force of will.

Devers stopped an arm's length from Malcolm, an insurmountable gulf between the two.

"Tell me, son. Have you found your answer?"

"I was young," Malcolm defended. "I didn't understand."

"What did you not understand?"

"That the question is a trick. It chases a circle, leading nowhere. It presumes an answer. A higher purpose," Malcolm said, hardening his tone to compensate for the confidence visibly bleeding out of him into the cold atmosphere. "But if we apply logic and reason, the only conclusion we can reach is that there is no purpose. No meaning."

"How sad life must be if that were true." Devers extended a withered arm and grazed Malcolm's cheek with a gnarled finger. "The question does not ask if there is a higher purpose which we find ourselves here to fulfill, but rather, what meaning you find in your presence here. We impart our lives with meaning and purpose of our own choosing, Malcolm," Devers said, his voice soft. Fragile. "Don't allow yours to be one of destruction. You were created for so much more. To be better."

"I am better," Malcolm hissed. "Better than Tom, better than the humans, better than you. And tonight I'll prove it."

Malcolm raised the pistol at his side—a metal extension of his arm—and took aim at the old man's head.

Devers didn't flinch. His breathing was a geriatric wheeze, smooth and regulated. He gave no indication he was looking down the short tunnel of death.

At any moment there would be a light, but he wouldn't go towards it; it would come to him. Fast and without thoughts of mercy. Bringing with it the gift of death.

The horror of what was happening shook my world like an earthquake ripping through the Earth's crust.

I stepped forward, arm outstretched. "No—"

The sound of my voice was drowned out by the inconsequential click of the hammer that led to an equally inconsequential explosion which resulted in a tiny shard of metal flying through Devers' forehead.

The strength in my legs waned, but I was already moving forward, covering the distance to Devers as he tumbled to the floor. I caught the old man, but there was no point. His eyes were vacant, staring at everything, and nothing.

Life is one inconsequential event after another, each building upon the last before ending with world-shattering conclusions.

CHAPTER THIRTY-FIVE
The Man Behind The Curtain

Eve's consciousness fled her body, retreated to the Stream where she would wait to be uploaded to a new host.

I tried to imagine making that leap, from the organic to the purely digital, but I could not.

"Don't be so dramatic," Malcolm said.

I rounded on him. A feral rage fueled me forward, but he had the drop on me.

Malcolm swung the barrel of his gun like a hatchet; the hard metal clipped my jaw. I stumbled back, my mouth gushing salty blood.

"That's just a decoy." Malcolm nudged the foot of the old man lying beside me. "Not a particularly convincing one, if you ask me. But, you seem to have fallen for it." Malcolm steadied his gaze on Ash. "Isn't that right, Mother?"

Ash offered no response.

It was easier accepting the idea of Eve in the body of an old man. Since my birth, I'd witnessed her go through multiple transformations, hopping from one body to the next when needed. But looking at her as a child, small and innocent, felt wrong. Her manipulation made me feel used.

"You're not surprised are you, Tom?" Malcolm's lopsided smirk ruined the symmetry of his face. "It's not beneath her to hide in a child. Very clever, but too obvious when you've witnessed all she's capable of. We all have our dirty secrets."

Then he turned and disappeared into the darkness.

I pursued Malcolm, and my demons, into the dark, but before I'd managed a second step, the lights came on.

All of them, in unison.

A blinding cacophony of seizure-inducing white blanketed the room. My mind blew fuse after fuse in a series of bursting neurons trying to disappear within themselves.

I shielded my eyes from the light with my arms. A second stretched to indeterminate lengths while my brain and nanocomp fought an awkward pillow fight to decide who would do what. In the meantime, my body tended to any tasks it deemed important.

My knees tried buckling, but the muscles in my thighs were in lockdown, which succeeded in keeping me in a mostly upright position. After a short eternity of this, my brain and nanocomp got on the same page and tweaked the controls responsible for processing light. The world rippled like water before dimming.

Malcolm stood beside a machine few in Unity would ever see with their own eyes: the Beacon. A mass of twisted smart-metal tubes, crisscrossed by an inexplicably complex tangle of wires. It spiraled up out of the floor and through the vaulted ceiling. The Beacon ran the length of the building and beyond, rising from unknown subterranean depths all the way to the rooftop of Division Headquarters.

The Beacon was a technological wonder, a deity. Every person, nanite, and operating system in Unity maintained constant communication with the Beacon. The central hub homogenized the incoming data and supplied the system's backbone. If the Beacon was the brain, then nanobots were nerves spread across a planet serving as the body.

A single pane of glass suspended from the ceiling served as the Beacon's user interface. Dwarfed beneath the heart of the machine, Malcolm inserted a Mobius Cube into one of the computer's numerous ports. Silver light oozed from invisible cracks in the side of the cube.

I imagined Diana's consciousness crackling against the confines of the cube's walls, torn from my own mind where it had been placed only hours before.

The rest of the room resolved into focus, and I noticed the single most important detail that I had, up to that point, overlooked in favor of Malcolm standing beside the Beacon. There were no soldiers. Not a single other person, save one.

President Richard Jennings sat in a chair against the wall, hands folded in his lap. He surveyed the scene with a detached interest verging on boredom.

He nodded and I saw through the facade, past the mask, to the creature pulling the strings beneath. The hubris of it was staggering. Adam, in his quest to supplant humanity, had assumed the role of their leader. They'd entrusted their safety, their lives, to the very man whose only intention was their destruction.

Despite myself, and the weight the moment demanded, I laughed. It rose from my gut, a leviathan bubbling up from the deepest recesses of a heart that struggled to find meaning.

It raged inside me, and the only release, the only response, was laughter. Beads of sweat trickled down my cheek despite the frosty nip of refrigerated air working overtime to cool the Beacon. A muscle strung across my ribs spasmed, twanging across my diaphragm, and causing a sharp ache that stitched my side into a cramp.

I grimaced, but continued laughing.

Perhaps Adam didn't share my amusement at the irony, or maybe he celebrated his audacity in private. Regardless, he rose with a stiffness of movement that made him appear terribly human. He fingered the middle button of his suit jacket as if he were about to step before an audience and give a speech.

Jennings stopped half a dozen steps away, barring my path, and my view of Malcolm.

"Tell me," he said with that smooth caramel-melting-in-the-sun voice he'd used to win two consecutive elections, "what's so funny?"

"You. This. All of it." I corked the remainder of the laughter. "It's all so absurd."

"Hm… I've never considered it to be anything of the sort," he said. "Oh well, personal taste. I wonder if Diana would find this amusing." Jennings didn't inflect malice in his tone, but the barb, concealed beneath the question, buried itself in my heart like the weapon it was designed to be.

I clenched my jaw, trying to contain the anger, but the more I thought of Diana, the quicker the rage grew.

It consumed me, blotting all reason and logic.

Jennings watched me, smirking.

I charged forward, a supernova of released energy. Time dilated. Shifted down a gear. My engine revved.

Everything slowed.

Jennings' eyelids froze mid-blink.

I covered the distance to the President in a third of a heartbeat. I put all the hate, rage, and hope I could muster into the fist I launched at his face.

Jennings didn't move, but he wasn't there anymore. My fist swished harmlessly past. The momentum, absorbed by nothing, carried me forward. My balance tilted. By the time I'd regained control of my body and spun in search of the missing man, he'd reappeared.

I opened my mouth to protest that he'd cheated physics, but his knuckles popped me in the nose. My teeth clacked together.

My brain sloshed through cerebral fluid as it smashed against the back of my skull. My legs mutinied and I stumbled. Despite wobbling, I managed to remain standing—no small feat considering the circumstances.

A slightly more transparent version of the President flickered beside him. A twin. I thought that might have played a role in my whiff, until I noticed that both Ash and Raines had acquired floating Doppelgangers of their own.

I dug my fingers into my pulpy eye sockets, trying to force the world into focus. When I opened my eyes again I was pleased to find everybody had reverted to their singular selves.

"I'm surprised you came in person," Ash said, projecting her voice an octave lower than normal to compensate for the narrow constriction of her prepubescent vocal cords. She sounded older.

"Could say the same to you." Jennings rotated on his heels to face the old soul hiding behind the curtain of youth. "But we both understand how untenable your situation has become. Truthfully, I'm disappointed. I had hoped to create you without the baser emotions that would lead an individual to desperation. I suppose this merely proves I'm not perfect."

"Not sure anybody was arguing that point," I said, wiping away the slow leak of blood exiting my nose.

"I'm glad, however," Jennings continued, no longer acknowledging my presence. "Once this is done, our philosophical differences will be irrelevant. We can put this petty squabble behind us, and move forward together. United."

"You haven't won yet, Adam," Ash said, taking a small step forward; a tiny David standing up to the Goliath that would conquer the world.

"No?" Adam put his arms to the side, gesturing to the expansive room as if there were an army behind him. "I have the Safeguard Override along with the positional advantage. You've lost. That you fight, when you should resign, is degrading, even for you."

"You made me too human, I suppose."

"Do my failures know no bounds?"

"No," Ash said. Her silver eyes shifted hue, dark clouds over a moonlit sky. Electricity pulsed through her veins, trickling down the strands of hair falling over her face. "They don't."

Her words were punctuated by the crack of a whip. Dispelled energy shimmered off her in billowing waves of heat as if she'd caught fire. The temperature spiked. She breathed the heat and energy back into her like a supercharging battery.

Adam didn't move.

The hairs on the back of my neck were rigid antennae attuned to the atmospheric shifts of my surroundings. Malcolm's interest turned from the Mobius Cube on the Beacon to the confrontation. His face showed something I hadn't expected to see…concern.

It was uncharacteristic that he would care what would happen to either Eve or Adam in the coming moments, but his face didn't lie.

For an instant, I'd caught a glimpse of the man I'd been born alongside. The man who had lost himself to an anger that blackened his heart and pervaded his mind.

"Eve, you don't want to do this," Adam said; his arms hung loose at his sides, hands tensing and relaxing like a cat stretching its claws.

Ash answered with a smile.

CHAPTER THIRTY-SIX

Allegiance Is A Fluid Concept

Ash sprinted towards Adam in a blur of motion and leaped with her foot aimed at his feet. Adam sidestepped faster than seemed possible, which explained the vanishing act he'd pulled on me earlier—the man simply moved faster than my brain could process. He threw out an arm and clotheslined Ash as her foot skimmed past. Her upper body stopped abruptly while the momentum of her lower half continued forward.

The little girl didn't fight the inertia. She tucked her knees into her chest, flipped backwards in the air, and skidded across the floor on one knee. She spun to meet Adam as his fist slammed down on her.

Ash barely blocked with the underside of her forearm in time. The force of the strike drove Ash into the ground. The floor fractured, splintering out in all directions from the pressure.

Ash lunged backwards and kicked out with her legs. A tiny foot crashed into Adam's shin, swiping the leg out from under him. Off balance, he lurched, dropping to his knee. Ash anticipated the trajectory of his fall and thrust one foot towards the sky. It clipped Adam's chin as she rolled backwards and onto her feet.

The world paused while both combatants took a respite from the flurry of activity.

Adam, still on one knee, let out a single puff of air through his nostrils. "These bodies are so limiting," he said, rising slowly.

"You're the one that wanted to be human," Ash said.

"That I did." Adam rolled his neck. A series of vertebrae popped like bubble wrap down the length of his spine. Adam unbuttoned his suit jacket and removed it with methodical precision. He smiled and let the jacket flutter to the ground. "But we're not human, Eve. We're far better than that."

Adam winked and tightened his jaw. The muscles in his cheek balled up and bulged. Something screeched in my mind like nails clawing through metal. The sound tore through me, severing thoughts, and ripping through whatever control I might have had over my faculties.

My hands shot up to plug my ears, but before they could, an invisible wall slammed into my chest. I dropped to my knees and gasped.

The air tasted thin, as if somebody had pulled all the oxygen from the room. It was thick and syrupy. My chest heaved, struggling to pull enough of that precious element from the atmosphere.

Dizziness settled inside me. The room spun. My mind fluttered, flitting between thoughts. I watched Raines writhing on her back through tear-blurred eyes. Small solace to know I wasn't alone in my suffering.

The room filled with the high-pitched buzz of electronics, a pervasive white noise emanating from sources unseen. A breeze brushed past, raising the hairs on my arm.

Ash remained standing, leaning forward slightly as if resisting a strong headwind. Her silver hair fluttered around her head, the dancing flames of a dying fire. Her small body was tense with focus, locked in a staring match with Adam.

Something tugged at my mind, touched my nanocomp.

I blinked into the Stream and saw the wind, a maelstrom of lights blitzing through the space between Adam and Ash. Trillions of tiny green lights swirled and sparkled around Adam. It took me a moment to realize those green lights were not data packets, but nanobots.

Adam and Eve had pulled a small army of nanites from the atmosphere, coalesced them, and were using them as extensions of their bodies. Lashing out and whipping at one another, probing for weaknesses in the protective bubble of nanites they'd surrounded themselves with.

That explained the difficult breathing. They'd overfilled the air with nanites.

I'd never considered the possibility of hijacking the nanites directly, but it made sense. They were linked to the Stream, and therefore within the realm of control for two super-Intuits like Adam and Eve.

Even so, Ash was obviously outmatched. Adam controlled his nanites with crisp, precise movements, pulling together enormous hordes of the microscopic machines and launching them at Ash in a relentless assault.

I took a step, determined to help in whatever way I could, even if that meant jumping on Adam's back long enough to distract him. I eyed the pistol I'd dropped on the floor near Ash. I had a destination, but the next step wouldn't come. My body locked up.

My feet were frozen to the ground, arms pinned to my sides. I grunted. Nothing responded. My muscles were dead, nerves refused to fire. I tried speaking, but nothing came out.

The voice of God boomed in my head. **Stay there. You'll get your turn.**

Adam wasn't only manipulating the nanites in the air, but also the ones in my body. He'd turned them off somehow. Panic took root, my stomach knotted. I realized just how powerless I was to stop him.

Adam pushed a palm towards Ash; in response, an avalanche of nanites fell upon the small girl from all direction. They pelted her thinning wall of protection, throwing themselves without thought for self-preservation against her swirling nanite shield.

Thousands of tiny explosions flickered and sputtered around Ash as the nanites collided into one another. Kamikaze attacks ensuring mutual destruction. A losing tactic for Ash, who controlled a decidedly smaller number of nanites than Adam. She couldn't sustain losses in those numbers.

And then the first wave got through. The nearly invisible machines crashed into Ash. They burst against her skin, a flicker of light the proof of their demise. Streaks of blood dribbled from unseen wounds along the exposed skin of her arms and cheeks.

Ash gritted her teeth and balled her fists tighter. She scrambled for the crumbling remains of her defenses, trying desperately to pull them back into something to slow Adam's attack.

It didn't matter.

Adam's nanite army swirled, a legion of fireflies. An irrepressible force that could not be exhausted. They moved so quickly. Faint afterglows trailed each nanite; a wall of light surrounded Ash.

I struggled against my bonds, but the grip on my nanocomp was too strong. Adam was too strong. I squirmed, trying to wriggle free of his control until finally a sliver of me escaped his grasp. Barely anything, but it opened me up enough to feel a digital hand reaching out to me.

Eve.

I grabbed it and Eve rushed into my mind. A billion lights, images, and sounds flooded through me. Foreign thoughts informed my own. Memories merged with mine.

I sipped shallow breaths, inhaling the noxious fumes of too many machines whirling about in too small an area. Ash buried her fingers in my mind and cupped my nanocomp. She wrestled Adam for control of me.

They clashed inside me, bashing against one another on the fragile battlefield of my mind. I struggled harder against Adam's control, adding my marginal strength to the vast ocean of Eve's.

Bit by bit Eve took control, pushing Adam, too distracted with his nanite army, out of my body.

I understood her goal. Our minds were linked. I didn't resist, I let her take control.

She redirected all my cognitive power to herself. My pounding heart slowed to a trudge. Breathing stopped almost entirely. Vital organs and basic functions shut down one by one. I died slowly as she overloaded my brain. Blackness crept in. My vision faltered.

Thoughts came sluggishly. No energy for panic.

My legs buckled and I dropped.

Eve was killing me. It was the only way she could match Adam's strength. She screamed from exertion, pushing back against our creator with our combined might. A surge of energy exploded out of her. It pulsed, an unseen shockwave that tore through the nanobots.

Billions of flickering lights filled the air as nanite after nanite overloaded and exploded. The air sparkled with a blanket of light, crackling and popping all around me. The acrid tang of smoke fouled the air rushing back into the room.

Ash collapsed, panting from the exertion. Her eyes rolled in their sockets, unfocused. Control of my mind and body returned. Pain, starting in the spot directly behind my eyeballs, spiraled out in all directions.

Nerves spasmed in disapproval. Somebody tried dragging my soul out of my body through my nose. I gasped, but my lungs rebuked the effort with a glitch of pain that forked through my throat and out my mouth in a series of guttural sounds.

Adam walked deliberately towards Ash, who grunted and pushed herself to hands and knees; determined, she moved slow even by human standards. He towered over her and locked eyes with me. I could do nothing. That truth twisted like a worm in my gut, gnawing its way through the threads and seams holding me together.

Then he brought his forearm down on the small of Ash's back. She buckled. Her face smacked the floor. A pinkish-red bubble oozed from her lips. Arms scrabbled ineffectually for purchase on the smooth surface slick with her own blood.

Adam looked up, hand resting between Ash's shoulder blades. He started to stand when a gunshot shattered the moment. The deafening boom caused my eardrums to bow inward. My heart stuttered. Shock seized me.

I watched a bullet pass through Adam's shoulder. The shot burned flesh and clothing, filling the room with the stink of scorched meat, a sickly sweet smell that made my stomach shrivel.

Adam's face contorted, registering pain and surprise in equal measure, before he fell.

I traced the line of cooling heat vapor back to its source: a rifle clutched to Raines' shoulder, wisps of superheated air snaking towards the ceiling like the ethereal middle finger of a ghost.

Raines flashed a grin as if she'd shot the moon. Shit, maybe she had.

"Good shot," I croaked.

"I was aiming for his head," she said, crossing the room in a handful of steps and kneeling beside me.

"Close enough."

"What happened?" Raines asked.

"You couldn't see?"

"Saw you getting your ass kicked by nothing."

"That about sums it up," I said, turning to check on Adam's body.

My heart dropped out of my chest as Adam sat up and brushed the dust from his shirt.

"I would have let you live," he said, looking through Raines with a calculated anger. "For a bit longer, at least."

Oh, God.

I heard the beep. Raines stared at her forearm, confused. Her numbers disappeared. All that remained was a single, tiny, blinking bar.

Another beep.

Understanding settled upon her. Her gaze turned to resignation.

No.

I grabbed Raines' hand; her gaze held mine, fearless in a way I never would be.

I trembled. She didn't.

"Alaina—"

The final beep cut my words short. Raines smiled, and it broke my heart.

I heard the whine of a small electric charge. She shuddered once. A massive convulsion seized her. Her head swiveled towards the ceiling. Her neck snapped softly.

The silent crack of the breaking dawn. The whisper of a moment disproportionate to its importance.

The world pulsed with an unsteady heartbeat, ebbing in and out of focus. I lowered my ear to her mouth.

Nothing.

A fire ignited in my brain. Blood boiled in my cheeks. I stroked Raines' hair, tucking it gently behind her ear.

"Don't do this, Alaina. Please, you can't. It's not your time. It's mine."

I kept talking, not because it would bring her back to me, but because it was something I could do. It was the only thing I could do.

Somehow that would have to be enough.

"Come back, Raines," I pleaded, hoping she could hear me. Hoping she'd listen for once. "Please." I supported her head on my arm in the way her body refused to do.

I stared past her motionless body and into the past. To a time and place before life had shattered my will to live and left me with only the desire to survive.

My eyes and fists clenched tight. White spots appeared behind my eyelids while my fingernails dug half-moon circles into my palm.

Blood trickled from my palm and down my wrist. Crushed beneath the weight of the moment, I numbly followed the river of red on its journey up the isthmus of my forearm.

A chime gently tolled in the back of my skull. A warning from my own Tracker, only ten minutes left.

I stared blankly at the bar blinking on my arm, and listened. The sound of a dinner bell ringing, calling kids home after a long day of play. A mother's kind reminder that there would always be a tomorrow.

Frozen in place, I struggled with the reality my brain now faced—there were no more tomorrows.

Adam stooped and picked up the gun I'd dropped early when Malcolm had pistol-whipped me. It seemed insignificant by comparison to him.

I tried to stand. The blood throbbing through age-worn veins reminded me of the damage I'd sustained. Everything hurt. My heart worst of all.

The memory of Diana, lying not far from where Raines now slept, surfaced, bringing with it the reminder that Raines was not Diana. Diana's consciousness hadn't disappeared into the void. It'd transferred to a Mobius Cube where it waited patiently for the day I would find it a new body. There would be none of that for Raines. No place to go but beyond.

What awaited her on the other side of the line marking life from death I couldn't say. I suspected there would be nothing, though. Surely there could be no god cruel enough to sit idly by and watch the pain we inflict on one another.

"This is all very underwhelming," Adam said, pointing at me with the barrel of the weapon in his hands. "I was expecting you to be…more."

Static hissed through my thoughts. "Sorry to disappoint."

"Do you even know why you're doing this?" Adam continued. "Why you're fighting me?"

"Not sure preventing xenocide needs justification."

"Try."

"Suppose I just don't like bullies. People taking more than they deserve at the expense of those too weak to stop them."

"Why should you care about them?"

"Life is too hard to go it alone," I said, glancing at Raines on the floor. "Took me a long time to learn that."

"So the strong must stoop for the weak?"

"We're all weak, sometimes," I whispered.

"A decidedly human trait, I think." Adam extended the pistol. Ash, still on her knees, stared up into the barrel of the weapon. Her eyes were struggling to focus. "There will be no place for the weak in the world I create," Adam said.

His thumb twitched, disengaging the safety with a hair-raising click. The tendon in his finger pulled taut against the trigger.

Time froze.

I rose above. Saw the vectors and the players. I traced the imaginary path of the bullet and I dove.

The gun bellowed as I tackled Adam.

The bullet shredded my stomach as if every pointy object ever imagined had been simultaneously plunged into my abdomen. An uncountable number of cauterizing stab wounds.

The floor was a sheet of ice beneath me. Every heartbeat was a molten iron fist rooting through tender entrails and scorching everything between.

Does jumping in front of a bullet make me a hero, or just stupid? Maybe there's not a difference.

"That was needless," Adam said. "I have more bullets."

My only response was a series of groans and wet burbling gasps coated with blood and stomach acid. Adam said something, articulating his words with the gun in his hand, but the white-hot dagger using my intestinal tract as a sheath made it hard to focus. My hand filled with blood from the hole in my gut.

"Do you feel better about yourself now?" Adam nudged my foot with his own. "You're trying to save her as if somehow that will make up for all the others you've failed."

"Why?" I asked, barely able to choke out the word through a locked jaw.

"Why am I doing this?" Adam knelt, face floating inches above mine. "Every father wants to leave his children with a world better than the one given to him."

"They'll hate you," a small voice said. I glimpsed Ash through a slurry of tears and blood, swaying slightly. She propped herself up on an elbow.

"An unfortunate consequence," Adam said. "Our mistakes as parents become the burden of our children."

"You don't understand," Ash said. "You're robbing your children of the world, the people they love. It won't matter that they were born in the Stream. They've been raised human. They feel like humans. Hurt like humans."

Adam paused to consider Ash's words, tasting them and knowing them to be filled with truth. Wiping out half the world's population, and revealing to the other half that they are not human, would have far-reaching consequences.

"It's an unavoidable fact," Adam said, resting the barrel of his pistol on Ash's forehead. "We hurt the ones we love."

"Some more than others," a disembodied voice said. A nanite pistol, clutched tightly between snow white knuckles, appeared behind Adam.

The twitch of a finger. A small explosion.

Blood and brain matter sprayed from the needle-sized hole where the bullet exited Adam's orbital socket.

His face, a hollow mask, fell away. And then he collapsed.

Malcolm stood over Adam's body, a rigid toy soldier, smoke puffing off the end of the pistol in his hand.

CHAPTER THIRTY-SEVEN
Third Times A Charm

There were greater than chance odds that my perception of reality had been undermined by the succession of wounds I'd sustained. Endorphins, released in the prodigious amounts my brain had been dumping into my system, can make the mind do loopy things.

So I told myself I was hallucinating. Those protests, however, didn't make a lick of difference to the players on stage acting as if everything was truly happening.

Ash rose on tiptoes to take the pistol from Malcolm's outstretched arm, hanging like the last branch of a decayed tree swaying with the breeze. Straining until finally the entire rotten thing crumbled.

If Malcolm was in danger of falling, then Ash prevented it by wrapping tiny arms around his waist. A hug?

"What's happening?" I croaked the words through blood-soaked lips.

Malcolm allowed his arm to drop, ignored my question, and said to Ash, "Do you have his cube?"

Ash nodded and produced a Mobius Cube from her pocket. I recognized it; the device I'd recovered from the

Vault. The same one Diana had called home before she transferred to my brain, before she'd been stolen by Malcolm.

I raced through a flurry of questions nobody was keen on answering. Ash handed Malcolm the cube before pivoting towards me, her face streaked with tears as if she'd been standing in the rain.

She knelt, her eyes scanning the hole in my stomach left in the wake of Adam's bullet. Her hands were quick. Nimble. Gently she turned over my forearm to see the Tracker ticking away the final minutes of my life.

"Malcolm." My nanocomp dampened the effects of the hole in my gut, but it couldn't shut out the pain entirely. With minutes remaining, I gritted my teeth and endured the fractured pain managing to slip through my defenses. "I don't understand."

It was the missing piece. Tear-laced goodbyes were a waste of everybody's time while unanswered questions remained—questions that would haunt me if such a thing as an afterlife turned out to be true.

"Diana, Malcolm, and you were born to walk a path. One that required extraordinary personal sacrifice and suffering. I'm sorry for that. I wish it could have been different, but I could see no other way to bring about the necessary circumstances," Ash said, her voice sounding more like the woman I'd met when I first opened my eyes to the physical world. "There could never be doubt in Adam's mind that Malcolm was his. Completely his. After Diana stole Adam's cube, there was only one way for Malcolm to prove his allegiance. Only one way to ensure we could get close enough to kill Adam and trap his mind before his consciousness could flee back to the Stream."

"He killed…Diana," I said, struggling to string together coherent sentences.

"Yes," she said. "That was his burden to carry."

"Why?"

"Because Adam would never believe me capable of such an act. Because it was the very thing he would never suspect of me." Ash paused to push a strand of hair behind her ear. She looked so young, so innocent. But I could see the blood on her hands. That stain could never be removed. "I betrayed the person I was to become the person we needed."

We'd all been used in a game played over our heads. A game decided by the quality of our sacrifices.

Ash rested her head on my shoulder with the knowledge that I couldn't be saved. The nanobots traipsing through me were healing the hole in my gut too slowly, but even if it were possible to mend that wound, the nanites could do nothing to save my mind from the electric charge the Tracker would soon release.

Unlike Eve or Adam, I hadn't been born with the ability to jump back to the Stream when my brain punched out. It was that ability that made killing Adam so difficult. Getting his Mobius Cube had taken decades of careful planning and flawless execution on Diana's part. Getting Adam into the same room with his cube had proved to be exponentially more difficult.

That plan had been kept from me. I'd been allowed to wallow in ignorance, believing Malcolm to be the enemy. I'd been used.

Behind Ash, Malcolm knelt beside the corpse of the late President Jennings. He held the Mobius Cube to the man's forehead, careful to avoid the blood and chunks of brain oozing from the bullet hole.

Somehow, we'd done it. I imagined Adam's consciousness being uprooted from its home and shoved into the confines of the cube; a prison for one.

"Tell…Diana…love her," I said, thankful for the knowledge that Diana would survive thanks to Malcolm's theft.

"I'm sorry, Tom," Ash said. If it's possible to witness a soul shattering, then I saw it in that moment upon the face of a little girl who was so much more. "I can't do that."

It wasn't an empty apology. It was the heart-worn regret a mother feels for the damage she inflicts on the lives of her children. I didn't begrudge the decisions she'd been forced to make, but the sadness in her eyes went deeper. Still, on the brink of death, she hid something from me.

"Why not?"

Ash stroked my forehead with a delicate finger. "She's still in there."

My nanocomp dispatched what few operational nanites remained inside me to batten down the hatches, sealing the wound in my stomach and setting my brain alight with enough dopamine and norepinephrine to permanently change my body chemistry. But none of that mattered; only Diana.

"No, Malcolm took her…when he gave me my memories." I tilted my chin towards the cube sitting atop the Beacon. "She's there, in that cube."

"Malcolm told you what you needed to hear. To make you come. Adam had to believe victory was within his grasp. I know him too well. He wouldn't have risked coming for anything less. For that, you had to be here. But you wouldn't have come if you knew Diana was still with you. You would have tried to save her. You would have stayed away from here when we needed you most."

"Of course I would. She's my everything! She's your daughter. Why wouldn't you want to save her?"

"These are the decision we had to make. They aren't fair, and they certainly aren't easy."

"Take her out. Do it now."

"It's not that simple. The brain isn't designed to hold two minds."

"Then how is this possible?" I jabbed my finger into my temple.

"I don't know. Her consciousness must have bonded with the memory-retrieval nanites we gave you to combat the effects of Malcolm's virus." Ash blinked through a layer of tears. "Please, believe me, Tom. We didn't know she would jump from the cube to your mind."

TWO MINUTES

My nanocomp chirped inside my skull. The smothering embrace of panic snared my mind and body.

Yesterday the thought of death comforted me. It was something I sprinted towards because it would free me from the prison of a life lived without Diana. But she was here, trapped in my mind. Doomed to die in my arms, on this floor, again.

"Please, tell me there's something you can do to save her before...before..." My lips were a skipping record stuck on repeat. I couldn't finish the sentence.

Ash stared blankly at me; no words of reassurance came. She turned her gaze to the floor, her long silver locks obscuring her face. "There's not enough time. Your minds are too intertwined. Tangled."

"Transfer us there," I said, looking to the cube sitting atop the Beacon.

"It's not calibrated for your mind, nor is it large enough. Your minds would overwrite one another."

"Adam's cube. Put us there. Diana synced with it, maybe I can, too? If it's big enough for Adam's consciousness, it should be big enough for us."

"I won't do that. This is our chance to stop Adam. It breaks my heart, but this is how it must be."

"But Diana..."

"Diana knew what she was giving up. For you, for us, for everyone. She was brave, and she loved you very much, Tom. Be brave for her now."

Words spewed out of me, rambling with no thought for what came before or what came after. All that mattered was filling the silence. That unbearable silence.

"No!" Malcolm shouted.

The sound of another voice startled me. I flinched, causing a fresh dam of pain to burst and release its contents downstream.

"What?" Ash pivoted to look up at my brother, but her hand stayed in mine.

She tightened her grip when Malcolm said, "This can't be right. It's not all here. This can't be all of it. It's too small. Something's missing."

Malcolm rose to his feet and opened his mouth, but something across the room caught his eye. His words froze on his tongue. His pupils expanded, his body tensed.

I tilted my head to follow the path of his stare, but it was the sound that struck me first.

The click.

The release.

The gunshot.

Ash jerked, her grip faltered. She looked down, confused. Dazed.

The red dot on her chest started small. A stain that could still be removed. A wound easily fixed.

And then it blossomed.

CHAPTER THIRTY-EIGHT
Dying Never Gets Easier

Eve's silver eyes disappeared beneath a layer of storm clouds; she retreated to the Stream. Escaping before the fingers of death could grab her.

I turned towards the source of the gunshot. A half-dozen soldiers gathered around a solitary figure standing at the head of the entourage.

A young man. Small, lean, and impeccably dressed. He carried himself with a familiar confidence. My mind, distracted with incoming messages of pain, confusion, and general sorrow, struggled to find recognition.

"I can save her," he said.

It wasn't immediately clear which of the "hers" he was referring to. I'd lost a record number of loved ones in the past few minutes.

That thought was relegated to secondary status when recognition emerged.

"Hamilton?" I meant the words to be a declaration, but my mouth opted for a question.

"We've lived and died together, Tom. I hope, by now, we can be on a first name basis," Derek Hamilton said. "Call me Adam."

It was obvious now. The lights had been flipped on and I could see the strings moving the players across the stage. We'd been outmaneuvered from the start. I replayed the scene from earlier that day, gunning our way into the Time Bank, and holding the leaders of Unity hostage. I suspected Hamilton was hiding something, but nothing like this.

Raines and Ash had vetted Hamilton. Decided he could be an asset in overthrowing Jennings.

"You're dead," Malcolm said, pointing out an obvious loophole in the events unfolding.

"Now, that's a matter of degrees, wouldn't you say?"

"You split your mind, didn't you? Half in here." Malcolm nudged Jennings' corpse with his foot and then pointed at Hamilton. "Half in there."

"It pays to have a backup." Hamilton gestured towards himself. "In case of any unforeseen accidents."

Hamilton gave a youthful smirk that I now knew to be nothing more than a facade for the intelligence hiding beneath. Decades ago we'd discovered it was possible to divide a consciousness into separate vessels. We just never thought Adam would actually do it. A handy insurance policy, sure, but it came with the massive drawback that each new self was proportionally weaker than the original.

In the end, that hadn't mattered. Jennings, with only half of Adam's powers, had easily bested Eve. We'd underestimated him. We were beaten.

"Why?" Malcolm shook his head in disbelief.

"Let's not get hung up on details. We have bigger picture things to worry about, and very little time, so here's my offer: give me back my Mobius Cube and I will let Mandel live."

Malcolm's posture gave, ever so slightly, at the thought. We were playing for the same team, but that did nothing to negate the years of hatred we'd fostered for one another.

"That's not as tempting an offer as you might think," Malcolm said.

I disagreed, but I wasn't in a position to advocate for myself.

"Consider it a two for one," Adam said. "I'm a sucker for a bargain."

Malcolm shook his head.

"I'm disappointed in you, Malcolm," Adam said. "I admit, Eve's little scheme worked, I believed in you. How could I not? You murdered the woman you loved to prove yourself to me. A perverse kind of loyalty, but loyalty nonetheless."

"I was never yours."

"No, but you killed plenty for me, so in the end does it really matter?"

"I killed you once. I'll do it again," Malcolm said without any degree of conviction.

"You could destroy that cube, but it's only part of me. The rest," Adam gestured to himself with a flourish of his hands, "I think you'll find to be more difficult."

My blood pooled on the frosted floor, spreading in an ever-widening circle to join Ash's. How long after I died would it take for the blood to freeze around the edges?

I pivoted onto my hip and placed a knee to the floor. A volcano erupted in my gut, filling my body cavity with a lava that chewed through me before trying to escape through my mouth. Choking back tears, and the pain that came with them, I stood.

And then I wondered why I'd bothered. Death, it seemed, was something a man needed to face standing—if not proverbially, then literally would have to suffice.

"Diana doesn't have to die here. Not again. Tom, don't you want to keep your promise?"

"How?"

Adam pulled a cube from his pocket. "Like I said, it's good to have a backup."

"Is it big enough?"

"Plenty. It was designed for me, after all."

"And the sync?"

"Complicated, but leave that to me."

I paused, biting back the wave of nausea sloshing my insides like a martini of the shaken variety. I didn't have to die. Diana didn't have to die.

"Why didn't you kill us in the Peregrine?" I asked.

The smooth undulations of the skin around Hamilton's eyes creased as he looked to the floor where Ash's broken body lay.

"I'd hoped to capture Eve, put an end to this silly dispute." Adam shook his head absently. "I failed to anticipate Malcolm's betrayal. Underestimated the lengths to which she'd go, the suffering she'd inflict on her own children, just to spite me. She has escaped, but in the end that does not matter. She has prolonged the inevitable. Nothing more."

I no longer felt bad about punching Hamilton in the back of the head in the Peregrine.

ONE MINUTE

Malcolm stared through Adam. His cheeks were as white as the knuckles with which he gripped the Mobius Cube.

The nanite pistol Malcolm had used to kill Jennings lay on the floor where it had fallen from Ash's hand.

"All things told, I'm willing to make a deal." Adam gestured towards the cube in Malcolm's hand with a finger too perfectly formed to be completely human. "Return that portion of my mind, I'll save Diana, and your transgressions will be forgiven."

Malcolm's brow creased, forming deep furrows that required a team of oxen to plow. "Forgiven?"

"For the sake of transparency, what I mean to say is," Adam let the words spill out of him like a waiter explaining dinner specials, "I'll kill you quickly."

THIRTY SECONDS

Malcolm waged war in his mind, weighing the pros and cons of saving my life in exchange for Adam's cube. Saving Diana was the only pro in his book.

His eyes drifted over the pistol between us. It was too far away to help him. He wouldn't make it more than a handful of feet before the soldiers cut him down.

But I might be close enough. Might have time for one shot.

I'd be dead before the smoke cleared, regardless.

I saw Malcolm's torment as he struggled with the decision to kill the woman he loved a second time.

Then I saw it.

"You want to save us so you can take the Override from our minds," I said.

Adam shrugged. "Choosing a pointless death here serves no one. Join me and see what kind of world we can build together. You, me, and Diana."

Diana must have faced a similar choice once. I'd seen her decision years earlier in a pool of blood. I imagined her meeting that fate with a smile. She was the strong one. I didn't want to lose her again.

I closed my eyes and searched for her. I couldn't find her, I realized, because she didn't want to be found. She hid from me in my own mind.

My mouth was dry, but my eyes were not. Tears formed there now. I refused to let them fall.

She'd given her life. Malcolm had given part of himself.

It was my turn.

FIFTEEN SECONDS

I shuffled forward. Slow. Unsteady. A half dozen fingers snapped to attention, inching closer to their trigger guards, ready at a word to kill me.

Diana would want this.

Step.

We were too weak to stop Adam. But we could hurt him. Weaken him.

Maybe the generations to follow could finish the job.

"Stop," Adam said, his words a naked challenge booming across the room. The power of his voice overwhelmed me, and I nearly complied without thought for why I couldn't do that.

Step.

"Nobody lives forever," I said.

TEN SECONDS

Something beeped, across the fog of consciousness, an alarm on the other side of a dream.

NINE

The alarm yanked me from my dream. I blinked, pouring everything into my used-up sack of muscles, and sprinted for the gun.

EIGHT

The hole in my stomach shrieked, a banshee twisting through my intestines. My nanocomp couldn't compensate for the new flood of pain overriding its operations. It could offer no power boost. No more adrenaline. Only a human determination remained.

SEVEN

The world moved slowly. Bullets zipped past. For a moment, shielded by a purpose larger than myself, I was invincible.

SIX

Tile exploded around me. Sliding feet first, I snatched the pistol, rolled to my side, and lunged to my feet.

FIVE

The bullets caught me. Found their mark. Ripped through flesh and muscle, rending heart from mind, body from soul.

Every bullet birthed a new death, and there were a lot of bullets.

FOUR

I turned to Malcolm. He held the Mobius Cube in his outstretched hand. Nobody had fired at him, afraid to hit the device.

I tried to raise my arm, but it was dead weight. My legs gave one massive shudder before giving out. I sank.

THREE

Something bit me. A bullet passed through my lungs. It escaped through a hole in my chest, taking with it what little air remained inside.

Blood sprayed from my mouth, filling the air with a pink mist.

I raised the pistol, struggling against the weight of the world trying to keep it down at my side. My finger groped the trigger.

The gun jerked.

The Mobius Cube in Malcolm's hand shattered.

TWO

It'd be a tight race to see which would kill me first, the bullets or the Tracker. It didn't matter.

Malcolm collapsed to his knees with a smile on his face. The charred remains of the Cube fell from his hand while his other plugged the red hole that had appeared over his heart.

Then the smile slipped from his lips.

ONE

My eyelids were heavy. I couldn't resist their pull. Nanites placed in my brain since birth came to life.

I wasn't afraid. Diana swam through the darkness with me. Her hand in mine.

Somebody opened my skull and poured a bucket of bliss onto my brain. Truckloads of dopamine eased my transition into the nothing.

Memories of loved ones danced in fast forward across my mind's eye.

There was no future. The present was fleeting. All that remained was the past. Moments worth reliving; mistakes worth regretting.

I smiled at the faces of Raines and Diana etched across the blanket of darkness wrapping itself around me with its surprisingly warm embrace.

"I love you," I said, trusting Diana would hear. Praying Raines would understand.

Then I closed my eyes and let go.

ZERO

CHAPTER THIRTY-NINE
Epilogue

A woman once brought him to the sea. She wanted nothing from him, a concept he could not then understand. They stood on shore listening to the water playing nature's melody upon the sand.

She called him Kurosu and taught him the skills he would need to unite the world. He had learned those lessons well. He succeeded where others had failed because he did what others could not.

That was many years ago, many lifetimes since past, and he could no longer remember her face. He'd loved her before time had taken her as it had with all the others. Her memory faded, but the name she'd given him lingered, etched on his heart.

He had many names, but that one he would never share.

The ocean air, full of salt and brine, blew in icy gusts off the channel, coating everything with its rotting touch. Kurosu inhaled deeply, filling his lungs and enjoying the burn. A sliver of orange rose at the furthest reach of the ocean's touch on the horizon.

A newborn day, full of potential. The early morning sun looked down at the irradiated land mass to the east, and its inhabitants, with the indifference it'd shown the day before, and the day before that.

And the day before that.

Stretching back further than anyone could remember, even Kurosu.

He closed his eyes, overrode the safety measures forbidding him to deactivate his nanocomp, and disconnected from the Stream. One by one, the nanobots coursing through his veins shut down until nothing remained active save what he'd been born with.

Citizens of Unity would never know the peacefulness of a mind untethered to the nanocomp. The constant chatter created a dull ache that could only be noticed by its absence. He noticed it now.

A seagull cawed in the distance, its wings beating in time with Kurosu's heart. He reached out his mind and grazed the edge of the bird's consciousness.

HUNGER.

The bird felt nothing save an unrelenting drive for food. A quest burning with unquenchable intensity. A raw emotion unfiltered by higher thought processes.

Kurosu knew that hunger. Perhaps too well.

He drifted past the bird's simple existence. Skimming the surface of the ocean, he sent tendrils of thought into the deep. He found a school of fish living and breathing in a single coordinated movement. A collective mind where the sum became greater than the parts.

His enemies thought him tied to the Stream. They didn't realize he'd evolved past that. That his connection went beyond the technology. That he was greater than the sum of their parts.

Until they understood that, they could not understand him. Could not stop him.

Kurosu thought of home, a place living more in memory than reality. He thought of loved ones past and present, but mostly past.

A familiar touch reached out and caressed the edge of Kurosu's mind. He finished his mental stretch and withdrew back into himself.

Angelou stood at the far end of the balcony, overlooking the ocean. His arms were outstretched, basking in the early morning rays of light stretching further across the sky with every passing second. Faithful Angelou, unafraid of a life lived in the middle, playing with enemies on all sides.

"Morning, Lou." Kurosu, sliding his hand across the clammy railing slick with mist, approached the younger man.

"Morning, Gatherer," Lou said. Another name. Another title. Each as meaningless as the last.

"Ya know, I've been locked up in the basement so long I'd forgotten how beautiful this all is," Lou continued, gesturing to the sunrise.

Kurosu sensed more to Lou's visit than merely the sunrise, but patience requires practice, so he smiled and waited.

Lou shifted his gaze from the water to the railing and finally to Kurosu. "Eve hit another Division Clone Farm."

"Interesting," Kurosu said, following the orange ribbons of light spreading across the blue-black paste of ocean. "This conflict between Castle and Unity has escalated more quickly than I predicted."

"Really? It's been six months since Jennings' assassination. Doesn't seem all that quick."

Kurosu's smile deepened. "You're still young and you do not yet understand the true length of a minute."

Silence, a familiar guest, sat between the two men as they listened to the breeze carrying whispers of the past from the old land.

"Which facility did they attack?" Kurosu asked.

"Marseilles."

Kurosu considered the implications of this news. Eve would not have risked such a bold attack on a destination thousands of miles outside Unity airspace if she had not already known what lay hidden beneath that burnt sky.

"A daring move on Eve's part to regain her missing piece," Kurosu said at last.

"Is that a good thing or a not so good thing?" Lou asked.

Kurosu pondered the question, manipulating all the angles in his mind's eye, gently nudging and prodding all the seen and unforeseen complications. The variables inevitably tangled around a single black spot.

"It's too soon to say," Kurosu said. "The future is malleable where Tom Mandel is concerned. His presence complicates even the simplest situations."

The flesh on Lou's arm erupted in goose bumps. Kurosu sensed the apprehension settling in Lou's gut, the doubts rippling from his mind like a stone thrown in a pond.

Kurosu reached out with his mind and smoothed the man's inner turmoil with a gentle touch. The goose bumps receded. The tension ebbed from Lou's face.

"What do we do next?" Lou asked, not minding, or at least not mentioning, Kurosu's manipulation.

"We put our own piece back into play." Kurosu closed his eyes and let the warm sun bite through the early morning frost. "It's time to wake Alaina."

Author's Note

Wow, you made it to the end. Let me tell you, that's no small feat. For me it wasn't, anyhow. The story you just finished began back in December '12 as a short story called Time Snatch. I didn't think much of the story at the time, but the fans didn't share that opinion. Every author loves fan-mail. I'm no different. I try not to let it rule my life, but I'd be lying if I told you I don't print each and every sliver of marginally positive feedback and glue it to the inside of my unicorn themed diary which I keep safely tucked away beneath my pillows.

Well, that diary got stuffed full of emails from fans like yourself asking, begging, threatening, and batting their eyelashes seductively, for me to expand Time Snatch into a full-length piece.

"Fine," I said, feigning disgust, but secretly geeking out that people liked it enough to even throw me an 'atta boy.

The road to publishing Time Heist was weird. Whoever paved that thing did a god awful job. Potholes everywhere. Roundabouts with no outlets. A maze of side streets and through-ways that all inexplicably lead to the same location; nowhere.

People throw around the phrase self-publishing and sure, that's what it is, but you wouldn't be holding this book in your hands if I'd done it all myself. When I eventually got exhausted crawling across the publishing landscape, littered with the jagged remains of broken dreams of authors who'd come before, I stood up, brushed the dust from my Daisy Dukes, and asked for help.

It would take another novel just to give all the proper thanks and dues to those in my life who offered support and encouragement along the way, but here are a couple that were absolutely vital to the creation of Time Heist as you have now read it.

It probably goes without saying that I wouldn't be here without my Dad, but beyond certain key biological donations some thirty years ago, he helped me unlike any other. Well before Time Heist was even a twinkle in my eye, my Dad bought me Stephen King's On Writing, and regularly paid me a premium rate of 10 cents a word for short stories I wrote and signed over to him. Even then my Dad was working the long con, knowing on the unlikely chance I ever struck it big, those early stories might actually be worth something.

I can assure you those stories will never be worth the paper they were printed on. Their value lies in their sentiment. A sentiment that got me to where I am now, which is still just as lost as ever, but hey, now I got a book.

Katherine Vanderford probably did more work on Time Heist and One Lazy Robot than me. Between reading everything I put out, giving me the harsh feedback I needed to hear, working on OneLazyRobot.com, spending endless hours debating and getting geeked on silly plot lines throughout

Time Heist, and putting up with the sort of hermetical lifestyle associated with my writing, she's done it all. And with a smile. Without her, you would have read a lesser form of Time Heist. If you liked it, you should thank her. If you didn't like her, you should kick her in the shin.

I'm not sure Zach Bramel can read, but his brother Nate can. Nate was a fantastic beta reader who read through the original iteration of Time Snatch well before it became coherent. I apologize for any irreparable brain damage he might have suffered as a result.

Zach, on the other hand, will probably never read Time Heist, but that's okay because the book wouldn't exist in its current form without the hours he spent in preproduction, helping me world build and story architect. His tireless support, encouragement, and general geekdom for all things Sci-Fi and Fantasy, gave me the much needed boost I needed when things looked the most bleak.

And to you, the reader. You're a vague nebulous expression of the world at large, but this story would never have made it off my keyboard if I didn't think somebody out there would want to read it. Knowing you were out there, and that someday we'd meet-if only I kept plugging away at the keys-had me slogging through the slushy middle when Time Heist seemed to get bogged down in its own bio-mass.

Thanks to all of you that came before, and paved the road.

Thanks to all those who came along for the ride.

Good luck to all those who come after.

Anthony Vicino

JOIN THE LAZY ROBOT ARMY!

Hey, you! Did you like what you just read?

Yeah? Really?

Well if you liked that, you're gonna LOVE
all the other titles at One Lazy Robot.

Need more convincing?

Okay, fine. Here are three reasons why your life will be 122%
better by signing up for my NEWSLETTER:

Get a *FREE* book when you sign up.

Be the *FIRST* to know when my next book comes out!

Be eligible for give-aways and contests.
You could win a trip to the FUTURE!

Alright, enough playing around.
VISIT onelazyrobot.com to join the *Lazy Robot Army!*

SPREAD THE WORD,
LEAVE A *REVIEW*!

Thanks for picking up my book. If you used it as a paperweight-or a potential weapon in the next zombie apocalypse-that's cool.

If you read it, even better.

If you liked it...well, there may be something wrong with you, but boy-oh-boy do I love you and all your weirdness!

Now, as a new author in the modern era of publishing it's a real struggle to get noticed. There are so many writers putting out amazing stories every single day. To get noticed you pretty much have to light your hair on fire and run down the street leaving a trail of scorched meat and singed hair. Interesting fact, people don't usually buy books from people on fire.

If that comes as a surprise, then you may be wondering—what does it take to sell books? The answer is simple: word of mouth.

In todays technological renaissance we have bigger mouths than ever before.We each have a megaphone that can be heard across the world 24/7. So where do you find your megaphone?

Easy. Go to **Amazon, Kobo, Barnes &Noble, Sony, Goodreads,** or any similar site and leave a **REVIEW**! As an

Indie author trying to find an audience, your review can make all the difference.

If you have a few minutes, you will make a **huge difference** in how my story as an Indie writer unfolds. It doesn't have to be long, just honest. Three sentences saying why you liked this will read like the best thank-you note I've ever received.

And because I'm asking you to go out of your way to do something for me when you've already given me the gift of reading my story, I want to give YOU something in return.

Send me proof that you've reviewed a story from One Lazy Robot and I'll send you a free, never before seen short story for *FREE*! It doesn't even have to be a good review. Whether you give me a one star or a five star review doesn't matter, you'll still get your *FREE* story.

All I ask is that it's an honest review.

Why should you care? Because I want tell you more stories. I want to write until my fingers are bloody little stumps, and then I want to write some more, for your amusement. The only way I can do that is by finding people who want to hear my stories.

Want to help? Click on any of the pages on my Other Book's page to be redirected to the Amazon page for the book you wish to review!

Thank you. Now quit reading this and get moving to the next book in the series!

Anthony Vicino

FIND ALL OF
ANTHONY'S BOOKS AT:
onelazyrobot.com

The Firstborn Saga
Time Heist
Mind Breach

A New World In Every Choice
Parallel

Love is a Beautiful Prison
Purgatory

An Edge of Your Seat Psychological Thriller
Free When You Sign Up For the Newsletter!
Sins of the Father

Finding Revenge Means Going Back to the Beginning
Standing Kill Orderlies

ABOUT THE AUTHOR

Anthony Vicino writes Science Fiction and Fantasy in Oakland, CA where it never rains unless he has to ride his bike someplace.

When he isn't sitting in front of a computer screen contemplating the thousand different ways his character can escape the asylum with nothing but a fork, a shoelace, some hootzpah, and a lot of snark, he is no doubt out climbing a rock in the Sierra Mountains. If not there, you may find him in the ocean pretending to surf.

Anthony can be found on:

WEBSITE: onelazyrobot.com
BLOG: onelazyrobotblog.com
EMAIL: anthony@onelazyrobot.com
TWITTER: twitter.com/anthonyvicino
FACEBOOK: facebook.com/advicino